Carol was born in Morton in Mar[illegible]
height of the Second World War. Having spent the greater part of her young life moving from house to house and home to home she arrived at Trewince on the Roseland Peninsula and felt that she had finally arrived home. It was here that Carol met and married Michael, the boy next door and a true son of Cornwall, and it is where the first two of their sons were born. Having been proud of her Irish and Welsh ancestry, it was with great delight that during recent investigation into her family history that she found that one of her great grandmothers was actually Cornish and came from Penzance; her name was Jane Luke. Circumstances caused Carol and her family to 'emigrate' across the Tamar in an effort to improve their lives, but their hearts remained on the Roseland and this is where they have returned frequently. When Trewince was finally sold Carol and her family were fortunate to retain the cottage by the river, and it is here at Quay Cottage that she finds the inspiration for the stories of Tremanyon and the Tremayne family. Carol and her husband now divide their time between their home in Cornwall, their family on the farm in Essex and their son and his family in Derbyshire.

This is a work of fiction, any resemblance to real persons, living or dead, is purely coincidental.

Tremanyon – Time Brings Many Changes

Published by:
Palores Publications,
11a Penryn Street, Redruth, Kernow, TR15 2SP, UK.

Printed by:
The St Ives Printing & Publishing Company,
High Street, St Ives, Cornwall TR26 1RS, UK.

ISBN 978-1-906845-42-1

TREMANYON
TIME BRINGS MANY CHANGES

CAROL SYMONS

To Val... with best wishes

Carol Symons

This book is dedicated to my beloved friend

Angela Mary Clarke 1946 -1999

Some people come into our lives and stay for a while:
Others come into our lives and leave footprints on our hearts . . .

and they can never be forgotten.

Tremanyon

Time brings many changes

Carol Symons

Palores

Acknowledgements:

My thanks continue to go to all the local families on the Roseland who made my own family so welcome all those years ago and I hope that they will continue to forgive me for basing my stories on Trewince and the Roseland Peninsula; especially for changing, just a little, the description of this beautiful headland and names of the villages to fit my fictitious story. For this is what it is, pure fiction; there are no persons living or dead that I have based my characters upon.

My thanks also go to:

Les Merton for his guidance and help with the sequel to the first book of the Tremanyon Saga 'A Shadow Falls'... and to my sister-in-law Cynthia who gets to read the first draft copy and tells me if the story line is going the right way; to Tobi and the staff at St Ives Printing and Publishing Company and not forgetting my good friend Tracy for her time and effort producing the covers.

Last but not least my thanks to my husband Michael and all my family for their support, suggestions and understanding over the years...and, of course, to you the reader; for if it wasn't for you I would not be able to continue to write about my second family... the Tremaynes' of Tremanyon.

Once again my research has been through on line research; it never fails to amaze me of the amount of information that is available just by typing in a few words and this has sometimes caused me to divert the story line. My visits to various locations in Cornwall when I am home have also been informative and inspiring... such as Geevor Mine, Botallack Mine and the East Pool and Agar Museum; in contrast the commercial Poldark Mine gives children and families a taste of what it might have been like back in these early days. Maybe one day I will write a story about a country far away and convince myself that I need to travel there in order to research another novel!

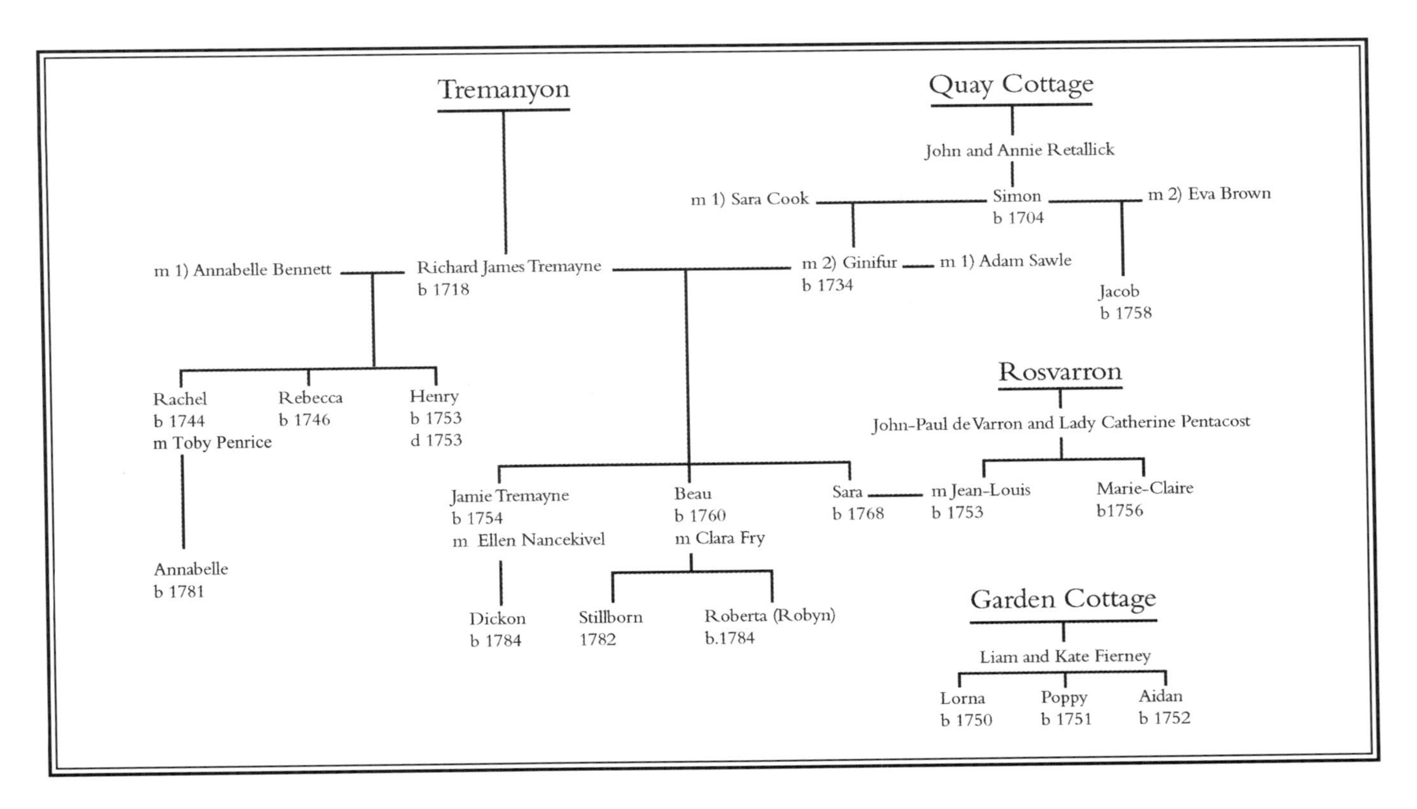

Tremanyon
Quay Cottage
John and Annie Retallick
m 1) Sara Cook
Simon
b 1704
m 2) Eva Brown
m 1) Annabelle Bennett
Richard James Tremayne
b 1718
m 2) Ginifur
b 1734
m 1) Adam Sawle
Jacob
b 1758
Rosvarron
Rachel
b 1744
m Toby Penrice
Rebecca
b 1746
Henry
b 1753
d 1753
John-Paul de Varron and Lady Catherine Pentacost
Jamie Tremayne
b 1754
m Ellen Nancekivel
Beau
b 1760
m Clara Fry
Sara
b 1768
m Jean-Louis
b 1753
Marie-Claire
b1756
Annabelle
b 1781
Dickon
b 1784
Stillborn
1782
Roberta (Robyn)
b.1784
Garden Cottage
Liam and Kate Fierney
Lorna
b 1750
Poppy
b 1751
Aidan
b 1752

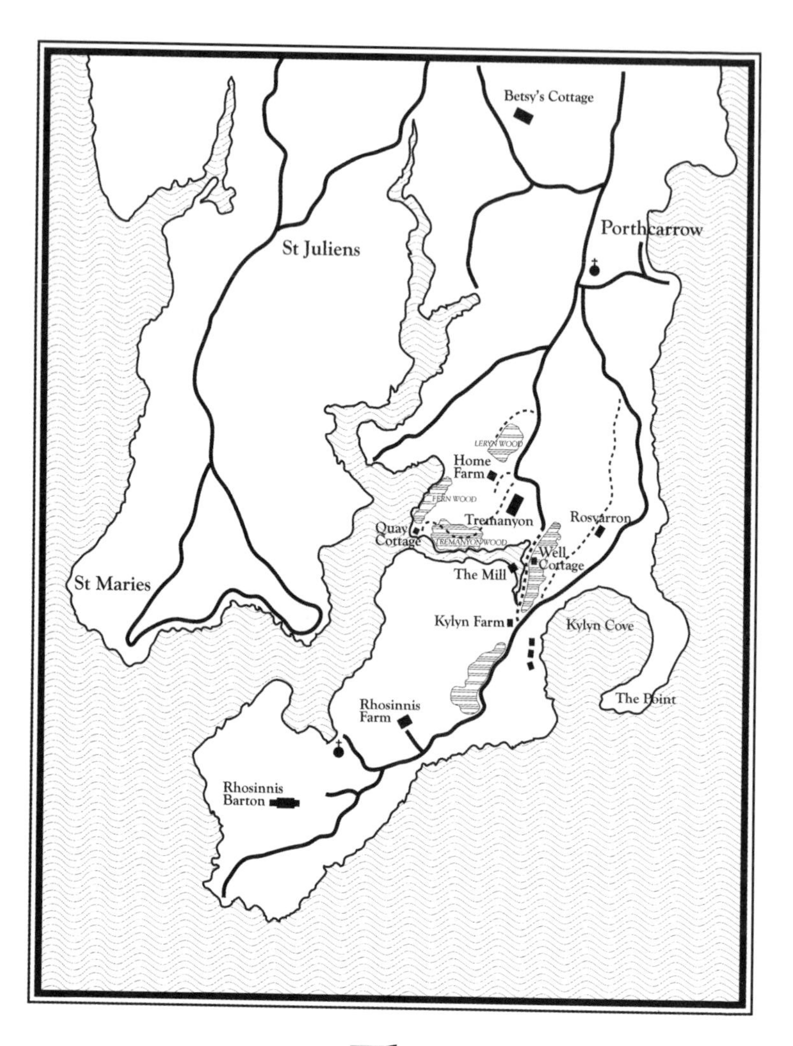

The Rhosinnis Peninsula

Chapter One
1781

THE ENGLISH FRIGATE was a fine sight with its sails stretched taught, taking advantage of the light breeze, as it made a slow approach past the headland; gliding gracefully into the Carrick Roads the sails were quickly furled as it hove to in the sheltered waters. The noisy rattle of the chain disturbed the silence of the late afternoon to be quickly followed by a resounding splash as the anchor hit the sparkling clear water of lapis blue and jade, before plunging to the sea bed in the deep bay where it soon took a firm hold in the sand and rock. With a shudder the *Tribute* slowly swung on the chain as she came to rest in the calm waters of Falmouth Bay.

"Detail a landing party, Mr Stephens." Captain Trenchard ordered before turning to the younger man in uniform standing beside him. "The cutter will take you ashore from here, and we will probably make a faster turnaround as you suggested; just instruct Mr Stephens as to where you want to make your landing."

Jamie Tremayne glanced hungrily at the bend in the river which was hiding Quay Cottage and his first view of home for over six years. "I am truly grateful to you for bringing me home; in all honesty I was not looking forward to the journey from London by coach."

"It was a pleasure to have your company Captain Tremayne but tell me, have you definitely decided to leave the sea for I understand that Admiral Kemp had high hopes for you?"

Jamie smiled. "My promotion was gained purely by the untimely death of Captain Ferris, and my being the most senior officer available when we were so far from home."

"You underestimate yourself. News of your courage and skill has been noted by those at the Admiralty, trust me. What is more, you will be greatly missed by your crew." Captain William Trenchard shook his head and glanced at the long boat being lowered into the calm waters of the bay. "I was sorry to hear the news about your father's untimely death. Are you going home to take over the estate?"

Jamie's brow creased into an unfamiliar frown. "No, it is more likely that my brother will take over the major part of the estate. But I believe that my father has left me Rhosinnis, it covers a large part of that headland there in front of us." Jamie indicated the rolling headland to the east of Falmouth Bay. "The land adjoins Tremanyon and I will be able to keep an eye on my mother."

"Surely your brother will do that! You have a promising career ahead of you in His Majesty's Navy. Admiral Boscawen was your Godfather I understand; he would have been proud of you. I beg you to reconsider; don't throw your life away buried in some backwater."

Jamie laughed. "It is no backwater, believe me. Admiral Kemp has given me a year to consider my future, but I have been away too long and I want to go home. I have confidence that my future lies here, in Cornwall." He glanced out into the bay at a fishing boat approaching from the Lizard. "I'm sure that is one of our boats." Jamie narrowed his eyes against the lowering sun. "Yes. It's *Guinevere*." The Cornish Lugger with its two masts and half deck was easily identified by Jamie for he had often accompanied his father to the boatyard whilst it was being constructed. She was a medium sized craft with a crew of six. A thought crossed his mind. "Captain, do you think that your longboat could intercept that fishing boat. I could transfer to her and you will be able to continue your voyage without more ado."

The older man put up his hand to shield his eyes as he followed the progress of the oncoming fishing boat. "I'm sure it could; but there is no need I assure you."

"I would be grateful. I quite fancy arriving home in one of our own boats."

"As you wish." Captain Trenchard glanced at the cutter, the eight men in place with their shipped oars. "The cutter awaits you. Give your orders to Mr Stephens and he will intercept the fishing boat. Captain Tremayne!" He extended his hand. "May I wish you well in your new venture? However, I must add that I hope that we will see you again, in uniform and back where you belong; on board as Captain and master of your own ship once more."

Jamie took a firm grip of the offered hand. "Thank you. I have promised to think things over very carefully before giving my final answer to Admiral Kemp. I wish you a successful voyage and a safe return to England."

Captain Trenchard's eyes followed Jamie as he clambered swiftly down the rope ladder slung from the deck to the cutter where he turned to give a final salute. William Trenchard returned the salute and then made his way back to the poop deck.

The order was given to release the boat hooks that held the small boat to the side of the ship and the seamen dipped their oars into the bay; with strong strokes they sped the cutter through the clear blue water towards the oncoming fishing boat.

Jamie stood in the bow, drinking in the sight and sounds of his surroundings; he had learned to sail in these waters with his mother and grandfather. The Rhosinnis Peninsula rose up out of the calm waters where its green pastures and woodlands swept down to the water's edge at some points and, at others, rocky cliffs gave a dramatic background to the secluded sandy beaches at their base. The peninsula also enjoyed fertile soil, with abundant grass for sheep and cattle together with land suitable to grow crops of dredge corn, wheat and potatoes. Hills and valleys, woods, streams and hidden creeks made it a diverse landscape encompassing the small village of Porthcarrow and the estates of Tremanyon, Rosvarron and Rhosinnis. He had walked and ridden over every inch of the headland with his father and mother, and much of the surrounding countryside too. He was home, and he should have been home sooner. If he had returned sooner then, maybe . . . No! Jamie pushed the thought aside and concentrated on the crew of the fishing boat.

The longboat had not escaped the interest of the fishermen as they headed for the quay hidden by the bend in the river; they had watched it leave the frigate anchored in the bay "Where d'ye thinks they'm goin'?" Tommy Sawle asked of no one in particular.

"T' be sure, I don't know. Tis a fine uniform that gentleman be wearin' though. Our Jamie's a Captain now and would be lookin' as grand as 'ee be too, I'm a thinkin'." The helmsman's accent was a rare mixture of Irish and Cornish, both soft and musical. He too watched the approaching boat and the uniformed figure standing in the bow shielding his eyes from the sun. Where the devil would they be going, he wondered, there was nothing but open water ahead of them? Unless . . . Aidan Fierney frowned. What interest would they have in a small fishing boat going about her honest business? He grinned to himself at the thought of the cargo that had been on board with the fish just two days ago.

Suddenly the figure removed his splendid hat and hailed them across the narrowing expanse of water that divided the two boats.

"Ahoy there *Guinevere*!" He called out. "Have you room for a passenger to Tremanyon?"

Aidan handed the helm to Ben Rowse as he watched the cutter draw nearer. "Bring her about Ben," he instructed as he took a closer look and a smile spread across his face. "Jamie! Jamie! Is that really you?"

The crew of the cutter shipped their oars as the tide carried them the last few feet and Jamie pulled out the boat hook to take a hold of the fishing vessel. Looking up with a grin on his face he answered. "It is that Aidan. Luck has been with me for sure, the *Tribute* saved me a long journey by coach and now I can travel home on one of our own boats." He threw his canvas sack over the side, into the well of the boat, and clambered swiftly aboard where he gripped Aidan firmly with his strong hand before putting an arm of friendship about his shoulders. "How are you my friend?" He asked before turning to call to the cutter. "Thank you, Mr Stephens. A safe journey to you and the crew." With a swift salute from the crew the cutter drew away and began its return to the *Tribute* and, as *Guinevere*'s sails filled once more and resumed her course, Jamie stood beside Aidan as they passed beneath St Maries.

"Are they expecting 'ee at the Big House?" Aidan asked.

"Yes, and No. I did write to Mother saying that I would be coming home, but I gave her no specific date. How is she?"

"She is well. Comin' t' terms with a life without y'ur father." Aidan took a quick glance at Jamie's face, which was turned towards the small cove ahead.

"My brother and sisters?"

Jamie didn't notice the slight hesitation before Aidan answered. "They're all well."

There was a moments silence as Jamie listened to the slip slap of the waves as they first broke upon the bow of the boat and then ran splashing along the hull leaving a frothy wake behind them. "Could you drop me off at Rhosinnis beach, Aidan? I have been too long at sea and have the sudden yearning to feel good firm Cornish soil beneath my feet. I will walk around the river to the creek and hail Gramps at the cottage to row across and fetch me."

Aidan frowned briefly. "Do ye fancy company? I could come with 'ee . . . the boys can take *Guinevere* in."

Jamie smiled his agreement. "That would be good. I've so much to catch up on."

Jamie's concentration on the approaching beach and the jetty running out into the water from the protected wall was such that he didn't see Aidan's expression darken, or hear him say quietly to himself. "Yes . . . there is. More than 'ee would wish, 'n not much of it will be t' y'ur likin', I be thinkin'."

Jamie was the first to jump ashore and waited for Aidan to instruct the crew and join him. As the boat pulled away from the shore he turned to his friend. "You have no idea how good it is to feel this earth beneath my feet." He unbuttoned the gold braided jacket and loosened the neck of his shirt. "Come on, let's go home . . . I have been away far too long."

Side by side, the two friends jumped the tiny stream that ran out through the wall and pushed open the gate which led to the footpath along the edge of the field beside the river. There was still some warmth in the fading sun and Jamie soon removed his jacket and slung it carelessly over his shoulder. "Where was my father going when he took that fall?"

The suddenness of the question surprised Aidan but he quickly recovered and offered the only explanation he had. "T'be sure I'm not knowing the answer to that one. Your mother believed that 'ee was goin' over to Killow Barton and that was why there was such a delay in findin' him. We was all searchin' in the wrong place. T'wasn't till mornin' we found 'im in the valley behind the Mill.

Jamie glanced back at Aidan as they followed the winding river path, too narrow to walk abreast at this point, but Aidan was looking down, watching the uneven ground. "He was going to see Robert Fry?"

Aidan gave a reluctant. "I s'pose so. Tis what y'ur mother thought anyways," whilst hoping that Jamie would not continue the subject. "Surely Mrs. Tremayne wrote and told you all the details!"

Jamie drew to an abrupt halt. "I only had a brief letter from Lady Falmouth. That was just six months ago, the first I heard of the news. In it she told me of Father's accident and begged me to request compassionate leave. It was forwarded by the Admiralty. I have received no letters from home for the last three years, just before father died. It isn't unusual for letters to follow us from port to port and not arrive until we get home," he explained unconvincingly. "However, I'm glad that Father and Mother have been keeping an eye on Clara. I haven't received any letters from her either. I expect she was miffed that I was so suddenly shipped off again when she was expecting me home on leave for our wedding. I only hope that they received my letters to them." When Aidan said nothing he continued with confidence. "Of course they did. Letters to home always arrive safely. But I did so miss receiving all the news about Tremanyon. You have no idea how much one looks forward to news from home."

Aidan did finally manage to find something to say. "I can imagine."

The tiny path along the river now rose through a plantation of trees. Jamie studied the undergrowth. "Why haven't the orders been given to keep this wood properly managed? What on earth is Jack playing at? I would have expected better from him." Aidan didn't answer. "Have you lost your tongue Aidan? You've usually got a lot to say for yourself."

"Jack Newton is no longer the bailiff at Rhosinnis." Aidan informed him in a rather terse manner.

"Jack! Not bailiff at Rhosinnis!" Jamie repeated parrot fashion. "He wasn't old enough to give up, and where would he go? Jack was born on Rhosinnis, Aidan; he was happy here and when the time came that he could no longer work he would have been given accommodation in one of the cottages on the estate. He knew that . . . what reason would he have to leave?" Jamie couldn't believe the news.

"Ye'd best ask y'ur mother," came Aidan's short reply.

"Ask Mother! What on earth could she have to do with it? Come on Aidan, just what are you trying to hide from me?" Aidan neither answered nor looked at Jamie, his gaze firmly fixed on the village on the opposite shore. "What happened to friendship Aidan? I thought that we had no secrets from each other."

Aidan looked sheepishly at his feet and kicked a stone off the path. "That was before . . ." he offered by way of an explanation.

Jamie was baffled. "Before! Before what? Before I went into the Navy? That didn't bother you . . . before, as you put it. Before I became a Captain? That shouldn't mean anything either, it's only a uniform and a fancy hat, Aidan. It doesn't change the man inside it, I'm still Jamie Tremayne. All I want is home here in Cornwall, on this peninsula." He sighed as he looked about him. "Why did Jack leave, Aidan?"

Aidan finally looked up at his friend, taking note of the set of Jamie's head and body language, and relented. "He didn't leave, he was pushed."

"Pushed!" Jamie shook his head in disbelief. "Pushed by whom?"

"The Squire, as y'ur brother wishes to be known. He gave Jack notice to quit. Said that 'ee no longer required his services, 'n 'ee could manage quite well on his own." They had halted by a style, where the path split, one path that would lead up over the hill and back down to the creek and the mill; the other path led to the head of the creek where Quay Cottage was perched on the other side. "That was nigh on three years ago now, after y'ur father died. Beau got rid of four men too, 'n 'ee went on t' tell them as remained that they would have t' work harder to make up for it or they would be out on their ears 'n all. He halved the workers at Kylyn too."

Jamie stared at Aidan in disbelief, before letting his eyes wander over the nearby fields. The hedges were overgrown, and in less than three years the brambles had taken hold and were encroaching on the fields. Gorse, docks, horse thistles and other obnoxious weeds were to be seen in pastures that had once been as clean as Tremanyons lawns. "Why? Why would Beau do that?" Jamie studied Aidan's closed expression and wondered exactly what had happened since his Father's untimely death, to bring this about. Aidan had always been so open, so easy to read, a close companion with whom he shared many secrets. It appeared that this was not the case now.

"I'd rather not comment till ye've spoken to y'ur mother and brother, Jamie." He added at last.

Jamie sighed unhappily. "I was so looking forward to coming home, Aidan. With all the fighting I've seen, I thought that the one place that would always remain the same would be Tremanyon." He placed a hand on Aidan's shoulder. "But I tell you this, Aidan; whatever else has changed, our friendship will always remain."

Aidan gave him a brief smile. "I hope it be so, Jamie . . . that I do 'n all. But time brings many changes, I fear."

With a heavy heart Jamie took the next step towards the head of the creek, where he expected to call out to his grandfather at Quay Cottage; the fisherman's cottage and Pilchard Cellar stood on the other side of the tributary known as Mill Creek.

Once only a single floor, the dwelling above the pilchard cellar and net locker had since been extended, with another floor added in 1757 when Jamie's maternal grandfather had re-married. This gave them two bedrooms and a box room with a living room and kitchen below. Simon Retallick and his new wife were thrilled with their extended new home and to everyone's surprise Eva gave birth to a son, Jacob, in 1758. Ginifur's mother had died when she was a child and she had been brought up by her father in this very cottage and with the help of her paternal grandparents who lived at Well Cottage. The result of this new union was that Jamie had an uncle who was younger than himself and Ginifur had a half brother younger than her son. Over the intervening years Jacob and Jamie's relationship had been that of brothers, but this relationship did not develop between Jake and Beau who was born in 1759

Guinevere's crew had alerted Jacob of the news of Jamie's impending arrival and he had sighted the two men as they came around the riverside path. By the time that Jamie and Aidan had clambered down to the rocks Jake had rowed the boat over and was waiting for them. "Welcome home, Jamie," he greeted his sister's son warmly. "Tis been a long time."

"Too long, I gather." Jamie added ruefully. "But thanks 'Uncle' for those kind words," he quipped and Aidan's and Jake's laughter at this joke lightened their spirits for a moment or two until they reached the other side of the creek. "Where's Gramps?" Jamie wanted to know. "I thought that he would have come down to meet me when he learned that I was home. Haven't you told him?" Then, as a thought crossed his mind, he added fearfully. "He is alright isn't he?" and Jamie glanced anxiously up at the cottage.

Jacob hastily assured him. "Yes, Da and Ma are both well; but I thought Ginny would 'ave written and told 'ee. Y'see, I was married two years back along; now me 'n Tess d' live in the cottage 'n Da and Ma have moved into Well Cottage to look after Gran. Gramps died last spring, but I 'spect you know that. Of course Da still keeps the books for the quay boats, but 'ee have more time for 'iself. He and Ginny go fishin' out of Kylyn Cove and it 'ave 'elped 'er too, I'm thinkin', since your Pa died."

Jamie shook his head. "Is anything the same? The sooner I see Ma the better." He stooped to pick up his bag. "Are you coming Aidan?"

Aidan shook his head. "No . . . But I'll see 'ee later, never fear. Don' go worryin' about y'ur bag and fancy hat, I'll bring 'em up when I'm finished 'ere." He watched Jamie's retreating back as he set off up the track towards the Big Wood. "Be Jesus . . . What a welcome home there be in store for him." Jacob looked bewildered and Aidan explained. "Apparently ee've 'ad no news from 'ome since before his father died, and then only recently from Lady Falmouth tellin' him of his father's death and beggin' him to come 'ome." Aidan explained.

"Nothin'! What, not even from Ginny? Nor 'er over at Killow Barton?" Aidan shook his head. "Dear God. What a welcome ee's gonna get, t'be sure." Jacob whispered.

Aidan turned his eyes away from the receding figure. "Ginny kept that quiet," he said, "she never said a word about him comin' 'ome."

Joshua pondered these words. "If tis true about 'im not receivin' no letters from 'ome, tis a fact that she've not heard from 'im in these last three years either. Not even after 'is father died."

"So Da said . . . t' tell the truth, I didn' know whether t' believe him."

"Never did believe 'ee could be'ave so . . . ee'd always written s' regular. I always thought there 'ad t'be a reason; though for the life of me I can't think what could 'ave 'appened." Jacob contemplated the question.

"Be Jesus . . . !" Aidan exclaimed. "If she's not expectin' him, she's goin' t' 'ave one devil of a shock. I'd best catch up with him before 'ee get t' the 'ouse." He made to leave but Jacob caught hold of his sleeve.

"Wait Aidan, as soon as I 'eard the news that Jamie 'ad arrived 'ome I sent young Timmy up with a note for Ginny. She will know by now." Jake assured him, "and Liam and Kate 'n the girls will be near by, never fear."

Aidan shook his head. "May God and the blessed Mary help them both," he said as he sadly turned away to see to the unloading of his boat.

* * *

Jacob's warning had indeed given Ginifur precious moments to collect her thoughts and prepare herself for her son's arrival. In the fine Georgian house that Richard had built in 1750, after a fire had destroyed the old one, Ginifur waited in the library; a fire had been lit in the grate to ward off the early evening chill and dusk was drawing in; it had been a warm spring but of late it had turned unseasonably cold in the evenings. Liam had placed a tray with decanters and glasses upon it on the table by her side, and Kate had water on the boil if she wished to call for tea. Beside her the Irish wolfhound peered up at her through slit eyelids, watching her every move, aware of her mistress's anxious state even though her face showed no sign of it. Ginifur heard the crunch of Jamie's boots upon the gravel as he approached the front of the house and at the sound of them upon the steps, bounding up them two at a time, her heart gave a leap; the sound of his footsteps was a sudden reminder of Richard, who had always been in such a hurry to get home. She waited with baited breath as she heard Jamie open the front door and step into the hall.

The library door was ajar and Jamie could see that the candles burned in their brackets on the wall and, although he could not see it, a lamp was lit upon the desk with its light spilling on the floor. But still he hesitated . . . he paused at the entrance and glanced about the hall. It all looked just as it had when he left over six years ago. A beautiful flower arrangement on the side table, the flowers no doubt picked by his mother that morning and just one of many that would be dotted about the house. His instinct told him that his mother was waiting for him in the library, just as he was certain that Jacob had sent word ahead of his arrival at Quay; Jamie put out his hand and gave the door a gentle push. As he had expected Ginifur was sitting in his father's oversized chair, making her look so small and vulnerable with an apprehensive look upon her face and her anxious eyes fixed on the doorway. At the sight of Jamie, Ginifur swiftly rose to her feet and mother and son stepped towards each other at the same moment.

Ginifur's arms reached out to embrace her son. "You will never know how much I have longed for this moment." she told him. "It sounds weak of me, I know, but I have missed you so much. Since Richard . . . your father . . ." She still found it so difficult to speak her husband's name, "Of course, Rachel, Rebecca and Sara have been so good. Rachel comes over at least three times a week and, of course, Rebecca and Sara are still at home."

Jamie swallowed the lump in his throat as he placed his hands upon her shoulders, pushing her slightly away from him to enable him to look down into her face. "Rachel!" he uttered. "Comes over from where?"

Ginifur stepped back to take a harder look at his face. "From where? From Nanshute of course. Where else?"

"Nanshute!" Jamie repeated foolishly. "But that is Charles Penrice's place. What on earth would Rachel be doing at Nanshute?"

Ginifur studied the confused expression on Jamie's face; the lines about his eyes. There was no feigning his look of bewilderment; he really did not know what she meant. "I wrote and told you that Rachel married young Toby Penrice. They were married over a year ago now."

Jamie turned to the fire. Suddenly he was cold and he held out his hands to the welcoming flicker of the flames.

Ginifur was left examining Jamie's back. It appeared to her that he had grown taller in the time that he had been away; certainly broader. Wide shouldered and narrow of hip Jamie was just like his father. Of course he was older too, she thought, he was twenty seven and she hadn't seen him for six years. Of her two sons it was Jamie who most resembled his father. He resembled him not only in his features but in his build, his honesty and steadfastness, in his courage and in his love for the family. It was this last characteristic quality that made it so strange that they had not received any letters since he was so suddenly seconded to the fleet patrolling the Americas. Richard had told her that if they had not heard from Jamie then there had to be a very good reason and in her heart Ginifur knew that this must be true but, nevertheless, she couldn't help having sleepless nights wondering about his wellbeing.

Jamie turned away from the cheerless flames; it seemed to him that even they held no warmth. "I received no letter," he said. "It isn't unusual for letters to take a long time to reach us when we are away at sea, but I received no letter. In fact none at all since I was seconded, except the one from Fanny Boscawen telling me of father's accident and asking me to request compassionate leave."

Ginifur was confused. "You are mistaken; it was I who wrote to tell you the news. You surely cannot believe that I would let you hear that from any one else?" she exclaimed. "And Richard died three years ago Jamie!!"

Jamie took her hand and guided her to a chair saying. "Sit down Ma, please don't look so troubled; there has to be an explanation. However, believe me the first time that I heard of the news of Father's accident was in a letter from Fanny Boscawen. I received her letter six months ago; it has taken all this time for me to obtain a release."

"No." Ginifur insisted. "It is three years since, and you have forgotten," she repeated in her distress, "and I found it so hard to understand why you never answered. A word of comfort would have meant so much in these last years." She stopped, fearing that she was expressing self-pity for herself and judgement on him.

A bewildered expression appeared on Jamie's face. "What do you mean . . . no letters? I have written to you regularly. Each time a ship was sailing for home I sent a letter in the Admiralties sealed chest. But I received no communications from home at all, neither from you or Clara."

Ginifur blanched at this statement. "I don't understand. I wrote to you every month, Beau brings the mail in with him, if there is any, and always takes any letters away with him when he goes."

"Beau is not at home either!" Jamie was finding it hard to take in the number of changes that had been made during his prolonged absence. "Where is he?"

Ginifur sighed. "When Beau heard that your father had changed his will, he refused to spend another night beneath this roof."

Jamie perched on the edge of his father's desk. "Then where is he living?"

Icy fingers clutched at Ginifur's heart, a sinking feeling began to grow in the pit of her stomach. "Killow Barton." She whispered.

"Killow Barton! The Fry family are letting him live at Killow Barton? Good grief Mother, what on earth has been going on here?" Jamie's confusion seemed complete.

Ginifur glanced at the crystal decanter on the table. "Would you pour me a glass of brandy, Jamie?"

Jamie finally found something to amuse him, and laughed. "Brandy! You . . . drink brandy? Has my arrival been such a shock to you? Believe me I didn't intend it to be so."

"Oh Jamie! A surprise, yes, but only one I have prayed for."

Jamie poured two glasses of brandy and handed one to Ginifur. "Beau! You were explaining to me about Beau being at Killow Barton," he pulled a chair closer to hers and sat down.

Ginifur took a good sip of the amber liquid. It sent a warm glow to the pit of her stomach, chasing away the sickness that threatened to engulf her, and gave her strength to continue. "After your letter, explaining that you had been seconded to the Americas we heard nothing from you. Neither us, your family, nor Clara. She wrote, pleading with you for an answer. She was distraught when she had no reply from you, no explanation about cancelled wedding plans, and no new date to look forward to. She truly believed that you had changed your mind. No . . ." Ginifur held up her hand as Jamie tried to speak, "please hear me through." Jamie sank back into his chair. "Beau offered Clara the comfort of friendship. He was patient, kind, and he was so young that we saw no harm in it. But in time the friendship developed." Ginifur took another sip of brandy to settle her nerves, watching as Jamie struggled to contain himself. "After they came to see Richard to ask for his blessing, your father said that he would write to you for an explanation. He wrote a letter and sent it to the Admiralty to have it forwarded to you. In it he informed you of Clara's belief that you had changed your mind. He said that if he didn't hear from you within six months then he would give his blessing for the marriage. The Fry's were quite happy for the marriage to go ahead."

Jamie could keep quiet no longer. "I received no such letter from Father and no letters from Clara either." He pushed himself out of the chair and strode to the window. It was now dark beyond the square panes. The darkness outside was exaggerated by the light from within, as dark as the thoughts in Jamie's heart. "Then . . . what happened then?"

Jamie's fears were equalled by the pain that lodged in Ginifur's heart. Pain from the blow that she was about to deliver to her own son.

Jamie's face softened as he stepped towards her chair and, taking her hand in his, he knelt down beside her. "Then Ma...what happened then?"

"Two months later Richard had a riding accident, Casper unseated him and he died where he fell. I wrote to you immediately, begging you to plead with Admiral Kemp to allow you to come home. I really did. But no answer came, I was so afraid that you might be injured . . . dead even. Beau was very good. He contacted the Admiralty and they assured him that you were well and acting under orders of war." Jamie was biting his lips so hard, to stop himself from interrupting, that a tiny spot of blood appeared on his lower lip. "Edward Franks finally came out to read your father's Will. We were hoping that you would be coming home so I had asked if it could wait, finally he said we could put it off no longer. Edward confirmed what I already knew; Richard had changed his Will. Edward told us all that it had been changed about six months before his death and, prior to reading it, he made it quite clear that there was no disputing the contents. Every precaution had been taken to ensure that there was no way it could be overturned, he said. Beau did object, most vociferously. He clashed angrily with Edward; heated words were exchanged and Beau blamed me for poisoning your father's mind against him. He left, saying that he would sleep no more beneath this roof." Ginifur took a deep breath. "I begged them to wait for a decent passage of time before they wed; but Beau's anger was such that he refused a period of mourning and married Clara a month later. They are living at Killow Barton, in the Dower House. It is Robert Fry's belief that Beau has been unjustly treated and that Kylyn Farmhouse is not a suitable house for his daughter to live in." Ginifur sank back into her chair and sighed deeply. "Oh Jamie! I am so sorry. We didn't know what to do... and then when Richard died so suddenly . . ."

Strangely Jamie found that he didn't feel as hurt as he thought he might have been. He felt anger, an unusual characteristic in his make up. He was completely baffled as to what had happened to all of the correspondence both to and from Tremanyon, and he felt an enormous amount of love and pity for the woman who sat before him. It was she who had born him, had gone through so much in the years before her marriage to his father. It was Ginifur who had raised him with her love and both she and his father had guided him carefully into manhood, instilled into him his values of trust and honour. So what had happened to Beau? Why was he so different? Ginifur was waiting for him to speak, her eyes awash with unshed tears. "So what was it in Father's will that upset him so much?"

Ginifur brushed aside a wayward tear. She reached into her pocket, concealed within the folds of her skirt, and retrieved a sealed letter which she thrust into Jamie's hand. "Perhaps this might shed some light upon it."

Jamie turned the letter over. The vellum was worn with constant handling but the ribbon that tied it was secured still with a blob of red wax, into which Richard had pressed his seal. Returning to the chair he had vacated, Jamie sat down and carefully released the seal. Having studied the opening words he glanced at Ginifur. "Do you know what he has written?"

Ginifur shook her weary head. "No. To be truthful, it worried me more than a little when he gave it to me. But Richard laughed it off and said that there was nothing to be worried about. It had been a whim, a mere whim on the spur of the moment, he said . .

. when a morbid thought had crossed his mind that he might not see you again. I understood that feeling, for it had happened to me on more than one occasion."

Jamie nodded. "Then I shall read it to you." He poured another glass of brandy and settling himself in the chair unfolded the letter once more and began to read aloud.

My dearest son, Jamie.

If you are reading this missive then my fears have not been imagined, and my eyes will see you no more. Be assured that you have been everything that a father could wish for in a son and that you have given me every reason to be proud of you. Although I may not have shown it, I love you dearly. A man is not supposed to express this feeling towards his children, for it is presumed the prerogative of the mother.

But I digress.

For some time now I have been troubled with fear for the future of Tremanyon and Beau's compulsive desire to inherit it. Perhaps it is just that he is too young, immature, or maybe it is that I just do not want to consider the thought of letting it go. Whatever the reasons for my fears I have returned from Edward Frank's office today where I have changed my Will. Every avenue has been explored; it is water tight and cannot be challenged in law.

As I promised, I will be leaving you the estate of Rhosinn-is, although Beau will benefit from the income until you return to claim your inheritance. To Beau I leave Kylyn Farm together with the Mill and Mill lands.

However, the major change is that Tremanyon and the Home Farm have already been transferred to your mother. In her hands Tremanyon will be safe for she loves it as dearly as I do myself. It will be for her, and her alone, to decide its future and to whom she will leave it.

Maybe it is only the senseless fears of a man who is progressing in years. Perhaps the incidents that have come to my notice have been exaggerated, or perhaps I have been misinformed and the accidents just that . . . accidents. In this case you will not be reading this letter and I will be possibly writing another.

However, should it come to pass that I do not see you again, I beg you to watch over your mother. Ensure that she is always in company, and that at no time should she be tempted to go riding alone.

I cannot go into details at this moment. I have no positive proof that either of us is in serious danger, it seems too foolish to even contemplate. However I finish this letter with an easier heart, knowing that all will be well in your hands.

My deepest regret is that I may not see you again,
I am, as always,
Your loving father,

Richard James Tremayne

Jamie folded the letter and, for a moment, mother and son sat deep in their own thoughts until Jamie finally broke the silence. "You truly had no idea about the contents of this letter?" He need not have asked for Ginifur's answer was clearly written on her face.

She shook her head in mystification. "No I can not believe that he really feared for our lives! Why should he? Who would have anything to gain?"

"I don't know. I agree, if it was anyone else but Father I would say that he was imagining it. No, it only brings me back to the letters and why they went missing. You say Beau always collected the mail?" Jamie frowned as he puzzled over the contents of the letter.

"Yes, Beau always collected the mail; you must remember he always liked to ride to the village to collect it. But, you don't believe that Beau . . . ? Surely you wouldn't think . . . ?" Ginifur was appalled that Jamie might have thoughts that his brother may be involved in the loss of the letters, even for one fleeting moment.

"Not the Beau I knew." he declared. "Not the boy I grew up with, nor the one I left behind when I first went to sea. But the one you have described to me, the one who has let Rhosinnis go to rack and ruin, the one who would turn Jack Newton out of his job and his home . . . !"

"Jack! Jack Newton has left Rhosinnis? Surely you must be mistaken. Jack would never leave Rhosinnis!" Ginifur interrupted.

"So. You really didn't know."

"Know what?"

"Beau has got rid of Jack, and four other men too. No, I don't know who they are but I intend to find out." Jamie informed his mother.

"Why would he do that?" Ginifur's concerns were real enough for she had known all of the men who worked on the Tremanyon Estate, and had done for the greater part of their lives.

"To enable him to withdraw more of the profit? I don't know, you tell me." There was the sign of anger in Jamie's voice. "According to Father's letter, Beau has been receiving all profits from Rhosinnis land until I return to claim my inheritance. Well I have returned; from now on Beau and his wife stand on their own two feet, or should I say four?" He gave a mirthless laugh which brought Ginifur up with a start.

Ginifur studied her elder son. Jamie wasn't given to displays of anger; it was not in his character. The grandfather clock chimed in the drawing room and Ginifur glanced at her watch, the one that Richard and Annabelle had given her for her eighteenth birthday; the one that she wore pinned to her dress to this very day.

Annabelle Tremayne had died in childbirth, in her attempt to deliver a son to her beloved husband. But she had always suffered with ill health and both mother and babe had died due to her weak heart and the extremely long labour that they had both been forced to endure; Richard had been left with two young daughters to bring up. Rachel and Rebecca were now Ginifur's step daughters, she had helped to bring them up during Annabelle's life and, in her mind, she could think no less of them than her own daughter by Richard . . . "My goodness! Look at the time! Liam and Kate will never forgive me for keeping you from them. They were so excited when Jacob sent word up from Quay that you had finally arrived home." She rose from her seat and took Jamie's hand. "It is so good to have you home again, Jamie. Whatever it was that Richard feared, I know that we can face it together. Let us sleep on it and talk again in the morning. You must eat, and I will get Liam to bring up some wine from the cellar."

"Where are Rebecca and Sara? I thought that you said that they, at least, still slept beneath this roof!"

Ginifur laughed for the first time since his arrival, the smile bringing back the first signs of the mother that Jamie had left behind six years ago. "They do Jamie, they do. They went over to Rachel and Toby to see the baby. I am a grandmother, would you believe it? Richard would have been so happy."

"At last a piece of good news to welcome me home. So I am an uncle! Do I have a niece or a nephew?"

"A niece. Annabelle is just three months old." Ginifur pulled the bell cord and far off they heard it ring. "She has been named for Rachel and Rebecca's mother of course, and if she carries the genes of her grandmother's beautiful nature she will be a gifted child indeed."

The sound of a closing door and feet hurrying along the passage preceded Liam and Kate. They had been waiting anxiously for Ginifur to pull the bell cord and Jamie was touched to see the expression of welcome on their faces, and to feel the warmth of their embrace. These two were much more than faithful servants, for Liam had become Richard's most trusted friend after their sojourn to the New World and their adventures there in 1753. They all had so many questions to ask, so many things to tell and before they knew it they heard the rattle of the carriage upon the drive.

"Here come Rebecca and Sara now." Ginifur headed for the door. "This will be a surprise for them."

"I hope a pleasant one." Jamie added. "I expect Rebecca will lecture me on my obligations to write home more regularly. I wonder if she will believe me."

Not knowing of Jamie's explanation, Liam answered. "Oh yes, whatever the reason. T'be sure she will," Liam had never lost the Irish lilt in his voice, "for Rebecca never believed, not even for one moment, that you had forgotten us. And neither did I, I might add, nor y'ur mother and father." his eyes followed Ginifur as she passed into the hall to greet her daughters. The sound of the girls' laughter drifted up the steps as they alighted from the carriage. "T'was only young Beau who commented about the absence of any letters."

"And I bet he put the knife in too." Jamie suggested.

Kate laughed. "Oh, 'ee put in his two pence worth, don't 'ee doubt it. But she wouldn't 'ear none of it . . . no not 'er." She nudged Jamie in the ribs. "I'll go and get some food on the table shall I?"

"Only if you and Liam will join us to eat it Kate. I want a real welcome home, up to now it's been somewhat lacking."

Kate grinned as she reached up to place a kiss upon his cheek. "Jest 'ee wait 'n see what Lorna, Poppy and me 'ave prepared for 'ee, 'n with so little time too. That'll bring a smile to y'ur face, mark my words," and with this she hurried out into the hall.

In the brief moment they had alone Jamie turned to Liam. "Tomorrow we must talk. If Father took anyone into his confidence it would have been you."

Liam studied Richard's son. As the years rolled by Jamie resembled Richard Tremayne more and more. If only things could have been different, he thought to himself. "T'be sure there is not a lot t' tell. What there is was mostly suspicion, nothing that I can prove."

"Nevertheless, we have to talk." Jamie repeated and Liam nodded his agreement. However, there was no time for more as Rebecca and Sara burst in through the door.

* * *

It was much later, when they were all in the drawing room that Liam reminded Ginifur about the box. He had thrown another log onto the fire when he remembered it. "Did ye think t' give Jamie the papers that Mr. Franks left, and the key for the box that ye keep in the safe?" he asked.

Ginifur's face was flushed with all the excitement. "No, of course I didn't. But you get them Liam and we will all enjoy Jamie finding out what the contents are," she handed Liam a bunch of keys. "I was too delighted at seeing him again that everything went out of my mind."

"What on earth are you talking about?" Jamie was sitting on the large comfy sofa with Rebecca; Sara was sitting on the floor at his feet, with her arms linked over his knees as he recalled an incident that had amused him. Sara jumped to her feet excitedly. "The box that Adam left in Mama's keeping when he died, you remember Jamie, and the key which was to be given to you on your 25th birthday. But you weren't here. The papers are something else I don't know about. Come on Mama, you sit here next to Jamie." She shushed her sister to another chair as Liam returned with the box, the key and a sheaf of papers tied carefully with red ribbon.

With a smile Liam handed them to Jamie. "Ye'd best open them soon, for t'be sure the ladies 'ere 'ave been filled with curiosity ever since Mr. Franks brought them over."

Jamie laughed. "Well, in that case, which do you think I should start with, little sister?" he asked Sara.

"Oh the box, Jamie. Who is interested in silly pieces of paper?"

Jamie studied the box and papers, as if weighing them up in his mind. He shook the box. "Well there certainly are no gold coins in there. I think I'll look at the papers first."

"Oh Jamie!" Sara pouted her pretty lips in mock anger.

Carefully Jamie untied the ribbon. With exaggerated movements he opened the pieces of paper and then proceeded to study each one with great consideration; Sara was almost beside herself with curiosity. Finally, folding the last sheet carefully he looked at the group of faces watching him with intent expressions. "What about these Ma? Did you know what these contain?"

"Not completely. When I married your father we decided to ask Mr Franks to invest the money that Adam left me, for your future. It was to mature on your 25th birthday, with the possession of your box. What the end results are I have no idea."

"Oh Jamie, don't tease us so. Tell us what it is." Sara jumped up and demanded.

Jamie grinned and shook his head at the same time. "I can hardly believe it. I owe you Ma, Adam and Mr Franks a great deal of thanks," he paused.

"Oh Jamie! Do tell us, please." Sara stamped her pretty little feet in exasperation.

Aidan had arrived from Quay in time to join the family for dinner and was relaxing on the window seat as Jamie waved the papers towards him. "Well Aidan, it looks like I will be able to get started on enlarging Rhosinnis Barton sooner than expected."

Ginifur glanced first at Aidan and then Jamie. "You mean . . . !"

"I mean that with Adam's money and your generosity, and with Mr Frank's knowledge, you have all raised me more than enough money to enlarge the old house on Rhosinnis." He folded some of the papers and raised the last pieces. "And this is the deeds to Rhosinnis, my portion of Father's estate, for which I will always be grateful."

"Jamie!" Ginifur's hand flew delightedly to her face. "Oh Jamie, I am so pleased."

Sara clapped her hands delightedly. "Well! Who would have thought that little pieces of paper could have such wonderful news? Now the box Jamie, please. Please open the box."

Jamie dangled the key in front of her. "Then you open it Sara. I have had enough excitement for one day."

Sara snatched the key with glee, and taking the box upon her knees she turned the key in the lock. Slowly she raised the lid and peeped inside. Her smile of anticipation vanished. "Papers!" she exclaimed. "Just more papers." Taking out the two sheets that lay on the top she handed them to Jamie. "You had better read these too," she said. "This one is addressed to you."

Jamie took them, opening the first and then glancing about him he announced. "It is a letter from Adam Sawle and is dated 1756." And for the second time that evening, he read aloud.

Jamie

By this time I have no doubt that you will know that I, Adam Sawle, was not your true father. Nevertheless it must be that you are the only son I will ever have.

I loved your mother very much and was proud to give you both my name when her need was so great. I have, I confess, been hard on both of you; on Ginny for not loving me as much as she still loves your true father and you . . . because . . . just because she loves you too.

You will also know, by now, that I have lived a precarious life and my future is uncertain. That is the reason behind me writing this letter to you now. The enclosed certificate relates to a share in a new Tin Mine (Wheal Jenny) which has opened on the edge of St Austell. The shares I leave to you and any interest on these shares will be deposited with Mr Franks who has been instructed to hold it and invest it in future shares should they become available.

It is Mr Franks who writes this letter to you, but I sign it in the hope that you will have a happy life and that Ginny too finds the true happiness that she deserves.

Adam Sawle

Jamie glanced up at Ginifur, whose surprise was most evident as she wiped the tears from her cheeks. Jamie opened the other piece of paper, a legal document in flowing script *Five hundred shares.* "Five hundred shares" he exclaimed. "Twenty percent of the shareholding of Wheal Jenny." He was speechless.

Jamie's news was greeted by stunned silence. Ginifur was quite taken aback by his announcement and Sara! Well . . . Sara couldn't understand why this piece of paper was such good news.

"No money? No jewels? Just another piece of paper!"

Jamie laughed and reached for the box and glanced in. "Yes, just a piece of paper. But obviously Adam thought it very valuable indeed. However it would appear that Wheal Jenny had just been opened and they had only just dropped the first shaft. Who knows, it may even have been closed down by now."

"Wheal Jenny!" Liam pondered. "On the edge of the moor, near St Stephens, I'm thinkin'. I'm afraid, if tis the same mine, they were in trouble back in seventy-eight." he informed them. "Apparently the seams of tin began to run out. The investors kept propping it up and lost a lot of money I seem to remember. Mr Fry included I believe. I think it closed a year or so ago. I can't be sure."

"There you are then. Easy come, easy go. But it was a kind thought of Adam nevertheless." Jamie laughed and raised his shoulders in resignation.

"Oh!" Sara exclaimed. "What will you do now?"

"Well, I shall have to see Mr Franks to thank him for his part in all this; no doubt he will enlighten me on the present position or demise of Wheal Jenny." His carefree laugh was cut short as he took his first real look in the box. "Hello! What's this?" Putting in his hand, he pulled out a tiny envelope that had been tucked up at the side of the box. "Well! This certainly isn't paper," he said as he felt something hard inside.

Sara's interest had been awakened. "What is it? Oh, open it Jamie please. Let us see what else Adam has left you."

Jamie opened the tiny envelope and withdrew an ornately decorated card which said 'To Ginny, with all my love. Adam'. The words had been laboriously written in Adam's own hand and Jamie read them aloud before tipping the remainder of the envelope's contents into his hand. A gold sovereign, elegantly mounted, a gold chain together with a gold cross, a delicately engraved gold broach and a small gold figure of a mermaid; he held them out to Ginifur. "I guess these are really meant for you Ma."

Sara, a rapt expression on her face, watched as Ginifur took the items from Jamie's outstretched hand. "Have you seen them before, Mama?"

"The brooch, yes. Adam gave it to me long ago, one Christmas. I often wondered what had happened to it. The cross and chain . . . No; nor the mermaid." Ginifur's voice trembled with emotion as she spoke. "But I think the mermaid is a reminder of Kiara, and Adam's and my childhood."

"I think that he must have loved you very much, Mama."

Ginifur bit her lip before answering. "I know he did, Sara. I know he did."

Jamie saved her from further examination by saying. "Well I have to admit that the day has ended much better than it started, was it really only a few hours ago?" he raised his glass. "It is good to be home and amongst my family and friends. I would like to drink a toast to you all and a give a big thank you to both my real father and to Adam, who treated me as his own son." They all raised their glasses to drink with him. "I assume that Mr Franks still conducts our business?" Ginifur agreed that he was still in practice but that Edward's son Daniel now conducted most of the business. "The hour is late," he concluded. "I want to ride over the whole of the headland tomorrow, and hopefully look at all Tremanyon Home farm accounts if Mother doesn't mind." Ginifur indicated that she didn't mind at all. "And I would like to do it all before Beau puts in an appearance. So I think it is time for me to retire. Will you be ready to go out with me at six tomorrow Liam?"

"T'be sure I will, 'n delighted I'd be 'n all." Liam agreed.

"Then I think that it is goodnight all round. I am looking forward to seeing Beau's face when he appears on the morrow. I expect news must have reached him of my unexpected arrival."

* * *

In spite of Jamie's long day, and his tiredness, he did not sleep well. For some time he lay awake with unanswered questions filling every corner of his mind. He tossed and turned in his bed until finally, giving up any thoughts of sleep, he rose and dressed in his civilian clothes which were hanging in his wardrobe. Unconsciously he sniffed at them. They all smelt fresh and aired, someone had taken great care to make sure that they were fresh and ready for him whenever he returned home. His Mother? Kate? It could quite easily be either of them. He glanced in the long mirror. The reflection which stared back at him was strange and unfamiliar; not entirely unsurprising, for he had been in uniform throughout the entire past six years. Jamie decided that he would need to make a visit to the tailor. His old jacket was now a very snug fit; his shoulders were much broader than they had been six years ago but he could wear his cape if needs must.

Before the dawn lightened the sky beyond the library windows, Jamie had made a thorough examination of Ginifur's accounts for Home Farm. He had familiarised himself with yields and commodity prices and, when he heard movements in the domestic quarters, looked at his watch to find that it was six o'clock. Closing the last of the books Jamie went to find Liam.

The news that Jamie Tremayne had returned to Tremanyon had indeed reached the village, and was greeted with great delight by all who heard it. However, whether it was by accident or design, no report of these tidings had arrived at Killow Barton; neither did anyone comment upon it when Beau rode through Porthcarrow the following noon.

There was nothing to indicate that today was different from any other day as Beau slid from his saddle and called out. "Joe! See to Bran for me. I shall want to ride over to Rhosinnis later, make sure he is ready for me." Not waiting for an answer he looped the reins loosely through the ring beside the stable door and strode off towards the house. Taking two steps at a time he bounded up to the side door and into the back hall. The door to his father's study was ajar; this was unusual for his mother usually attended to the estate accounts in the library, preferring the light and the view over the gardens. Beau tapped his boots with his short whip, then threw off his cloak and tossed it carelessly over the back of the chair that stood in the corner. He was about to ignore the open door and call out for his mother when curiosity got the better of him. He paused at the door and listened but could hear no movement in the room and then, irritated with himself, pushed open the door.

To give him his due Beau hid his surprise extremely well, for undoubtedly Jamie had the advantage on him. "Well! So the prodigal son has returned. I expect Liam has already sorted out the fatted calf. What has brought you home without warning?"

Jamie smiled as he inspected his young brother; they had never been really close but Jamie had always put this down to groundless sibling rivalry that would eventually wear off. Beau had always taunted Jamie that their father favoured him, and he also believed that Jamie was closer to his mother; he was unnecessarily jealous of Jamie for in truth Richard favoured neither of them. As for his sister Sara, this was a different matter. In Beau's opinion Sara counted for nothing, she was just a girl and only the baby of the family, although he was firmly convinced that she was both spoiled and Papa's little darling. Yet even from an early age Beau believed that it would be he, his father's namesake, who would inherit Tremanyon. After all, he was the true heir; Jamie had been born out of wedlock whilst Ginifur was married to Adam Sawle. In his eyes the fact that Jamie was Richard Tremayne's first born son and that he had legally adopted him following his marriage to

Ginifur counted, for nothing. Beau had been only a boy when Jamie left home to go to sea on his first voyage, and barely considered a man when Jamie left on his last tour of duty . . . just a youth of seventeen.

There had been times in his youth when the finer points of Beau's character disguised his obvious flaws. Back then his good looks, imaginative flair, sense of humour and his blatant charm tempted one to overlook his failings; but Beau was a child no longer.

In the few brief seconds that it took for Jamie to answer him, all these things flashed through his mind. "I did write to Mother, telling her of my intention to return home." Jamie smiled pleasantly. "It's good to see you Beau," he pushed himself out of his father's chair to greet his brother in an endeavour to put their differences to one side; they were full brothers after all.

"*Richard!* My name is Richard. Richard Tremayne . . . as my father was before me." Beau snapped and with a side stepping movement managed to place a chair between them, thus avoiding any physical contact. "What on earth possessed Mother to call me Beau I cannot imagine."

Jamie obviously found something to amuse him as a laugh escaped his lips, infuriating Beau even more. "It wasn't Mother, actually it was me. At first it was 'Brother' then 'Bro' and finally 'Bo'. It wasn't long before you became Beau to everyone."

"That figures." Beau spat the words out contemptuously. "I should have guessed that you would have had a finger in it." He glanced idly around the room. "Making yourself at home I see. Just couldn't wait to sit in Father's chair," he added sarcastically.

Jamie suppressed his rising anger. "It is still my home, I believe."

"Well it's Mother's, for now. Don't go making yourself too comfortable."

"For now?" Jamie wondering what answer he could possibly have and repeated himself. "For now?"

"It will be my son who will inherit." Beau snapped. "Not yours."

Jamie nodded wisely, unaware that Ginifur had made any decision as to succession. "I did not know that you were about to become a parent Beau. However I understand that congratulations are in order; I do hope that you have made a wise and considered marriage. How long is it now? Three years? I am only surprised that you have not produced an heir to date. Anyway, may I offer my felicitations to both you and your wife, and I sincerely hope that you will both be very happy."

"Do you indeed?" Beau sneered suspiciously.

"You find that hard to accept?" Jamie raised his shoulders in a careless manner. "Believe me it is the truth."

"Humph!" Beau huffed, but his eyes took on a wary look as he pushed the chair away and, spinning on his heals, made for the door. "Where's Mother?" he demanded.

By the time Jamie had followed him into the hall Beau had opened both the library and drawing room doors. "Mother and Sara have gone to Well Cottage to see Grandfather; apparently he is not well." He informed his brother.

Beau made no effort to disguise his distaste. "Why does she waste her time with that old man? If she sees Father's family once a year it's a minor miracle."

Jamie ignored this churlish remark, refusing to be drawn into a fruitless conversation. It was a sad but true fact that the Tremayne family at Mevagissey had all but broken off contact with Richard's second family when he remarried. They had thoroughly disapproved of his marriage to his housekeeper and if it had not been for Rachel and Rebecca, their grand daughters by Richard's first marriage to Annabelle, Jamie suspected contact would have ceased all together. "Did you want anything in particular?" he enquired, agreeably.

"No." Beau snapped. "Naturally I call frequently to see if Mother is well, or find out if there is anything I can do."

"Like bring the post?" Jamie suggested.

Beau's expression did not change and he chose to ignore the subject of the post. "How long are you home for this time?" Beau put the question uppermost in his mind as he spied the account books open upon Ginifur's desk.

"This time?" Jamie appeared to consider the question. "This time . . . ?" and he waited until he had Beau's full attention before placing his cards firmly upon the table. "This time I am home for good . . . I shall not be returning to the sea."

Beau's face showed the impact of this information and, infuriated by Jamie's revelation snapped peevishly. "You won't find it easy to make a living at home here."

"No." Jamie agreed with him. "Certainly I won't, if I continue farming Rhosinnis in the manner that you have for the last few years. Out of interest, what were the yields like this year?"

Beau blanched and his eyes flashed with blatant hostility. "I don't need to answer to you. Father's instructions in his Will were quite explicit; I had all the profits from Rhosinnis until you saw fit to return home. You certainly took your time, didn't you? In any case when harvest is over all the crops are mine to sell." Jamie's smile only fuelled his anger further. "I brought the mail with me." Beau indicated the two letters he had thrown on to Ginifur's desk.

"Ah yes. The mail, it's good to know that the Royal Mail does such an efficient job, don't you think?"

"Meaning?" Beau scowled.

Jamie chuckled. "Whatever you make of it Beau."

"*Richard!*" Beau exploded. "*My name is Richard!!*" He pushed angrily passed Jamie and headed for the door. "Tell Mother I shall call on her tomorrow."

"Why not call in at Grandfather's if you are heading that way, and somehow I think you are. I am sure that he would be delighted to see you." Jamie suggested, finding the whole situation extremely humorous. He was rewarded by an incensed backward glance from Beau as he stamped furiously towards the front door.

Liam found Jamie shortly afterwards, in the library staring absently out of the window. "I heard young Beau's voice. A right brotherly welcome he gave 'ee too, I'm thinkin'." Jamie didn't answer immediately. "Don' 'ee mind 'im." Liam added comfortingly. " 'ee be all talk that one, and unfortunately opens 'is mouth before 'is brain be functionin'."

"But why has he got himself into this state? Something must have happened for his childish jealousies to consume him to this degree."

"I'm afraid that Beau's attitude is the culmination of all 'is self-centred belief in 'imself, and 'is continued idea of your father's preferment for his eldest son; although illegitimate in Beau's eyes of course, 'n therefore not worth consideration."

"Me?"

"Yes. I mind that Dickon was right too; t' leave Tremanyon in Beau's 'ands would be its downfall, mark my words. But pay no mind to 'im, are we not goin' back to Rhosinnis? To be honest I was looking forward to it."

Jamie brightened at this thought. It was a bright spring day and he wouldn't need a cape. He picked up his riding jacket, he was already dressed for riding, and closing the library door behind him they made their way to the stables.

* * *

By mutual agreement Ginifur was alone when Beau arrived at Tremanyon the following day, Jamie was paying a visit to Jack Newton in the overcrowded cottage at Portloe and Sara was helping Rebecca in the tiny schoolroom that Richard had provided for her in the village. On Ginifur's instructions, to appease Jamie and discreetly out of sight, Liam was on hand to offer her support, should she feel the need to call for him.

Beau's attitude had not improved and the glass rattled violently in the front door as he slammed the door behind him. He had seen Ginifur seated at her desk as he walked round to the front door, angrily avoiding entering by the side door, and immediately turned towards the library.

Beau's raised voice was countered by Ginifur's usual calm manner and the more her patience with him was displayed, the more rattled Beau became. The point which caused him to raise his voice even louder was her continued insistence on referring to him as Beau. On this point Ginifur was not moving. "Your father is very much still alive in my heart, Beau, and it would cause me too much grief to use his name for you. I will admit that you were given your father's name; however the intention was to use your second name to distinguish between the two of you. Perhaps that would have suited you better, maybe you like the name Claude . . . personally I don't, but it was your father's choice. You have been called Beau all your life and I am not about to change the habit of a lifetime. Why you suddenly have this obsessive desire to revert to your given name I cannot imagine, for Beau has been quite acceptable to you all these past years." What ever Beau had to say about the subject it didn't cut any ice with Ginifur and the subject was finally dropped.

Ginifur would not be drawn into a discussion on the fairness of Richard's settlement or on Jamie's decision to return home and give up his career at sea. She did not mention the missing letters or the fact that Beau had drained Rhosinnis to the very bottom. Neither did she discuss Jamie's feelings when he learned that his brother had married 'his girl', and when Beau finally took his leave he was none the wiser about Jamie's plans for the future or what actions to expect from him.

In fact, at this time Jamie had no confirmed plan in his mind. He was fairly certain that he would not return to the sea and in the meantime he would begin the enlargement of the main residence at Rhosinnis for, who knew, he might get married one day. For the time being he was happy to be back at Tremanyon, amongst his family and friends. He would just take each day as it came until he felt in a position to make any real plan for the future.

At first he had been confused by his reaction to the news that Clara had reneged on her promise to marry him, for this was how it appeared to him, and she had managed very soon to transfer her affections to his brother Beau. He tried to analyse his own feelings without great success; in truth he found that it bothered him little about her change of heart. Of course he realised that it was quite feasible that his extended period at sea had lessened his own ardour. That now, in hindsight, he had begun to see aspects of Clara's character that were not so appealing. He began to wonder if by readily accepting the proposition to send him to the Americas on an extended tour of operations it had been an unconscious action on his part to give him time to reconsider his own position. Clara's continual preoccupation with his future prospects, which he had once seen as her natural desire for security, he had begun to think of as obsessive. It was as though, her considered marriage to him was based on the fact of money and position alone. She had shown little interest in anything that did not directly involve herself or her family. Like Beau, he now realised, she was both self centred and haughty. The more Jamie considered the situation the more he wondered how he ever became betrothed to Clara Fry.

It had been, he presumed, a physical attraction in the first instance. The Fry family had only recently moved into the area when they first met and the fact that they had a daughter of marriageable age soon brought about the invitations. Jamie had been introduced to Robert and Margery Fry and their daughter at a celebration at the home of Martin Harris, who was still the standing Member of Parliament for Tregony. Clara was petite in stature and possessed a pale complexion with delicate features and white blonde hair. She was like a piece of fine and fragile porcelain, and it brought out the protective instinct in all the young men who were introduced to her. But it was Jamie's strong, dark and handsome features that had drawn her to him in the first instance, she had said, and he had been flattered. Yet now he found himself wondering if even this was true.

To all outwards appearances Jamie was the elder son of Richard Tremayne and Richard Tremayne was a prominent Member of the

Parliament, a wealthy landowner in his own right and also connected to a family of quality whose family estate was near Mevagissey. Although born whilst Ginifur was married to Adam Sawle, Jamie was in fact the true son of Richard and when Ginifur married Richard he had insisted in a full adoption whereby Jamie took his rightful surname. Of course it was local knowledge . . . but it was history. Few people ever thought of Jamie's beginnings. He was a Tremayne . . . not only was he a Tremayne, he was well liked and respected, as was his father. The Fry's had no reason to think anything other than that Jamie would be Richard's heir. Of course the fact that this might have coloured Clara's, or her parent's view of him as an acceptable suitor had never occurred to Jamie either, till now. He had been flattered by Clara's attention and by the hospitable manner that the Fry's welcomed him into their home, and yet, had he imagined it? Even whilst in the midst of the planning for their forthcoming wedding Jamie had felt a cooling in their relationship.

Whilst Jamie had been at sea there had been little time to consider these things. Now with time to recall what had seemed like trivial incidents, Jamie came to view them objectively and, finding that he was not in the least emotionally disturbed, came to the conclusion that he had lost nothing of true significance. Beau, he decided, was welcome to Clara Fry . . . and they were a well suited pair!

* * *

Caught up in the excitement of returning home, arranging for the return of Jack Newton and engaging replacement workers for those who had been put off by Beau and had found further employment, Jamie had little spare time on his hands and continually found reasons to prevent him making his promised visit to Truro. In fact there were only a few days to go before Christmas when Jamie made the overdue visit to Daniel Frank's office.

Daniel was the son of Edward Franks, and Edward had been the family's solicitor, and friend, who had dealt with all Richard's private matters since he first purchased the fire damaged ruin of Tremanyon in 1748. He welcomed Jamie into his office at the end of the Mews, ushering him through to a private sitting room beyond, and towards the chairs set on either side of a roaring fire. "I am glad to welcome you home Jamie, but you took your time in coming into Truro!" he grinned wickedly. "You'll have a drink?"

Jamie nodded, returning the grin. "Just a seasonal one, of course."

"Whisky, Brandy? Do you have a preference?" Daniel opened the doors of a cabinet to reveal a row of decanters and glasses.

"Brandy would be good; it has been a cold ride in to Truro. On reflection I should have come when the weather was warmer. It almost feels as if it could snow." Jamie waited with his back to the fire, warming his hands, whilst his host poured two glasses, handed one to him and then he took the offered chair. "I have found so much to do since returning home that this is my first visit to Truro," he explained.

"No problem." Daniel assured him. "I just thought that curiosity might have got the better of you, I presume that Mrs Tremayne gave you the documents!" Jamie indicated that she had. "I informed Father of your intended visit and he wanted to come in to see you. He should be joining us at any moment, I heard him arrive a short time ago."

"It is some time since we saw each other. I have been away at sea for more years than I care to remember, so it must be at least six years." Jamie remembered their last meeting. "It was certainly under happier circumstances than those that have brought me home."

"Yes. It was the New Year Ball at the Assembly Rooms, I recall. You introduced us to . . ."

Jamie smiled. "Yes . . . I introduced you to Clara, my once fiancé."

Daniel looked embarrassed. "I should have remembered, I am sorry."

"Don't be. I'm not." Jamie laughed. "I truly mean it Daniel, but let us forget an unpleasant subject."

"You were also accompanied by your sisters, Rachel and Rebecca. They were both belles of the ball that night I can tell you, and received many an admiring glance. Your eldest sister is married now I hear, and Rebecca? She has not given her heart away?"

Jamie stole a swift glance at Daniel's casually turned head. "No. Not as yet, I understand. But . . . am I mistaken in believing that you two were very close at one time?"

Daniel fidgeted with the decanter which he had placed on the small table at his side. "Yes, as friends only; there was no romantic attachment of course," he turned abruptly as the door opened. "There you are! Look who's here Father. The spitting image of Captain Tremayne don't you think?"

An elderly gentleman entered the room. His hair was white and his face lined, but a mischievous pair of pale watery eyes twinkled below hooded lids. An ivory topped cane assisted him to walk quite upright as he held his free hand towards Jamie. "Welcome home young Tremayne. Welcome home, if indeed it can be termed welcome under the circumstances. Such a dreadful thing! Dreadful without a doubt. A man in his prime still, with so much to look forward to," Edward Franks shook Jamie's hand warmly.

"Thank you, Sir; it is thoughtful of you to say such kind words."

Edward Franks lowered himself into the wing backed chair that Daniel brought forward. "Nonsense! Utter nonsense! Kind indeed! It was the truth. A finer man you couldn't wish to meet was Richard Tremayne. A great loss to Cornwall and an even greater loss to your family, no doubt." He eyed the tall dark young man. "Indeed you are the image of him. He was about your age when we first met, you know. Yes . . . yes . . . Back in . . . forty-seven . . . forty-eight? Yes that was it, forty-eight. Just after the fire gutted the Durance place." He was silent for a moment. "Not so long ago really, yet a lifetime it seems, sometimes." Edward studied the young man. "Yes, yes. You are indeed your father's son, no one could doubt it. It was his dearest wish that you should inherit Tremanyon you know. In the end we found a way to bequeath it to your Mother and she will be able to pass it on to the descendant of her choice, male or female."

"It is no matter, and in my view the right decision." Jamie assured him. "I am more than content with my own inheritance. One day Rhosinnis will be my home and this will be possible sooner than I believed with the good fortune of the investments that you have made on my behalf."

The old man nodded sagely. "I only wish other's were as satisfied." Then he chuckled. "Did quite well didn't we?" He waved a hand at his own son standing behind the desk. "Don't hide the decanter boy. Poor me a glass too, and sit down . . . do." he indicated the chair Daniel had vacated. "Come on, I want to hear all the news. I want to hear how Jamie's dear Mama is fairing."

"She is well, Sir, thank you." Richard informed him whilst Daniel poured a small glass of brandy, handed it to his father and made to resume his place in the vacant chair.

Edward Franks brought his glass to eye level and peered at the contents before reaching it out to his son. "Fill it up boy, what's this? Half measures? I thought that we were celebrating."

"Father!" Daniel attempted to reason with him. "You know what the doctors have said."

"And I listen to them 365 days of the year. Today I have no intention of doing any such thing. Today I am celebrating the return of the son of my greatest friend . . . and one drink is not going to make any difference to my health at my age. Fill it up." he insisted.

Daniel reluctantly did as he was told and handed his father the nearly full glass. "But just the one," he proclaimed.

"Just the one." Edward Franks agreed reluctantly, having got his own way.

Like old friends do, they passed more than a few moments in familiar conversation until Edward broached the subject that had brought Jamie into Truro. "So, young man. What do you want to know first?"

Jamie placed his empty glass on the small table at his elbow and looked directly at his senior. "Did you know Adam Sawle, Sir?"

"I did indeed." Edward assured him but added no more.

Jamie paused. "What was he like? If you don't mind me asking, I would like to know. Mother has said very little, I think the memories still hurt."

Edward Franks lent on his ebony tipped cane and glanced into the flames of the fire, as if they would conjure up an image for him. "A bright young man; born into other circumstances I think that he could have been a brilliant business man. He had such a head for figures and an uncanny knack for seeing an opportunity. I acted on his behalf a number of times over a couple of years. I don't know where his initial investment came from, I didn't want to know then and I don't want to know now, but his investments were shrewd. Young Adam instructed me to purchase the initial shares in Wheal Jenny when they were first launched and investors were sought. He asked me to continue to purchase any shares in the mine that came on to the market, which I did with the profits until the troubles set in. On the information given to me back in seventy-five, I made a loan on your behalf to the company to follow a fresh seam. But they failed to find the mother lode and two years later I refused to make a further loan until they matched it with funds from the other shareholders."

"So the mine closed." Jamie assumed.

"No . . . !" Daniel entered the conversation. "Far from it," he allowed his father to continue.

"It was shortly after this that we were paid a visit by a young man named Davey Rawe; his father had been the mine captain at the Bottalick Mine before the cave in there. Young Rawe told us that he was convinced that they were following the wrong seam, a false lead; he believed that the seam divided further back the shaft and that the mother lode was in a totally different direction. I asked him what made him so sure. Young Rawe said that he had been mining with his father since he was a mere boy, and that he had taught him to look for the signs. He had come to me so that I may inform my client of the true facts before he invested more capital. After a great deal of discussion we decided that there was a possibility that he was telling the truth. I informed the other shareholders that my client stood by his agreement to issue further capital when they matched the funds. When further funds were not forthcoming I said that we would fund a maintenance program until they did. To date they have not done so, and in fact some wish to dispose of their shares. I have not purchased any since."

"Has anyone investigated this false lead, or where this young man says the division is made?"

"No. The mine Captain, name of Hawes, is convinced that he is right and that there is no mother lode; unfortunately the shareholders agree with him. Their views are that young Rawe is an upstart with no experience."

Jamie considered this information. "How many shares do I own now?"

"Thirty one percent of the total issue." Edward informed him.

"Thirty one percent!" Jamie was stunned. "How are the others distributed? That is if you know."

"As I remember, and if things haven't changed, Nancekivel still holds his twenty percent, Martin Petherick still holds his ten percent, Charles Bolitho down to eight and Robert Fry is down to fourteen percent. The remaining seventeen percent is made up of small shareholders holding just one or two shares each. The major shareholders initially were Nancekivel, Fry and young Adam Sawle. 500 shares equated to twenty percent of the shareholding."

Jamie was amazed at the ability of Edward to remember this list of figures without the need to refer to written notes. "I see." He thought for a moment. "What is the chance that I might meet with Davey Rawe and visit the mine?"

"I'm sure that it could be arranged." Daniel declared. "I think you will agree that he seems a very genuine young man."

"Will you arrange it then please? After Christmas, sometime in the New Year. I would rather my shareholding in the company is kept quiet a little longer if possible."

Daniel said that he would make the arrangements for a meeting and then allowed his father to proceed to discuss other aspects of Jamie's inheritance. Furthermore Edward Franks was able to give him an insight into the man who had been just a name to Jamie. In the few short years that the elder man had known Adam he had come to hold him with some regard. The outcome was that Jamie was indeed surprised at his own wealth, bequeathed to him by a man who was not his biological father but had treated him as such in his final will.

This was the first Christmas that Jamie had spent at Tremanyon since he left home six years ago and he looked forward to it with undisguised delight.

Christmas day was spent with the family, with the exception of Beau and Clara who announced that they would be spending Christmas day with Beau's grandparents at Mevagissey. In truth he wasn't missed. After attending Church the whole family, with Liam, Kate and Aidan, sat down to an excellent early dinner prepared by Lorna, and Poppy with the help of Mabel and Lottie. Afterwards they enjoyed an evening of music, singing and parlour games.

Rachel and Toby, together with their new daughter were staying over for a few days and on Boxing Day Edward and Daniel Franks arrived to spend a night under the roof of Tremanyon at Ginifur's invitation. She had done little entertaining since Richard had died she declared; in truth she had done none.

Ginifur had just distributed her gifts to her children when Beau and Clara put in an unannounced visit. Beau was attending under sufferance and was making it quite plain and when Mabel brought light refreshments into the lounge, for Kate and Liam were spending the day with their own family, Beau suddenly proclaimed they were leaving.

Naturally Ginifur declared her disappointment but Beau insisted, informing them that Clara needed her rest. "For we have only called to give you the good news that Clara is with child." Jamie was the first to congratulate the pair, followed by Ginifur who professed her delight at the news. Beau assumed a smug expression. "So, come the summer, you will have yet another future heir for Tremanyon Mother."

"Always, of course, pre-supposing the babe is a boy, Beau. Or do you have divine information about the sex of your unborn child?" Jamie remarked, his amusement increasing as Beau turned on his heels. "I am not a gambling man Beau, but I don't advise placing a bet on the outcome."

A fuming Beau placed a comforting arm about his wife, who was upset by the obvious hostility between the two brothers and had found the whole aspect of the visit distasteful. But Beau's confidence had been dented; it hadn't occurred to him that the child Clara was carrying might indeed be a girl.

Rachel and Rebecca endeavoured to lighten the mood of the visit, but Beau and his wife clearly felt that they had fulfilled their family duty and were eager to leave. As the front door closed behind them and their carriage drew away Ginifur released a sad sigh. "I have searched my heart to find where I made a mistake with Beau," she voiced her thoughts. "I believed that I had treated you all the same."

Rachel clasped Ginifur's hand. "A better mother we could not have had. No," she stopped Ginifur interrupting, "not even if our own mother had lived. She loved us dearly Ma I have no doubt but, although I do remember her, in all honesty it was to you whom we turned to even before her death. Rest assured you meted out love and correction in equal measure; never favouring one more than the other, including Rebecca and I who were not of your own blood but always in your heart your daughters too." Her declaration eased Ginifur's mind for a time, but it was always a recurring dilemma.

Chapter Two
1782

THE DAY BEFORE Jamie's first visit to the mine, he and Daniel travelled to Hewas Water where they would stay at Trelander Barton, situated just outside the village which was a little to the west of the town of St Austell, with an acquaintance of Daniel's. The purpose of the visit, the Quintrell family had been told, was ostensibly for Jamie to inspect a young stallion at a nearby stud farm in his search for a new stallion for his stables, to breed with his own mares at Tremanyon and soon at Rhosinnis. Their story was not entirely false as Daniel had arranged for Jamie to visit a farm for this very purpose, conveniently situated less than a short ride away from where the Rawe family lived in a diminutive stone cottage beside the babbling stream that ran down through the valley.

The unseasonable warm and spring like weather vanished with the night and Jamie awoke to the sound of rain beating upon the window and wind howling through the bare branches of the trees that had been planted to afford the house a modicum of protection from the worst of the elements. Brief interludes in the driving rain afforded glimpses of a moor rising above the hill at the end of the valley. Having been born in a gentler landscape Jamie found the open aspect wild and alien. Further in the distance, he knew, rocky outcrops would provide little more shelter for the grazing stock than the expanse of heather and moorland grasses. It was a hard life on the moors for the tenants of some of the poorest land in the county, or for those who held moorland grazing rights at the very edge. The opening of the few tin mines on the edge of Goss Moor had provided a few jobs for the fit and healthy, for those with the courage or simply desperate enough to work below the ground in miserable and dangerous conditions. Young boys helped to add to the family income by pulling trolleys filled with ore along tunnels running with water and working long hours for little pay, whilst above ground young girls toiled with their mothers, sisters and cousins as 'bal maidens' carrying out the laborious task of sorting the ore at the large trestle tables, tearing their hands to shreds on the jagged rock until their once tender skin became hard and calloused. Jamie shuddered and turned away. This was the ugly truth behind his inheritance and he began to wonder at the fairness of it all.

Alone in the dining room Jamie gazed briefly at the portraits upon the panelled walls. Ancestors of the occupants he thought as he recognised a likeness in the males. He had turned his attention to some landscapes when the door opened and he was joined by Daniel with his friend Bertram Quintrell.

"Well you couldn't have chosen worse weather!" Bertram barked in his brusque manner. "S'truth man you can't really mean to tramp up the valley in conditions like this?"

Jamie smiled to himself, thinking that the climatic conditions were in his favour, for who in their right minds would be abroad in this weather, worsening by the minute, to see him inspecting the mine workings with young Davey Rawe. Turning to his host he grinned. "I've seen far worse conditions at sea."

"Hmph! Guess you're right there me lad. Still, no point in going out when there's no need I always say." He headed for the side table already set out with platters and silver covers and helped himself to a plate of freshly prepared food. "Well! If you intend to continue on this foolhardy venture of yours, and tramp about in the rain, you had better make sure that you have a hearty breakfast inside you to keep you warm. I'll make sure that there is enough hot water to send to your rooms so that you will be able to soak yourselves in hip baths on your return. For as sure as my name is what it is, you will be frozen to the marrow when you finally get back here." He placed his plate upon the table and waved a knife in the direction of the food.

Talk soon turned to horses, as Bertram had a fine stable of his own, and to the difficulties of estate management. Bertram Quintrell had, of course who hadn't, heard of the untimely death of Jamie's father. "Good man Richard Tremayne. He will be greatly missed. Most odd, if you don't mind me saying, the manner of his death! Never was a finer horseman than Richard Tremayne, never thought there was a horse could throw him. Still find it odd. New horse was it?"

"No, actually he is the horse I am riding today, Casper. They seem to think that the horse was spooked. It was a narrow track and uneven. Father came off, saddle and all, so they tell me. They think that Casper caught Father's head with his hoof." Having repeated it aloud Jamie appreciated how unlikely it sounded. Richard Tremayne was an excellent horseman and Casper a tried and trusted mount, even if a handful. "If he had been found sooner . . ." Jamie left the sentence unfinished.

"Hmph!" Bertram shook his head again. "Most odd, most odd."

Daniel, having mopped the egg from his plate with a piece of fresh bread, wiped the crumbs from his mouth and pushed his plate away. "Well Jamie, let us not waste any more time. If it continues to rain like this we'll be able to go up the valley in a boat." he quipped.

Having been pressed to take some extra oilskin cloaks, repeating the directions given to them and promising to return as soon as possible they finally took their leave, collected their mounts from the stable and headed north up the valley towards St Stephens.

The road was well used and would, in dry conditions, be hard surfaced with rock and stone. But the rain had brought mud down from the fields on higher ground at either side, making the conditions unfavourable and the going slow. At least Jamie was correct in his assumption that there would be few people abroad in these weather conditions and they passed neither man nor beast on their journey towards the village.

Just before the village of St Stephens they came upon a small collection of cottages huddled together beyond a stream that ran beside the muddy track. In normal conditions the stream would babble melodiously as it flowed along in front of the cottages. But now, after twelve hours of continuous downpour, the tiny stream was a turbulent rush of water that had spread outwards in its endeavour to escape its narrow confines and was now only inches away from the doors of the cottages that were its neighbours. Worried faces peered anxiously from behind small windows whilst a few wrapped up individuals, clothed insufficiently for the inclement weather, were hurriedly filling hastily constructed sacks with mud and shale and placing them around the doors. Apprehensive women stood in their doorways wondering when they would be forced to abandon their homes.

As turbulent as the water was, the river bed was hard and made of rock, it could be forded easily enough on horseback although the thought crossed Jamie's mind that he would not like to do it on foot for the force behind the water was quite strong enough to carry a man away should he have the misfortune to fall. With a reassuring word to his mount Jamie pressed his knees gently against the horse's flanks; urging him forward he set Casper's head towards the noisy rushing water.

A tall young man picked up another sack to fill and glanced across at the horsemen fleetingly before attending to the job in hand. Davey Rawe paused briefly as his brother nudged his arm and said, "Look 'ee yonder," then he completed the task of filling the sack, tied it firmly with a piece of cord and placed it beside the growing heap before straightening his back and pulling himself to his full height. Davey was six foot in height and then some more. He didn't know for sure; for he had never been measured. However it was true to say that he was the tallest man in the village. Not only was he tall but he was well built, strong and not an ounce of surplus fat on his body; for their diet, though meagre, was a healthy one. Davey and his neighbours were some of the lucky ones and were treated favourably by their landlord Squire Nancekivel who owned the whole of the settlement beside the edge of the stream. Included in the rent for each cottage was an allocated plot of land on which to grow vegetables, or keep a pig or a few chickens. By necessity a close community they had implemented a barter system between themselves and they managed to live a far better existence than the average family in either countryside or township. Some of Davey's neighbours were employed on the Squires land, a few walked to St Austell daily and others worked in the tin mines situated close to Goss Moor and a few, like Davey, were some of those recently employed in Wheal Jenny. Davey was luckier than most, he had been selected as one of the caretaking crew. One of those whose job it was to see that nothing was removed or stolen from the site, that the workings did not flood, that general maintenance was carried out and the winches greased.

Jamie would have picked Davey Rawe out from a crowd as one different to his companions. He was tall and his back was straight, unusual in a miner but he had a miner's look about him, and Jamie noticed that as the man made a move towards them he held his head up high. To some it would infer that he had a somewhat rebellious nature and that perhaps he felt that he was no man's inferior. However Jamie, looking into the man's eyes as he approached recognised, him to be a man who was sure of himself within the confines of his position in society; and Jamie knew for certain that this was a man whom he could learn to trust. Instinctively he knew that this was Davey Rawe. Until this moment they had referred to him as *young* Davey Rawe; in point of fact he was probably no younger than Jamie. Jamie reined Casper in and waited as he watched the proud young man approaching them. Davey Rawe had adjusted the less than waterproof sheet about his shoulders and stepped towards the horse, his trousers were hitched up away from the quagmire about his feet and tied with cord to keep them from falling into the mud. His head was uncovered and his hair was dark like Jamie's own, but wiry curls gave the impression that it had a life of its own as uncontrollable strands of hair twisted and corkscrewed in the wet. Usually miners were of pale complexion, but his swarthy skin reminded Jamie of the Romany gypsies, who sometimes attended the Tregony fair, and yet his features were more refined. Thick brows were set above evenly spaced slate grey eyes, a long straight nose above a well defined mouth that twitched at the corners, hinting at a man who could see some humour in life even when there was little obvious to smile about. Jamie judged that this young man would be within a year or two of his own age for, although first impressions were that he could be older, no doubt his life had been a far cry from Jamie's own privileged lifestyle. Even if Jamie's mother had not married Richard Tremayne of Tremanyon, as life had turned out Adam Sawle had left Ginny and her son well provided for and they would have had a comfortable life in the cottage on the cliff above Dingerien Bay.

Davey came to a halt a few steps from the horses head. Looking up he smiled briefly. "Good day t' ye Sir. St Stephens be a long ways from nowhere so t' speak, are 'ee lost, in need of directions p'raps? Unless y'ur lookin' for St Stephens o' course, but that be still a ways from 'ere."

Jamie took his cue from Davey Rawe. "We are near St Stephens you say; well at least we've managed the first part of the journey. Perhaps you would know where we might find John Polton? A farmer in the district I believe." He turned to Daniel. "What was the name of the farm Dan? Polhendra?"

"Old John of Polhendra? Yes 'ee d' live nearby. Tis nought but a few acres though, breeds a few 'orses." Davey continued to play along, speaking loudly enough for him to be heard by ears tuned in on the conversation. "Tis a bit out of the way mind. If'n 'ee don't know the way, in this weather ye could get lost in no time. Tell 'ee what though, I'm a goin' that way meself. We'm nearly finished 'ere. If'n it don' stop rainin' soon there's nought we can do t' stop it floodin' the cottages." He glanced back at the men filling the last of the sacks before adding, "'old on a bit, 'n I'll get me things t'gether." The young man hurried back to the cluster of men and women and explained that he was going to guide the two *gents* up to Polhendra on his way to make the check of the mine.

A young woman, huddled in the doorway of the nearest cottage, called out. "Don' 'ee be doin' nothin' stupid Davey. If the mine be floodin' then leave un be 'n get back 'ome. Bloody mine 'as bought nought but bad luck to we. Don' 'ee let un bring us no more."

Davey pulled the sheet more firmly about his shoulders and threw his head back as he laughed at the rain and his sister. "Nora, ye'll eat y'ur words afore long, ye mark what I d' say. I don' belong t' believe that Wheal Jenny is through with we yet."

Davey Rawe suggested that Jamie re-cross the stream and said that he would cross further up, where there was a rough foot bridge. Jamie wheeled Casper round and made his way back through the tumbling water to firmer ground on the other side, where Daniel waited. With a backward glance at the group huddled about the cottage doorways he hoped the water would rise no further and headed up the valley. Although the rain had eased slightly, there was no noticeable difference as the trees continued to shower down a constant stream of water on to their heads but, in a few short moments, they had found the rough bridge that Davey had described to them and he was already there waiting for them in the shelter of an abandoned stone shack beside the lane.

Jamie hurriedly dismounted and followed Daniel to join the young man, taking what little shelter there was from the rain.

"Mornin' Mr. Franks," a brief smile lit the young man's face. "Ye could 'ave chose a better day t' come a visitin'."

"You are right there, Davey; I hope that this rain won't indeed flood the workings at the mine. Will it be safe to take Captain Tremayne below?" Daniel expressed his concern.

"Oh 'es, tis dry as a bone below ground, don' 'ee worry none 'bout that. All the water will 'ave run away afore it could get down t' the levels," he assured them. "We put the 'orses on the pump wheal t' take away the surplus this very mornin', but most of it runs away through the adits anyways."

Daniel waved his hand, making the introductions. "Jamie this is Davey Rawe and Davey this is Captain Tremayne, now the largest single shareholder in the Wheal Jenny. However this is privileged information and what happens today is to be kept a secret between ourselves. Captain Tremayne wishes to remain anonymous for the time being, you understand?"

Davey nodded emphatically as he took note of the man who would possibly be his new employer. In truth he was his employer this very day; for it was he who had paid the wages to take care of the mine. "Ye've got me word on it, Sir," he shook the excess water from his hair "I'm pleased t' meet 'ee, Sir. Wheal Jenny be a good mine, she'll bring ye a good profit if ye've a mind t' watch the signs. I tried t' tell 'em that they was followin' a false lead, but 'em wouldn' listen t' the likes o' me. Can't say as 'ow I blames 'em really. After all I'm only a miner in their eyes. But I knows I'm right, 'n Da says so too. I took 'im below, ill as 'ee be, 'ee wanted t'see for 'isself. 'ee d' recon as 'ow the mother lode i'nt far away. One blast . . . maybe two . . . no more."

Jamie smiled. "I'm pleased to meet you Mr Rawe. It's a wise man who will listen and learn from his father. I shall be pleased to make his acquaintance sometime in the not too distant future. However, first I would like you to take us below, into your mine, and instruct me further. You will understand that I know nothing of mining, I was brought up on the land and have spent the last years at sea."

Davey screwed up his face and grinned. "Me name is Davey, Cap'n. Mr Rawe don' sound right some'ow. But if what ye say be true, if'n 'ee don' mind me askin'... what on earth made 'ee buy into Wheal Jenny?"

"Ah!" Jamie tapped his boot with his crop. "I was left some shares by . . . by a relative of my Mother. Mr Franks assures me that they have been a wise investment and on his suggestion I intend to increase my share holding," he studied Davey's open face for some seconds before adding, "and if you are proved to be correct . . . Davey, I assure you that I will not forget your information or your loyalty to the mine."

"I didn' ask Mr Franks for no reward." Davey protested. "It jest didn' seem right t' keep takin' money t' follow the wrong seam."

Jamie laughed at the angry expression that had appeared on Davey's face. "Easy now. I did not mean to infer that you did expect reward. But come, let us make a move, I think that the rain has eased a little."

Indeed it had and, with Davey leading the way, the party made its way up the valley on foot towards rougher land that could, now and then when the mist and rain allowed, be glimpsed in the distance.

As the trio left the valley floor the trees came to an abrupt halt. Stone hedges marked the boundaries, with a few blackthorn bushes bent by the wind and growing between the gaps. Narrow lanes led to isolated farmsteads and off to the left Davey Rawe pointed out the winch frames of Wheal Jenny which were clearly visible. Jamie studied them and the few stone buildings surrounding them. They etched a desolate picture upon the skyline, in stark contrast to the large house that he had glimpsed through the trees to the right. "Who lives in that large house over there?" He asked Davey who now walked at his side.

"That's Squire Nancekivel's place. Lives there with 'is daughter," a frown formed upon Davey's forehead, "t'be 'onest with 'ee, Squires all right." He bit into his lower lip before continuing. "T' tell 'ee the truth, I nearly went to see un, but . . ." his voice trailed off.

"But!" Jamie prompted, and Davey shook his head as if to say he hadn't an answer. "You didn't know how far it would go, or if it might put your job at risk. Was that it?"

"Some'ut like that, I s'pose." Davey kicked a stone which rattled ahead of them. "Anyways, folks kept tellin' of a mysterious investor and the legal man that represented 'im at the share'olders meetin's, 'n I got t' thinkin'. Well with legal men, it's a bit like church in't it? They mus'n tell what other folk tell 'em. Be that right?"

Jamie nodded and smiled. "Something like that," he agreed.

"Well I waited till there was a share'olders meetin' 'n it was the mine captain who pointed Mr. Franks out t' me, 'n 'e looked all right if'n ye knows what I mean. So I followed 'im 'n waited outside the Inn where 'e was stayin'. Ye knows the story from there, I 'spect." A group of stone buildings appeared at the edge of a stone track beyond the hedge. "There's Polhendra, shall I wait whilst ye look at the 'orses?"

Jamie examined the assortment of stone sheds and buildings and nodded his head thoughtfully. "Yes . . . if you don't mind. I don't expect to be long, I feel a little awkward to tell the truth for I only made the appointment to cover my visit to the mine. Nevertheless, now I am here I might as well take a look. My favourite stallion is getting a little long in the tooth, and I might as well start looking here as anywhere else," he handed Casper's reins to Davey, and turned to Daniel. "Would you like to come with me Dan or stay here and mind the horses with Davey whilst I make a quick visit?"

Daniel smiled and informed him that he would rather wait with young Rawe. He declared that he had never chosen a thoroughbred horse for himself or helped anyone else either for that matter. He always left that kind of decision to others more qualified than he and he didn't feel that now was the time to alter the habit of a lifetime. The rain had now well and truly eased and he and Davey wandered across the lane where they lent against the stone hedge admiring the view whilst Jamie conducted his business.

Jamie was not long. The blood lines were good, he told them as they made their way back towards the mine; there had been a young filly for sale and a two year old gelding with promise, but Jamie really wanted a stallion and nothing he had seen took his fancy. Talk had returned to the mine and Davey was telling Jamie about the levels at which he was working when the mine closed. When asked why it didn't flood with all this rain, he explained that the underground streams and springs at this point were mostly south of the mine and those to the north and west ran the other way down the hill. It was only the spring to the east that caused any problem at all. That was managed by the adits, that took the water away, and the maintenance team Davey Rawe had managed to pull together.

As he lifted the catch to the gate at the entrance of the mine Davey glanced back at the house in the trees. "If'n ye're really interested in 'orses then ye could do no better than to see Squire Nancekivel. My brother Hal works in the stables there. They breed horses for the 'unt. Hal says that they've some of the best bloodlines in Cornwall, 'n some would say the whole country. Lord Falmouth and Lord Godolphin 'ave both bought 'orses from 'im. Squire took Hal t' Ireland with un last time 'ee went looking for new bloodstock; them visited Dublin, Wexford and Tipperary too."

Jamie glanced thoughtfully at the grey granite house peeping through the protective plantation which screened it from the worst of the weather and thought that maybe that wouldn't be such a bad idea.

There was only a small team retained to keep the mine open and Davey had made certain that this shift would be his. The only other person at the mine would be his younger brother, John. John had relieved the previous shift and was the only person there to greet them. Davey made the introductions and then led them to the main shaft.

Having entered the granite building Jamie paused beside the guarded shaft, the only access to the workings deep below ground. Stepping nearer he glanced into the gaping void, only the first few feet were visible, showing a ladder securely clamped to the side and vanishing into the unfathomable darkness below. He raised an eyebrow. "And this is the only way down?" There was no fear in his voice, purely a genuine question.

Davey nodded. "For the moment, yes. Each level is connected by a series of ladders between levels, the only way up or down. We use a horse whim driven by ponies for the rag and chain pumps; it's worked by the system of cogs and wheels bringin' up any water left in the lower levels of the mine. When they finished this mornin' I tol' 'em t' give the ponies the day off, we've managed t' keep the levels down quite well of late. I'm sure there must be a way to take men down and up the workings using a similar system. What we need be one o' they high pressure boilers them keep talkin' about down at Hayle, then us could p'raps add some steps to it. He picked up his stiffened felt hat and placed it on his head. Picking up two more he held them out to Jamie and Daniel. "You'm not really dressed for clambering about a mine, if ye don' mind me sayin'; but if ye really want t' go below then these'll maybe 'elp 'ee stop 'urtin' y'ur 'ead." He glanced into the depths. "Are 'ee really sure ye want t' do this?"

Jamie took the offered stiff, thick wool hat and placed it on the low stone wall, threw off his cape, divested himself of his jacket and withdrew, from the package that he had had strapped behind him on the horse, a thick woven smock that he had used when he and Aidan went fishing. Pulling out a second one he handed it to Daniel. "There you are Dan, that should protect your clothes from the worst and hopefully stop any awkward questions when we return to Trelander." He pulled the first smock over his head and shoulders and waited for Daniel to do the same. Both then warmly clad they placed the thick hats on their heads and Jamie added. "Well . . . lead the way then Davey. You don't think that I have ridden out here in this dreadful weather just for a view of a hole in the ground. Mr Franks has paid to keep the mine open, with my money I might add, on information given to him by you. Now it is for you to convince me that his decision was the correct one and that there really is a future for us all in Wheal Jenny. I don't have to tell you that there is a lot riding on this young Davey or tell you that I know nothing about mining either but, believe me, I am a quick learner. It is up to you to convince me that what you believe, may be true. If you do then, and only then, will I consider the next step."

Davey Rawe indicated that his brother should lead the way. He handed a candle lamp to John, which he fitted to the leather belt round his waist. "Climb down t' the first level John and wait there until us d' join 'ee, then us'll go down to the next level till we'm all on the fifth level." He turned to address Jamie. "I will explain the situation as we go." Jamie nodded. "I will follow both ye and Mr Franks with another lamp. Ye won't be able t'see the bottom of the shaft, but be sure ye don't fall. I wouldn't like t' 'ave t' explain why 'ee were 'ere." Jamie watched as John stepped onto the ladder and took a firm hold of the top rung until he felt the strength of the securings in the side of the shaft before taking his first steps into the void "I can assure ye that we 'ave maintained all the ladders . . . they'm safe." Davey added with a smile as he watched Jamie swing his leg over the side and grinned as he too tested the strength of the fixings.

"I am a sailor. I never take anything for granted; it is second nature to check before stepping into the unknown." Jamie replied as he started the downward climb.

Assembled on the fifth level Jamie commented on the rise in temperature as they had descended ever deeper into the mine. It was almost warm, there with the heat rising up from the bottom of the shaft which continued down for some fathoms below them. Davey removed the shutter from the candle lamp about his waist, lit some candles and placed them on a crude shelf in the rock, he also fitted some to the brims of their hats with a spot of melted wax and, in the gloom, indicated the narrow tunnels that led from the assembling point where they stood. All of the tunnels were hewn from the rock. One was a little larger than the others and it was to this one that Davey led them. With Jamie by his side, when space allowed, he acquainted him with the operations of the mine explaining the methods of extracting the ore, showing him the traces of the lode that they had been following, and where the tributers had been digging the ore and removing it from the tiny tunnels, no bigger than a man could crawl in, off the side of the main level in which they walked. Davey explained the tribute system, where miners bid for a pitch according to its assessed value by the mine captain and these were then auctioned to the miners who were prepared to work for the lowest tribute. He showed how the walls were shored up for added strength, and explained where gunpowder was used carefully to create a controlled explosion without bringing about a fatal collapse in the mine. The information seemed endless but Jamie seemed to absorb it all, asking pertinent questions when the occasion arose. At first there was room for two to walk together along the rough walled tunnel, picking their way carefully along the uneven floor, avoiding a discarded barrow here and there or a pile of assembled ore which had not been removed. But as the tunnel narrowed they were forced to walk in single file with their heads down and, as the roof and walls began to close in on them, there was nowhere near enough room for them to walk upright and they had to walk with a considerable stoop; with their heads down and their shoulders almost touching the sides. Jamie almost walked right into Davey as he came to an abrupt halt, holding his lamp level with his head as he examined the walls carefully. Jamie and Daniel watched in silence, the only sound came from the water which dripped constantly around them and the tapping noise made by Davey's investigation of the rock surface surrounding them as if, for the umpteenth time, checking that his thoughts were correct.

Suddenly Davey stopped and returned to where they waited. "There!" he pointed a few feet ahead of them, where there was a change in the direction of the tunnel. "Ye can see 'ere, where the lode all but vanished. The last ore took from 'ere were from that tributary, yonder. Mr Hawes, the mine Captain, made an investigation and decided t' take samples. They set the charge 'ere." Davey pointed to where a section of the wall had been blown away, forming a large cavity. "Further investigation led 'im t' believe that the lode continued t' the left 'n the new tunnel went that way."

"But you don't believe him?" Jamie suggested.

"No." Davey hesitated. "I know I'm only a boy compared t' a man of 'is years. But me Da, 'ee knew 'is job, worked the tin mines all 'is life. I went underground with 'im as soon as they would let me, and learned me trade from 'im. Ask anyone who worked in the Bottalick Mine, there was none better."

"It was his health that stopped him?"

"They said it were an accident. A badly laid charge collapsed the tunnel 'n 'ee were trapped for three days. 'ee were the lucky one they said, many did'n live through it. Lucky! Da could'n work again, could 'ardly walk. Da lost 'is job 'n us all lost our 'ome."

"Then why do you do it?" Jamie puzzled.

"Don' rightly know I c'n answer that. Ye've an instinct for it I s'pose. Bit like fishermen maybe, but fur the life of me I would'n want t' do their job, no more 'n them would want t' do mine. Guess it's bred into we by generations of miners afore us. It gives 'ee a feelin' ye can't explain, there's just y'urself 'n the tin . . . man matched against mineral."

"So what led you to believe the mine captain was wrong?"

"I did'n, not at first. T'was only when us could'n find the new lode that I started t' question it. Cap'n said I were wrong, it were only a matter of time. One Sunday I tunnelled in from the explosion site aways, till I found where the seam continued, that's when I showed 'im the fissure in the rock and the tell tale sign of the lode t' the right, 'ee dismissed it, said I knew naught 'n not t' waste 'is time nor the shareholders money." Davey explained.

"But you didn't believe him then?"

"No, neither did Da."

"How would he know? Are you telling me he came down to see it?"

"Not right then 'ee did'n. I drew a plan of the mine, described the signs 'n took samples up top for 'im t' look at, 'ee were quite convinced I were right, but 'ee didn't come down the mine till she be closed. Then John 'n me brought 'im down. T'was easier then, 'ee could take 'is time, like. Lowered 'im in the kibble us did, John 'n me." Davey smiled at the memory. "Made 'im some wheezy mind, on top o' the accident the tin dust 'ave got into 'is lungs over the years, but 'ee insisted on goin' on. Us crawled in there with a couple of lamps 'n 'ee made 'is own examination. Took un nearly an hour afore 'ee were satisfied, 'n 'ee were real crook after I c'n tell 'ee."

"And . . . ?" Pressed Jamie.

"Well like I said. Da agreed that the new lode d' go off t'other way completely. Silly thing is we both believe tis only a short ways away. Not only is . . ."

"Yes?"

Davey drew a deep breath. "Of course us may be wrong. If'n it were me only, then maybe I would'n be so keen t' say, but there be Da, y'see. Tis what 'ee believes, 'n Da! Well, ee's never been wrong afore."

Jamie controlled himself with difficulty. "About what?"

"About the size of the lode."

"And what about the size of the lode?" Jamie asked patiently.

Davey looked slowly from Jamie's shadowed face to Daniel's. This bit of information he had never given out, hardly believing it himself, let alone to suggest it to someone else. He returned his eyes to Jamie, studying his face to see whether he should divulge the information. Supposing that they were wrong, supposing for the first time Da had not read the signs right. He hadn't been down a mine in a long time now; he wasn't as young as he had been! Jamie returned his scrutiny, assessing the honesty of the young man before him. Asking himself what the young man would have to gain by all this. If the information was wrong the worst that could befall him would be that he would be out of a job. There would be little action that could be taken against him for misinformation.

Davey made his decision. "Us d' believe . . ." he said confidently, "me, 'n Da that is, that the lode we've been followin' t' this point, were but a tributary of the mother lode. A good one, tis true 'n 'ee could easily confuse it. The one we was following yielded well, tributes from the side was good 'n there were really no reason t' think otherwise. But the mother lode lies beyond this face, 'n in that direction. Da's sure of it, 'n 'ee d' say tis a big'n. And, 'ee say that what's been took out of this mine is nothin' compared t' what lies beyond for ee's convinced there be copper there too."

Jamie just stared at him, he opened his mouth to speak but nothing came out and he turned to Daniel. "You didn't tell me this!"

If Jamie could have seen better he would have noticed the colour drain from Daniel's face. Daniel shook his head. "I didn't know," was all he said.

Jamie turned back to Davey. "Take me in there and show me what you are talking about."

Davey was taken aback. "In there! You'm want t' crawl in there, on y'ur belly 'n in all this dust . . . 'n in they clothes!"

Jamie pushed his hat firmly on his head and turned towards the opening in the rock face. "Too damn right I do. It's my bloody mine and it's my bloody money. If I am to take your word and your father's for spending more of it, I want to see what you are talking about. And I am warning you young Rawe, you had better be good. Don't miss anything out, you tell me everything. Everything, is that clear? Not only your future, but mine also, will depend on the outcome of this visit."

Davey argued no more, adjusted his hat and said. "Tis no wider than ye c'n crawl through t' start with, but at the end tis wider. I dug it out afore bringin' Da down, so's it'd be easier for un, 'n us could work side by side." He shook his bewildered head. "Ye'll follow me, be that right?"

"You've got it in one. I'll be right behind you . . . Daniel, you'll wait here. Yes?"

Daniel nodded, feeling that he would rather sit down and take this all in. Could young Rawe really be right in his assumption? Surely not? Surely an experienced mine captain would not have missed such a sign if it really did exist? He looked about him and spied an upturned barrow. Stumbling across the uneven surface of the tunnel floor he slumped upon the wooden barrow and buried his head in his hands.

"Be ye alright, Sir?" John's concerned voice almost made him jump. "I've got a jar of fresh water if ye're feelin' a bit faint like," he offered.

Daniel peered into the gloom beyond and behind him. It was like being entombed, he decided, and the thought did not serve to improve his condition. Daniel held out his hand for the offered flask and gave a husky. "Please . . ." He sipped the water, so cold it was almost like iced water, and his head cleared as he put his mind to the information and quickly assessed the possible outcome of the news that young Davey Rawe had given them.

In the confined quarters out of sight of Daniel, Davey attempted to instruct Jamie on the wonders of tin mining. Coming from a long line of miners, and a miner himself all his life, the significance of the rock strata and the way a seam of ore ran through it would usually point to the obvious conclusion that large deposits of ore lay not far away. If the mine captain couldn't see it how on earth was he supposed to convince a layman like Captain Tremayne? Davey needn't have worried. Jamie listened intently to all he had to say, studied the rock face and the ore samples that were handed to him and made observations that were relevant to the problem that faced them. Having shown Jamie the evidence of tin most likely not far away Davie pointed out a section of rock going off in the other direction. "See this . . .'ere?"

Jamie lifted the lantern to get a better look. "You mean this damp green patch? Yes, what is it? Mould or algae?"

In the dark Jamie could even hear the smile upon Davey's face. "Neither . . . tis copper. Tis only the tip of it mind, the copper is below the tin 'n us'll need to go down deeper for it."

“And what does your father say about that?”

“Well y’see, next mine over be Magdalene Mine, she be a copper mine. Done well over the years but she be nearly mined out, ’n with copper prices so low ’cos o’ the copper from Wales floodin’ the market, she ’ave cut back ’n put men off work.

“Does that affect Wheal Jenny?”

“Not dreckly, no. But Father is convinced that there be big deposits of copper beyond this rock and we are quite a ways within the boundary marks of Wheal Jenny land.”

“Big? How big?”

“Well . . .’ee can’t be sure o’ course, but in ’is words ‘I believes it could be even bigger than that there tin.” Davey indicated the tin seam on the opposite side. “What’s more . . .” he put a hand in his pocket and drew out two pieces of rock which he handed to Jamie to inspect.

“I suppose you expect me to say something.” Jamie held them close to the candle lamp, twisting them one way and another in the dim light. “Is there something shining there? I can’t be sure, glass like . . . what is it?”

“We think that one piece contains pieces of amethyst and t’other be garnet. These are only small tis true, but it shows they’m ’ere.”

If Jamie had any lingering reservations about Davey Rawe’s honesty they were dispelled instantly. “Where were these found?”

“Right ’ere, just where the first copper signs come on the left. May not be much, might never find anythin’ bigger, but it shows they’m ’ere. The Magdalene ’as mined a few worth mentionin’ over the years.” Jamie took one last look around the small cavern and finally pocketing a few samples of the ore to inspect at ground level, he confirmed that he had seen enough for the time being and they returned to the main tunnel.

Once more above ground Davey showed them where and how the ore was sorted and at the sorting tables he broke some of the samples to show them what he was looking for. Jamie thanked the brothers for the tour of instruction, bade Davey and his brother to keep his visit strictly to themselves and requested that Davey paid a visit to Trelander Barton around noon of the following day; just in case he had thought of any question that had not been covered.

Jamie and Daniel spoke little on their return ride to Bertram Quintrell’s home, each in his own thoughts. The rain had dispersed, patches of blue sky appeared from between the thinning clouds and, as afternoon wore on, the sun peeped out more frequently until, by the time Hewas Water was in sight, it hardly seemed possible that the morning had started so dreadfully.

After dinner, over port and brandy, Jamie told their host of the disappointing outcome of his visit to the Stud at Polhendra.

Bertram drew on his cigar, blowing a perfect circle into the air as he exhaled slowly and watched intently as the circle drifted upwards until it finally vanished. "Hmm . . ." slowly he lifted the brandy glass, swirling the amber contents gently round the glass. He sniffed the bouquet appreciatively before taking a sip. "Excellent brandy, truly excellent. Wouldn't care to tell me where you got it I suppose?" Jamie grinned. "No. Didn't think you would somehow," he took another sip. "So you want to acquire a new horse, do you?" Jamie nodded, explaining that his own favourite stallion was getting a little long in the tooth for any real hard work. It had been fine whilst he only needed it for visits home, but now that he was resident again, and trying to establish himself and help his mother to carry out his fathers love for his stables, he would need to bring on a new horse.

"Set your heart on a stallion have you?"

"Yes. I want to improve our already good stock. Casper too needs to be replaced and a well bread stallion would be a good start."

"Surprised that you didn't visit Benjamin Nancekivel whilst you were up there! Didn't who ever told you about John Polton tell you about the stables at Penhallow?"

"No . . . Good are they?" Jamie feigned unawareness of its existence.

"Some of the best in the west." Bertram laughed heartily at his own humour and then nodded his head seriously. "Some would say it is truly the best. Stay an extra day and pay him a visit. Believe me, you'll not be disappointed."

"I can't just turn up without an appointment!" exclaimed Jamie.

Bertram laughed. "Take it from me; you'll be made most welcome. Ben Nancekivel doesn't get about much nowadays; they have infrequent visitors at Penhallow since his wife died. You would be made most welcome, I can assure you. The place is in the back of beyond mind; Penhallow means on the edge of the moor and that's about right. But, see here, I'll send one of the stable lads up with a message, first thing in the morning. Tell him you will call on him in the afternoon. How's that?"

Jamie smiled appreciatively. "It sounds perfect. It seems that my visit may not have been in vain, Daniel," he remarked.

Daniel nodded his agreement. Finding that he was, for the moment, speechless.

Later, alone by the fire, they discussed the findings at the mine, young Davey Rawe and his father and, of course, the suggestion that there was a great deal of ore left in Wheal Jenny; and Jamie enlightened Daniel of the conversation that had taken place out of his earshot. If any, if not all of what they had learned was true, then it was possible that a small fortune was still to be made and the mine was not played out as had been suggested. Jamie considered his proposed visit with Squire Nancekivel. Daniel had met with him on a number of occasions for he was a shareholder in Wheal Jenny, but knew very little of him personally. Jamie decided that he would play it by ear and, after a great deal of consideration, declared that they would definitely visit Penhallow and take Davey Rawe with them.

* * *

The butler announced Davey's arrival shortly after noon and after a brief interview they set off to visit Benjamin Nancekivel.

There had been a sharp frost in the early morning and it showed little sign of thawing; it had taken Davey all morning to walk to Trelander. The return journey was somewhat quicker as Bertram Quintrell had insisted that they take his carriage. Jamie satisfied his curiosity by saying that he had loaned young Rawe a cape to protect himself when he kindly offered to guide them to Polhendra and that, if it was acceptable to him, they would give him a lift back to St Stephens. Bertram had not been witness to Davey's arrival, so would not have been aware that he had not returned a cape.

The crisp, bright afternoon continued without a thaw; there was no warmth in the sun. The stiff easterly breeze kept the temperature low and the puddles left from the day before still had a thin coat of ice covering them as they turned into the drive at Penhallow.

Jamie's initial impression was that of many others, it was a fine Manor House. However, on closer inspection, there was sign of neglect. The walls were good and solid but the paintwork required attention; potholes were appearing in the drive and a fresh layer of shingle would not go amiss. The grass in the paddocks looked well kept but the hedges badly needed a trim, as though there was not enough labour to attend to this mundane yet essential work. As the carriage drew up to the front door, and Jamie alighted, he noticed that the gardens too were showing signs of decline. He reflected on this as he waited for Daniel and Davey to join him on the drive. In his opinion Squire Nancekivel needed money, yet he retained the share of his original holding in Wheal Jenny when everyone else was selling out. Why? Jamie was keen to find out.

The door was flung open, not by a butler or manservant but by the jovial faced Benjamin Nancekivel himself. Short, stocky, with the ruddy complexion of a man who spends a great deal of time out of doors and sporting a neatly trimmed beard, he was dressed casually as though he had just returned from a walk. He bounded down the steps with a large hound at his heals. "Welcome to Penhallow," he declared. "I received the message to expect you, now then which of you young gentlemen is Captain Tremayne?" He glanced from one to the other, his eyes briefly settling on Davey Rawe. "No. I know it's not you young Davey. I wonder how you come to be here? I'm sure they could find their way without your guidance . . . never mind." An intelligent pair of twinkling blue eyes scanned Daniel, registering the fact that they had met before at the mine meetings and quickly determining that this was not the gentleman he was expecting. He immediately turned his attention to Jamie, instantly aware that this had to be Captain Tremayne, and smiled. "I am pleased to meet you," he said, and held out the hand of friendship.

Jamie accepted his firm handshake. "I hope that I have not inconvenienced you. I felt that it was too much of an imposition to call with so little notice, but Bertram Quintrell insisted that you would not mind."

"And neither do I, no, no. It's good to see a new face. Don't get about much these days, not one for socialising, standing around making polite conversation. To be honest I prefer horses to people. You are looking for a horse I gather. For yourself or your good lady?" he asked.

Jamie grinned. "Myself. There is no Good Lady . . . yet."

Benjamin Nancekivel cocked his head on one side in a puzzled attitude. "No! Forgive me, but I thought that Bertram said that your name was Tremayne. Are you not the son of Richard Tremayne . . . of Tremanyon?"

"I am." Jamie confirmed.

The squire's confusion was obvious. "I thought . . . then. But are you not married to Miss Carla Fry? I was invited to the wedding but, the circumstances you see."

Daniel glanced briefly at Jamie, wondering what his reaction would be, but he need not have worried. Jamie burst out laughing. "No. I see the mistake. That is my brother Beau. Beau is my young brother, I am Jamie. I have been away at sea until quite recently. As soon as word got to me of my father's death I returned home and now I plan a new career, one linked to the land. To be honest, on reflection, I don't think that I should have really entertained any other."

Squire Nancekivel was still not entirely satisfied. "You are the eldest son of Richard Tremayne?"

"Yes, that is true. I am Captain Richard Tremayne's first born son, but I was born before my Mother and Father were married," he admitted honestly.

"I see. I see," said Squire Nancekivel, who clearly didn't, wondering why he had not heard of this other son from Robert Fry when he was boasting about his son-in-law. Still, Benjamin thought to himself, Fry was a sly old bugger anyway. Not the sort that he would trust very far. "Well!" he addressed Jamie returning to the matter in hand. "For yourself then?" He considered his options. "A stallion I think. Young, with good breeding and a bit of spirit . . ." he looked at Jamie for confirmation.

Jamie smiled. "Go on."

"I think that I have just the one for you. You'll have to wait a bit, not quite a year yet, but he has promise. Oh yes, he's got promise. Bassett wanted him; he thought he would make a good horse for the hunt . . . made me a good offer too," he eyed Jamie up and down. "Are you acquainted with Francis? Helped to form the Cornish Metal Company you know. Didn't know then why I turned him down; perhaps now I do."

"I remember him vaguely. I went with father, once when home on leave, to ride with Basset's hounds at Illogan . . . I presume you refer to the Bassets of Tehidy?"

"Mm . . . yes. Sir John Rogers wanted him too, he founded the Four Burrow Hunt with the Vivian brothers a couple of years ago; Basset rides with them too y'know . . . turned Roger's offer down too."

"And now?" Jamie reminded.

"Now . . . ? Well something tells me this time it is different. He needs a special owner this colt, and instinct tells me that you may be the person." He turned to Davey. "Young Rawe, run down to the stables and tell Hal to bring Merlin out. Tell him I have a prospective buyer with me."

With a quick glance at Jamie, Davey did as he was bid and Squire Nancekivel and his visitors followed on at a slower pace. Jamie was given a conducted tour of the stables, he inspected the brood mares, the stallions and the young stock of varying ages, and he was impressed by the knowledge of the owner. He was truly a man who loved horses, his love of breeding showed in all his stock and he could discuss each ones lineage without recourse to records. Merlin turned out to be white, as were both his parents, and although Jamie had never considered a white horse in the past he was particularly impressed with the young stallion and, even taking into consideration that he was not really ready for a replacement at this point in time, he was drawn to the young stallion immediately. The feelings were mutual. The young colt threw up his head, sniffing the air for a moment, and then nuzzled at the hand that was held open to him while Benjamin nodded happily to himself. The bargain, once made, Jamie was offered refreshment to seal the deal and the party made its way back towards the house. The squire was a little taken aback when, afterwards, Jamie asked if he might bring Davey Rawe into see him as he had a proposition to put to him which involved information which Davey was party too.

In the study Davey glanced uncomfortably about him; Jamie noticed and immediately went out of his way to put him at his ease before addressing Benjamin Nancekivel.

"Sir!" he began.

"Well I don't know that I like the way this is starting?" the squire exclaimed. "Is it really necessary to be so formal? I fully realise that I am old enough to be your father, young man, but I would prefer it if we could start off on first name terms, I think that I would feel more comfortable. You have told me that your name is Jamie, my name is Benjamin, but my friends call me Ben." Benjamin Nancekivel was stunned to hear what Jamie and Daniel had to tell him, and listened carefully to Davey's theory of the mother lode lying in a different part of the mine. Having heard them through, he sat for a few moments without saying a word, quietly trying to absorb the information before addressing Jamie. "And so it has been on your behalf that Mr Franks has been acting all this time." Jamie nodded. "So why, might I ask, have you not come forward before?"

Jamie gave him the brief explanation that he had only now come into his inheritance and, having had no knowledge of it, the administration had been in the hands of Edward and Daniel Franks until his 25th birthday. This birthday had occurred whilst he was still away at sea and obviously he had no knowledge of it until he returned.

"And now? You think that young Rawe and his father may be correct in their assumption?"

"I am willing to fund further exploration and would like to call an extraordinary meeting of the shareholders of the mine, but I think that I would like you behind me in this, particularly in view of the fact that you are the second largest shareholder in Wheal Jenny."

"Second?" questioned Ben Nancekivel. "I actually thought there was an equal allocation. So who is the largest shareholder might I ask?" His look encompassed both Daniel and Jamie but it was Daniel who answered.

"On the last purchase of shares for Captain Tremayne, it is he who holds the largest number of shares." Daniel informed him.

Benjamin Nancekivel digested this information before surmising. "Fry has sold out, has he? Got no guts that man! Only came in for a quick profit, never really showed any interest in the mine, who's the other? Petherick too, eh? Quick enough to take the money when it came in, grabbing it like it was going out of fashion, though not so quick to invest when it was needed," he said scathingly.

"Bolitho still holds ten percent, Petherick eight percent and Robert Fry still holds the most with fourteen percent at the last count." Daniel informed him.

"Then, I take it that you could be prepared to stand beside me on the renewal of exploration, Ben?" Jamie asked eagerly.

"Wouldn't I like to see the expression on Fry's face if you are proved right? Damn me if I wouldn't." Ben Nancekivel considered the problem further before adding. "Why don't you stay for dinner and we'll discuss this in greater detail, stay the night why don't you? I'll send word to Quintrell to expect you in the morning sometime and I will send you back in my own carriage."

After consideration Jamie and Daniel agreed to spend the night at Penhallow, sending Davey home and charging him not to divulge what he had heard and to await further instructions.

It was not until they entered the formal dining room that Jamie and Daniel were finally introduced to Benjamin's daughter, already seated at the far end of the mahogany dining table.

Outwardly Ellen Nancekivel bore not the slightest resemblance to her father. She was slender and, Jamie quite correctly guessed, not as tall as the average female. She was blessed with remarkable bone structure whilst her perfect oval face was framed by a mass of dark chestnut curls. A pair of matching brown eyes was set below finely arched eyebrows and above a delicately formed nose with a shapely pair of lips tilting upwards in a welcoming smile. Her flawless complexion was more olive than the usual pallid pink and white that was the desire of most young ladies of the time . . . her age? Possibly mid twenties! She extended a perfectly manicured hand. "Captain Tremayne! It is a pleasure to welcome you to my father's home, please forgive me for not greeting you earlier."

Jamie was enchanted; there was almost a musical tone to her voice. "There's nothing to forgive," he assured her, "and the pleasure is all mine, I can guarantee."

Squire Nancekivel smiled inwardly, ushering them to their chairs and taking his own at the head of the table. Any dissimilarity to her father ended with their physical appearance. She shared the same happy and outgoing personality with Ben Nancekivel; shared his interest and love of horses and showed a genuine interest in others. The conversation flowed easily backwards and forwards and she listened avidly to the talk of the possible mother lode of tin ore at the Wheel Jenny mine.

"Why Wheal Jenny?" prompted Jamie, at the end of the meal.

"Jennifer was my Mother's name. Father proposed that the mine be named after her, Wheal Jenny." Ellen gave the simple explanation, but did not further the subject.

"A strange coincidence." Jamie mused. "My own Mother's name is Ginifur. It was her first husband who bought the shares in the mine, increasing them because he thought the name was a good omen. I inherited my shares from him."

Ben Nancekivel smiled. "Then he was right. I've always been sure of it; can't fathom out why no one listened to young Rawe before now." Ben pushed the empty desert plate away from him. "To be quite candid Jamie, and there is no point in being anything else, I do not have the funds to finance further operations. Everything I had was sunk into the mine, excuse the pun; the horses just about keep the wolf from the door. That's it, in a nut shell. I've been tempted more than once to sell my shares, I can tell you. But I've always held on to the belief that I would be proved right in the end." He shook his head. "I am afraid I can offer you only moral support, I have no more money at my disposal."

Jamie paused for thought. "How about I propose a bargain."

"A bargain!"

"If I put up the money and we are right, and you become a rich man, you reward me with that colt we've made a deal on."

Benjamin laughed out loud. "A man after my own heart. I like you young Tremayne, yes I do. Come . . ." he pushed his chair away from the table, "let us retire to the drawing room. My dear . . . !" he addressed his daughter with a raised eyebrow.

Ellen replaced her napkin on the table and with a gentle push her chair slid backwards, revealing the fact that she was seated in a wheeled basket chair. She turned a brilliant smile on Jamie and said. "Perhaps you would care to assist me?"

Jamie, his face showing none of the shock that he felt inside, stepped forward. Taking the concealed handles in his hand he said. "It would be a pleasure."

* * *

The Extraordinary Meeting of the shareholders of the Wheal Jenny mine was one of the most extraordinary events of the year at which Benjamin Nancekivel addressed the shareholders from the raised platform with Daniel Franks by his side and informed the meeting that their sleeping partner had expressed a desire to continue funding the mine with a new exploration. He went on to say that he had consulted with the gentleman in question, taken advice on the matter, and believed that on the information he had received the suggestion made sound sense; however, before a decision could be made a meeting had to be convened to address the point.

One after another, questions were fired at the platform and Squire Nancekivel and Daniel fielded them expertly. In fact the discussion became quite heated as questions were asked as to why it had taken so long for these facts to be made known. "These are points," Squire Nancekivel asserted, "that we would like to take up with the absent mine captain Mr Hawes, and if anyone knows of his whereabouts perhaps they would let Mr Franks know so that these questions might be answered." This was the point at which Jamie had decided he would make an appearance but, before Daniel could introduce him, there was a commotion at the back of the hall and the door opened to admit a tall forceful gentleman followed by the doorman protesting that it was a private meeting.

The gentleman brushed him aside and strode to the front of the hall. "Good evening Nancekivel, Petherick . . . Bolitho. I'd be obliged if you would allow me to address both you and your shareholders." Henry Bishop, owner of the Magdalene Mine, brushed aside any objections . . . he didn't wait for an answer; he simply turned his back on the platform and Ben Nancekivel and addressed his captive audience. "Wheal Jenny is played out, the tin has run dry as you all well know, and I fully understand that some of you here are naturally aggrieved at your company's failure. With prices so low, with tin and copper being brought out of Wales at less than it costs us to get it out of the ground, things are bad for all of us. The Magdalene Mine is better prepared to weather the storm and will be able to turn the corner. Wheal Jenny has been out of commission for far too long and it will take big money to get her up and running again, have you got that money? I don't like to see a mine go down when she's so close to another that is thriving and I propose that I will buy any shares that you may wish to sell and join the Wheal Jenny to the Magdalene Mine. The tin is run out at Wheal Jenny but we need more land to tip our spoil."

A hush had fallen over the hall which was now shattered by questions. "How much are you offering?" "What's in it for you?"

Henry Bishop fielded the questions confidently without giving a definite answer until Ben Nancekivel, having recovered from the shock of the arrival of the owner of the neighbouring mine, with a sharp rap on the table he called the meeting to order. "This is a private meeting of the shareholders of the Wheal Jenny, and it is in progress. You have no right to push your way in here and take it over like this, Bishop." Ben used his surname purely to show his displeasure.

More voices from the hall called out. "I'll sell if the price is right." "We've got nothing to lose, the mines made no real money since '75."

Benjamin Nancekivel struck the table with the gavel once more to bring the meeting to order and slowly the commotion diminished to a mumble as Benjamin spoke again. "You will all be aware of the fact that Mr Franks has been conducting the affairs of one of our shareholders, who has spent most of the last few years abroad. Mr Franks has asked if he may address the meeting with an important announcement. So without more ado, I give you, Mr Daniel Franks."

Daniel briefly outlined the fact that he had been instructed to handle the affairs of someone who would not inherit until he became of a specific age. As it was the trust of the deceased Adam Sawle, all business had to be continued without disclosing the name of the beneficiary. That time had now come about; the beneficiary had come of age and Daniel's time as the agent in respect of the mine known as Wheal Jenny had come to an end. He would be continuing to act as legal advisor to this new client, but for now he would like to introduce the now major shareholder to his partners. "Gentlemen it is my pleasure to introduce to you, Captain James Tremayne."

Jamie stepped out from a door to the side of the platform to be greeted by stunned silence as he made his way to the front of the platform. From behind him came the sound of shuffling feet and of a scraping chair as someone arose from the major shareholders chairs behind him. "What is the meaning of this?" Robert Fry demanded. "What skulduggery has been going on?"

A smile played on Jamie's lips as he turned. This was the first contact he had had with Robert Fry in six years or more. "Why should you suspect, skulduggery, as you put it?"

Robert Fry's face was puce with anger. "Are you telling us that it was you who owned those shares all along? Why the hell didn't you tell us? Of all the deceitful . . ."

Voices joined in the mumble of discontent, as Jamie looked about the room. "There was no deceit on my part, I can assure you. I was not aware that I had inherited the shares in Wheal Jenny until after I arrived home. The news has been as much a surprise to me as it is to you, believe me."

"Don't come the innocent with me!" Robert Fry interrupted. "You've been buying my shares all this time, haven't you? Conning me into selling something that you obviously think is worth a lot more. Why do you want my shares, or all the others that you must have brought in the last few months?"

"No one forced you to sell your shares Mr Fry. I understand that you expressed the wish to dispose of them and Mr Franks agreed your price. It was all above board as you are well aware and I will be happy to buy any other shares that you may wish to dispose of, but first hear me out."

"That is true," a voice put in. "Robert Fry asked me if I would be interested in them at one time."

Jamie glanced about the room. "Why did Mr Franks wish to purchase them? The answer to that one is quite simple, Adam Sawle believed in the mine and Mr Franks was acting on his wishes. Why would I now continue to buy the shares? Because I do not believe that Wheal Jenny has yet shown us her full potential. I believe in the mine and I will do everything in my power to keep her open." Jamie looked down at Henry Bishop who had taken a position against the side wall. "Why not ask Mr Bishop why he's really interested in Wheal Jenny? Do you really believe that he would pay you good money just to tip his spoil from the Magdalene Mine? Well I don't. At the last meeting Mr Franks put to you a proposition that would have kept the mine open. None of you took that offer and it is therefore my money that has paid for the maintenance team since that day. I ask you all once more to share with me in the further exploration of the Wheal Jenny. Take my word for it . . . The Wheal Jenny is indeed ready to start up again."

There was more shuffling of feet and mumbled voices uttered words such as "Good money after bad." and "Haven't I lost enough money in that bloody mine?" until someone at the back of the room, Jamie couldn't see who it was, asked. "And what makes you think there is more ore to be found in that mine, Captain Tremayne?"

"Quite simple. I believe that they were looking in the wrong place; I have been down there to see for myself. I can only wonder why such an experienced mine captain as Walter Hawes failed to see it." Jamie waited whilst angry voices rose in the air.

"What would he know about it?" and "What does the mine captain have to say?" It was at this point that someone actually asked the whereabouts of Walter Hawes, the mine captain. Then as they looked about them for the absent Mr Hawes silence fell upon the room.

Jamie moved to the front of the stage. "Mr Hawes is, apparently, absent from home," he informed them. "Mr Franks, Mr Nancekivel and I have all tried to track him down, without success. His family have let it be known that they have no idea where he might be, or why he has gone. It would appear that he was made aware of the possibility that they were following a false lead and I, for one, would like to question him on this subject. His absence is, to say the least, puzzling." Jamie suddenly looked down on Henry Bishop who was beginning to look decidedly uneasy. "You wouldn't have any idea where our Walter Hawes may be found, I suppose?"

Henry Bishop straightened up and came forward to the platform. "Just what are you suggesting, Tremayne?" he blustered uncomfortably.

Jamie smiled coolly. "I am not suggesting anything; I just asked if you had heard of the whereabouts of our mine captain, Mr Hawes, who couldn't follow a tin seam. Maybe he applied for a job at the Magdalene! If he did, I wouldn't recommend him Mr Bishop."

The statement was met with sniggers from the floor, bringing discomfort to the owner of the Magdalene Mine as he blustered. "Indeed he did not . . . and my offer is a good one to shareholders of a mine that is played out."

"But it's not played out, is it Mr Bishop? Wheal Jenny hasn't yet delivered the mother lode of the false lead that Walter Hawes was following. What's more he even missed the signs that suggested there were copper deposits too."

More angry voices filled the air. "False Leads?" "Copper!" and "Where's Hawes?" and "Who else knew about this?"

Henry Bishop's anger was evident when he shouted out. "What would a sea captain know about tin mining? You are all being deceived."

But Jamie's voice rose above them all. "Nevertheless my offer stands and whatever you are prepared to pay for the shares in Wheal Jenny, I will pay more."

At these words Henry Bishop turned on his heals and fought his way out of the hall as shareholders in the Wheal Jenny clamoured for answers. But it was Robert Fry's voice that rose above the uproar.

"You knew this all along didn't you, Tremayne? You and that tame lawyer of yours have been scheming to do us honest shareholders out of what is rightfully ours." he accused.

Daniel stood up, gesturing for Jamie to take a seat, his voice unwavering as he answered the accusation. "Both your shares, Mr Fry, and those of any one else that I purchased at Adam Sawle's request, were purchased from you at a price considered more than fair by yourself and, I might add, above the figure of the only other offer of purchase that you had received. The purchases were made in accordance with the wishes of Captain Tremayne's benefactor, who made his original purchase at the opening of the mine. I confirm that Captain Tremayne, as he has mentioned, was completely unaware of his inheritance until very recently. However, his belief in the mine is as great as his predecessor; therefore this meeting has been held to find a way forward. I suggest we table a break in the proceedings, allowing us all time to take refreshments and reconsider the situation. We shall reconvene the meeting here in two hours hence . . . at three o'clock." Daniel gathered his papers up before the unnaturally quiet audience and, motioning to Jamie to follow him, they left the room.

When the meeting reconvened Jamie explained why he believed that the mine had a future, telling the shareholders that he believed that they were not far from the mother lode of tin, that he had taken advice on the matter (without mentioning Davey Rawe, as he had requested) and that there were signs of possible copper extracts. He didn't further this subject nor mention the amethysts or garnets; these were subjects that would be covered after further exploration. The early angry accusations made by Robert Fry, and those he had managed to convince that they had been duped, were soon overcome when one of the smaller investors swung the remainder of them over to Jamie's side. At this point Robert Fry stomped angrily from the room, leaving Daniel and Jamie to reveal their proposed plans for the re-opening of Wheal Jenny.

* * *

Beau and Clara's daughter was born in the early hours of the morning on 1st June 1782. The news reached Tremanyon with the mail, when Jamie returned with it from the village. Unlike Ginifur's own children the baby was weak and sickly, apparently refusing to suckle, and died within forty-eight hours. Ginifur never saw her grandchild, not even in death. She was baptised hurriedly at the home of the Fry family and buried in Ruan Churchyard with only Beau and Clara and Clara's parents present.

* * *

Aidan leaped across the short distance of water between the boat and the shore, pausing briefly to see it on its way back to the quay. The haul had been a good one and there would be plenty of work for the women and children for a day or two. He glanced at the sky, if the weather held perhaps they would get another good haul tomorrow. He turned to the headland and in long strides set out to Rhosinnis where the house was set on high ground with outstanding views across the headland to Falmouth and The Lizard to the west, and sea and rocky coastal views to the east. From the back of the house the land sloped gently down to the river with St Maries cottages hugging the hill above the harbour on the opposite side.

New foundations had been laid out to extend the old manor house at Rhosinnis to Jamie's specifications and Aidan heard the sound of cheerful whistling, its source hidden from view behind the new walls. Picking his way silently amongst the stone Aidan came up from behind. "Well now! Tis a cheerful tune I'm hearin'. Do I take it that everythin' is goin' along as ye'd wish it then?"

Jamie didn't turn round, and mimicking the mixture of Celtic accents answered. "And if ye'd be thinkin' I didn't see 'ee acomin' Aidan me lad, ye're much mistaken," he turned, grinning. "It's good to see you; did you have a good catch? I saw the boat was way down in the water, so it's either a lot of fish you have caught or you've put a hole in her and she's shipping a lot of water." he joked.

"Just thought I'd stop and see how the house is progressin'. My . . . ! Ye've got on some since I was here last! Are ye pleased me lad?"

Jamie stepped back to take a wider look. Stonemasons were busy laying the stones that the apprentices were gathering and placing near to hand, and yes . . . it was going ahead quite fast. Luckily he wasn't strapped for cash, through Adam's prudent initial investment and the 'Franks' continued management far from it. Therefore he had been able to employ some excellent craftsmen from all around the district. They were presently living in the empty cottages clustered around the farm house and buildings a half a mile away until completion. A couple of the older men had brought their wives with them and they cooked and cleaned for them all. Jamie had made them a more than fair offer, and if the contract was completed before schedule they would receive a handsome bonus. Therefore they worked with a will, and although the evenings were pulling in they worked until they could no longer see. "Yes . . ." Jamie smiled again, "she's going to be a fine house Aidan."

"A grand house like that, do 'ee 'ave anyone in mind t' share it with Jamie? For ye'll be a bit lonely rattlin' about in that all on y'ur own like," a sly smile spread across Aidan's face as he saw a hint of colour rising above Jamie's collarless shirt.

"I most certainly do not." Jamie explained. "My experience of women has made me consider that a bachelor's life has much to commend it. Anyway . . . I won't be lonely. I have a feeling that it will take a few members of staff to manage."

Aidan followed Jamie as he headed for the doorway. "Me Da tol' me that ye'd broken through t' the new lode at Wheal Jenny. If tis as ye'd hoped for, I gather ye'll be a rich man in y'ur own right Jamie, ye'll need a house t' fit y'ur status."

Jamie laughed. "Fit my status eh? You make me out to be a right pretentious ass."

"No, that ye'll never be. But I know someone who would 'ave been, if it'd been them, 'n I bet t'other one'll be thinkin' maybe she should've stuck t' the brother she was first betrothed to 'n all," he gave a snigger. "I bet ol' man Fry be kickin' hiself too."

Jamie aimed a punch at Aidan's mid section. "Well my friend, and I'm thinking that I was lucky that young lady changed her mind. Take heed Aidan, you may not be so lucky when the time comes." They had come to a halt at the front of the building. "Hold on whilst I go and see George Stevens, then I'll walk home with you."

"Didn't ye ride over?"

"No Jacob and I sailed round; he was going over to St. Maries so gave me passage. He'll be waiting for me to walk back to the creek."

Whilst he waited Aidan took a seat on the low wall as he watched the fishing boats returning with the tide to the harbour on the other side of the river. The view through the valley was a fine one, he thought, but the house was a lot more exposed to the elements than Tremanyon, perched high on the headland as it was, with no tree belt to shelter it. When Jamie had seen to his workers they walked homewards along the river, talking of this and that. Aidan, trying to find out if his friend had truly settled down to shore life, and whether he was truly unhurt by his fiancées marriage to Beau. Certainly, outwardly, he showed no sign of distress. He talked animatedly about the progress at Wheal Jenny, of the farm at Rhosinnis and the building work in progress. He voiced his concerns for his mother's advancing years and for the future of Tremanyon if it should end up in Beau's hands; and outwardly he showed no remorse for his failed romance with Clara Fry. Aidan touched on the much talked of financial position of the Fry's. It was said that they had mounting debts which the Fry's had expected would be covered by their daughter's marriage into a wealthy family. This amused Jamie, who said that had Robert Fry kept all his shares in Wheal Jenny, their future would be quite rosy. As it was, the signs suggested that he would still be no pauper.

As they approached the bank of the river opposite Quay Cottage Aidan brought up the subject of Jamie's new stallion. "The first horse for y'ur new stables arrives t'morrow, I hear. Ye'll 'ave t' make a start on the stable block at Rhosinnis shortly."

"Mm . . ." Jamie acknowledged Jacob's hail from across the water with a wave. "I'm planning a cottage on the end of the stable block, like the one at home. Don't know of a good stable master do you?"

Aidan screwed his face up. "Don't tempt me."

Jamie continued the conversation as though the subject had not been mentioned. "Ben Nancekivel is bringing him over tomorrow. They are going to stay over for a few days. It will be good for Mother to entertain again, she keeps herself too much to herself of late. They are very nice people, and I am sure Mother will find a lot in common with them, they too are very private people."

"The daughter comin' too, I gather."

"Yes. She doesn't get out much either." Jamie watched the small boat approaching. "Ellen cannot walk you know."

"So 'ee said. Ma said that ye told her she was quite a beauty though."

"Kate talks too much." Jamie laughed. "And she's too keen to get me married. Once bitten, twice shy Aidan. After my experience with Clara I'm not too sure that marriage is for me."

"They'm not all like that one."

"No . . . possibly not. You've certainly found good lass in Prudence, Aidan. Will you marry her?"

Aidan fielded this suggestion with a shrug. He picked up a smooth stone and skipped it out across the water. "I can't think of marriage before I get a house to start married life in."

Jamie paused before answering. "No . . . I will need someone to look after the horses sometime in the future though. Perhaps you would like to think on it. I know you love the sea Aidan, but you have an Irishman's love of horses too." As Jake nudged the boat into the bank Jamie held on to the bow as he signalled for Aidan to climb aboard for the short row across the mouth of the creek.

* * *

Ginifur was indeed much taken with the Nancekivels. Benjamin's genuine warmth and cheerful personality, without airs and graces, made for easy conversation and if she had privately admitted to any fears for what she felt was a growing friendship between her son and his daughter, they were quickly forgotten. Ellen's remarkable confidence and wonderful smile captured her heart, and within moments of meeting her she realised that one completely forgot that she was confined to her basket chair. On their arrival Ginifur had greeted Ellen from beside the carriage at the foot of the steps, and then Benjamin had scooped her up in his arms and whisked her, without ceremony, to her chair which had been placed at the top.

Ellen gazed out across the lawns and remarked. "What a wonderful setting. Your family is truly fortunate to live in such surroundings. I love the moors, and I have visited the north coast on occasions, where my uncle lives, but it is so different here. The countryside is so much more, gentle . . . so beautiful . . . and to be able to see the sea!" She raised a pair of smiling eyes to make contact with Ginifur's. "Thank you so much for inviting us to visit your home. We have both been looking forward to meeting you all since Jamie issued the invitation."

By the time Jamie had returned home they were happily settled in the drawing room, ensconced in comfortable chairs and in deep conversation on equine blood lines, and the remainder of the afternoon and evening passed quickly. Rebecca and Sara too were captivated by Ellen Nancekivel, who showed a genuine interest in Rebecca's school room in the village. Before the evening was over, and they retired to their rooms, Jamie offered to show Benjamin over the headland on the following day and before he had the chance to continue the excited Sara jumped in.

"Are we going to make it an outing?" she asked eagerly.

Jamie laughed. "It looks as though we are going to now."

"Oh! Perhaps Ellen would care to join us?" Sara turned to their visitor "I would be happy to accompany you and drive the pony and trap." she suggested.

"Oh! I would love to join you all. But . . ." Ellen's voice trailed off and Jamie feared that she had been offended.

"What Ellen is trying to say, Sara, is that although she cannot walk, she can sit on a horse. Ellen and her father both ride out with Sir John and the Vivians at the Four Burrow Meetings; in fact I agree with Ben, Ellen rides quite well, for a woman," he teased. "I don't suppose you thought to bring Ellen's saddle did you?"

"We have a special saddle for her at home," Ben explained "but, if you have a spare horse and side saddle I am more than confident that she will manage just as well with that."

Sara was delighted. "Oh how wonderful!" she exclaimed. "You must ride Willow; can she Mama? And you can use my new saddle, the one that Da bought me; I can use my old one."

Ginifur smiled at Jamie. "Then that is settled. We will all go for a ride over to Rhosinnis tomorrow, weather permitting and, if it is fine I shall get Lorna and Poppy to pack a hamper of food and Joe will take it over to Rhosinnis for us all to partake refreshments before we all ride back."

Benjamin Nancekivel beamed. "A champion idea . . . champion indeed."

With this decision taken they retired for the night with Jamie carrying Ellen to her room before leaving her with Jane, Rebecca and Sara's maid, to assist her to get ready for bed.

The following morning, after breakfast, the family assembled at the stables. Sara had found a riding habit to fit Ellen, their size being similar it fitted her very well, and Jamie lifted her easily into the saddle on Willow. Gathering the reins in one hand Ellen stroked Willow's mane as she spoke reassuring words in her ear and, led by Jamie with Benjamin and Liam riding beside him, the party set out for the headland. Ginifur followed on, riding beside Ellen and mounted on Whisper; her aged horse Damson had died some years before. Willow was out of Damson and sired by Richard's stallion, Star. Whisper had been bred from Willow in more recent years. Rebecca and Sara brought up the rear, sometimes riding alongside Ellen and Ginifur when the track allowed or as they rode in the fields set high above the cliffs.

In spite of her disability Ellen was a fine horsewoman indeed. "When I am riding," she declared, "I can forget that I cannot walk, and think that I am the same as anyone else. It's a bit of a shock at the end of the day to have to return to my chair." Her face briefly showed a wistful look, which she quickly masked with her bright smile. "But I must be grateful for small mercies, I may not be able to walk now but my injuries could have been far worse and left me unable to ride as well," and she went on to describe the coaching accident which had caused the death of her mother and had left Ellen permanently disabled at the age of twelve. With her father's help and her own perseverance Ellen had learned to ride again. Like Ginifur she had, as a child, learned to ride without a saddle but after the accident she learned to appreciate the more genteel side-saddle favoured by ladies of quality, and this helped her to regain her balance. Of course she would always need assistance to get herself into the saddle, she admitted, but once seated upon a horse she could once more move without the aid of her father or one of the servants and from that moment on she was able to enjoy her new found freedom. Ginifur, Rebecca and Sara were much moved by Ellen's story and admired the plucky way she faced the future. Indeed, as she rode out confidently on Willow, a stranger would not have been any the wiser.

At the site of Rhosinnis Barton they dismounted. Lorna and Poppy had arrived earlier with rugs and cushions and the hamper with three bottles of wine which were being chilled in a bucket of water from the well. Jamie carefully lifted Ellen from her saddle and placed her on a blanket with pillows for her support. As they settled around her conversation flowed along with the wine and the food.

This was the first of many visits by the Nancekivels' to Tremanyon and at the same time as the fortunes of Wheal Jenny improved so the relationship between Jamie and Ellen grew, and any reservations that Ginifur might have had were soon dispelled by the couple's obvious happiness in each others company.

Jamie made frequent visits to Penhallow, staying there on the occasions that he visited the Wheal Jenny Mine, and it was on one of these occasions that Sir John Rogers sent over an invitation for Jamie to ride out with the newly formed Four Burrow Hunt. The Four Burrows hunt covered a large area between the west of Bodmin and the Lizard but on this occasion they were riding out from Roger's own home. Ben suggested that after the long ride over from Tremanyon Jamie rested his horse and ride Geraint, Merlin's sire; the young stallion, Merlin, was a virtual clone of this fine beast and Jamie was keen to take the opportunity to try it out on a hard ride. The Tremanyon Stud had never had a white stallion in their breeding stock and they had only ever had one white horse and that was Rachel and Rebecca's first pony. In truth, white horses had never appealed to either Jamie or his father, but from the very first moment of their introduction Jamie knew that he was fated to own this special animal.

As they rode to the meeting Jamie spied Francis Bassset amongst the riders; although slightly miffed to learn that Ben had sold the young stallion to Jamie he expressed his interest in the proposed combining of the Tremanyon and Nancekivel breeding programme. "Your father always did have a good eye for a horse," he acknowledged "I have more than one of his horses in my own stables as I am sure you are aware." The conversation then progressed onto the fortunes of tin and copper mining and Francis Basset's formation of the Cornish Metal Company before the Master of the Hounds blew on his horn and the riders assembled for the hunt. Ellen was indeed an accomplished rider, fearlessly setting her horse at jumps that could unnerve another rider less handicapped than herself and she was greatly admired by all for her courage in overcoming her disability. Today Ellen was riding her favourite horse, Blaze and it was as she landed after clearing the stream that Ellen lost her hat. Jamie and Ben were riding close by and saw the incident. Reluctantly they allowed the other riders to continue without them as Ellen turned her horse round and returned to the spot where her hat lay on the ground, looking down forlornly as she was unable to dismount to retrieve it. As Jamie turned his horse back to the stream Ben decided to leave it to him, smiling on indulgently as he watched Jamie dismount, pick up the slightly damaged headgear and brush off the worst of the offending mud and grass before offering it back to his daughter. Even from this distance Ben could see the expression on his daughter's face and gave up a silent prayer that she would manage to capture the heart of this fine young man. Ben was himself already extremely fond of Jamie Tremayne and was quite certain that his daughter was also.

In fact it was probably this day, and possibly this incident that cemented Jamie's own feelings. As he held the hat aloft to return it to its owner, Ellen's eyes misted over as she smiled down at the handsome, red coated figure; just once finding herself wishing that she was not so disabled and therefore perhaps could have a chance to win his heart and maybe one day share a life together. In the few brief moments that Ellen paused, any reservations that Jamie had entertained were blown away and he knew that he wanted to love and care for this charming and courageous young woman.

Chapter Four
1783 - 1784

1783 SAW THE fortunes of Wheal Jenny turned round. The mother lode had been exposed in '82 and although tin prices had fallen, not only was the tin ore of a high grade but further explorations produced a good yield of copper. Wheal Jenny began to flourish as other mines began to fail and close. As Davey and his father had predicted the first yield was good but as they proceeded further there were larger deposits of tin. Exploration on the other side of the level proved that copper was indeed to be found at the Wheal Jenny; and these deposits were to prove both rich and of a high quality. Henry Bishop and the shareholders in the Magdalene Mine were struggling to hold on as copper smelters were now operating in Wales and the price of copper had plummeted leaving many Cornish copper mines in desperate situations. Wheal Jenny was not one of them. With the new high powered boiler, and the ore being of high grade, the copper from Wheal Jenny was much sought after and with the improved working conditions at the mine the men worked with a will. So far there had only been small deposits of rock that contained either amethyst or garnet, but this was no great disappointment; it would have been a bonus on top of the copper deposits which had made Jamie and his partners in Wheal Jenny wealthy men.

Davey Rawe was made mine captain and this proved to be a popular choice with both the miners and the investors. Under the new management, headed by Jamie and Ben, the tributers were treated fairly and the conditions underground improved. The smaller shareholders were rewarded by receiving dividends far in excess of any that they had received in all the years before and Jamie and Ben's faith in Wheal Jenny was proved justified. Following pressure from Rebecca and the added persuasion from Ellen, Jamie had agreed on reducing the children's hours below ground to be replaced by compulsory attendance at the small school house that Jamie had given the order to build. It was well attended and the children enjoyed the spell above ground.

Even Robert Fry's circumstances improved with the interest on his remaining ten percent holding in Wheal Jenny. It turned out that he had in fact sold shares to Henry Bishop, but this had not come to light until after the meeting of the shareholders. In spite of the failure to take over the Wheal Jenny, Henry Bishop refused to sell the shares back to Robert Fry. Nevertheless the return on his ten percent holding was sufficient to save him from bankruptcy and allowed him to remain in his family's house in Ruan. However, Jamie's fortunes only served to increase his belief that he had been defrauded in the purchase of his shares and, in turn, this attitude and suspicion were added to Beau's jealousy until it all but consumed him. If only Beau's child had lived, and been a boy, things might have been different. It was only by convincing himself that Clara must conceive again, and soon, that his thoughts were channelled in a different direction. Beau's aim in life was to produce a son and heir, after that he would concentrate his efforts on securing Tremanyon and what he saw as his birthright.

With their finances somewhat improved the Fry's lifestyle also improved. Margery was happier and in turn was able to offer support to her daughter. With better nursing and her husband's and mother's support, Clara was finally able to shake off her gloom and despondency and turn her thoughts to the future.

The romance between Jamie and Ellen blossomed and Ginifur was pleased to see her son enjoy such happiness, giving him her support and encouragement when he informed her that he wished to make Ellen his wife. Jamie had no reservations that she would make him a good wife, it was only Ellen's own fears that he might be making a big mistake that got in the way. Benjamin Nancekivel was, without a doubt, delighted to give his blessing. He could think of no better son-in-law than Jamie, almost thinking of him as the son he never had even before this news.

Ellen's fears were finally overcome and she and Jamie were married quietly in St Stephens' Church on 15th December 1783. Ellen declined the offer of a honeymoon in Italy, preferring to return to Tremanyon to spend Christmas with the family and ride out on Boxing Day with the Four Burrow Hunt. On this occasion the whole family set out in the grand carriage very early in the morning, the horses having been ridden over to Truro and stabled with Daniel's horses before Christmas. They arrived at the Franks' home in time for a celebratory breakfast and returned to Tremanyon the next day.

Jamie and Ellen's wedding was not the only wedding to be held that year at St Stephens. Davey Rawe married Mary, the young school teacher who had been employed to run the school room at Wheal Jenny; they were offered accommodation in the adjacent cottage at Penhallow in return for caretaking the property during Benjamin's planned absences following his daughter's marriage.

Aidan also married his sweetheart, Prue, going to live in the cottage at the end of the stables built for them at Rhosinnis. Jamie's plans to establish stables meant that he would need a good stable-master and Aidan's love of boats was only rivalled by his love of horses. With his impending marriage Aidan had made his choice, but until the horses were established at Rhosinnis he would carry on fishing at Tremanyon. Jamie was delighted with this decision and in truth Ginifur was very happy too, for Prue was a lovely girl and had agreed to help Ellen when they moved into the farmhouse at Rhosinnis when it was finally complete.

1784 was to be a year of births in the Tremayne family starting with Rachel and Tobi's son, David who was born at home in the house near St Maries. The Tremaynes' of Rhosinnis had hoped to move into their new home by the summer of eighty-four; however, this was delayed by the news that Ellen had conceived shortly after their marriage and was with child. The baby was due to be born in October and it was deemed better that they should continue to reside at Tremanyon until after the birth. Initially this news infuriated Beau, for it appeared that Clara was finding it hard to conceive a second time. However, in April Clara told him that she was once more with child and all his attention was concentrated on the forthcoming event, due around Christmas time.

Dickon Tremayne of Rhosinnis was born at Tremanyon on 14th October 1784. Every member of the family, with the exception of Beau, was delighted with the news. Jamie's fears for Ellen's ability to give birth naturally were unfounded and she produced a healthy strong baby boy in the image of his father and grandfather.

Beau and Clara's second daughter was born on the 20th of November at Killow Barton. It appeared that, although a strong and healthy baby, she was not treated to a rapturous welcome. Clara burst into tears as soon as she was told that she had delivered a beautiful and healthy baby girl, and Beau . . . ! Well! Beau, after a moment of stunned disbelief, turned on his heels and left the house for some hours before arriving home in the back of a cart, courtesy of the landlord at Ruan.

The babe was to fair no better with her maternal grandparents, for they had all hoped for a boy child, believing that all their futures would be secure when Richard produced an heir for the Tremayne family. Margery Fry's initial response of joy at being a grandmother quickly faded. "After all," she was reported to have said, "I have a daughter, what do I want with yet another girl in the family?" If Clara had felt anything at all for her tiny daughter it quickly disappeared with her mother's rejection of her, leaving her only feelings of misplaced anger, aimed at the baby as if it were her fault that she was not born a boy. Clara refused to have anything to do with her child; even to the point of refusing to feed her.

Margery Fry briefly showed signs of remorse, recalling the Doctor in fear that the baby may die. Initially Doctor Craven was not concerned, saying that it was not unusual for a young mother to turn away from her new born child. New mothers often suffered from feelings of despair after their baby had been delivered. He recommended a wet nurse be engaged, and in a short time Clara would recover and accept her baby. Clara did not recover and the baby soon became sickly and cried constantly. Beau's anger increased daily and the Fry's tempers became short. For fear that the same fate might befall their second grandchild Margery Fry arranged for a quick baptism of the baby, forced into the position of choosing a name for her herself as none was forthcoming from Beau or Clara.

And so it was that Ginifur and Rebecca visited the Fry's household two weeks before Christmas and they arrived to find Clara yet again dissolved in tears, Beau obviously still angry and holding himself in check, and both the Frys' silent and morose. The baby, lying in her crib in the nursery adjoining the room set aside for Clara and Beau during Clara's confinement, was anything but beautiful. Tears streamed down her red puffy face and her little fists beat furiously at the air as her lungs let loose to the outside world.

Ginifur studied her grand-daughter. "She is a sad little thing, and that's for certain," she remarked as she glanced at Beau. "May I pick her up?" Ginifur carefully asked for her son's permission before handling his daughter. "What have you named her, Beau?"

"Roberta." Margery Fry informed Ginifur. "I had to think of something quickly for neither Richard nor Clara would give it any thought, convinced as they were that she would be a boy and would be Christened Richard like his father and grandfather." Ginifur winced at the mention of her husband's name; it was still a raw wound in her heart. "Roberta! After her grandfather." Margery explained; then as an afterthought "It should have been Holly, for she's as prickly as a whole bough of it in my mind." Having imparted this information Margery and Robert Fry left the room to return to their daughter's adjoining bedroom.

Beau shrugged his shoulders indifferently. "If it pleases you. Personally I can see no pleasure in handling the brat myself. If it's to be so sickly it would have been best if it had died at birth, rather than cause so much heartache and grief to poor Clara. The constant crying is making her ill."

Ginifur refrained from answering and lifted the baby gently from her crib. Taking a nearby shawl of fine wool she wrapped it carefully about the tiny frame, gently rocking her as she walked towards the nursery window. Slowly the yells of anger and frustration subsided. The angry wails became heartfelt sobs and eventually the sobs became tiny whimpers until, finally, her breathing became even and she fell into an exhausted sleep in Ginifur's arms.

Margery Fry appeared at the nursery door. "What's happened?" she cried in alarm. "Why has she stopped crying?"

"She's asleep, that's all." Ginifur peered down at the sleeping child. "There! You look much better already without that angry frown on your face little one. Now if you can only learn to smile a bit, you will have us all treating you like a princess in no time."

"Princess!" Beau exploded. "Princess! That monster! First time it's stopped making a noise since it made its arrival; it even cries in its sleep . . . the bloody misery."

"Beau!" Ginifur reprimanded him. "This is your daughter we are discussing! Even a puppy would deserve better recognition than to be referred to as . . . IT."

"She's no daughter of mine. She's naught but a bloody miserable brat."

"Beau!" Rebecca spoke for the first time. "She's a baby. Just a baby. Look at her. A tiny frightened baby in a very strange world," she stroked the soft downy hair on Roberta's head as she slept peacefully in Ginifur's arms. "After the safe and secure world she has come from, who can blame her for finding it hard to adjust?"

"Best she'd never set foot in it if she can't cope. Best she'd died at birth, sickly thing. What good is a girl to me?" Beau yelled, followed by a wail from Clara in her bedroom.

The baby flinched at the new onslaught, screwing up her face in displeasure and Ginifur renewed the rocking motion until the child settled once more. Pursing her lips at the display of behaviour of her son and daughter in law she continued. "I think . . ." then, after a slight pause, Ginifur added thoughtfully, "perhaps, if her environment were a little calmer, a little quieter . . ."

"Calmer! Quieter!" Beau could no longer control his anger. "That monster has come into our lives, disrupting us all and causing nothing but grief and disharmony. I wish I had never spawned it, let alone seen it."

"IT! She has a name Beau." Rebecca spoke quietly but firmly. "I am sure that with a little love and care she will grow into a very beautifully little girl and make you a very proud father."

Beau's anger was complete. "*Richard! My name is Richard.*" He thumped on the fragile table at his side, sending the fine porcelain vase flying to the floor where it shattered into a hundred tiny pieces and causing Margery and Robert Fry to take a step backwards into their daughter's bedroom. Roberta's eyes flew open, appearing to lock onto her grandmother's face. Her tiny rosebud mouth trembled briefly, her fists clenched tightly as she drew her tiny legs up to tuck herself into a tight ball. She opened her mouth and took a deep breath as though making ready to let rip once more, but the face stayed firmly in place above her and the gentle rocking movement continued to sooth her. Roberta yawned and closed her eyes.

Beau took a step forward and viciously stabbed a finger at Rebecca. "If you think you are so wonderful, then you take her. I doubt you'll ever get the chance to bear one of your own." Ginifur let out a gasp of horror which made Beau turn away from his half sister and direct his tirade at Ginifur. "Spending all her time teaching the useless illiterate village brats to read and write is the nearest she'll ever get to bringing up a child. She's too cold and frigid to get a man, let alone keep one."

Rebecca blanched and turned away as Ginifur's calm but firm voice silenced the room. "Enough. That is enough, Beau." Her eyes scanned the room taking in her son, Carla's huddled form in the big bed in the room beyond and her parents hovering nearby. "Obviously you have all been under a great deal of emotional strain caused by the arrival of your daughter and her not settling in too easily to your routine. You are not thinking rationally Beau," she excused him. Rebecca stared, unseeing, out of the window at the river and the woods beyond. The baby still slept in Ginifur's arms and she made to return her to the crib. "I think that it is best that we leave now. I will return in a few days to see you all when Roberta has settled in to your family routine."

"NO!" Beau's voice was hard and as cold as the expression on his face. "If you leave that brat here, so help me I will smother her and damn the consequences." Ginifur drew the baby closer to her as if for protection. "If you think that her life is so precious then you take her Mother. I give her to you, if you think that you can put up with the mewling monster. From this moment on she is yours, ***not*** mine. As far as I am concerned she never was, and never will be part of my family." Beau had uttered his last words on the subject, turned on his heels and strode through the door to his wife's bedroom, slamming the door firmly behind him.

Ginifur reached out her hand to her step daughter. "Come Becky." she took her hand and turned her away from the window seeing the hurt on her face and the tears in her eyes. "He didn't mean it." Although she wanted to believe this she knew that her words sounded hollow. "When he realises what he has said he will be filled with remorse." The bedroom door opened and Robert and Margery Fry returned to the room. "The strain of a new baby is obviously making your lives very difficult at the moment, and Clara is obviously far from well enough to care for her newborn child. My son's attitude, I am sure, is brought about by his fears for his wife's health. Both of their feelings for their daughter will, I am sure, change with the improvement to Clara's health and the babe settling into your lives. If it would help, and only with your agreement, I would be happy to take Roberta to Tremanyon until Carla feels well enough to take charge of her daughter."

Margery Fry glanced at her husband's stern countenance and plucked nervously at the fine lace shawl clasped across her breast. Robert Fry ground his teeth as he frowned, then nodded briefly before taking hold of his wife's arm and steering her towards the door to the landing. Looking back over his shoulder he grunted. "Just take her. Do as he says, take her away from here and do not bring her back." He paused at the door briefly and then looked Ginifur straight in the eye. "If her life means anything at all to you, I repeat, do not bring her back here." With these final words he ushered his wife through the door and it closed quietly behind them.

Left in the room with her granddaughter Ginifur glanced from one door to the other, placed an arm around Rebecca's shoulders and drew her into her embrace with the baby. In the silence Beau's daughter opened her eyes once more and Rebecca gazed down at her perfect tiny form. "I think that if I lived here then I would be crying too, little one," she said as she touched the child's diminutive hand with her long slender finger. Roberta opened her firmly clenched fist and grasped the finger tightly bringing a smile to Rebecca's face. "Now what?" Rebecca asked as she glanced about the room.

"I think that it is time to take our leave." Ginifur settled the baby carefully in her arm and shepherded Rebecca to the door. "I think that we have all outstayed our welcome for the time being," she added with a rueful smile. "But before we leave we must go and see the wet nurse and then we will go home."

"Are you sure that you should take her, Ma?" Rebecca was uncertain.

"I do not think that there is any real alternative."

"He wouldn't really hurt her . . . would he?" Rebecca was filled with alarm.

Ginifur stared at the tightly closed door separating her from her son. "I fear that it is a very real possibility," she whispered.

Doctor Craven had recommended Rosie Pascoe as a wet nurse and she was found rocking her baby in the crudely fashioned crib at her feet beside the fire in the warm kitchen. Rosie quickly scrambled to her feet. "Tis no use Ma'am." she stammered unhappily. "Nothin' I do will satisfy 'er. Not milk nor a cuddle. I never knowed a cheeld cry so in all me life, I never." She glanced at her own sleeping baby. "I got more milk than I knows what t' do with, tis not that, honest, but she don' seem t' be able t' keep it down. She d' cry so much up it all comes again. Then when she'm cleaned 'n dry again I 'ave another go. If we'm lucky she be so tuckered out with all the cryin' 'n all, she takes a bit but falls asleep afore she'm finished. Me milks alright, just look at 'er," she pointed to her own baby, her face puckered in contentment yet lying on a hard wooden base with no mattress.

Ginifur laid a hand on the young woman's shoulder. "Don't worry Rosie; it is no fault of yours. Some babies take a little longer to settle into a routine. Anyway, I will be taking Roberta home to Tremanyon for the time being."

Rosie's face crumpled with alarm and a tear slid from her eye and trickled down her cheek as she reached to pick up her own daughter. "What? Right now?"

"Yes, I think that it will be for the best, at least for the moment. We will have to wait to see what the future holds for her. Hopefully it won't be too long before she is returned to her rightful place."

"Oh dear!" Rosie whispered. "Whatever shall I do now? Where on earth will I go?"

Rebecca's compassionate nature made her reach out to touch her as she turned a pleading glance at Ginifur. Putting a comforting arm about Rosie's shoulders she asked. "Was your husband Robbie Pascoe?"

Rosie nodded. "Yes Ma'am, 'ee was aboard the *Silver Dawn* when she went down."

Ginifur remembered the boat that had sunk without trace during a freak storm in August, loosing all hands. "He never saw his daughter then," she said as she pondered the baby's fate. Rosie was no more than a child herself Ginifur thought as she studied the young mother's face. Sixteen perhaps, no more than seventeen.

"No Ma'am. 'n 'ee was so lookin' forward to it too. Said 'ee wanted a daughter, 'ee did, 'n 'ee wanted t' name 'er Elizabeth." She gazed lovingly at her daughter. "Bit posh for the likes o' we really, so Lizzie it be," she said as the silent tears fell. "They'll not want we 'ere now."

Rebecca's pleading looks were quite unnecessary as Ginifur's eyes swept the room. "Weep no more Rosie, and gather up your things. The little girl in my arms will still need you, for one thing is for certain . . ." Rosie looked up into the smiling face of Ginifur Tremayne as she finished the sentence with a laugh. "I can't feed her myself."

At this Rebecca chuckled and Rosie grabbed hold of a tattered carpet bag that was tucked behind the chair explaining. "This is all I got Ma'am. The owner of *Silver Dawn* give us lodgin' with Robbie's job. When the boat didn' come 'ome 'n they was all given up for dead, 'ee were kind enough t' let me stay in the cottage till babe was born. Lizzie was born two days afore your grand-daughter. When Doc Craven reckoned they needed a wet nurse 'ee was kind enough to send me along 'ere. I were some pleased, cos I'd 'ave 'ad no roof over me 'ead, no 'usband 'n no ma nor pa either."

"Well we will need you for some months yet, Rosie, and after that . . . well we will see." Ginifur gave a final glance about the kitchen as Rebecca made an attempt to pick up a pile of baby's clothes on the table beside Rosie's chair. "Leave them Becky. Until her future is settled, this babe will need nothing more from this house. Come . . ." as she turned away she saw Rosie glance at the discarded pile of clothes and relented. "Pick them up Rosie, if you feel that they will be of use to Lizzie. We can't waste them now can we?" She smiled as Rosie quickly picked them up and Ginifur led the way to the door. "Let us go home."

As she settled herself into the carriage Ginifur studied the sleeping baby's face. "Roberta," she mused, shaking her head. "Roberta, I wouldn't wonder you even objected to the name they chose to saddle you with. Roberta, indeed! An ugly name, I don't even like it in its masculine form," she looked at Rosie. "Except when it's used in its informal way as Robbie."

Rebecca and Rosie seated themselves opposite her as Joe replaced the carriage steps and closed the door. "Home, Mrs Tremayne?"

"Yes Joe . . . please. The quicker we are away from here the better." As the carriage and horses drew away from the silent house Ginifur glanced out of the window thoughtfully. "What was that Margery Fry said?" she asked of nobody in particular. "She should be called Holly for she's as prickly as a whole bough of it?" Becky nodded, puzzled at where the conversation was leading. Beau's baby daughter chose this moment to open her eyes. The rocking movement had changed, but it wasn't unpleasant, just different. She could still hear the quiet voice that she had heard before and it continued to sooth her. "You are not a Roberta, that's for sure, and as pretty as the name Holly is you are certainly not prickly so we won't use that name either." She brightened as a thought entered her head. "Robyn!" she tried the sound again as the baby gurgled in her arms. "Robyn! I think she likes it. What do you think Becky?"

"I think it is lovely. Yes, Robyn." Rebecca agreed.

"Then Robyn it will be." Ginifur decided as she settled herself back in the carriage with the tiny baby awake and gurgling in her lap.

* * *

From the moment Robyn was picked up by her grandmother she became a different baby. She slept silently in her arms all the way home to Tremanyon and, when Liam had unearthed the old crib and Rosie had successfully fed and changed her, she briefly opened her eyes as she was laid in her new bed and then quickly fell asleep again.

The nursery wing was once more in demand, and at Christmas, Robyn and Dickon were joined by Annabelle, who was now three years old, and her brother David just six months. Ginifur once more had all her family around her with the exception of Beau and his wife. Ginifur had written a letter which had been hand delivered to the Fry's home, inviting them to join the family for Christmas but she had received no reply. Her initial reaction of disappointment was soon pushed to the back of her mind by the arrival of Rachel and her husband and children.

Jamie, Ellen, Dickon and Ben Nancekivel were to continue to live at Tremanyon until the spring, when they would move into their new home at Rhosinnis. As well as receiving an invitation for the New Year celebrations this year, Daniel Franks and his father were to share Christmas with the Tremayne family.

Chapter Five
1785 - 1792

ROBYN SETTLED HAPPILY into her new life with her grandmother. The miserable scrap of humanity who had been starved of the love of its parents at birth, quickly turned into a bright and happy baby with a healthy appetite. In spite of the improvement to her condition, when approached Beau and Clara refused to take their daughter back into their family, saying that they would hear no more talk of the subject; Beau stated that Ginifur could have her made her official ward if she so wished and they would sign the papers to that effect, but from the day she had left the house at Ruan she was no longer their daughter and should make no claim on them in the future.

Ginifur had been deeply hurt by her son's refusal to acknowledge his daughter, and vowed that Robyn would grow up to be a happy, well adjusted child believing that she was genuinely loved and wanted. Ginifur never hid the fact that she was the child's grandmother and not her mother, or the fact that Beau and Clara were her true parents; and Robyn, when she was old enough, seemed to accept this fact.

Whether Beau's hurtful remarks had any lasting effect on Rebecca or not would probably never be known, but Daniel's perseverance finally paid off and they were married after a very short engagement in September '85. Rebecca was to spend less time in her beloved school room and a teacher was sought to replace her. It was the only chance that the children of the village had to better themselves and Daniel said that he would pay for the school to continue. Daniel and Rebecca were to live at Philleigh, near to the ferry, and Daniel would stable a horse on the other side of the River Fal and ride into Truro when the weather allowed or, if not, would stay at his father's house if necessary. The unusual arrangement worked well and they were very happy and it wasn't long before Ginifur was to learn that she was to be a grandmother again. Not only was Clara again with child, Rebecca too brought the news to Ginifur that she was expecting her first child.

The sad event of the year in 1786 was the death of Simon Retallick, Ginifur's father. He suffered a heart attack and died on July the 2nd between the birth of Richard Charles Tremayne who was born on the 1st April 1786 and Tamsin Franks who followed on the 7th July. Ginifur was devastated by the loss of her father.

She felt utterly bereft. The four most important people in her life had been taken away from her. Her grandparents, her father and her husband. Jamie was desperately worried. It took the birth of Tamsin to force her to realise that she was in danger of neglecting Robyn and slowly she began to rally.

Beau was elated for his wife had finally given him a son but, once more, Clara had given birth to a sickly child who would subsequently be both cosseted and pampered by his mother and grandmother. He favoured his mother in looks with fair hair and skin, and there was no resemblance whatsoever to his paternal grandfather whose name he carried. But for Beau it was the culmination of all his hopes and dreams. Beau had a son and heir and he was convinced that now Ginifur must leave her estate to him. Preferably sooner than later.

However, where Tamsin Franks, who also had inherited her mother's fair curls and complexion, was a strong and healthy babe who would soon be following her cousins about on sturdy legs, Richard was to continue to grow into a child who was less than his father had envisaged. Dickon and Robyn were already strong and healthy children and as Dickon increasingly spent more time at Tremanyon, it was inevitable that the two children spent a lot of their time together both in the schoolroom and out of it. At an early age Robyn would be seen perched in front of Ginifur as she rode around the estate accompanied either by Liam, or Jamie with Dickon proudly sitting in front of his father. Naturally it was not long before the two children were introduced to their first mounts, initially following Ginifur or Jamie or accompanied by Liam and later alone on Home Farm

Richard was everything Beau despised in a child. Where Dickon and Robyn were healthy and happy, Richard was a sickly morose child, and where his cousin and sister were energetic children spending a lot of their time out of doors, equally at home in a sailboat as on horseback, Richard would most frequently be found clinging to his mother's skirts or enveloped in his grandmother Fry's arms where she would tell him fairy stories and feed him with sweet comfits. To make matters worse Clara and her parents would insist on calling the child Charlie, this being the name of his great grandfather on his mother's side of the family, and nothing that Beau said could persuade them to use his given name. Dickon and Robyn soon became proficient equestrians but from his first introduction to these four legged animals, young Richard Tremayne had turned crying to his mother. His real or imagined fear and his reaction to horses was to increase with the passage of time and there appeared to be nothing that Beau could do to tempt him to sit astride the white pony that he had bought for him. He would scream and kick even if anyone attempted to lift him up to ride in front of Beau when he rode around the district, but he was quite happy perched beside his mother when she went out in her little gig at a gentle trot.

Jamie involved himself in everything on the farm at Rhosinnis and the similarity to his father became more pronounced with the passing of years. On Ginifur's request he also took an interest in the affairs of Tremanyon, holding regular meetings with Jacob regarding the fishing boats and fish cellar, and young Henry Polaughan, Harry's son who had taken over from his father as bailiff at Home Farm. Ginifur had involved herself in the running of the estate soon after Richard died so suddenly; she had done a remarkable job and the employees had given her incredible support. But Ginifur still had enough to organise at Tremanyon alone and besides, she was now virtually a mother again, even if not in the true sense.

Robyn adored her grandmother and was both loving and obedient and her love was returned not only by Ginifur but Sara, Rachel and Rebecca and all their families. At seven years of age she was a slight child, small boned and tiny for her age, petite Ginifur said. She had dark wavy hair and a dark complexion, resembling Ginifur in her youth, but her eyes were the blue of her grandfather; as were Jamie's and Dickon's. In truth she could easily have been mistaken for Jamie's daughter for she resembled her parents not one bit. Robyn was polite to her father when he came into contact with her on his few visits to Tremanyon. She always smiled as she acknowledged him but escaped as soon as she was able, which wasn't difficult for he was not eager to spend time in conversation with her.

It annoyed Beau that Robyn insisted on calling him 'father' and he raised the matter frequently with Ginifur. Robyn never came into contact with her birth mother, as Clara never visited Tremanyon. She had seen her on occasions from a distance, her brother also, but she gave her mother only a passing thought never thinking that she had missed anything, for she was firmly convinced that she had the best mother in the world in her grandmother. What's more, she didn't need a father or a brother either, for she had Dickon and her beloved Uncle Jamie.

The arrival of Robyn had been a blessing for Ginifur. In spite of her great sorrow at the loss of her husband, Ginifur had never wallowed in self pity. However, having a new young life to focus her attention on did give her a new reason to live a long life. In both Dickon and Robyn she saw so much of Richard Tremayne that she felt that his heart and soul continued to live in them and Jamie, and that he was still nearby, watching over her.

Richard's, Liam's and Jamie's fears for her safety seemed misplaced and it would seem that Richard's accident must have been just that; an accident. Nevertheless, Ginifur never rode out unaccompanied however much she missed the times when she had ridden alone, and if none of her men-folk were available then Joe would ride along with her. Joe had married Rosie and Rosie and her daughter had moved in to the coach cottage in '89.

The yields at the farm had been good in recent years, and since Jamie had arrived home Rhosinnis had flourished. The crops had been good, the sheep flock healthy and had increased in numbers, the cattle too, and the stables and horses were giving added interest. With the combination of the stables at Tremanyon, Rhosinnis and Penhallow they had the making of breeding a good bloodline. With the land at Rhosinnis and Tremanyon and the Wheal Jenny Mine, Jamie's spare time was at a premium but his family never suffered for he always managed to find time to go riding with Ellen or Dickon. He was always home by late afternoon and at Rhosinnis Dickon dined with his parents and grandfather who now lived with them permanently; although both Dickon and Ben divided their time between Tremanyon and Rhosinnis.

Wheal Jenny continued with good yields of tin and copper, even though there were mines closing throughout the west of the county. She produced a healthy profit for her shareholders, much to the relief of Robert Fry and Beau, for Beau could not manage on the income from the Mill and Kylyn Farm. In fact both of these concerns suffered greatly from neglect of their owner. The bailiff at Kylyn did his best but short of staff and the lack of interest and investment made profit almost impossible. Jamie's good fortune only increased Beau's feelings of jealousy. He blamed Jamie for his own lack of money, for the lack of income from the farm and not once considering that it might be for Jamie's hard work and interest in his affairs that had turned a falling income into a profit at Rhosinnis.

Beau was firmly convinced that Jamie had cheated his father in law out of his shares in the mine and that because of this he and his family were forced to live in poverty.

Chapter Six
1793

GINIFUR WAS IN the library, books open upon the table. Dusk was falling early and the light fading fast beyond the windows, darkening the room. She heard Liam's soft footfall as he moved about the house lighting candles and lamps in the hall and drawing room and, as he opened the library door, she heard a horse canter up the drive. Ginifur didn't need to look, she knew it was Jamie and this was confirmed by his hurried feet on the steps up to the front door. He was just like Richard when he used to come home, Ginny thought to herself, forever in a hurry.

"What's bitten you, me lad?" Liam quipped as he lit Ginifur's lamp and Jamie burst into the room.

"Guess who I've seen?"

Ginifur laughed. "I haven't any idea. Who have you seen?"

"Jean-Paul," he informed her, smiling at the surprise on their faces. "Truly, I met his carriage in the village. Jean-Paul has come home to Rosvarron and Jean-Louis is with him. He looks a lot older, Jean-Louis that is, but then we all do I suppose. I haven't seen Jean-Louis since . . . when? Well it must be at least ten years ago." Jamie continued excitedly.

"Does Jean-Paul look well?" enquired Ginifur.

Jamie pondered the question. "Yes. Older of course, but still the same as I remembered him. He asked after you. He hadn't heard about Father and was genuinely upset by the news. He went very quiet whist Louis and I caught up on the news. But he sent his condolences and said that he would like to call on you."

"What brought him back to England?" Ginifur asked. "I thought that when he returned to Canada, after Caroline died, he would not return to England again.

"I don't know, Ma. He didn't say. On reflection I guess there must be a reason!"

"I wonder if it has anything to do with the dreadful events in France." Ginifur suggested. "I was sure that he had cut all ties there long ago. Was Marie-Claire with them?"

"No, and I didn't think to ask."

"It will be good to see him again." Liam added, remembering the adventure that the three of them, Richard, Jean-Paul and he had shared in '53 and '54 in the New World. Their shared friendship with Running Bear as fur trappers, and the dreadful experience of the Indian attack at Elly's cabin that had resulted in Richard's dreadful wound that had almost killed him. It had been a true miracle that he survived the journey back to England. Even then it had been doubtful that he would live. He wouldn't have lived, if it hadn't been for Ginifur. Ginifur and, of course, Old Betsy.

Betsy was now seventy-six years old and still combing the hedgerows for her herbs and berries. Both Ginifur and Jamie made regular visits to her cottage beyond the village. They always took with them a basket of provisions to ensure that she had something to eat, including some honey from the hives in the walled garden. Ginifur usually returned to Tremanyon from these visits with potions and salves that they needed for any coughs, colds or pains that they, or any of the employees, were suffering with at Tremanyon. Betsy continued to take a keen interest in Jamie's life and especially enjoyed his visits with Dickon and Robyn. The name of Old Betsy finally fitted her for there were few in the village that were as old as she. Netty Teague, the old cook from Tremanyon, had died two years past at the age of 87 and her husband Tom, once upon a time the head gardener, three years before that.

Of course Betsy could see Dickon's future too, and Robyn's, but she kept these to herself. It was Ginifur who caused her the most concern.

Jamie came alone on his last visit, this time he found her sitting in the rocking chair he had gifted to her. Betsy's cat was curled up on her lap and her feet were stretched out towards the fire on this March morning. Jamie looped his reins through the ring at the door before opening it. "Hello, Betsy, what's this? You are finding time to put your feet up now and dream are you?"

Betsy let out a low cackle of laughter and turned to face the door. "Ye're too cheeky by far, me boy, but still a good sight for these ol' eyes o' mine. But no, there be no dreams, jest worries."

"You have nothing to worry about Betsy; you know that Mother has promised that she will always make sure that you are cared for." Jamie assured her.

"Tis not me I be affeared for, tis y'ur Ma." She stirred the cat and pushed him gently off her lap. "I tried t' warn y'ur Da, 'ee didn' laugh at me tis true, but I did warn 'im not t' ride alone too."

"You have not told me this before, Betsy." This was the first Jamie had heard Betsy mention the fear that she had had for his father. "When was this?"

“Jest a week afore ’ee fell, that were the last time. Tol’ ’im more time’s than that over the last month or two though.” She peered up at Jamie. “The ’ard thing was I knawed I couldn’ do ought about it.”

“You are not trying to blame yourself are you?”

“No.” Betsy’s head bobbed up and down as if it were attached to her body with a spring. “Couldn’ ’elp ’im. I’m sorry me boy, but it was writ y’see.” She stood up and put another log on the fire before turning back to him. “But Miss Ginny! Tha’s a different matter, it’s not writ in stone. I tol’ Cap’n, ’n I be tellin’ ’ee now, she must not ride alone, ’n check the ’orse afore she d’ ride un too. D’ye ’ear me young Jamie? Ye watch over y’ur mother mind.”

“Betsy, what are you trying to tell me?” Jamie was alarmed, to say the least.

“Y’ur Pa ’ad a fall. Don’ ’ee think that be strange? ’ee wasn’t ridin’ ’ard, not chasin’ a fox . . . jest ridin’ through them valley fields. ’Is ’orse all lathered ’n edgy, ’n the saddle off when ’ee turns up at Tremanyon? ’n Cap’n ’ee ’gets ’it on the ’ead by ’is ’orse! Tid’n fitty in my mind. No, tid’n fitty atall.” She took the basket of food and placed it on the table with the herbs she was preparing for a remedy. “Nought anyone could do t’ stop it, I read the signs ye see. But young Ginny, tid’n so clear. But tis an ’orse again. Mark my words young Jamie, tis an ’orse again.”

Jamie felt a chill run through him, of course he had been shocked that his father had died due to a fall. But it seemed that Ginifur and the family had all accepted it as such, just an unfortunate accident. However, his father-in-law had found it almost beyond belief, Jamie clearly remembered their first conversation. Betsy unpacked the items from the basket and then replaced them with remedies and herbs that Ginifur had asked for. This barter system made her feel that she wasn’t accepting charity, for Betsy was a very proud woman. The previous conversation did not return as Betsy’s mind turned to Dickon and Robyn, then to the girls Rachel, Rebecca, Sara and Ellen and Ginifur’s other grandchildren. She did not mention Beau or Clara or Richard. Satisfied that Betsy was well, and promising to send someone over with some wood for the fire, Jamie headed home with a heavy heart. Could he, or should he, tell his mother of Betsy’s fears? Perhaps he should confide in Liam. Jamie rode home slowly as he went over his conversation with Betsy.

Two horses from Rosvarron were tethered outside the stables at Tremanyon when Jamie returned; in haste to see who had arrived he handed the reins over to Joe asking him to tend to his horse. Carrying the basket to the kitchen for Kate and Lorna to take charge of, he hurried to his room with a jug of water and quickly washed and changed out of his riding clothes before making his way to the drawing room. Jean-Paul and Jean-Louis had arrived shortly before Jamie's return and were engaged in a conversation with Ginifur, which quickly ended and they both greeted him warmly before seating themselves once more. Jamie asked about their lives in Canada and Ginifur was pleased to hear that they had kept in touch with Elly and her family. All Elly's children had married now and Tuck had enlarged the family farmhouse where Elly continued to live. In recent years, Running Bear had headed farther north, not wanting to live his life out on a reservation. He had lived a solitary nomadic life since his wife and son had been killed by the French invaders and didn't wish to live in confinement amongst people . . . even with his own kind. Jean-Paul had not heard news of him for nearly five years. Ginifur would always be grateful to Elly and Running Bear for the attention that Richard had received after his injury caused by an arrow during the raid on Elly's cabin in Canada. If it hadn't been for Running Bear and his herbal remedies in the first instance he would never have returned home. Then if it had been left to conventional medical treatment by the local doctor he would have died if Ginny hadn't plucked up the courage to ask Betsy for help. Yes, Ginifur owed a great deal to these people but she could only repay Betsy with help in her old age. It was her deepest regret that she had never been able to thank Running Bear in person. Richard had managed to make just one return visit where he travelled to see Elly and her family. When Running Bear had received word that his blood brother had returned to Twin Forks, he travelled overland for many days to see him. Apparently it had been quite an emotional reunion.

Ginifur's mind had wandered for a moment but she picked up the mention of Marie-Clair when Jamie asked after her.

Jean-Paul and Jean-Louis glanced uncertainly at each other before answering, but Ginifur rescued them by explaining herself.

"I am afraid that Marie-Claire is in France, Jamie. She met a young man, Pierre de Wandler, in Montreal whilst they were both on a visit there and she returned to France to marry him. It is for this reason that Jean-Paul has returned to Rosvarron, he has received no news of Marie-Claire for the last twelve months and is naturally concerned for her welfare."

From his position behind Ginifur's chair Jamie studied the faces of his childhood friend and his father. "I am so sorry. These are difficult times in France we hear. The news of the execution of the King and his family . . . just dreadful. But surely, Marie-Clair is in no danger?"

Jean-Paul shook his head. "I am afraid that she is. When Jean-Louis and I left for England a trusted friend returned to France to find Marie-Claire and report to me at Rosvarron. I received a communication today. Pierre has been taken into custody, whether he is alive still I have no idea for executions are being carried out with no trial or evidence other than on someone's word. However, due to a warning of a well-wisher he was able to have enough time to send Marie-Claire into hiding." He glanced briefly at Ginifur. "I was just telling your mother that I will need a boat to take me, and Jean-Louis, to France. We have to try to find Marie-Claire and bring her safely home. I need someone who is willing to ferry us over and bring us back, assuming that we are successful. Needless to say, when we left Canada I had hoped that, should the need arise, Richard would assist me. Not for one moment did I think that . . . Of course I had no idea that my good friend Richard . . ." The unfinished sentence hung in the air.

Jamie glanced at Ginifur wondering what her thoughts were. Of course if his father had been here he would have assisted Jean-Paul and probably gone along as well.

"You bring us the most terrible news." Jamie agreed. "I am sure that we can find a boat for you, of course the crew would have to volunteer for we could not order them to make such a dangerous expedition. I am sure you will understand."

Ginifur nodded her agreement, not adding anything as she waited for the full extent of the request to unfold.

"And you Jamie!!" Jean-Louis joined the conversation. "Will you join us? Your naval skills, your command of our language is as good as ours, no one would believe you to be English. We could really do with you beside us."

This was a request that Jamie had not expected. He should have, of course, but the expression on his face showed that he hadn't. "Me!" Jamie found his voice. "You want me to join you?" Jean-Paul and Jean-Louis nodded in unison. "Oh! I don't know," he glanced at Ginifur to see if she understood his predicament. "It is not that I am afraid of danger, for I have faced enough of that in my time in His Majesty's Navy; but as you know I am married now and Ellen, unfortunately, is not able to care for herself. Should anything happen to me, how would she manage to bring Dickon up alone." Ginifur had already acquainted Jean-Paul with Jamie's marriage and Ellen's disability. Jamie's response was not a great surprise.

To say that he wasn't disappointed would be totally untrue. Jean-Paul had counted on Richard to help him, although second best Jamie would have been a good choice. "I understand Mon ami; yes . . . yes I do, truly. If she were my wife I would feel just as you do." He turned to Ginifur. "The offer of the boat and a crew, if one can be found, I will accept with gratitude. We still have some time, as it will take a while for us to set up a rendezvous, and friends are still trying to find where Marie-Claire is hiding. As it stands we would be searching blindfold." He rose from his chair and held out his hand to Jamie. "Thank you Jamie. But I ask you to be very careful about whom you approach. I wouldn't want word of this to get out to the wrong people."

"You can be assured that anyone I approach will be sure to keep their mouths closed. Most of them will probably have had some contact with the free traders; they know when to keep quiet." Jamie grasped Jean-Louis by the shoulders. "Have faith Mon ami, you have to believe that Marie-Claire will be found."

Liam chose this moment to knock on the door and entered when Ginifur answered.

Liam headed straight for Jean-Paul. "I heard that ye had returned to Rosvarron, I was just going to visit ye when Kate told me ye was 'ere, with Ginny." He grasped Jean-Paul's hand in friendship and even accepted the kiss on both cheeks without embarrassment. "I hope that all is well with ye and your family." He turned to eye up Jean-Louis. "I see ye have brought this young reprobate along with ye, not got shot of him yet? Marie-Claire . . . where is she?"

The friendship which had sprung up between Richard, Jean-Paul and Liam whilst on their journey to the New World had never wavered and, following their return, their children Jamie, Aidan and Jean-Louis had become lifelong friends. Both Jamie and Aidan were now fluent in French as it had become their favourite means of communication when playing together, making their games more exciting.

Jean-Paul hesitated only briefly before repeating his story for Liam. Liam was equally sorry to hear this news, as he knew Aidan would be too. He asked Jean-Paul to keep him informed of the progress of his plans and said that he would let Aidan know of the awful news.

Having agreed to return the following week, or earlier if they had more news, Jean-Paul and Jean-Louis took their leave and Ginifur and Jamie and Liam went over the planned escapade to try to rescue Marie-Claire. Jamie felt bad at refusing to assist their friends, but Ginifur assured him that he had made the right decision.

When Aidan heard the news he quickly found Jamie and told him that he wanted to offer to take the boat to France with Jean-Paul and Jean-Louis. His French was as good as Jamie's, he declared, as in truth it was, if a little rusty. Jamie was partially relieved that the first member of the crew had been found but he still suffered with bouts of guilt and Ellen didn't help when she told him that he should aid his friends in their foray into France, believing as she did that it was sure to be successful if he went with them; for Ellen had such faith in her husband.

However, Jamie would not be persuaded to change his mind and after judicious discussions with Aidan a list of possible crewmembers was drawn up and every one of them volunteered to go. It only now remained for news to come for Jean-Paul from France.

With no news having arrived from France Jamie rode in through the back gate of Tremanyon to find Ginifur, Dickon and Robyn getting ready to ride out. Liam's mount was tethered waiting for his arrival. "Where are you off to?" he enquired.

"Just over to the headland. Down to the Mill, up the valley and out to Rhosinnis. We will come back along the coastal lane." Jamie was taken aback by a cold feeling that swept over him and Ginifur must have noticed his hesitation. "I have to do this Jamie, I have to ride that way sometime, I can't keep ignoring it forever. I am ready, really."

Jamie wasn't convinced but kept quiet; anyway Liam was going with her. He alighted from his horse to assist Joe with the tacking of the horses, he remarked on the side saddle and Ginifur laughed.

"I have to set an example to Robin. I can't expect her to ride side-saddle if I don't."

Satisfied that everything was to his satisfaction he turned when he heard Lorna call Ginifur's name.

"Mrs Tremayne . . . Ma . . . She has taken a fall. She fainted and fell down the steps to the west wing. Can ye come, Ginny . . . please?"

Ginifur turned to the children. "Wait here you two. I don't expect I will be long, there is still plenty of time for our ride," and she and Jamie followed Lorna back to the house.

Beau chose this moment to make one of his infrequent visits and, most unusually, drove in with Richard in the gig beside him. The sight of Dickon and Robyn dressed and ready for riding did nothing to improve his demeanour. These visits always brought to the fore his dissatisfaction with his life and they only emphasised the differences between his son Richard and his sister and his cousins. However, Beau did his best to disguise his feelings as he said hello to Dickon and nodded to Robyn with the acknowledgement. "Roberta."

Robyn smiled politely as she returned his greeting. "Father."

"Out for a ride are you?"

Dickon replied for them both, as he usually did. "Yes, we are riding out to the headland with Grandmother when she is ready."

"Are you now?" Beau alighted from the gig. "That will be nice for you," he approached Ginifur's horse. "She has turned into a fine mare, I remember her when she was born," he said as he fondled the horse.

Robyn and Dickon turned their attention to Richard. The differences increased as the years passed by. Richard pale skinned, plump and blonde. Dickon and Robyn both dark skinned, dark haired and lean. The three cousins regarded each other, weighing the other up. Dickon was quite ambivalent, having no real feelings one way or the other but Richard hated Dickon with the intensity that his father hated his brother. There was only one person Richard hated more, his sister Roberta. Roberta lived here in Tremanyon, in the house that should be his father's home . . . and his . . . Richard Tremayne's. His grandfather had built this Georgian Manor house in 1750 and it should be handed down to his heir. In his father's eyes this should have come to him when Richard's grandfather died, and then to his son in his turn. But Tremanyon had been gifted to Richard's grandmother. Richard's feelings for his grandmother were only a few points higher than his feelings for Dickon and Roberta. Ginifur had done little to deserve this rejection, if anything at all, but these feelings were exacerbated by the fact that Roberta was now her legal ward as well as her grand-daughter.

Lorna returned with the news that Ginifur had decided to postpone their ride until tomorrow, if the children wanted to ride over the fields at the Home Farm they could, but they were to go no further.

With a curt. "Well, your grandmother will be too tied up with her loyal Kate to find time for us." Beau climbed back into the gig and drove off, meeting Ellen as she drove in the gates in her light trap.

Dickon was just telling Joe to return Willow to the stable as his mother drew to a halt. "I thought your grandmother was taking you riding?"

"Kate has fainted and taken a fall. Grandmama has to see to her." Robyn informed her.

"We can go tomorrow." Dickon showed no sign of disappointment. "Kate must come first."

"There is no need for the children to miss their ride, Joe. Willow has a side saddle already on her, I'll take the children out for a ride myself."

Joe looked uncertain. "But Mrs. Tremayne said as 'ow I was to stable 'er, Ma'am."

Ellen laughed. "Joe, you have seen me ride often enough. I can't walk . . . I can ride as you well know, and it was Willow I rode on my first visit to Tremanyon you will recall and it was Willow I rode to the hunt in Truro with Jamie."

"I knows that, Ma'am, it's just . . ."

"Yes I know . . . Mrs Tremayne said that you were to stable Willow. Don't worry about that Joe, I will explain to her when I get back, I am quite sure that she has enough to cope with right now." She applied the brake to the trap and looped the reins loosely on the hook by the seat. "Now, bring Willow over here Joe, and help me into the saddle."

Reluctantly Joe did as Ellen bid him; she had done this manoeuvre enough times that it was accomplished quite smoothly and, with two happy children to accompany her, Ellen led the way out of Tremanyon and down the hill.

Ginifur was concerned about Kate. To her knowledge she had never suffered dizzy spells in the past. She had fainted at the top of the short flight of steps down to the west wing, which was built slightly lower than the original part of the ground floor of the main house. She had taken a nasty bump to her head and Ginny was particularly concerned about this, but she had also hurt her leg and arm and Ginifur wasn't sure if there was a break in her leg or just a nasty strain. To keep the leg straight she sent Poppy to the walled garden to get one of the men to bring up a large enough piece of wood to carry Kate upon, and when Peter Cutler arrived with a centre section from a plank from the timber yard he helped Jamie and Liam to carry her to one of the spare bedrooms in the house for it would not be easy to carry her up the narrow winding stairs in the cottage. When Kate was lying as comfortable as they could make her, Ginifur carefully examined her. She applied a cold compress to her head and looked carefully at her eyes before turning her attention to Kate's leg. After a thorough examination she was confident that Kate had not broken her leg but was concerned that she had fainted and fallen. Kate admitted that she had been suffering with dizzy spells and for this reason Ginifur asked Jamie to send someone over to ask Dr Craven to call as soon as he could find the time.

There was no sign of the children, and Beau and Richard had been and gone without Jamie knowing that his brother had called at Tremanyon. He was puzzled to see Ellen's empty trap with the horse happily tethered to the rung in the stable wall. "Joe!" he called out as he made his way down the stables to the harness room.

"Yes Captain Tremayne." Joe appeared at the end of the passage.

Jamie shook his head with a grimace on his face. "How many times must I tell you? I am just plain Mr Tremayne. There can only be one Captain Tremayne, and that was my father. Where are the children, and what is Ellen's trap doing outside?"

In spite of Ellen's assurance Joe was worried that she had countermanded Ginifur's request to stable her horse. "Young Mrs Tremayne said she would take the youngsters for their ride. She said it be alright, Sir. Tol' me not t' worry Mrs Tremayne, she 'ad enough t' do with Kate she said." His concern that he had not done what Ginifur had asked was clear to see. "Did I do wrong, Sir? Young Mrs Tremayne, she be a fine rider, 'n she 'ave ridden Willow afore."

Jamie dismissed his concern. "No, no. If Ellen makes up her mind to do something even I can't stop her," he assured Joe. "No, of course she is more than capable of managing Willow, even on one of her bad days." So why did he have this sinking feeling in the pit of his stomach, why the icy fingers clutching at his heart?

The sound of horse's hooves cantering into the drive and up to the stable door brought Jamie and Joe quickly outside to find a flushed and dishevelled Robyn jumping from her pony, tears streaming down her face as she headed for the steps at the back of the garden cottage.

"Robyn!" Jamie called. "What's happened? Where is Dickon? Where is your Aunt?"

Robyn halted abruptly and turned to Jamie. "Oh, Uncle Jamie! She's fallen. Aunt Ellen, Willow got upset and reared up, something must have disturbed her. It wasn't that though. The girth strap broke and the saddle came off, Auntie with it. She's hurt Uncle Jamie. Aunt Ellen is hurt and Dickon is with her. My father too, he was driving past The Mill and saw us on the other side of the valley. He came across to help."

"Joe, have you unsaddled Merlin?" Jamie asked

"No Mr Tremayne, only loosened the girth. Was about to unsaddle him when you called out, I'd just decided p'raps ye was stayin' a whiles."

"Bring him out then." He knelt down beside his niece. "Robyn, go and warn grandmother that I am bringing your Aunt Ellen back here. Tell her all you know about what injuries she may have." Robyn nodded tearfully but turned to do his bidding. "And tell her to send someone for the doctor," he called after her.

Joe appeared with Jamie's horse, adjusted the girth strap and held his head whilst Jamie leaped into the saddle. "Follow with the trap Joe, but fetch some blankets first, I'll see you at The Mill." With this Jamie cantered down the drive and vanished from sight. Joe hurriedly followed Robyn to the house meeting a concerned Ginifur at the side door. Joe told her what he knew and collected the blankets as Jamie had directed him.

Liam had followed Ginifur to the door and went to aid Joe in harnessing the horse to the trap, saw Joe off to The Mill and then saddled another horse and rode off to get the doctor. Kate was not in need of urgent attention he was quite sure, but it may be very different for Ellen.

Jamie found young Richard in Well Lane, sulking agitatedly in the gig as he pointed across the valley to where Beau and Dickon were sitting beside the fallen Ellen. Tying his horse to the side of the gig Jamie bounded over the stream and ran up the hill.

Dickon was white and shaken. "It's alright Dickon. Mama will soon be well, don't worry now." To his brother he said. "Thank you for stopping to help, Beau. I am in your debt."

Beau didn't answer immediately, just stood up and looked down at Jamie's wife. Jamie knelt down beside Ellen. "She's hurt, not dead." Beau informed him. "She spoke to Dickon only a moment ago."

Jamie glanced at Dickon who rubbed his eyes on his sleeve as he acknowledged that Beau spoke the truth. "Yes Pa, she did," he agreed between sobs. "Said I wasn't to worry and that she would be fine soon."

"And so she will Dickon, so she will." Jamie assured his son as he made a quick investigation of Ellen's limbs. She seemed to be lying quite straight. Not twisted in any way. He made the decision to move her, it would take too much time to get medical aid to her here, in a field, and Jamie had to get Ellen back to Tremanyon. "Can you help me to carry Ellen to the trap, Beau?" Beau glanced back at Richard sitting in the gig and Jamie followed his eyes. "No, Joe will be here any minute with the trap," he informed his brother. "There would be no room to lie her down in your gig."

Beau glanced down at Ellen. She was a slip of a thing, he thought to himself, with her tiny frame and withered legs. What on earth had his brother seen in her? "Of course." he agreed. "How would you like to go about it?"

Jamie glanced about him. Willow having lost her saddle was still edgy but grazing nearby and beside her stood nervous Pebbles, Dickon's pony, wondering what was going on. "If you can handle the horses Dickon bring them along, if you can't, don't worry they will be safe enough here." To his brother he instructed him to support Ellen's useless legs whilst he carefully carried her upper body, mindful to support her neck and head. Jamie was grateful that she was not aware of them carrying her, she felt no pain throughout the difficult attempt to carry her across the uneven ground to Joe's waiting trap. Ellen was indeed very small compared to many young mothers, and therefore also light to carry but the uneven ground contained many pitfalls as they found out, and Jamie wondered whether Willow's foot had caught in the uneven ground and pitched forward. Dickon followed with the horses, struggling with Willow's saddle but Jamie was too busy occupied with Ellen to notice. Joe had arrived with the trap and saw Dickon struggling with the horses and saddle on the uneven hill. He quickly jumped across the stream to help him; taking the saddle he made a cursory inspection of the girth strap before taking Willow's reins.

Back on Well Lane they lay Ellen carefully on a blanket on the floor of the trap and covered her with another. Jamie instructed Dickon to climb up beside Joe and asked Beau to tie the horses behind his gig and bring them back to Tremanyon. This arranged he climbed in beside Ellen and cradled her head in his lap. Joe had already turned the trap around so they headed straight back to Tremanyon and where Ginifur was waiting with a bed ready for Ellen and the news that the doctor should already be on his way. By the time that Liam had helped Jamie carry Ellen up the wide staircase, Lorna came with the news that Dr Craven had just ridden in.

A quick examination proved that Ellen was suffering from concussion but although Dr Craven was confident that she had no broken bones he was not satisfied that there were no internal injuries. Liam had ridden out to Rhosinnis to take the news to Ellen's father and Benjamin Nancekivel arrived as Dr Craven was taking his leave from Jamie and Ginifur. Jamie hurriedly returned upstairs to Ellen with his father-in-law close behind him.

Tears filling his eyes as he gazed down on his daughter's lovely face, Benjamin spoke to his son-in-law. "She will be alright, won't she Jamie boy?"

Jamie was far from certain. Ellen was as white as the sheets that she lay between. Now and again her blue veined eyelids fluttered briefly, but she hadn't opened her eyes since they had brought her home. "Dr Craven says that the next forty-eight hours will be critical."

The next two days and nights were the longest in Jamie's life. Jamie, Ginifur or Ben sat beside Ellen's bed the whole time, sometimes all of them. Once or twice she opened her eyes and spoke briefly, once asking for Dickon. Her son was brought to her room and conducted himself bravely in her presence, but afterwards wept in his grandmother's embrace with Robyn watching on with tears in her eyes. Robyn had never seen Dickon cry before and there had been many occasions when he could have done. The sight of him like this made her want to cry too. Dr Craven called three times each day, but could offer them no hope for improvement. Ginifur wondered whether to fetch Betsy in to assist, but after second thoughts believed that there would be nothing that she could do this time.

In the early hours of the following morning, when Benjamin Nancekivel entered the room to relieve Ginifur and Jamie, Ellen opened her eyes. She looked briefly at three of the most loved people in her life, gave them a beautiful smile and passed quietly away.

* * *

Like his father before him, Jamie sat at the desk in the library with the remains of a bottle of red wine in front of him and another empty glass in his hand. Liam knocked on the half opened door before entering and Jamie glanced up to acknowledge him. “Liam?”

His father’s manservant and friend noticed the near empty bottle and glass but made no comment. “I’ve got Joe outside; he has asked to see ye Jamie.”

“NO! Don’t bring him in here.” He slammed his fist on the table. “Ellen was an accomplished horse woman, she shouldn’t have taken a fall. First Father, now Ellen! Who else is going to die due to neglect? Two girth straps breaking! I thought that Father said that he was as good as Sam Sawle. Never! Sam would never have let a horse out without checking that everything was in good order.” This was the first sign of Jamie’s anger at the incident that had killed his wife.

“But, Joe . . .”

Jamie’s fist struck the desk once more. “NO, I said NO Liam. I don’t trust myself to even see him at the moment. Make sure that he stays out of my way.”

Liam took one last look at Jamie’s contorted expression and decided to leave the room.

In the hall Joe was ashen faced, clutching two girth straps in his hand. “Leave him be, lad. T’be sure the man has just buried his wife, Joe. Give him time, just give him time. He’ll see the truth of it when he be ready t’ see it.” Liam attempted to reassure Joe.

“I think that ye’ll ’ave t’ find someone else t’ do my job, Liam. Ye ’eard ’im.” Joe turned on his heals.

“No Joe. Ginny has insisted that she does not hold ye t’ blame. There be no need for drastic action.”

“P’raps not. But ye ’eard ’im, ’ee does.” Joe left the hall and headed back to the stables and Liam went to the kitchen to tell Kate what had happened.

A further knock on the library door bought an angry Jamie to his feet. “I said NO, damn you . . .” he grasped the door handle and flung the door open to crash against the wall.

Aidan took a step backwards. “No! No what?” he had backed almost to the other side of the hall, facing a distraught Jamie whose face was contorted with rage, such as Aidan had never seen before.

Jamie held his position in the doorway bringing his emotions under control as he became aware that he was not facing Liam, but Liam's son, Aidan. "Aidan! I'm sorry. Did you wish to see me?"

Aidan recovered his composure. "Only if ye 'ave the time, Jamie. I don' want t' disturb ye."

"No, come on in Aidan and we'll open another bottle of wine. I need a friend at this moment in time." Jamie turned back into the library, picked up the near empty bottle and pulled the bell cord before slumping into one of the comfy chairs and indicating the other to his friend.

Aidan did as he was bid, then studied Jamie. He had lost a lot of weight in the past week or so, and bags had formed under his eyes with the lack of sleep. This wouldn't help the state of his temper, but no one had ever seen Jamie loose his temper before, whatever the provocation. Poppy had presumed that more wine was being called for and entered the room to place another bottle on the desk, with some fresh glasses. Picking up the empty bottle and the dirty glasses she bid a hasty retreat and Jamie gave a mirthless laugh as she scuttled from the room. "Well that certainly shook them up." he retorted with a mirthless laugh. "Is this just a social call Aidan, I'll admit that I'm not feeling very sociable at the moment . . . or did you want to see me about something?"

"A bit of both Jamie. We are all worried about you, and Dickon most of all." Aidan sat forward in his chair. "Also, I 'ave t' talk to 'ee about the French trip."

Jamie's eyes seemed to come into focus. "French trip! Oh yes, Jean-Paul's daughter. Marie-Claire . . . news is there?"

"Yes. We 'eard from France on the day of the funeral. I'm sure that ye're aware that the boat is ready! I've just come t' let 'ee know that we will be leavin' first light, day after t'morrow."

Jamie's face was now alert and concentrating. "I wasn't aware that things had gone this far."

"Ye 'ad other things on y'ur mind Jamie. This was something that Jean-Paul, Jean-Louis and meself could see to." Aidan explained. "I just didn' want t' make final preparations without consultin' 'ee first."

Jamie agreed that he had been somewhat engaged in other matters but asked what news they had received and Aidan explained that apparently Marie-Claire had taken refuge in a Convent somewhere outside St Malo. Even Convents were not safe from searches by government forces or being ransacked and Jean-Paul was anxious to be on his way. A rendezvous place and time had been arranged and they would leave as planned.

"You have a full crew? Everyone fully aware of the danger?"

"Oh yes, they knows there be danger but 'em still want to play their part."

Jamie rose from the chair and glancing at the bookshelves he retrieved some leather bound rolls of vellum. He selected a chart of the northern French coast line. "Show me where you plan to land; I am guessing that you do not intend to sail right into St Malo harbour!"

Aidan laughed. "No I don't think so." Jamie laid the chart on the desk, finding heavy items to prevent it from rolling up tight once more, and Aidan joined him to indicate where they proposed to make the rendezvous. Jamie fetched another map of St Malo which showed the surrounding area, noting any convents where Marie-Claire might have received shelter. Jamie took it all in and then wished Aidan a safe trip and a speedy return home.

When Aidan left him Jamie began to empty his third bottle of wine, this time accompanied by the partially empty bottle of brandy too, and it was the early hours of the following morning when he stumbled up the stairs.

Once again reliving one of the lowest periods in her life, Ginifur lay awake until she heard Jamie's footfalls on the landing before she turned over; with tears drying on her cheeks she closed her eyes and finally fell asleep.

* * *

Dawn was breaking as he made his way down the hill and the river and St Maries were still cloaked in semi darkness and the light morning mist. The silence was what struck him the most. There was no sound of men making ready to go to sea, no sound of voices carried on the light breeze. It occurred to him that he was too late. There was no need for them to hide their departure as it was the normal time that a boat would depart to fish in the bay. At the bottom of the slope he turned to face the quay, a lamp was lit in the cottage and he saw that they were gathered there in readiness to leave. He knocked and opened the door.

"Jamie! Mon ami! Have you come to see us set sail?" Jean-Paul stepped quickly towards him. It was the first time that they had met since Ellen's funeral. Since that day Jamie had kept himself shut away in the library at Tremanyon, refusing to see anyone but his family, and even they saw precious little of him he understood. "It is good of you to think of us when you have so much more on your mind."

Aidan, Jean-Louis and Jacob studied Jamie's stance and were not surprised when he announced that he had not come to wish them well on the venture, he had come to join them.

Jean-Paul was stunned. "No Jamie. You have too many responsibilities here at Tremanyon and Rhosinnis to put yourself in danger for the sake of friendship."

"I have made my decision. My reason for not going in the first place, no longer exists. Dickon will be brought up by his grandmother now; he will need her in the months to come. I know Aidan knows the French coast as well, if not better than I, this is his command. But I am coming too Jean-Paul, I am coming too."

The crew of the Sara-Anne was delighted that Jamie was to sail with them. Jamie had sailed the high seas, surviving many sea battles and come home. For them this was a good sign.

The Sara-Anne rode on her deep water mooring in mid stream, a Cornish Lugger too she was larger than Guinevere. This fine Lugger was the largest of the fleet which sailed from the quay, it too was clinker built, had three stepped masts and was half decked. With all sails set she could make the journey from Cornwall to Roscoff in around nine hours. Aidan was allowing twelve hours to reach their destination. The tide was not quite high enough to bring her into the quay, and the crew were ferried across by Jacob who would stay behind and watch as his friends and sister's son set sail on this venture.

* * *

It turned out to be an uneventful crossing; the crews on the fishing boats out of St Malo were familiar with the sight of the Sara-Ann and her crew. In fact the Bretons and Cornish had often been brothers in arms throughout history. Many village names were similar, the languages too had a lot in common and the Cornish language was still in use in the outlying districts in the west of the county where English was considered very much a second language. Many Cornish men and women still believed that Cornwall was a nation in its own right. Indeed they still had their own Parliament; The Stannary.

Aidan had often visited these waters and the one or two fishing boats they could not avoid hailed them cheerfully. They made pretence of fishing during their outward journey and as dusk fell they began to make their move towards the French coast.

The rendezvous point was east of the fishing port of St Malo and the chosen beach was in a sheltered secluded cove where there was no coastal village and the fishing boat could safely get close to the shore at this state of the tide.

Jean-Paul and Aidan studied the cliffs and the valley as the boat drew slowly nearer to the narrow stretch of beach.

"There!" Jean-Paul exclaimed in a hushed voice, for sound would carry far over the water at this time of the night and in this silence.

"I see it." Aidan acknowledged. "Are we agreed, we go in?"

Jean-Paul, Jamie and Jean-Louis indicated their agreement and the boat edged slowly forward with Tom swinging the lead, checking on the depth of water to ensure they weren't left stranded, high and dry on a falling tide. Jamie thought that he noticed movement along the valley at the eastern end of the beach and not long after, heard the muffled oars of a boat dipping into the water and taking long strokes as it approached the fishing boat from the nearby rocks. With some yards still to cover Aidan hove to and ordered a quiet drop of the anchor; it slid smoothly below the slight swell and held at the first attempt. The small boat pulled alongside and a swift conversation was held with Jean-Paul.

"We must leave quickly," Jean-Paul informed Jamie. "There are armed men not far away and it is essential that this boat is well away from the shore and out of sight before anyone can see it. It might make it impossible for them to come back to pick us up if suspicion is raised."

"I understand." Jamie agreed. "Jean-Louis . . . Aidan!"

Aidan spoke briefly with Ben Rowse who would take the Sara-Anne back out to sea, closer to the English coast where they would resume their supposed fishing activities until it was time to make the planned pick up, then he joined his companions in the small boat. With all of them aboard it was heavily laden, therefore quite low in the water and they did get wet, but it was only a few yards to the beach where the boat was dragged quickly ashore by their French accomplices. Jamie glanced back to see that their life line, the Sara-Anne, was already well away from the shore. Even from this distance it would be hard to be convinced that she was not indeed just another French fishing vessel.

As soon as the little boat had discharged the quartet onto the beach it had been returned to the water and was soon back amongst the rocks where it was quickly disguised with net and sea weed.

From the top of the rocky escarpment it would be invisible. The oarsman quickly returned along the beach and the whole group made their way, single file, up the shallow incline. The valley above the beach was well hidden with bushes, giving them cover until they reached the point where it joined another track and the leader of the group signalled a halt before continuing alone until he was sure that the coast was clear. When he returned, he indicated that they were safe to continue the ascent and keeping tight formation the group climbed silently to the top of the cliff. With no words spoken and only sign language given, the group pressed on along the coastal track up through the wooded valley and here, at another junction with the track coming from the west of the beach, the French leader spoke in hushed tones with a waiting compatriot. Speaking in his own tongue he explained that the armed men were closer now and travelling fast along the road from la Guimarais. They must pick up their pace if they were to reach and cross the road before they were cut off. With half their companions escorting them ahead, and the other half to the rear, they increased their pace to a steady jog.

In spite of his age Jean-Paul was fit and healthy and he was pleased to find that he had no difficulty in keeping up with his son and his friends. He was eager to receive clearer information about Marie-Claire for it appeared that things were moving at a rapid pace in France during this revolution. Many members of the aristocracy who had not already met their maker beneath the guillotine were either under arrest, in hiding, or some more fortunate were attempting to flee for their lives. If they had been fortunate enough to find shelter with a willing supporter they would live with the daily fear of either being discovered or betrayed. Fleeing was a dangerous undertaking with the ports controlled by the new government troops; all ships arriving at the mainly fishing harbours were boarded and searched. A fortunate few managed a secret rendezvous in a secluded cove such as the one that Jean-Paul and his son and friends had landed at, but these were subject to regular investigation and there was always the possibility of infiltration by a secret supporter of the revolution posing as a loyal member of the rebels. At this point of the revolution even the ordinary man in the street and the peasants feared for their lives. To mention that maybe the new government was not any better than the old one could bring about arrest and imprisonment with immediate execution without trial. Throughout the country the populace lived in daily fear.

At the junction to the main coastal route another member signalled them to cross quickly, and now they headed south across tiny fields with few hedges for cover. Silently, still at a jog, they made their way along the hedgerows and field borders which gave them little in the way of cover, apparently aiming for a small farm a few kilometres from a nearby village.

Unconsciously they picked up the pace, shortly turning to the east to make a pass of La Mare from that side. A few lights filtered out of the cottages they passed and Jamie thought that if there were any locals abroad at this time, they risked very real danger of being discovered. However, out of the darkness in the distance Jamie noticed a group of farm buildings, a secluded farm yard possibly, to which they appeared to be heading, and he was considerably relieved to find that his assumption was correct. As they entered the sheltered yard and congregated in the open fronted shed, there was a very evident sigh of relief from every member of the group. Thank goodness that they had had the cover of night to hide them.

There were ten of them in all. The two men they had met on the journey had vanished once more into the night after they had crossed the road. Now there were six rebels and the four men from Cornwall. By agreement there were no introductions to the rebels, knowing their names could put them in mortal danger; if captured torture would be used to extract vital information.

The farm buildings formed a square around the stone farmhouse, which was little more than a cottage in reality. The low door opened and Jean-Paul, Jean-Louis, Jamie and Aidan were hustled inside. They entered a large kitchen and living area whilst the leader of the rebels spoke briefly to the remaining men before they too dissolved away into the darkness. The kitchen took up virtually the whole of the ground floor with a steep staircase at one end, not much more than a ladder really, but it would give the farmer and his wife access to possibly two bedrooms above. A large iron range dominated the far end wall whilst an assortment of pots and pans hung above. Two old comfy chairs were set nearby, a wide dresser showing off the wife's few prized china pieces and a large table and chairs in the centre furnished the downstairs room. It was to the large pine table that the farmer's wife bade them sit whilst she ladled out bowls of potato and vegetable broth with chunks of freshly baked bread and a plate of goats cheese. The sheds surrounding the cottage obviously housed a small number of farm animals. Jamie had noticed a small cart containing probably the last of the root crops for feeding both the animals and owners alike. They were the lucky ones, for those who lived in towns and cities were now suffering from starvation. Food of any kind was scarce and bread was fought over in the streets if there was any to be found in the bakeries, and fresh meat was never seen. The populace was so desperate for food there was not a wild bird to be found on the wing in the skies overhead, and desperate men and women ranged far and wide to scavenge any morsel of food that they could find.

By agreement they decided to call the rebel leader Francois and it appeared that he was to remain with Jean-Paul and his companions. Francois explained that they would have to settle here for the night and tomorrow then, as soon as it was dark, they would set off for Saint Coulombe and on to the Convent at la Croix Blanche. This was where Marie-Claire had sought refuge they were finally told. One of the rebel's sisters was a Nun in the Convent and he had received news that Marie-Claire was well but feared for her life as word had reached her that her husband had been tried, condemned and executed within twenty-four hours of his capture. She was the only refugee in the Convent and the Nuns were confident that news of her presence there had not leaked out. Nothing could be certain though for in these terrible times brother was informing on brother, friend on friend and neighbour on neighbour. You could trust no one, sadly not even your own family. However, Francois assured them that he trusted his men implicitly but other groups had suffered infiltration. On the occasions one was found before bringing about the groups end, the consequences were dire with the group implementing their own severe punishment.

Having eaten their frugal meal, the group was led out to a hay loft where they would have to spend the remaining hours of the night and the morrow. This period of inaction would be difficult to fill, and they would have to remain hidden in all that time. The farmer's wife had given them a basket which contained a loaf of bread, some cheese and a stone jug of water for the morning. She would try to bring them something else during the day if there was no one about to see her. By agreement they decided to eat and drink sparingly as they didn't know when more would arrive.

Many outlying farms had suffered searches of their buildings, and this one was no exception, as republican soldiers endeavoured to hunt down rebels in hiding or, even better, members of the elite society seeking escape across the channel. For this reason Jean-Paul said that they didn't wish to take anything else that they may have to try to hide should the need arise; there was only the scattering of hay left over from the last summers harvest and four sacks and a small heap of root crops in the far corner. Having agreed both a night and day watch of the surrounding countryside they heaped the hay into three piles and Jamie took the first night watch as the others attempted to get some sleep during the remaining hours of darkness.

With no windows to give all round vision it was difficult to keep continual surveillance of the whole of the surrounding countryside with one watch, but gaps between the planks of the upper walls made it a little easier and moving about kept them alert. There were two doors to the loft, one at the far end of the building and the other over the farmyard where the fodder crops could be forked into the yard to feed the stock. The farmer had told them that there was precious little left of either stock or fodder. Most of the animals had been pillaged by either starving peasants or government troops when they searched the premises. The farmer and his wife had hidden the last of the grain in the house, the milk cow was tethered with the goat in the small shed which was adjacent to the mean dwelling where they lived, and a small pen in the yard held a sow and her litter of pigs which they hoped to fatten for meat if no one came and stole them too. They used to have more cows, a few sheep and goats, chickens and ducks. Now all that was left was the cow, one goat, the sow with her new born piglets and seven chickens that were kept in a small pen over night.

It wasn't long before the first slivers of light crept silently across the landscape. Jamie paused to take a last look around before waking Jean-Paul to change the watch, when the sound of a commotion in the village was magnified in the early silence of dawn and woke them all. Jamie studied the outskirts of the village from the crack beside the end door. Beyond the sparse hedging and few trees, he could see figures searching cottages and outbuildings. He turned to his companions. "I don't like it. This doesn't look like a random search."

Jean-Paul followed Jamie's directions. "It wouldn't appear so . . ."

"A traitor!" Aidan suggested.

"We are unfortunately living in a time when today's friend is tomorrow's enemy." Jean-Paul regretted the depths to which his country had fallen. The farmhouse door opened quietly and a few moments later the farmer's head appeared at the top of the ladder. In rapid French he assured them that neither he nor his wife would give their hiding place away. His fears were the same as theirs but the fact that they were searching in the village proved to him that they had no firm information to go on. This wouldn't be the first time that their small farm had been searched and they had always maintained a good relationship, on the surface, with the searching soldiers. Hopefully their search would not be too intense. He then returned to the yard and soon the aroma of freshly baking bread was wafted to them from the open kitchen door. The farmer first fed the pigs with a bowl of swill and then, letting the chickens out from the coop, he chased them out of the yard eastwards into a small area of scrub, away from the approaching soldiers. Then he took up a stool and bucket and settled himself beside the back door to milk the cow.

Jean-Paul and Jamie considered their options; there were few. Not enough hay to hide in and too many of them to pose as members of the farming family. All they could do was watch as the searchers closed in on them.

"No dogs." Jean-Louis observed.

"Small blessings." Aidan added as they watched them fanning out to search the hedges.

When the first soldier entered the farm yard the farmer was just finishing the milking. He moved the bucket of milk to one side, wiped his hands on the sack tied around his waist and took a hold of the rope halter on the cows head.

The leader signalled the following soldiers to halt as he approached his countryman and quickly made it clear that he and his men were going to search the small farm.

The farmer smiled. "I am a loyal Frenchman," he declared. "You are welcome to search my property, but for what are you searching . . . perhaps I could save you the trouble if I know what you are looking for. I have little in the way of food left as most of this has been either shared or taken over the past months. I now only have the cow, a goat and the pig." He explained.

"We have reason to believe that enemies of the state are in the vicinity. Have you seen anyone . . . been asked to hide someone for the night?"

The farmer assured the sergeant that he had nothing to hide and that he had no sympathies with enemies of the new order or members of the aristocracy. He complained that they were living from hand to mouth but the sergeant and his friends were welcome to share what little food they had.

The soldiers, their noses twitching at the aroma escaping the kitchen door, reluctantly spread out across the yard. One by one they checked the ill assortment of buildings, tipping the roots out of the cart to make sure that nothing was hidden beneath them, and finally came to the lower floor of the barn where the friends had taken hiding.

A young man, barely fifteen or sixteen, poorly dressed and with an ancient gun carelessly held in one hand opened the lower door and looked into the gloom.

"Nothing here!" He called back across the yard. "No horses or cows. Just an empty hand cart and some tools."

"Is there a ladder?" the Sergeant asked, and the boy reluctantly had to admit that there was one on the floor. "Search the loft then." he instructed.

Reluctantly dragging the ladder across the floor and placing it against the open hatch to the upper floor, the boy looped the webbing strap of the gun over his shoulder and climbed the unsteady ladder until his head peered through the hatch into the dusty and gloomy loft. A sparse layer of hay or straw covered the floor of the loft and a pile of root vegetables were scattered in the far corner with a few filled sacks and a basket of roots beside them. "Roots!" He mumbled. "Only fit for animals and wouldn't even boil up to make a decent bowl of broth. Nothing here," he called back to the leader. "No hay, no straw and nowhere to hide."

The farmer's wife chose this moment to bring out some bread rolls and a jug of buttermilk with an assortment of pottery mugs. The aroma of fresh bread was too much for the hungry young soldier who decided not to climb into the loft and investigate further and clambered down quickly to take up the offer of free food before it was all eaten by his compatriots. Food was scarce for all, including the loyal forces of the people.

The farmer and his wife sympathised with the soldiers who had to scour the countryside, with little or no food in their bellies, to track down enemies of the state and wished them success in their endeavours. They even pressed a bottle of apple wine on the sergeant, the last they had of last year's efforts he told them. The soldier was much impressed with the loyalty of this peasant couple and, happier with food in their bellies, the group bade the couple farewell and moved on to resume their search elsewhere.

The farmer's wife returned to the kitchen and the farmer, with a small bucket of grain in his hand, led the haltered cow out of the yard to tether it on a patch of grass a short distance from the house yet still within sight of the back door. Then, keeping an eye on the still searching soldiers, he shook the bucket of grain to encourage the hens back into the farmyard where he spent the next few hours doing mundane tasks.

When the couple were convinced that the danger had passed the farmer once more climbed the ladder to find out where his visitors had managed to hide. The sacks of vegetables had been emptied on to the floor and Aidan showed him how they had hidden in the large Hessian sacks. They admitted that they had been certain that they would be discovered and it was only due to the quick action of the farmer's wife that had distracted the young soldier from his search by offering them the bread and buttermilk. The farmer chuckled at their explanation and handed over some of the remaining bread and buttermilk to see them through the rest of the day. Jean-Paul pressed him to take some payment for the food that they had sacrificed for them; he had come prepared for such an event.

Taking it in turns they continued their lookout over the countryside but the searchers did not return and they watched and listened with some amusement as locals arrived to discuss the search of the village. They said that one of the villagers had been beaten when he objected to his house being searched, but no one had been found. All of them wondered who on earth they could have been looking for and the farming couple could offer no explanation either and appeared as baffled as they were.

When Francois returned that evening he brought with him a selection of well used local clothing that he wanted them to change into; insisting that they would blend in better should the occasion arise that they had to explain their presence in France. They had already decided on their cover story.

That evening they sat around the farmhouse kitchen table, sharing the family meal of cassoulet and fresh bread. Picking up on the nervous demeanour of the Frenchman Jean-Paul asked. "Something is bothering you mon ami, what is it?"

The rebel leader and the farmer shared a brief exchange before he answered Jean-Paul. "Four of our group were arrested last night on suspicion of being enemies of the new order. Two of them were the men we met on the road, and did not know where you would be hiding; others escaped and are in hiding themselves. I am afraid that we have been betrayed by someone within."

"Something to do with the search today!!" Suggested Jamie.

"*C'est possible*. The fact that they did not come directly here and find you suggests that it was none of those who were with us last night."

"Does that mean that our venture is in jeopardy, how much information could have been passed on about my daughter and our effort to rescue her?" Jean-Paul above all of them was concerned. "You have placed yourselves in great danger for us."

The rebel leader dismissed this suggestion with a casual wave of his hand. "Nothing to worry you . . . we must not let these people ruin our country. We have to make a stand and hope that in the end common sense will prevail. Only I, and the brother of the Nun at la Croix Blanche, know of the destination we are aiming for, and I will lead you to the Convent tonight. The information that I have is vague but the troops are searching the countryside around here, though they are obviously not aware of your actual hiding place. Your host and his wife here have aided many of our countrymen and women to escape Madame Guillotine and they are becoming quite adept at distracting the soldiers from searching the buildings.

"What is the plan when we reach the Convent?" asked Jamie

"We should arrive before dawn and they will be waiting for us, I arranged this myself. I have other things to see to in La Croix Blanche and will return as soon as I have finished, to lead you all back to the coast."

An inspection of the alternative clothing convinced Jamie that they would have a greater chance of passing undetected, and they each took their pick of the various items and left their own clothes for the farmer to hide, distribute or burn if they failed to return. When all was ready the five comrades bade a farewell to their hosts and set off for la Croix Blanche.

There was a clear sky and this made the going easy as they made a wide circle around any groups of cottages that lay in their way but, as darkness fell, most of the locals decided that the safest place to be was behind their own closed door, so there was nobody abroad to see them pass through the villages *en route*. By alternately walking and jogging they covered the ground more quickly than they hoped and Jean-Paul was surprised when their guide pointed to the outskirts of la Croix Blanche. It was a small village, similar to those in Cornwall. The small houses long and low, built of cob or stone, together with a few tradesmen who had set up shops to trade close to the cross roads at its centre. The village was as silent as the grave and so they decided not to make a detour but walk right through the centre. They all recognised the fragrant aroma of freshly baking bread as it wafted on the air from the *boulongerie;* the baker was already at work but any other early risers were still in their homes. The last establishment in the village was the blacksmith's shop; in the open fronted workshop the fire in the furnace was burning low ready for the blacksmith to bring it to life with his large bellows and all was quiet as they passed by. About a kilometre further on, at the edge of a wood, lay the Convent of la Croix Blanche.

Stealthily they approached the convent walls, pausing whilst they still had cover of the trees and bushes to search the surrounding area for a possible trap that they might fall into. Satisfied that there was no ambush set up, Francois indicated that they should continue around the side of the convent to the two large doors at the entrance. Beside the door was an ornate large iron handle which, when pulled, would ring a bell within. Francois gave it a good tug and they all stood back, waiting. As thick as the doors were, the sound of footfall came to them followed by the sliding of the cover of the opening, set in the middle of one door. Beyond the protecting grill Jean-Paul could see the face of a Nun in the light of the lamp that she carried.

"Bon nuit, monsieur. It is late, how can I help you? Are you lost?"

Francois spoke for them. "God Bless you Sister. We are travellers, looking for a safe resting place for the night."

"We are living in difficult times for travellers. Few places are safe to rest one's head." The Nun agreed. "I will speak with our Mother Superior." The shutter slid back into place and they waited again.

The next time the shutter slid open an older face looked out at them. "Sister Dolorosa tells me that you seek rest for the night. The hour is late."

"But we have the moon to light our way and the good Lord to guide us."

"With the Lord beside you anything is possible."

"Then may he guide us to that which we seek."

Jean-Paul wondered if the responses would have been different if the sky had not been clear and the moon hidden, but the Mother Superior smiled and instructed the sister to open the door. The heavy door opened just wide enough for them to pass into the vestibule. The Mother Superior stood solemnly before them, her hands clasped together in front of her, and they all bowed their heads in greeting.

"Welcome, my sons, we have been waiting for you and thank the good Lord for your safe arrival. We are prepared for your early departure as we have received unsettling news of government soldiers on route to disband our Order here at la Croix. It is possible that they will be here on the morrow and you must leave as soon as possible."

"Do you think that they know of your visitor?" Francois was dismayed at the news.

"I cannot be sure. If they do it cannot have come from within these walls for no one has had contact with the outside world since Marie-Claire arrived."

"Perhaps it is a false alarm!" Jean-Paul suggested.

"Perhaps . . . But you will want to see your daughter. Come follow me."

From the vestibule, a long corridor ran the length of one side of the convent and, on either side, doors opened on to Nuns bedrooms. Half way down the corridor Mother Collette stopped beside a door and indicated to Jean-Paul that this was the room where his daughter had received sanctuary. Hesitantly he knocked, and they waited.

The door opened to reveal a novice Nun demurely dressed in grey habit and white wimple. She too had her hands clasped before her and her head was bowed.

Jean-Paul frowned, puzzled he glanced at Mother Collette; surely she had indicated the wrong room and he glanced beyond the Nun expecting to find Marie-Claire behind her.

"Marie-Claire!" Jean-Louis tentatively spoke his sister's name.

The young Nun lifted her head and smiled, and in spite of her demure attire, with a happy "Jean-Louis." She turned and flung herself at Jean-Paul. "Oh Papa! I feared that you would not get here in time. I was so sure that they would find me and . . ." with this she divulged into tears. From the day that she had arrived at the Convent she had been stoically brave, outwardly always believing that her father would rescue her. But recently news had arrived that members of the rebel group had been arrested and this was followed by the news that government soldiers were on their way to the Convent at la Croix Blanche.

Jean-Paul hugged his daughter close to him, comforting her for a moment or two. Finally he gripped her shoulders and held her away from him as he looked down into her face. "We are here Marie-Claire. Look, Jean-Louis, Jamie and Aidan," she blinked away the tears and gave them an enigmatic smile. "But we still have a long way to go and you must continue to be brave." Marie-Claire nodded. "Francois will lead us back to the coast where a boat awaits our return."

"*Merci, Merci.*" Marie-Claire grasped Francois hand and kissed him on both cheeks.

"It is a pleasure Madam, to help you to freedom." The Frenchman assured her. "We will leave as soon as it is light, but now I have to pay a visit to someone in la Croix Blanche who should be able to give me information on these government soldiers who are heading this way." He turned to Jean-Paul. "The news is disturbing. We must leave at first light. If I fail to return you will have to make your own way to the coast, can you do this?"

"If needs must, we can. But I sincerely hope that you will return for I fear for your safety too." Concern was written in the expression on Jean-Paul's face.

"*Merci, merci*. May the news not be as bad as we fear." The rebel leader bowed to each of them in turn.

"May God be with you." Jean-Paul kissed him on both cheeks.

"You also and *bon voyage*." With these parting words Francois turned and left with Sister Dolorosa.

In spite of their determination to get some rest it proved impossible. The Nuns provided them with bowls of fresh broth, some bread and cheese and also fresh fruit and a jug of goats' milk, and they sat around the refectory table discussing the current situation. Imperceptibly the sky outside the small high window began to lighten as Mother Collette joined them. She came hurrying into the room in an agitated state.

"You have bad news?" Jean-Paul pushed back his chair. "What has happened?"

"Jacques, an orphan from the village has run up with the news that Pierre, Sister Isobel's brother, has been arrested. Francois escaped but the soldiers are hunting him down as we speak. Whatever plans he had made for your journey to the coast must be abandoned. We have to come up with an alternative, she glanced at Marie-Claire who had removed her Nuns clothing and now wore a simple dress. "However we dress Marie-Claire she will stand out as more than a peasant if you are challenged. We must find a disguise to fool them."

Jamie studied the sister of his friend. Marie-Claire had always been a rare beauty. Her long dark ringlets bounced with health even after being contained beneath the head dress of a Nun. Her skin was flawless, devoid of powder or paint and she had a natural grace. These were not the attributes of a hard working peasant girl from the countryside. He glanced at the Mother Superior and the Nun at her side, they did have a natural grace and their complexions were clean and clear also. "Marie-Claire completely fooled me when I first set eyes on her. If there is to be any disguise I suggest, with your consent Mother Collette, that this be the one to adopt. Marie-Claire will not pass as a peasant however we dress her; it really is our only feasible option."

"I agree." Jean-Louis backed him up. "She almost had me fooled too, and I'm her brother."

It was finally decided that this was the only option, but the method of travel had to be considered. A Nun walking with four men was out of the question, so how were they to travel?

It was Sister Dolorosa who came up with the solution. The convent possessed a small cart and a pony which they used to transport produce to and from the markets. They grew most of their own produce and some meat but occasionally they would drive the cart to the coast to buy salted fish, taking with them any surplus vegetables that they had to trade. They had not made a trip for some time, so it should not cause much interest. They all agreed that this was possibly their best option, but it would be unusual for a Nun to make this trip without being accompanied by a reliable man from la Croix. Mother Collette suggested that the most suitable person for this role would be Jamie or Aiden.

"Without wishing to cause offence," she added. "I think that your Papa or brother may raise suspicions if you are stopped for questioning. You are both very French aristocracy in spite of your clothing. I suggest you stay hidden if possible."

Jamie grinned. "And Aidan and I . . . ?"

Mother Collette smiled back at him. "I think that you both have some of . . . what shall we say . . . the common man in you. I think that you have been accustomed to perhaps living and dealing with people who are not so affluent. You have the dark looks of the people of Brittany and their build. Monsieur de Varron and his son do not have this. I mean no offence."

"None taken." Jamie assured her. "So be it . . . you agree Jean-Paul?"

"Of course, but we must make haste."

Mother Collette took Marie-Claire's hand and led her away instructing Sister Dolorosa to lead the men to the stables to harness the pony and cart, and to send someone to the outhouses to fetch any vegetables that they could spare for market.

The sun was rising above the horizon when Marie-Claire joined them at the stables clad in Nuns clothing. With her came Sister Dolorosa and the boy from the village.

When all was ready the pony and cart was led to the gate at the lower end of the Convent grounds. It had been decided that Jamie would drive the cart and he helped Marie-Claire climb into the seat.

"I am coming too." Sister Dolorosa informed him. "We have to bring the cart back," she said matter of factually as she placed a hand on the boy's shoulder, "Jacques will ride in the back to help me on my return journey."

Jamie glanced at the Mother Superior, who had just arrived to see them off, and when she indicated that she was in agreement he helped Sister Dolorosa to mount the cart before joining them on the wide seat and taking up the reins.

Jean-Paul bowed low. "I will not forget your courage in helping my daughter. When these dreadful times are over I hope that we will meet again and I will be able to show the extent of my gratitude."

"Bless you my son. Now please make haste and may our good Lord and the blessed Mother Mary watch over you and keep you safe." Jean-Paul bowed again over her hand. "*Bon voyage, monsieur*. We have come to love your daughter as one of our sisters. We pray that she will find safety on a foreign shore."

Jean-Louis added his thanks and Aidan too, and then the pony and cart set out into the French countryside.

* * *

Sister Dolorosa had made the journey to the coast a number of times, and as dangerous as it could be they decided to follow the normal route that would have been taken on previous occasions, for any deviation from the norm could, or would, arouse suspicion.

It was still early as they approached la Croix Blanche but here and there people were huddled together in groups, as they discussed the events of the dawn; they looked up as the cart approached but after a cursory glance they carried on their conversation. It would appear that Sister Dolorosa was correct; the cart raised no suspicion with the local populace. But what would happen if they came upon soldiers manning a check point.

They were about to find out.

Ahead of them, at the cross roads, Jamie spied a group of poorly clad government troops. Glancing back at the cart, Jacques grinned at him from his perch on a sack of potatoes but of Jean-Paul, Jean-Louis and Aidan there was no sign. They had vanished between the cottages at the side of the road. With a brief glance at Marie-Claire and the Sister by her side he didn't let the pony hesitate in his stride and confidently headed towards the road block.

In spite of the new government's distrust of religious orders and the sacking of monasteries and imprisonment of members of the church, much of the general populace still held both Priests and Nuns in esteem. As the sound of the pony and cart became noticeable the soldiers looked up to see who was approaching before parting to stand on either side of the lane.

As the cart drew level with the soldiers, Jamie brought it to a halt. *"Bonjour."* He greeted them "Is something amiss in this lovely village that brings the loyal forces of our new order to this area?"

"*Mais oui, citizen*. We have arrested a dissident and seek another who has escaped. Have you seen anyone acting suspiciously?"

"*Non*. But then we have only come from the Convent, barely a kilometre."

"*Bonjour* Sisters." The soldier greeted the Sister and Marie-Claire. "You are out early. Where are you bound?"

"We are making our monthly trip to the coast to fetch salted fish and to sell the few vegetables that we have left over from the winter store." Sister Dolorosa informed him.

"Doesn't usually take two of you." Put in one of his companions who had obviously been recruited locally.

Sister Dolorosa didn't hesitate. "No. Sister Maria will have to make the trip alone next month, so she is coming along to make herself familiar with the route and whom she will need to contact at the coast for our supply of fish."

"And the boy?"

"Jacques wanted to see the sea, so I said that he could come along for the ride." Jamie told him.

"Are you from round here?"

"No, St Coulombe. I have been engaged by the Convent to carry out repairs and, as we are passing through the village I can pick up some things that I need from my yard on our way back." The soldier looked sceptical. "There is only one pony and cart, it seemed sensible to do one trip," Jamie explained.

The soldier glanced at his companions as if to ask their opinion then with a shrug of his shoulders told them to be aware that there was an enemy of the revolution on the loose and that he may be armed.

"Thank you for your concern for our welfare." Sister Dolorosa's smile encompassed them all. "We will take great care and should we see anyone behaving unusually we will report it at the earliest opportunity."

The soldiers stood back from the cart. "Take care sisters, and a safe journey."

"May God bless you my son. Drive on Andre."

Jamie lifted the reins and with a brief flick of the whip the pony set of once more.

Once out of earshot Jamie congratulated the Sister on her handling of the soldiers before turning to Jacques. "Where did the others go?"

"They slipped away between the houses and will meet us on the other side of the village."

The boy's grin was infectious and Jamie found himself smiling back at him. "Where is your family, Jacques? Won't they be expecting you back home?"

Jacques shook his head. "I have no family. My mother died and my father went off to fight for the revolution. There's no one to worry about me. As far as I am concerned I am an orphan of the revolution."

Jamie glanced at Sister Dolorosa who nodded her head. "How old are you?" he asked.

"Thirteen, old enough to look after myself."

"You don't have the same views as your father, I take it." Jamie smothered a grin.

"*Non*. I certainly do not, but I wouldn't want them to find out." He aimed his thumb at the air behind his head. "Our King may have had his faults but what we've got is far worse. Beheading people just 'cos they have more than the rest is not justifiable in my opinion, and turning on the Church, burning religious books and imprisoning our Priests for preaching the word of the Lord is totally unacceptable. Now they are arresting ordinary citizens for minor offences either real or false, and beheading them also just on the word of another. I hope that it never comes to this in your country."

Jamie could only agree. The thought that such a thing could happen in England was something that he could not contemplate.

"*Monsieur!*" Jacques called his attention. "Ahead, under the trees."

"It is Papa and the others." The relief at the sight of her father and brother was quite evident in Marie-Claire's voice.

Jamie reined in the pony and cart. "I'm pleased to see you my friends. Did you meet up with any of the soldiers back there?"

"No, we managed to slip through the cottages and gardens. We saw evidence of house searches still going on but managed to avoid confrontation." Jean-Paul smiled at his daughter. "I never thought to see my daughter as a bride of Christ, but you are a beautiful sight however you are dressed."

"Do you think that we will find soldiers in St Coulomb?" Marie-Claire voiced the thoughts of them all.

"Possibly, but we must take the normal route to the road at Haut Pays." Sister Dolorosa insisted, and Jamie agreed.

Setting off once more the pony and cart kept to the uneven road, whilst walking abreast of them their companions attempted to conceal themselves where possible amongst the trees and bushes alongside the fields.

As it was any fears they had about St Coulomb were unjustified. The long main street through the township only occupied by the locals who raised their hands in greeting to Sister Dolorosa, asking for news of the Convent and Sisters; some had sisters or cousins who had taken the Order. Jean-Paul and the others skirted the town, agreeing to meet up on the other side as at la Croix Blanche. Pausing at the pump in the centre of the town, Jamie alighted and led the pony to the horse trough before taking the dipper from the cart and pumping some fresh water into it to offer to the two Sisters before taking a drink himself. Young Jacques had jumped down from the cart and hailed a group of youths on the other side of the street. Soon they were in earnest conversation and Jamie, after a brief glance at them, returned the dipper to its hook and led the pony away from the trough where he had taken his fill and was soon contentedly nuzzling at a clump of grass. Marie-Claire and Sister Dolorosa had climbed down to stretch their legs.

"Are you ready to move off, Sisters?" Jamie asked as he approached them, assisting them aboard when they agreed. "Jacques!" The French youth waved back at him. "We are setting off again."

"*Oui monsieur, un moment sil vous plait.*"

By the time Jamie had taken his seat, collected the reins in his hands and released the brake on the cart, Jacques had clambered aboard and with a wave to his friends they set off once more. They rode in silence until the houses were once more behind them before Jacques clambered over to Jamie. "There are soldiers in la Mare," he informed him. "One of my friends spent the night there with his grandparents and they arrived last night but aren't searching the houses. They have set up a camp outside.

"Is there a road block?"

"Not when he left, *non*. Doesn't mean there won't be though."

"No. It would be too much to hope not. I suppose that we still have to go through the village Sister?" Jamie posed the question.

"You can not go round it, unless it is on foot through the fields. A Sister or two of the Order on foot with four gentlemen and a boy would draw suspicion, I can think of no reasonable explanation. Our only course is the one we have set out on." Sister Dolorosa pointed out.

At this point their companions emerged from the hedge to join in the conversation and it was agreed that they would have to continue through la Mare and hope that there was not another road block.

It was mid afternoon when la Mare came into view. The encampment, if it was truly there, had to be on the other side of the village as there was no sign of tents on the approach. Any hope that they would be able to drive straight through was dispelled by an obvious roadblock in the centre.

The road had a barricade across it, soldiers to right and left. This was not the only problem; the soldiers were tired, tetchy and had also been drinking. There also appeared to be no serving officer in charge of the men and the highest rank visible was a young sergeant, younger and more inexperienced than those manning the barrier. As he reined in the pony, bringing the cart to an easy halt, Jamie's first thought was that this would not be as easy as it had been at la Croix Blanche.

"Well! What do we have here?" One of the older soldiers approached the cart. "*Mon Dieu, mon amis*. We 'ad better be on our best behaviour, we 'ave two Sisters of Mercy 'ere; p'raps they could pray for us, eh! What d'you think t' that Sister?" He addressed Sister Dolorosa who was on the outside of the seat.

"We would be very pleased to say a prayer for you my son." Sister Dolorosa agreed with a smile.

“Yes I bet you would,” sneered the soldier. “Just like the aristocracy, you think yourselves better than us don’t you?” He ignored her denial. “This New Order should put an end t’ the aristocracy and the Church in my opinion. Let the people rule the country, confiscate the land and let us all ’ave the same rights in law.” Receiving no comment in return he continued. “You don’t agree with a suggestion like that, I take it?”

Jamie intervened. “I am sure that the good Sisters have done nothing to incite your anger. We are only on our way to the coast to sell the Convent’s vegetables and to purchase some salt fish for the Sisters at la Croix. You surely have no quarrel with the Nuns do you?”

“Nuns! Whose word is it that they’re Nuns and not two members of the aristocracy on the run?”

Jacques joined in before Jamie could stop him. “Of course they’re Nuns. Sister Dolorosa makes this trip regularly, ask anyone in la Mare.”

“Shut up boy, or I’ll arrest you for obstruction,” the soldier snapped. “I didn’t ask you for your opinion. When I do you’ll know it,” he turned to Jamie. “And who are you?”

“Andre, an odd job man at the Convent at la Croix Blanche.”

“One man and all those women!”

“*Non*. There’s a stable hand and one to help in the gardens.”

“Still the odds are in your favour I take it. Is it different with a Nun?” He made a lewd suggestion then added contemptuously. “No, I guess not. They’re all the same with a bag over their head.”

Jamie felt his blood boil but was aware that the soldier was trying to provoke him to make a move that would result in a confrontation so, with difficulty, he held his tongue.

Sister Dolorosa was not so circumspect. “What on earth are you insinuating? May God forgive your blasphemous thoughts.”

“God! Haven’t you heard Sister? The New Order does not recognise your God,” he looked around his companions. Some joined in with jeering comments whilst others, like the young sergeant, were not so comfortable.

“Well lads, what do you think? Are they Nuns or members of the aristocracy fleeing for their lives?” He came closer to the cart. “The young’n there, take a good look at her.” Levelling his gun with the occupants of the cart he ordered them to get down onto the road and to produce some evidence of themselves and for the journey.

Jamie was glad that the Mother Superior had thought ahead to cover such an event and reached into his pocket.

"Halt." The gun was levelled at Jamie. "What are you doing?"

"I was only going to produce my papers." Jamie explained.

"Down here, at once. All of you . . . you too." He pointed at Jacques.

Jamie reached the ground first and quickly came round to assist the Sister and Marie-Claire. Jacques followed.

The soldier, of indeterminate age, studied the two women lasciviously. Their religious and modest attire proved to be no barrier to his thoughts. Marie-Claire, realising just how dangerous their situation was, demurely clasped her hands in front of her and cast her eyes down to the ground. Sister Dolorosa was angry and her eyes flashed at their tormentor. "We have a lively one here; bet she'd make a good ride, eh? What about you my lovely?" He approached Marie-Claire. "Why don't I believe you are indeed a bride of Christ, eh?" Jamie began to wish that he had his friends beside him, it really looked as though the game was up and they were about to be exposed.

"How dare you make these accusations and stop us from going about our legitimate occupation." Sister Dolorosa had really got her heckles up.

"By the powers of the Government of France anyone suspected of treason can be stopped and searched." As the soldier lowered his gun Jamie was about to take a breath when the Frenchman brought up his hand and tore off Sister Dolorosa's head dress, revealing her shorn head and uneven clumps of hair.

Sister Dolorosa held her head high and, in defiance, declared "May God forgive you."

Jamie glanced uncomfortably around him. Were the others nearby, dare he make a move? If the soldier should do the same to Marie-Claire the game would be well and truly up. No Nun ever had lustrous ringlets like hers.

For a brief moment the soldier regarded Sister Dolorosa, a murmur from his companions causing him to pause. But swiftly he turned and snatched at Marie-Claire's head. Jamie closed his eyes in despair and kept them closed at the gasp that escaped the soldiers' lips. But no shout of jubilation followed and Jamie slowly opened his eyes to see Marie-Claire's head still bowed demurely with her hands clasped serenely in front of her. There was no sign of her beautiful head of hair, the shining ringlets that used to tumble over her shoulders, and Jamie fought back the tears that came unbidden as Jacques stifled a laugh. No one spoke a word for a moment and suddenly the silence was shattered.

"What is going on here?" The young sergeant, unable to handle the situation for himself, had decided that his best option was to go for help. A well dressed officer thrust his way through the crowd that had been drawn to witness the proceedings. Having fought his way through the press of bodies the officer came to an abrupt halt in front of the two Sisters. "*Mon Dieu*!" He stared in disbelief at the sight before him and Jamie took the opportunity to retrieve the head cloths and hand them to the women. The officer spun round to the soldiers. "Who is guilty of this offence?" he demanded.

The angry soldier recovered himself. "They are members of the aristocracy making an escape," he made the accusation as he pointed to the aggrieved Sister and the silent demure Marie-Claire.

The officer raised an eyebrow as he took in Jamie and Jacques.

"Sir, they are Sisters of the Convent at la Croix Blanche; we are on our way to sell vegetables and collect salted fish from the coast at the request of Mother Collette." Jamie offered the papers that The Mother Superior had supplied.

"You are?"

"Andre, odd job man at the Convent. When required I accompany the Sisters on their journeys in the outside world.

"You?" The officer pointed to Jacques.

"My name is Jacques, from la Croix. The Sisters said I could come with them to see the sea."

In spite of the situation the officer found a smile curl his lip. He turned to see the two women attempting to cover their shorn heads. The older one lifted her face to his, glancing at the insignia on his breast and the stripes on his sleeve. "Sister?"

"Sister Dolorosa, of the Convent at la Croix Blanche, Captain. I must thank you for your timely intervention; I was beginning to genuinely fear for our safety. We make this trip to the coast once a month, as anyone in la Mare can confirm. I cannot understand why anyone should accost us in this manner."

"You restrained yourself well citizen." The soldier addressed Jamie. "It must have been hard not to come to the aid of the good Sisters."

Jamie wondered if there was an underlying suggestion in this remark. "It was hard, I agree. But interference or objection might have made matters worse for I fear drink has been involved."

"I think that you may be correct." The French Captain rounded on the offending soldier. "You are a disgrace to your unit. Sergeant, place this man under arrest and arrange for the good

Sisters to be escorted through the village. Please accept my sincere apologies for this disgraceful incident. If you will wait *un moment* I will write you up a letter giving you freedom to pass any barriers erected on the remainder of your journey to the coast and back. Jamie didn't want to wait any longer than necessary, Lady Luck had been with them so far but could it continue? He reflected on the wisdom and foresight of the Mother Superior and wondered how Marie-Claire had found the courage to allow her beautiful hair to be cut off so badly. He could imagine the expression on Jean-Paul's face when he saw her shorn head, cut so short it was almost bald, with clumps of hair standing on end. Marie-Claire remained silent throughout, hands clasped in her lap and head bowed as if still suffering from the shock of her treatment. In truth, Jamie wondered if she indeed was shaken, he had to admit that he was. They really had had a very close encounter.

Returning with the letter the French Captain handed it to Jamie with instructions to show it immediately should they be stopped again. Jamie assured him that he would and thanked him again for his timely appearance and intervention on behalf of the Sisters.

Finally the Captain stood to attention and saluted. "May God watch over you Sisters."

Sister Dolorosa smiled radiantly as she returned the blessing "May God also be with you, Captain; and thank you once more."

Yet again Jamie lifted the reins and, with a light flick of the whip, the pony and cart moved forward and, this time, were escorted through the remainder of the village till the cottages came to an end. The soldiers came to a halt, stood to attention and saluted as Jamie drove the pony and cart forward.

For two or three hundred yards no one spoke a word. Not until they had turned a corner and the village was out of sight was the silence broken.

Jacques expelled a deep breath. "*Mon Dieu*, that was close. I thought the game was up for sure."

"You kept your nerve Jacques, well done." Jamie at last addressed Jean-Paul's daughter. "Marie-Claire! Are you alright?" He ventured to put his arm about her shoulders.

Marie-Claire raised her head, looked into his eyes and smiled at him. "I am fine Jamie. I very nearly refused to let the Nuns cut off my hair. I thank God and Mother Collette that I was convinced that it might save all our lives."

"Your father will have a seizure when he sees you." Jamie also thanked God and Mother Collette; for once again she had been quite right.

Jacques tapped Jamie on the shoulder. "Speak of the devil, he is up ahead with your friends."

Jean-Paul, Jean-Louis and Aidan came hurrying forward to meet them. "What did ye do to have the honour of an escort, *mon ami*?" Aidan joked.

"I think that is a question you will wish you had not asked." Jamie told him, but the torn and disturbed head dresses of Sister Dolorosa and Marie-Claire indicated that they had been involved in some trouble and they had to retell the events in la Mare as they had happened. Jean-Paul had been horrified that it had been such a close call, if the soldier ever found out that he had been perfectly correct in his assumption he would be justifiably angry. Jean-Paul complemented Sister Dolorosa on her calm handling of the situation and did indeed shed a tear at the sight of his daughter's nearly bald head. Nevertheless, he too was grateful to Mother Collette for her foresight.

Now only a short distance from Haut Pays they drove the pony and cart into a small wooded area, away from the main track, to await nightfall.

They ate the meagre ration of food that they had brought with them and then rested beneath the trees. After a sleepless night and the long day, they even managed to snatch a few moments of sleep; they would have another sleepless night ahead of them.

As darkness fell, Jamie informed them that he was going across the road to the valley to reconnoitre the land that surrounded the small bay where they had landed. Jean-Paul wanted to go with him but Jamie insisted that he stayed with his daughter and son; Aidan would go with him. If neither of them returned then they should move away as soon as they could. He handed the pass to Jean-Paul, telling him to keep it safe and signalled Aidan to follow him.

At the head of the valley they paused in the scrub and, speaking in whispers, Jamie went over his plan of action. "It'll be just like those games we had as boys," remarked Aidan.

"But far more dangerous, Aidan. This is no game I am afraid."

"Don't worry Jamie, I know it. You can count on me."

"I know that Aidan, or I wouldn't have even suggested that you come with me now, are you ready?"

"Aye. If either of us sees anything we'll give the night owl call. After the count of five the other will answer and we'll draw back to here."

Jamie gripped his hand. "Take care my friend."

"You too."

Jamie found a damp patch of earth and rubbing it onto his hands he spread the dirt over his face, Aidan did likewise and they both melted into the darkness. There was light cloud cover; the moon appearing briefly now and then.

Without a sound Jamie crept nearer and nearer to the coast, pausing now and again to listen. He had covered a good stretch of ground when he stopped again. He could hear the waves as they broke upon the shore, he couldn't have far to go, perhaps his fears of an ambush were just that . . . fear. He was almost convinced that his fears were imaginings and that there were no soldiers and no ambush. Everything was silent. It felt too good to be true.

It was.

Jamie was about to move less cautiously when he heard the sharp snap of a twig beyond the thicket in which he had paused to rest. The moon chose this moment to light up the clear patch of ground ahead of him and Jamie crouched low as a dark shape emerged from the deep shadow and he heard the sound of rattling stones ahead of him. The latter could be a rabbit of course, but not the dark shape . . . that was a man.

"Sh . . . silence." The whispered order came from the clearing and at the same time the haunting cry of a night owl floated on the night air. Jamie counted to five and putting his hands together blew to produce an answering call.

"What's that?" The querulous voice asked from beyond the bushes.

"An owl you fool, and it's mate." The quiet voice of authority answered. "You've seen nothing?"

"No Captain."

"Just keep quiet, and your ears and eyes open."

Jamie heard another twig snap and light footsteps moving away from him. What should they do next? If they gave a signal the boat would stay out at sea, but would they recognise a false signal and come in. Somehow he had to warn them, meanwhile he must get back to Aidan and silently he retraced his steps.

Jamie reached the rendezvous spot ahead of his friend and hid in a nearby copse to wait. He didn't have long and had just settled his back against the tree when the hoot of an owl broke the silence once more. It was a good imitation, Jamie agreed with a smile, and gave an answering call.

Aidan cautiously made his way from the surrounding bushes immediately sensing where Jamie hid.

Jamie uncurled himself from the base of the tree. "What did you see?" he came straight to the point.

"Tis a trap, t'be sure. I came upon the first sentry in a copse beyond the fork in the track. There be a score of men or more coverin' the track to the beach. We'd never make it to the beach let alone the boat . . . and you?"

"A sentry on the other side, plus a Captain so you can safely assume there's a good number lying low."

Aidan studied Jamie's expression. "Ye'r not worried that the boat will come into the beach are 'ee? There's no way that they can know the signal to bring the boat in."

"You would think not, but they appear to know too much of our moves to chance it. We must cause a disturbance that can warn them to head back out to sea. When will they make another attempt to pick us up here?

Aidan smiled. "They won't make another attempt."

Jamie couldn't believe that his crew would abandon them in France, and said so.

"I didn' say they would abandon us. It's just that they won't make another attempt to pick us up here. Ben Rowse will already have made contact with Jean-Paul's old accomplice. If this attempt fails we are to make speed to a fishing harbour east of here. There we will trade our goods for fish and leave the village to return at dusk and board his Lugger to rendezvous with Ben at Mont St Michel.

"Who made those arrangements?"

"Truth is, I did it meself. Didn' tell no one, neither Jean-Paul nor Louis, or the crew. Only told Ben as we left the boat."

James expression relaxed. "Good thinking on your part. I don't think I would have thought of it."

"Yes ye would, if ye'd been planning this venture ye would."

Jamie wasn't convinced, but Aidan had a point, he had no part in the planning of this escapade. But he was damned sure that he was going to get everyone out and back home safely . . . somehow. "Well we have to cause a disturbance to warn the crew off landing. Can you get safely back to the other side of the track?"

Aidan agreed that there was a safe place to cross and a good spot behind the picket line where he could get a good view of the track after it forked east and west, if only the clouds would disperse.

"Then this is what we'll do."

* * *

Captain Mathieu silently walked around his hidden company on the western side of the track; to the east another company also lay hidden. He was proud of his men; they were disciplined regular soldiers not a hastily assembled collection of untrained peasants in an ill fitting assortment of clothes made to resemble a uniform . . . of sorts. If he didn't know where his men were hidden he wouldn't have seen them himself. Not one of them had been tempted to disobey the order not to smoke, for the slightest scent would give them away. He was convinced that his mission to capture the fleeing aristocrat with her collaborators, enemies of the state all of them, would be a success. The problem was they had no idea how many people they were looking for or what disguise they might have adopted. The boat should be somewhere out in the bay by now, waiting for the signal. He glanced up at the sky as, for a brief moment the moon slid out from behind the swiftly moving clouds . . . and immediately dived for cover as a volley of shots rang out from behind his men. Another volley followed from the other side of the valley, behind the men hidden there. They were trapped in the valley, how on earth could this have happened. Before an order to hold fire could be given the sentries opened fire quickly followed by the hidden soldiers. It was some time before order was restored and the Captain made his rounds to find that his men had sustained injuries caused by guns used by their own fellow men at arms.

Jamie and Aidan had already slipped safely away and the little company of travellers was already on their journey. The pony was refreshed and with the men taking turns to run alongside, alternating between riding in the cart, they had managed to put a good distance between them and Haut Pays before pulling into the cover of trees to rest for the few hours before daylight.

The following day was to prove unexpectedly uneventful, with no sign of soldiers or road blocks and they concluded that the soldiers had concentrated their efforts on the events around la Croix to Haut Pays. Aidan insisted that they kept up the pace for they were to reach the fishing village before dusk began to fall.

After some careful attention to their head dresses, Sister Dolorosa had improved their appearance and she and Marie-Claire stopped to purchase some fresh bread and cheese and glean any information of unusual activity. Jacques too chatted with the local *garcons* on route, but neither of them heard anything that gave the impression that soldiers were in the area through which they travelled. Confident that there were no soldiers or barriers, no one to contest their right to travel, they continued at a pace once they left the villages and hamlets that they drove through, and it was mid afternoon when the coast came into sight and Aidan pointed out the fishing village with a small harbour.

Jamie drove the cart down through the village, towards the harbour. The Sisters attracted a little attention when it got about that they had potatoes to sell but the men and boy were all dressed in ragged trousers, and one of them wearing a red cap of liberty, so they let them pass without interest.

Glancing around at the few boats still moored up at the quay, Jamie spied a Lugger tied up near to the harbour entrance. "What was the name of your friend's boat, Jean-Paul?"

"The *Helena-Louise*. Her owner is Marcel Bertrand."

"I think I see the boat . . . a Lugger on the far side. Look they have seen us and are starting to put some fish baskets on the quay." Hesitantly Jamie edged the pony and cart onto the hard area in front of the row of fishermen's cottages and they looked around. The only activity appeared to be that which would be deemed normal in a coastal village. Men, women and children worked industriously mending nets strung on timber drying frames, a group of women chatted together at the corner of the packed earth main street with babies slung in shawls over their shoulder or small children clutching at their skirts or kicking stones.

Keeping alert Jamie encouraged the pony forwards to the stone jetty that protected the harbour and boats moored within from rough seas. Not that protection was needed today, beyond the harbour wall there was a swell which wouldn't deter a fisherman putting to sea.

Having placed his fishing baskets on the quayside the fisherman bounded ashore and made his way towards them. Short in stature his wiry frame disguised his strength, for Jamie had been watching him throw the fishing baskets on to the quay as if they contained nothing more than hens' feathers. Jamie knew just how heavy those baskets would be for he had lifted many like them whilst helping to unload the boats at Quay Cottage. The fisherman drew level with the cart and addressed the occupants. "*Bonjour*, Sisters, I trust that you had a good journey." Although he was expecting Jean-Paul and Aidan he had no idea what disguise they would assume, but the sight of the sisters was so unusual that he rightly judged that this was them and played along. "My daughter heard you had some potatoes to sell and ran ahead of you . . . perhaps we can trade. Would you like to inspect our fish; caught fresh today. There are pilchards that you can salt down and some large cod from which you can take your pick." Taking the pony's halter he led him towards the iron ring set in the protecting wall. Jamie jumped down and tethered the pony before helping Sister Dolorosa and Marie-Claire to the ground. Once assembled on the quay the fisherman studied their faces. He dismissed Aidan immediately, considered Jamie briefly and casting a quizzical eye at the red hat addressed Jean-Paul. "At last we meet monsieur,"

"The pleasure is all mine, Marcel." Jean-Paul greeted him. "I am in your debt."

"No problem monsieur. We who love our country must keep our friendship through these trying times and pray for a satisfactory conclusion. But don't thank me yet, I have not yet delivered you to your boat."

Sister Dolorosa and Marie-Claire made an inspection of the fish for the benefit of those watching and Jacques opened the sacks for Marcel Bertrand to give cursory approval and they made a play at bartering before the fish were loaded on to the cart and the potatoes placed on the quay.

The crew were due to return in about an hour they were told and Jamie suggested that they make a move to leave the village, giving the impression that they were making the homeward journey, and come back to board the boat as soon as the dusk began to settle.

Marcel eyed the Sisters. "I am presuming that one of you will be our passenger. I am afraid that you will look a little conspicuous in that attire clambering into the boat. It could prove difficult to explain at a later date. I have an idea . . . hold on . . . *un moment*." Climbing aboard the boat he rummaged in the aft locker and returned with a bundle of clothes and a dark navy Breton cap. "They belonged to my youngest son. About your size he was, they should fit and you'll be less conspicuous."

Jamie wondered what had happened to his son but thought it best not to ask. He took the clothes and placed them on the seat, handed the Sisters back up and clambered in beside them. With a wave they said *au-revoir* and left the village.

At a safe distance, once again they took shelter in a belt of trees where Marie-Claire changed her clothes and donned the blue woollen cap, pulling it well down to hide her badly shorn head of hair. The sight of her emerging from cover brought a smile to Jamie's face.

Nervously she approached him. "What do you think Jamie? Personally I am afraid I will fool no one."

Jamie was inclined to agree, but attempted to reassure her. "You make a very pretty boy indeed, but with this rough and ready collection of masculinity around you, you will be well hidden, *Garcon.*"

Jean-Paul was dismayed to see her clad as a boy but hid his feelings, just grateful that she was alive. Jean-Louis and Aidan made a joke and she seemed to relax a little until Sister Dolorosa stepped forward to bid her *bon voyage.*

This proved too much for Marie-Claire and she divulged into tears. Sister Dolorosa took her in her arms and told her that she had been so brave over the last weeks and she didn't have much longer to be stoic. She added that the Sisters at la Croix Blanche had loved having her stay with them and Marie-Claire must get word to them that she had arrived at her destination safely. Jacques had already taken Jamie's place on the seat of the cart and was waiting with the pony's reins in his hands. Jean-Paul handed Sister Dolorosa up onto the cart and thanked her for all she had done for his daughter, expressing concern for her return journey should she be stopped.

"We will return by another route, *monsieur* . . . never fear, steering well clear of la Mare and St Coulomb. And, besides, we have the letter of safe conduct," she grinned as she reminded him.

It was a sad parting and it was a sombre group that settled down to wait for dusk.

All was quiet as they re-entered the village for the second time that day. With dusk falling most people were inside eating their supper whilst they could still see it. Here and there an oil lamp burned in a cottage window, a cat leapt over a wall to go on his nightly prowl and a small terrier gave noisy chase. The fishing boats that would go to sea tonight had already left, there was only the *Helena-Louise* still moored at the harbour entrance making ready to sail.

With their hearts in their mouths the men surrounded Marie-Claire as they stepped out onto the quay. Every step of the way to the boat they expected to hear a sharp order to halt, and they were within a few yards when Marcel called out. "Be quick. Hurry . . . hurry." He pointed to the coastal track to the east of the village where they could see a troop of soldiers hurrying along the cliff path. The soldiers were still too far off to be able to distinguish the boat or stop it leaving and Jamie and his friends hastened aboard. Before they had even managed to gain their balance the boat slipped away from the quay and they were moving quickly into the open water.

"Who else knew you would leave from here?" Marcel's boat was well clear of the harbour village before he asked the question.

"Only me. I didn't tell Jamie about the alternative plan until after Haut Pays and even then not the name of the village." Aidan was truly puzzled. "There is no way any of the crew could give us away."

"Just coincidence then." Marcel assured him

"There have been too many coincidences." Jamie pointed out.

"*Oui,* true. But true also that the soldiers regularly patrol our villages. This visit comes a bit early but they possibly thought they might try to catch us out. They search our boats for gun powder, you see, smuggled in for our rebel fighters."

"How long before we get to Mont St Michel?" Jean-Paul asked as he and Jean-Louis sheltered and supported Marie-Claire who was finding it hard to gain her sea legs.

"We've arranged a rendezvous at midnight. You had better pray that there is no 'man of war' out there tonight."

They sighted Mont St Michel before midnight and Marcel and his men dropped their nets over the side to do some fishing while they waited out the time till Jamie's boat arrived. Fishing boats came and went but there was no sign of the man of war that Marcel warned them might appear. As the hour of midnight approached Aidan caught sight of a familiar sail to the south west. Confident that it was the *Sara Anne* Aidan pointed it out to Marcel who immediately ordered the nets to be shipped.

The last of the catch was being emptied from the net as Ben drew alongside. "Fine firework display us had the other night," he quipped. "Guess ye'd best be quick 'n climb aboard and let's run for 'ome."

"T'be sure, I never 'eard sweeter words." Aidan made a quick boarding and turned to help Marie-Claire clamber aboard, with Jamie's assistance from Marcel's boat.

Jean-Paul expressed his gratitude to Marcel Bertrand and his crew and hoped that they would meet in better circumstances next time, then bade him farewell before jumping across the short gap with Jean-Louis following promptly behind. With calls of farewell and *bon voyage* ringing in their ears Aidan took the helm and turned the boat for home.

The homeward journey, like the outward one, was accomplished with no unpleasant incidents until they were sailing off Mevagissey when Jamie spied a revenue cutter putting to sea and hauled them up. Issuing the order for the Cornish Lugger to hove to the revenue men came aboard to search the boat for contraband. Marie-Claire managed to keep hidden, huddled amongst the crew, until the disgruntled revenue officer was forced to admit that there were no smuggled goods on board and had to abandon the search.

The sun was about to sink below the hill on the other side of the river as the *Sara-Anne* tied up to the buoy opposite Quay Cottage. For the last three days Jacob had been anxiously looking out for them and it was with relief he hailed them from the quay and made ready to bring them ashore.

Whilst Jamie organised the carriage and horses to take the *de Varrons'* home to Rosvarron, Ginifur and family, with Kate and Liam, listened open mouthed to the story of their escapade. The women were aghast to see Marie-Claire without her cap on her head but she made light of it saying that she had always wondered what she would have looked like with either blonde or red hair. Now she would be able to find out, she declared, as she would have wigs made in all colours.

When Jean-Paul, Jean-Louis and Marie-Claire finally left for their home, Jamie and Aidan collapsed into the comfy chairs in the library with a good measure of brandy, savouring it whilst they remembered some difficult moments of the last week.

Dickon was overjoyed by his father's homecoming; Robin too for Jamie had been more of a father figure to her than her own father.

* * *

Absenting himself from Tremanyon and Rhosinnis to embark on the rescue mission to bring Marie-Claire safely home to Cornwall had forced Jamie to put aside his personal grief for a time. For a full week it had been necessary to focus only on this issue for the sake of the safety of them all. The reality of accepting that his life had to continue without Ellen beside him was still difficult to come to terms with, and he missed her dreadfully; however the adventure in France, and it had indeed been an adventure, had made him realise that life must go on. He still had a wonderful son, he was living in a free country . . . in the place that he loved most and surrounded by a loving family.

Within days of being home he was once again involved in the day to day running of the farm at Rhosinnis, making trips out to Wheal Jenny on the outskirts of St Stephens and helping Ginifur oversee the estate at Tremanyon.

Jean-Paul and his son and daughter took up residence at Rosvarron, deciding not to return to Canada and six months later Marie-Claire sported a head of tight curls. Jamie joked that she looked like an elf and suggested that if she dressed in green she would be mistaken for a Cornish Piskey.

Chapter Six
1794

JAMIE WOULD CELEBRATE his fortieth birthday in June and Ginifur was determined that it should be just that, a celebration.

Ginifur was in her sixtieth year. It was a point in life, considered by some, to be a great age; a time to sit quietly in a chair and take life easy, if you were lucky enough to still be alive that is. This description did not apply to Ginifur Tremayne. Ginny was still fit and active, taking a keen interest in the running of Tremanyon and in her children and grand-children. She continued to ride frequently with the faithful Liam at her side and was often accompanied by Dickon and Robyn who were both now ten years of age and growing fast.

Since Ellen's untimely death Dickon had lived with his grandmother at Tremanyon. Jamie also had temporarily made his home there with his father in law, Ben Nancekivel, but of late he had been spending a few nights at Rhosinnis.

Dickon still missed his mother, but his recovery had been eased by the love that he received from Ginny and Robyn and the whole family, including his beloved grandfather Ben. Nowadays Dickon mentioned his mother with ease and a smile on his face, his recovery almost complete.

Since his return from France Jamie had at first buried himself in his work; this became the focus in his life and during the day gave him little time to grieve over his loss. The night times were not so easy of course and he would stay up late working on figures for improvements to the mine or at Rhosinnis, until he was too weary to keep his eyes open and would tumble into bed with exhaustion.

Ben Nancekivel was at first inconsolable, for Ellen had been the focal point in his life for many years. In spite of his own loss Jamie was acutely aware of his father in laws love for his daughter and the devastation that her death had caused him. Concentrating on helping Ben through his period of mourning actually helped Jamie to come to terms with his life without Ellen.

The fact that the *de Varrons'* were still in residence at Rosvarron also aided his recovery. Jean-Louis was a frequent visitor to Tremanyon and often accompanied Jamie when he rode over to the mine where they would spend a night or two at Penhallow.

Marie-Claire was also a frequent visitor, and her happy disposition always lifted Jamie's spirits, bringing a smile to his face and frequently raising a laugh. In spite of her jesting about the variety of wigs to disguise her shorn head, as soon as there was enough growth to create tight curls she refused to wear them further. In fact the short hair suited her elfin face. Now after two years her hair almost reached her shoulders the familiar ringlets were forming once more and she was a rare beauty. Marie-Claire too would frequently ride out with Jamie, sometimes with Jean-Louis and sometimes alone. The two siblings played an important part in Jamie's recovery from the loss of his wife.

Since Ellen's accident, Beau's visits to Tremanyon were still few and far between and Ginifur did not have the opportunity to build a relationship with his son, and her husband's namesake. *Young Richard*, as Beau called him, was eight this year. In no way did he resemble his grandfather; he continued to grow into a pale carbon copy of his mother. His fair curls hung loosely on his shoulders; he had an unhealthy pallor and even more unhealthy stature. Richard's mother, Clara, had also increased her size since the birth of her son and no longer resembled the pretty young girl of her youth. She spent her life lying on the sofa eating sweet meats and fancies; her teeth were rotting in her mouth and her once svelte figure was now hiding beneath rolls of fat and loose dresses designed to hide it. *Young Richard* also had a sweet tooth and refused any form of exercise. No matter how hard Beau tried to persuade him to eat more healthily or to exercise, it was all to no avail and if Beau could see that there was no resemblance to the child's paternal grandfather, he would not admit to it.

Due to the good fortunes at the Wheal Jenny Mine, Robert Fry continued to maintain a good standard of living but Jamie's continued rise in the community, rankled both him and his son in law.

From the moment that Ginifur removed Roberta from the Fry household the child's name had never been mentioned. It was as though Clara had never given birth to a daughter. If Margery Fry ever gave her grand-daughter a passing thought she never showed it but she, her husband and her daughter doted on *Young Richard*, or Charlie as they still continued to call him. Anything the child wanted he had, anything he did not like was not forced upon him.

To say that the situation didn't cause Ginifur any heart ache would be wrong. Beau was her son after all, and born out of love as Jamie and Sara had been and Ginifur continued to ask herself where she could have gone wrong, feeling that the blame must indeed lie with her.

Jamie's accusation of Joe's negligence was never raised again, and his actions since did not suggest that he continued to hold him to blame. Jamie had always taken an interest in the stables, whether they were at Tremanyon or Rhosinnis, and he never questioned Joe's capability whilst his own horse was stabled within his precinct. But Joe did not forget those hurtful words that he had overheard.

When Rosie's time as wet nurse for Robyn had come to an end Ginifur had offered her a domestic place at Tremanyon, which she had gladly accepted. Rosie and Joe had become fond of one another and at the previous summer were wed. Rosie didn't have to change her name, or Lizzie's; for their surname was Pascoe already.

* * *

Marie-Claire was visiting Tremanyon whilst Jamie and Jean-Louis were riding over to Penhallow and Wheal Jenny; Ben Nancekivel wanted an update on a young filly that Hal Rawe was bringing on for him and he wanted Jamie to consider bringing her over to the stables at Tremanyon to breed with one of Ginifur's stallions. It was the first time, since Ellen's death, that Ben had shown an interest in his horses and Jamie was keen to cultivate it hoping that he was finally coming to terms with the loss of his daughter, as he felt that he had managed to do.

Once again Ginifur brought up the subject of Jamie's birthday and Sara and Marie-Claire were soon helping her to plan what format this should take. June was still some time away, three months to be precise, but Ginifur was persuaded that preparations should proceed as soon as possible if it was to be a success, and soon they were occupied in drawing up a guest list.

As the list grew Ginifur had to remind them that Tremanyon was not a large country house and the list should be tailored to fit. Sara pointed out that Jamie's birthday didn't fall until the end of June and that the weather should be fine; with a long summer evening they would be able to hold some of the celebrations out of doors. They could have an ox roasted over a fire pit and a grand buffet rather than a formal dinner, but Ginifur was not convinced by the suggestion that they should celebrate with a masqued event.

Preparations for the surprise birthday party were well under way at the beginning of May when Jamie rode in early from Rhosinnis and Liam informed him that Ginifur would be found in the drawing room. Jamie headed for the house and was surprised to find his mother alone with some sewing in her lap staring dreamily at the fireplace. "What's this? Time to sit and daydream? Are you feeling well Mother? It's unusual to find you sitting down at this time of the day."

Ginifur tore her attention away from the beautiful fireplace that had been installed in Tremanyon by Richard, her late husband, when the Georgian manor house had been built in 1750. "I was just remembering, Jamie. It seems a lifetime away and yet just like yesterday at the same time. Does that make sense? Your father loved this house, it was his dream. I was thinking about the day Mr Gibbons came to instruct the Italian workers on his designs for the ceilings. Richard was so proud of what had been achieved." She brushed a tear from her cheek and Jamie knelt by her chair and took her small hand in his. "I miss him so much Jamie. If I didn't have you and the family I don't know how I would bear it."

"I know Ma. We all miss Father, but none of us as much as you."

"You are so like him, Jamie. Each year that passes you become even more like him. Dickon and Robyn too, they have inherited so much from their grandfather."

"Their grandmother too, I hope. Does it hurt? Seeing so much of Father in me and the children?" Jamie wanted to know.

"Oh no! In truth it is a comfort. I feel that he is always with me when I have the three of you around me." Ginifur set her needlework aside and affected a brighter countenance. "Where are you off to today?"

"Jean-Louis and I are going over to Wheal Jenny. I am going to meet Davey there tomorrow."

"Tomorrow! Tomorrow is Sunday. Isn't the mine closed on Sunday?"

"Yes and no. We are replacing the Watt/Burton condenser engine. It has served us well and saved some fifty percent of coal usage since it was installed. But Richard Trevithick's new High Pressure engine is going to revolutionise the mining of copper. I am extremely grateful to him for allowing us to do trials for him. It was fitted last week."

"Is there something wrong? Is that why you are going over there?"

Jamie stood up and stretched his legs. "I don't think so, but obviously there is something that Davey wants to talk about. I thought that it would be good to take Dickon over to the mine as well. He is of an age now when he should learn how hard others work to give us the lifestyle we have become accustomed to."

"That's an excellent idea, why don't you take Robyn too. It would be good for her to see another side of life." Ginifur suggested.

Jamie wasn't certain. "Are you sure? I know we'll only be gone for a few days, but you will miss her if she is not around surely?"

"Don't be silly. Liam and Kate are always with me. Sara is still at home, when she is not teaching in Rebecca's schoolhouse. Robyn is a sensible girl and will not require a maid. She will cause you no problems. I assume that you will stay at Penhallow."

"Yes. We'll be there for two, maybe three nights. If you are sure?" Ginifur smiled and said that she was. "How quickly can they be ready?"

"No time at all. They are in the west wing so I will go up and pack some saddle bags for them. They will be so excited they will be ready to leave as soon as you are."

True to her word Dickon and Robyn were ready to leave and were mounted beside Jamie when Jean-Louis and Marie-Claire rode in from Rosvarron.

"Hello Marie-Claire." Ginifur greeted her warmly. "Have you come to see your brother off or pay a visit to Sara?"

"Neither, Mrs. Tremayne. I thought that it would be helpful to Jamie if I was to accompany them if Jamie did indeed decide to take Dickon along with him. As it is I see that Dickon's little shadow is with him too. Besides, I would love to see Wheal Jenny for myself; my brother speaks of it so often."

Ginifur admitted that it would indeed be helpful, for no doubt there would be times when Jamie was occupied elsewhere; she would be able to rest more easily knowing that Marie-Claire was with the children.

The journey to Penhallow was accomplished within the hours of daylight and they arrived before dark to find that Davey and his young wife Mary were away from home. Along with Hal they were attending a family wedding, so the young stable lad informed them.

"Knowing how the celebrations for Davey's own wedding carried on well into the night, we won't see him till the morning." Jamie commented with a smile. "I just hope that he hasn't forgotten that I am due to meet him at the mine at noon tomorrow."

The house and beds were always kept aired for unexpected arrivals, but Jamie was puzzled to find that there was no fresh milk, butter or bread on the slate shelf in the larder. Mary would normally have left them there with a selection of cold food for supper. Luckily Ginifur had left nothing to chance and Robyn informed them that her grandmother had instructed Kate to pack a basket of food which was strapped at the back of her saddle.

The fireplace in the drawing room was laid with paper and sticks and a bucket of coal beside it, as was the range in the kitchen. Jamie soon had both of them blazing and a kettle quickly set in place to provide them with a hot drink. Robyn helped Marie-Claire to prepare supper, and they gathered in the warmth of the kitchen to eat it round the scrubbed pine table. The adults smiled benevolently as the children found it increasingly difficult to keep awake, and as soon as they had consumed their supper Jamie signalled for Marie-Claire to help him take them up to bed.

Mary bustled in early the next morning, complaining bitterly that Davey had not informed her of their proposed visit and apologising for not being there to welcome them and prepare dinner. Within no time at all she had conjured up fresh bread, milk and eggs and informed them that Davey had left for the mine before light. No doubt he would see them there before the day was out.

Jamie was puzzled by what appeared to be Davey's casual attitude when his message to him had appeared to be urgent.

Nevertheless they enjoyed the simple breakfast that Mary rustled up for them and then set off for Wheal Jenny with Mary promising them an excellent dinner on their return.

It was a dull grey day as Jamie led the little party up to the gates of the Wheal Jenny Mine. He would have liked the sun to be shining for it looked so different on a bright sunny day. "Good morning Tom." Jamie greeted the elderly ex-miner on duty at the gate. "Is Davey Rawe up at the mine?"

"Mornin' Sir. I'm thinkin' 'ee must 'ave come afore I come on duty, 'is brother John come lookin' for 'im 'bout an hour ago," the old man said.

"I'll go on up then, and find him. I've brought my son and niece with me to show them how hard our employees work on their behalf." Tom nodded as he watched the visitors pass through the gate and head on up the track to the mine and soon they were hidden by the bushes growing alongside the track.

As the turn in the track hid the gateman from him Jamie espied a miner heading towards them. He was quite tall, wore a hat pulled well down on his head and a long coat covering his clothes. Jamie drew his horse to a halt as he greeted the man. "Good morning. I don't recognise you, do I? Have you been taken on recently?"

The man touched his cap respectfully. "Yes Mr. Tremayne. Davey Rawe took me on this last week. He be up at the mine waitin' for 'ee. Tol' me t'say 'ee would meet 'ee down the mine."

"Thank you. You're off home now are you? You must have had a late shift," the miner nodded. "Then I'll not detain you any longer." Jamie watched the miners retreating back as the man headed homeward before turning once more to the expanding group of buildings at the pit head. The stamps were silent now and only the maintenance team on duty. At the pit head another new employee confirmed that Davey was indeed below waiting for Jamie to join him. Once more Jamie retrieved his long fishing smock from his saddle bag, he always brought it with him to cover his clothes when he came to the mine, then he instructed Jean-Louis, Marie-Claire and the children to await his return to the surface when he would show them around Wheal Jenny.

Dickon and Robyn watched apprehensively as Jamie lowered himself on to the top rung of the ladder and took his first steps into the dark void. Dragging her eyes away Robyn looked up at Marie-Claire. "I don't like it. I wish Uncle Jamie hadn't gone down there."

Marie-Claire smiled reassuringly. "Your uncle has been below ground on many occasions Robin, he is quite used to it I promise you."

Robin wasn't convinced, something felt dreadfuly wrong. "I know . . . but . . ."

"But what?"

"I don't know. It just doesn't feel right. . . I'm sorry."

Marie-Claire placed a comforting arm about her shoulders. "It's your first visit to the mine, isn't it?" When Robyn agreed, she continued. "Anyone seeing the reality of the life of a miner would be fearful for their loved ones going below ground. But Wheal Jenny is a good mine, with a good safety record and a management that considers its miners. There is nothing to fear Robyn," she looked about her. "While we wait, why don't we take a look around above ground? On a working day there is a lot going on, noise and bustle. The Bal Maidens sort the ore on those trestles over there." As Jean-Louis, Marie-Claire and the children picked their way around the site a figure emerged from the engine house.

John Rawe approached them. "Good mornin' Monsieur de Varron. What brings ye all t' Wheal Jenny without Mr Tremayne?"

"Oh no! We're not alone. Jamie is meeting Davey on the ninth level; we are only waiting for him to return."

"Mr Tremayne! Meetin' Davey on the ninth level? Ye must be mistaken."

"No." Jean-Louis shook his head. "He received a message from Davey that he wished to see him this morning. We rode over last night. A miner on the path near the gate confirmed it, and then the man at the pit head told him to go to the ninth level where Davey was waiting."

Any colour in John's face drained away as a look of horror spread across it. He turned and called urgently. "Bill, fetch Davey immediately. Tell him to go to the pit head." Turning back to Jean-Louis he told him to repeat what he had said and tell Davey that he had already gone down the mine to bring Mr. Tremayne out. With this he turned and ran across the open ground to the access shaft.

"Marie-Claire, you had better take the children back to Penhallow, for I fear that something is dreadfully wrong."

Dickon squared his shoulders. "I am not leaving here until I know that my father is safe," he stated adamantly.

"Nor me." Robyn added a little tearfully.

"I think that they speak for all of us Jean-Louis." Marie-Claire said. "If Jamie is in any danger we will stay here together. But what on earth is happening?"

At that moment Davey Rawe appeared at the door of the mine office and hurried over to them. "What's this about Mr Tremayne meeting me here today?" he asked impatiently. Jean-Louis repeated the story he had related to Davey's brother John. "I sent no such message to Mr Tremayne. What do you mean he has gone to the ninth level?" Once more Jean-Louis described the two new employees who had directed Jamie to go below. "But we have taken on no new workers, above or below ground. Captain Tremayne knows all our men," he was totally confused. "Are you sure they told him to go to the ninth level?"

"Yes. . . quite sure."

"Dear God! If the fault line in the eighth level should split now he'll be buried alive."

The few men on duty were congregating from around the site, wondering what the commotion was about. Davey turned to the youngest. "Frankie, run to the village and get more men. And pray to God we won't need them. Captain Tremayne has gone to the ninth level and we must get him up right away."

As Frankie turned to run, the earth began to tremble beneath their feet as a rumble emanated from below the ground. Jean-Louis, Marie-Claire and the children could only look on as Davey and the men leapt forward.

* * *

Jamie had just stepped off the last rung of the ladder when Betsy dragged her eyes away from the flames in the fire. She needed a fire both in winter and summer now that she was beginning to feel her age. Anxiously she reached for her cloak and her stick and hobbled out of the door. Betsy didn't wander far nowadays; finding most of the herbs she needed closer to home; her bones ached as well and it wasn't so easy for her to get around. Nevertheless, today she would have to walk to Tremanyon to see Ginifur Tremayne. Betsy and Ginifur went back a long way and, as she walked, Betsy was remembering the day that she had met the young woman for the first time, with baby Jamie on her hip, whilst she was picking herbs near Tremanyon. Ginifur, Richard and Jamie had been the family Betsy had never had. Healer or White Witch, whatever she was they had never let her background come between them since Ginifur had called on her to treat Richard Tremayne when he returned from the New World. Never a week went past now without one of them calling to see her, to bring her wood, food or honey; Ginifur worrying that she wasn't eating properly. Richard was gone now but one of them, Ginny, Jamie or Liam would be here in a day or two, but that would be too late. She must see one of them now, preferably young Jamie if he was at home. Betsy had never been a praying woman, but she prayed now that her vision was not too late.

Betsy had hobbled as far as the Church, it had taken her a long time and her back ached, her legs ached and she was breathless too. She paused to take a breath and as she did she raised her head and saw Liam pull the trap up outside Rebecca's schoolroom and Sara jumped down and waved him goodbye. It was a struggle but Betsy managed to get level with him by the time he had turned the horse and trap around in the square.

"Well. . . Hello Betsy. A bit far from 'ome aren't 'ee? If ye needed somethin' why not wait till Ginny comes, she'll be down t' see 'ee in a day or so."

"No Liam, it can't wait, I must see Jamie or Miss Ginny. Tis urgent."

"Well now, Jamie's not at home right now, gone on a visit t' Wheal Jenny. Taken the children with 'im too,"

"Oh No!" Betsy clutched the stick to support herself as she felt her legs tremble. "Liam, I must see Miss Ginny. Please 'elp me t'get t' Tremanyon, Liam. Please."

Liam studied the old woman's anxious face, something was frightening her. What ever it was it was real to her. He jumped down from the driving seat, opened the small door at the back of the trap, picked her frail body up and placed her on the seat. "Whatever it is Betsy, don' 'e worry, I'll get 'e up t' Ginny right away." Returning to his seat Liam picked up the reins and they left the village at a good trot. The sight of Betsy in the Tremanyon trap with Liam did not pass un-noticed and word quickly spread about the village.

At Tremanyon Ginifur was tidying some books in Richard's old office. Jamie used it now, she supposed that one day he would move it all down to Rhosinnis but there was no hurry on her part for him to do so. She heard Liam's voice before he entered the side door, and wondered who he was talking to. The last person she expected was Betsy.

"Betsy, my dear! What are you doing making this long walk? It is too far for you, why didn't you find someone to bring a message if you needed me?" She was full of concern, for Betsy was now getting on in years.

"I couldn', no one near by 'n I 'ad t' come t' see 'ee right away. Now young Jamie's gone 'n I might be too late."

"What on earth are you talking about Betsy?" Ginifur felt a tremor of alarm. "No... come on in first. I'll get Kate to make us a nice cup of tea. Come, come. . ." she led the way to the library whilst Liam gave Betsy his arm.

Once seated Betsy explained that she had seen Jamie in the flames. One minute he was quite clear and the next enveloped in a cloud of smoke. . . or dust. She couldn't be sure which but Betsy was convinced that he was in danger, and said so.

"Are e sure t'was not just the smoke from the fire?" Liam offered a solution.

"D'ye thinks I doesn't know the difference between a seein', 'n real smoke. I'm not that far gone yet Liam."

"But you didn't see where he was?" ventured Ginifur. "Nor when?"
"No. I didn'. But it were Jamie right enough, 'n 'ee were in trouble I'm telling 'ee. Trouble is I don' know if tis trouble t' come or as 'appened already." Her whole body seemed to collapse down into the chair so that she looked no bigger than a small child. "But I'm feared for 'im. . . Ginny we must warn 'im."
Ginifur stared at her for a long moment before turning to Liam. "I don't know what to think Liam, Betsy has always had the knack of foretelling. Sometimes I know I have been guilty of dismissing them as inconsequential, but in all honesty I know there have been occasions when she was proved correct in her prophecy. Is Jamie in danger? I just don't know. . . but what I do know is that I don't feel easy about things. What should we do?"
"I could ride to Penhallow Ginny, if that would make ye feel any easier." Liam offered.
Ginifur looked out of the window. "I know the days are still pulling out but no, Liam. . . I am not sending you out on horseback to ride all that way through the dark. No."
"Then we either wait till mornin' and ride over to Penhallow, or I get Joe t' hitch a team t' the coach and we start t'make our way there right now. Whatever ye says, Ginny. . . tis your call. If we should leave now, it won't be an easy or a quick journey but, we'll be there afore dawn."
Ginifur studied Betsy's hunched form. "You are sure of this, aren't you Betsy? You don't get yourself in to this state for nothing." Betsy was exhausted she could hardly acknowledge her. "Liam, pick her up and lay her on the couch there. I will get Kate to bring her some warm food and a drink and some blankets. She must rest here until tomorrow and then we will send her home." She bent down to the old woman. "Betsy, listen to me. Liam and I are going to find Jamie. I am sure that you have warned us in time; please do not fret any more. Now you are to stay here till morning, Kate will look after you, and I will come and see you as soon as we return." To Liam she said. "Please go and fetch Sara right away, and get Joe to harness the horses to the carriage, and tie some spares behind. I will ask Kate to pack some clothes for you and I will pack some for Sara and myself. We should be able to get away before dark don't you think?"
"Easily, I'll go now then," Liam glanced down at Betsy, lifted her with ease and placed her tiny body on the large couch. "Kate'll look after ye just fine," he assured her.

* * *

"Marie-Claire!" Jean-Louis looked at his sister. "The children . . . !"

Marie-Claire clasped the hands of Dickon and Robyn. "I will not force them to come away; neither will I let them hinder what I believe is a rescue attempt. We will wait in the mine office for you to bring us news." With this she led a tearful Robyn and a stunned Dickon away towards the building recently vacated by Davey.

Clouds of dust particles rose from the open shaft as Jean-Louis approached Davey and the miners of Wheal Jenny. They were already tying wet kerchiefs and cloths across their noses and mouths and arming themselves with extra tools to carry below ground.

Davey was issuing clear instructions that they were to wait until they had all assembled at hopefully the ninth level, if not it would have to be the eighth. "Remember John is down there too, 'ee may 'ave reached Cap'n Tremayne in time and they both might be 'eading on up as we speak, so don' go down so fast that ye risk knockin' 'em off." He waited till the last man had lowered himself onto the ladder before turning to Jean-Louis. "When the men arrive tell 'em that I think that we 'ave 'ad a cave in from the eighth level t' the ninth, 'n that I suspect that Cap'n Tremayne, and possibly my brother John too, may 'ave been buried on the ninth. Tell 'em t' be prepared t' come below 'n set some of 'em t' get the kibbles working for we might need t' remove some of the rock t' get t' them. As soon as I 'ave seen what us 'as t'do , I'll come back topside with further instructions."

Jean-Louis looked down at the shaft. "I want to come too," he insisted.

Davey nodded his head. "I understand, but not just now. Let me assess the damage first. If ye c'n 'elp I will ask 'ee. I give 'ee me word."

Jean-Louis indicated that he understood and watched as Davey lowered himself onto the ladder, then he turned away to wait for the arrival of a rescue party. It wasn't long in arriving, men, women and children all hurrying to the pit head. Each of them receiving the news that Captain Tremayne and John Rawe may be buried alive with horror, for if it hadn't been for Jamie, and Davey and John Rawe, the mine might have been either closed or in other hands by now and their lives not as good as they had been over the last few years. John Rawe had gone below to warn Captain Tremayne, now it was not clear whether there were one or two men missing. There was not a man woman or child there who hadn't been affected by a mining accident at some time or another and they knew that the waiting was the worst part. Or was it? No the worst part was when they brought a body up and you found that it was no more than that, a body. A father, husband or brother that had once been such an important part of your life was no more. The breadwinner of the family gone. Mining was a hard life, and accidents happened.

The dust, emerging from the shaft, was lessening as they waited impatiently for news, and it was some time before Davey's head appeared above ground followed by the dejected men of the advance party.

Davey headed for the mine office and climbed the steps to the hard flat area in front of the office door to address the miners and their families. The men who had returned with him were coughing hard, in an attempt to rid their lungs of the dreadful dust. But as Davey made a stand and looked down on the assembled crowd a silence, like nothing Jean-Louis had ever experienced, settled over the compound. "I'm afraid tis as I suspected, the fault line on the eighth level 'as split open causing a cave in on the ninth," a murmur of voices travelled around the crowd. "Accidental, or man made, tis too early t' come to a conclusion. But the fact remains that Captain Tremayne and my brother John are not on this side of the fall."

"What do 'ee mean, accidental or man made?" One man asked of another.

The murmurs increased until Davey held his hand up to quiet them, but he did not answer the question, instead saying. "It may be that they'm both safe on the far side of the fall, or 'ave taken shelter in a side tribute. This can only be an 'ope, as ye are all aware, and time is not on our side. We must start on a rescue attempt immediately and will need t' work in relays. Y'know the drill, form y'urselves into teams under y'ur appointed leaders; I will come and tell 'ee what each team will 'ave to do. We 'ave been fortunate at Wheal Jenny, with few accidents and no deaths since Cap'n Tremayne took over the runnin' of the mine. Let us all pray that we will be able to say that t'morrow."

As the men attached themselves into groups and Davey walked among them issuing his instructions they were all too busy to notice the stealthy emergence of another figure from the shaft, covered in dust and a hat pulled well down over his head he struggled to control his coughing as he slunk away into the shadows.

Until the dust had cleared, the men had to work in short shifts in their attempt to clear the debris from the tunnel. Jean-Louis insisted that he was going to help and Davey did not deter him, allowing him to work alongside him. Moving the sharp rock soon cut his hands, but after accepting a leather glove from Davey he continued to work out the shift. When he returned for their break above ground he insisted that Marie-Claire bind his hands with strips of linen torn from her petticoats for he was determined to return to work with the men until Jamie and John were found.

One after the other the teams returned above ground and were replaced by the next, and dusk was falling when Davey led his men below ground with Jean-Louis stubbornly accompanying him. This was when they came upon John. Jean-Louis had been helping a miner lift a larger piece of rock and uncovered one of John's boots. Davey came forward to decide the next move and slowly they uncovered John's lifeless body. Sombrely they lifted him in turns, each man helping to carry him to the surface where Davey's mother, sister and John's young bride waited for news. It had been John's wedding yesterday; they had been married barely twenty-four hours. John's father was too ill to make the journey up to the mine; he waited at home with his eldest daughter for company. Grace Rawe let out an agonising cry when she recognised the dust covered figure of her young husband as Davey reverently lifted him in his arms and made his way towards his family. Hearts and hands reached out in a wish to give some comfort to the grieving family, but suddenly all eyes were drawn to the faces of the children and young woman on the steps of the mine office.

Dickon looked up into Marie-Claire's face with the unasked question on his lips.

"No Dickon, it isn't your father. It is Davey Rawe's brother John."

"Is Uncle Jamie dead too?" Tears trickled down Robyn's cheeks.

"We don't know yet Robyn. It is not necessarily so. As Davey explained, he might be sheltering on the other side of the fall."

"But you don't think so" added Dickon.

"Don't put words into my mouth now young man. You never give up hope, until all hope is gone." Quickly Marie-Claire cast up a prayer for the lost miner and made the sign of the cross before adding another fervent prayer for the good Lord to spare Jamie's life and another to the blessed Mary and any other saint who might be listening to intercede on her behalf.

Holding his mother briefly in his arms, as a group of miners' wives took charge of his brother's body and two men were allotted the task of carrying him home, Davey and Jean-Louis insisted on returning to the rock fall and doubling the attempt to rescue Jamie. The fall was bigger and went further than Davey believed was natural, and they had all but given up on the chance of finding Jamie by midnight when a shout from the pit head brought Davey and Jean-Louis running. They had only been above ground for barely five minutes, but tired and weary as they were they scrambled back down once more.

Miners stepped aside as Davey and Jean-Louis made their way forward to the rock fall where a large slate like section of rock had fallen at an angle across the tunnel, supporting smaller unstable rock above. Beneath that, covered by dust and rock one could make out the shape of Jamie's body lying inert, face down amongst the debris.

Jean-Louis drew a deep breath and covered his face with his hand wondering how he was going to convey the news to both Jamie's son and Ginifur, his mother.

Davey studied the site carefully, trying to decide whether any movement would bring the rock down upon Jamie's body and anyone else beneath if they tried to move him. He called for pit props to be brought forward and then carefully placed them in position before attempting to uncover Jamie's body and bring it out.

Laying him on a clear space in the tunnel Davey carefully wiped the dust from Jamie's face, his eyes were closed, his jacket was torn and he opened it to lean over and put an ear to his chest; there was no recognisable heart beat and he looked up at Louis and gave a regretful shake of his head. All the miners in the tunnel removed their hats briefly as they stared down at the body of the largest shareholder in the Wheal Jenny Mine. Tragedies such as this had touched all their lives, it was a hazard of the work that they undertook every day, yet there was hardly a dry eye amongst them.

As with John's body before, the miners worked together to lift Jamie and carry him above ground. Word had quickly spread and Marie-Claire, holding tightly to the children's hands waited and watched from the mine office as they placed Jamie's body carefully upon the ground.

Davey looked up as someone detached himself from the crowd. "Your mother sent a message to me that Captain Tremayne was trapped by a rock fall. She hoped that I might be needed and that his life would be spared."

Davey almost smiled. "That's typical of Mother, thinkin' of others even when she be grievin' the loss of 'er own son," he said proudly. "But I fear ye c'n do nothin' for 'im either, Dr Jessup."

The good doctor placed his bag on the ground. "I don't doubt you are a good miner, Davey Rawe, but why not let me take a look. Perhaps I'm the best judge to decide whether Captain Tremayne is dead or not."

Chastened, Davey agreed. "Of course doctor. I meant no disrespect." He took a step back and indicated that space should be given for Dr Jessup to make a thorough examination.

Dr Jessup quickly ran his hands over Jamie's limbs and body before carefully lifting one eyelid after the other to study his eyes before and finally his wrist to feel for a pulse. Opening his black leather bag he removed a mirror, and undoing the buttons on Jamie's shirt, he exposed his chest, leaning over to place an ear against his body. Not a word was spoken, the night was still and quiet and if a pin had been dropped it would have shattered the silence. Satisfied with his examination the good doctor took the small mirror in his hand, Jean-Louis was wondering what use a mirror could possibly be when he placed it near to Jamie's nose and mouth briefly before examining it thoroughly. Wiping the mirror he repeated the process before standing up. "Captain Tremayne is alive. . . just, but nevertheless, at this moment he lives. He has a very weak heartbeat, I can discern no alarming breaks or fractures to his arms or legs, but he is suffering from severe concussion from which he may, or may not, recover. If you can construct a stretcher to carry him to Penhallow, I will be able to carry out a better examination there. But we need to be quick, I cannot express the urgency to get him inside and warm. His temperature is alarmingly low and time is precious."

Davey quickly instructed men to help to prepare a stretcher, and then assisted with the carrying of Jamie back to Penhallow. Mary had run ahead with two other women to prepare a bed and put water on to boil. Ashes were still warm under the fire in the range and these were placed in warming pans. The bed was warming up before they carried Jamie into the house.

In the drawing room Dr Jessup paused and looked at the small boy beside the young French woman. He was staring up at him, trying to be so brave. "I understand that you have no mother, young man."

"No Sir. She died in a riding accident." Dickon's voice cracked as tears formed in his eyes.

"The children live with their grandmother." Marie-Claire explained.

"Ah yes! Ginifur Tremayne, Richard's second wife. I had the pleasure of being introduced to her by Lady Falmouth. A charming young woman. Captain Tremayne's mother do I assume? She is still alive I take it?"

Jean-Louis managed a smile. "Very much so."

"Then I suggest that you get word to her quickly, for I truly fear that Captain Tremayne may not recover from this disastrous accident."

Jean-Louis made for the door. "Then I must ride to Tremanyon immediately," he declared. "It is imperative that Mrs Tremayne is informed before it is too late."

Davey stepped forward and put his hand out to stop him. "You are in no condition to undertake such a ride. Hal will ride to Tremanyon for you. Ma'am." He turned to address Marie-Claire. "P'raps you would write a message for my brother to take with him."

"Of course." Marie-Claire gave the children a hug each and then went to the bureau from which she extracted paper, ink and a quill, sat at the desk and wrote a brief note of explanation, asking Ginifur to make haste to Penhallow. This accomplished she handed it to Davey at the very moment they heard a knocking on the front door. Jean-Louis went to open the door. . . to Sara Tremayne.

* * *

As Ginifur's carriage approached Penhallow they were astonished to see the drive crowded with men, women and children from the mine; their faces illuminated by the flares they held in their hands as they waited in silence. Respectfully they moved back from the drive to make way for the carriage and horses as it approached and the men removed their hats as Liam helped Ginifur to alight from the carriage. Ginifur looked about her, recognising Davey Rawe's brother Hal at the front of the crowd. With fear in her heart she approached him. "What is going on Hal? Why are you all waiting here?"

Hal didn't want to be the one to tell her the news, it should be from one of her own, but he had no option. "Tis the Cap'n,

Ma'am. Cap'n Tremayne 'ave 'ad an accident, 'ee were caught in a 'cave in' y'see. I'm sorry t'be the one t' tell 'ee Ma'am. We'm all just waitin'. . . t' 'ear the news, like."

"I see," said Ginny, who didn't understand at all, and was stunned by the news in spite of Betsy's warning. "Thank you for your concern, I am sure they will come and tell you as soon as there is news." She turned away and grasped Liam's arm. "Sara, knock on the door please. They will not be expecting us and won't know that we are here."

Sara ran up the steps to do as her mother bid her and waited impatiently for the door to open. When it did she could hardly recognise Jean-Louis for the dirt and dust and the state of his clothes.

* * *

Jean-Louis stared in disbelief. "What on earth. . . How did you know. . . ?" He stepped aside as Ginifur appeared at the door accompanied by Liam. Jean-Louis turned to see the doctor at the foot of the stairs. "Dr Jessup, this is Mrs Tremayne, Jamie's mother, and his sister Miss Sara Tremayne."

Dr Jessup came forward and extended his hand. "I am sorry that our meeting this time is in such different circumstances, Mrs Tremayne." He glanced at the blood-stained rags wrapped around Jean-Louis hands and said "I will need to see to those before I go."

"In time, in time." Louis dismissed him. "What about Jamie?"

"Let us take Mrs. Tremayne into the drawing room," the good doctor suggested. "She has just arrived and I am sure this is not the place to discuss her son."

"Of course, of course." Jean-Louis headed for the drawing room door. "I still do not understand. . . "

Marie-Claire had taken a seat on the chaise with a fearful child snuggled up each side of her struggling to keep awake. At the sight of their grandmother both Dickon and Robyn ran to her for comfort. Quietly and calmly Ginifur soothed the children with her serene acceptance of the situation and raising all their hopes when she told them of her confidence in Doctor Jessup whom she had met at Lady Falmouth's home, when he had been called to treat one of her own sons. Turning to him now she said. "Now, I would like to see my son."

The good doctor suggested that he made a better assessment of Jamie before she visited him, explaining that they had, only this minute, arrived from the mine and Mary was washing Jamie in readiness for him to examine him in full. Ginny wanted to see Jamie immediately, but she agreed and Dr Jessup picked up his bag and left the room.

Whilst Dr Jessup went to see his patient, Marie-Claire and Jean-Louis were eager to hear what had persuaded Ginifur to make the sudden trip to Penhallow, and Ginifur wanted more information about the accident at the mine. Ginifur managed to persuade the children that all would be well and that they should allow Marie-Claire to escort them to bed. This was accomplished when the exhausted children fell asleep in the same room with Marie-Claire seated between the beds in case they should waken. Ginny also managed to persuade Davey to go home to see his family. As tired as he was he had a duty to be with his mother and father at this time, but he would only leave when he was assured by Mary that she would stay and help.

Finally, when Dr Jessup returned to the drawing room Ginifur offered him a seat. He also looked tired and drawn, he was no young man either and Ginifur offered him a glass of brandy which he gratefully accepted when Liam poured one for him. He took a sip and placed the glass down on the table, entwining his fingers he looked across the room at Ginifur. "I am fairly confident that Captain Tremayne's head injury has not caused a fracture of the skull but he is suffering from severe concussion. It is too early to discount brain injury, and concussion is a funny thing. There is no knowing when, or if, he will recover from that."

"What do you mean?" Ginifur had arrived fearing the worst; it had been a relief to find that he was still alive.

Dr Jessup composed his thoughts. "Mrs Tremayne. . . I can heal your son's physical wounds, the cuts and bruises, these are nothing; but the head injury that he has sustained is something else. In all honesty, my dear lady, I fear that he may not recover and you should perhaps prepare yourself for this. I am sorry that I should have to give you this news. It was such a tragic accident and I understand that another life has already been lost."

"Yes. . . David Rawe's youngest brother. He went down to try to warn Jamie and bring him back to safety but was caught in it himself. It was an act of true bravery, for he knew how unsafe the tunnel was. I just cannot understand why Jamie was there at all."

"Mary Rawe has bathed your son's wounds and I have dressed those that need immediate attention and given him a thorough examination. Although unconscious he has been made comfortable and I will go home for a little 'shut eye', but I will make my call here the first visit tomorrow."

"Thank you doctor. May I go and see him now?"

"Indeed, and I must dress those wounds on your hand young man." Dr Jessup turned to Jean-Louis. "Perhaps you would be kind enough to ask Mary to bring me some hot water, Mrs Tremayne?"

"No! Don't worry Mother, I will get some hot water and cloths from the kitchen." Sara said.

Ginifur acknowledged her daughter, saying that it would be good for her to have something to occupy her; she held out a hand to Liam saying. "You will come with me Liam."

"If you wish it Ginny."

"I do Liam, I do."

Ginifur and Liam made their way up the stairs to the bedroom where Jamie lay in the large four poster bed. He looked so small and frail that Ginifur took a sharp intake of breath as the memory of Richard's return from the New World flashed before her eyes. Mary Rawe was sitting beside the bed and made to leave as Ginifur approached.

"Thank you, Mary, for what you have done for my son."

"Think nothing of it Ma'am. It is no more than you would have done for my Davey." She picked up the bowl and cloths from the table. "Call me, Mrs Tremayne, if you need me. I'll only be in the kitchen, waiting for Davey."

"I will. Thank you again and I will see you later."

As Mary left the room Ginifur stepped nearer the bed studying the pale face of her son, Jamie. His face showed signs of bruising and the cuts had been attended to, but it was the lack of colour in his face that caused her greatest concern. It was as though all the life had already been drained out of his body. She sat down on the vacated seat beside the bed and took Jamie's cold hand in hers. "Oh Jamie. What are we going to do now? You will have to want to recover Jamie, dig deep down inside you and remember all the important things in your life. You can hear me Jamie, I know you can. Dickon needs you, and Robyn too, we all need you. You have never given up without a fight Jamie; you must find it in you to fight your way back now. I will stay here until you do." Ginifur caressed her son's hand as the tears flowed down her cheeks and Liam placed a comforting hand upon her shoulder, also remembering their long vigil all those years ago beside Richard's bed in Tremanyon.

For the next week, night and day someone sat beside Jamie's bed. Jamie could survive without food for a while, Ginny knew that, but he needed liquid and her determination that Jamie would eventually recover made her deal with this herself. Hourly she would have Liam lift and support Jamie whilst she painstakingly managed to get some water and honey past his lips, one teaspoon at a time. It wasn't much more than a quarter of an egg cup full at a time, but over the period of twenty four hours it was enough to keep him alive. All the while she continued to talk to him, telling him what the children were doing, of the well wishers who called and the small gifts they brought with them. She told him of Davey Rawe's attempt to find the mysterious men who had directed him to the ninth level and how the fall of rock had uncovered the beginning of a new lode of copper. When Ginifur was too exhausted to carry on Jean-Louis and Marie-Claire continued to administer the water and honey for her.

Doctor Jessup called daily and was increasingly surprised that Jamie continued to hang on to life; slowly Jamie's pulse became stronger but, even so, he showed no signs of recovering consciousness.

Since Rebecca and Daniel's first visit, Daniel had ridden over on his own to see Jamie and Ginifur wasn't surprised when he made a further visit. The curtains were drawn back and the window open to let in some of the warm May air as Ginny watched him riding up the drive. "Here comes Daniel again, Jamie," she said as she glanced at her son lying in the bed. "I wonder what news he brings with him today?" Ginifur tucked the needle safely into the piece of embroidery and moved the frame away as she rose from the chair. "It is nearly time for you to have another drink of water; if Liam doesn't come soon perhaps Daniel will help us," she turned as she heard voices beyond the door and wasn't surprised to see Liam come in with Daniel.

Daniel looked a little flushed but Ginny dismissed this as an effect from the long ride. "It's good to see you again so soon, Daniel, but you have your own work to attend to. We can manage and I would let you all know if there was any change in circumstances."

"Yes. . . I know. But it isn't just about Jamie's health I am afraid." He glanced at Jamie. "Perhaps we should talk about this downstairs."

"About what?" Ginifur was mystified, what could be important at this time when Jamie still hovered between life and death.

"The mine, Wheal Jenny."

"Can't it wait Daniel; can it really be that important?"

"I think so, and I need some help on this." He glanced again at Jamie wishing so hard that he would make a recovery. "Let us go down stairs to discuss it."

Ginifur bit her bottom lip as she thought about it, then made her decision. "No, Daniel. I have been talking to Jamie for the last week about stuff and nonsense. About the children, who are no such thing of course, but of inconsequential occurings that have happened day to day. Wheal Jenny is an important part of Jamie's life, what ever you have to say he should hear it for himself."

Daniel looked puzzled. Jamie was still unconscious; he couldn't hear what he had to say. What on earth was Ginifur saying?

"I will not believe that Jamie cannot hear what is going on. As far as I am concerned he is in a dreamlike state from which he cannot find any reason to return. All his other injuries are healing well, now all that is required is a reason for him to wake up."

"Is that what Dr Jessup has told you?" Daniel inquired hesitantly.

"No." Ginifur was forced to admit. "He is a good doctor, I don't doubt it, and he has treated Jamie well. But there are some things that I just know, and this is one of them. So speak up Daniel. Speak to me, if you prefer, but loud enough for Jamie to hear too." She took her seat by the bed and took Jamie's hand once more into hers. "Jamie, Daniel has brought you news of the mine. I know that you can hear us Jamie, it might be important and you should hear it for yourself."

Daniel hesitated, looking from Jamie to his mother and back again to his friend's motionless body. Ginifur, still holding Jamie's hand, gestured for him to speak. "It's about the mine, Jamie! Wheal Jenny. Well. . . not only about the mine, I guess. Robert Fry too."

"Robert Fry! What on earth is he up to now?" Ginifur asked

"To tell the truth, he has called an extraordinary meeting of the shareholders of Wheal Jenny. It has been put about that Jamie will not recover from his injuries and that it is only a question of time. Without Jamie, Wheal Jenny is like a rudderless ship. I just don't know what to do." Daniel sat down and put his head in his hands with a groan. Ginifur, searching for something to say jumped with alarm as Daniel suddenly leapt to his feet and shouted. "Damn it

Jamie, your mother says you can hear. Well hear me now. If you don't pull yourself out of where ever it is you are, you will loose everything that you have worked for since you came home. Wheal Jenny and perhaps Rhosinnis too. Not only that, what about Davey Rawe and his mother and father? Young John lost his life trying to warn you of the danger on the ninth level. He has left a young wife of just twenty four hours, and his parents have lost their youngest son. Don't let it all be for nothing Jamie. John thought you were worth saving; now it's up to you. And while you are about it, spare a thought for Dickon. The boy is out of his mind with worry, he has lost his mother, are you really considering leaving him without a father too? " The outburst had drained him, and Daniel sank back into the chair.

Ginifur studied Jamie's face wondering, for the first time, whether her instincts were wrong and he actually heard nothing at all when suddenly she felt Jamie's hand move within her grasp. "Daniel, he moved. Jamie moved his hand."

Daniel looked up. "Are you sure? Perhaps you imagined it."

"No I didn't, I tell you he moved his hand. Jamie, Jamie. . . can you hear me? Don't try to speak, just squeeze my hand if you can hear me."

Daniel got up to watch, not really believing that he would see anything at all, and wasn't surprised when he didn't. He was about to turn away when, very slowly, Jamie's fingers curled around Ginifur's hand and gave her a very light squeeze. "He did, Ginny. Jamie has moved his hand. I think you are right, Jamie can hear us." He was so exited he wanted to run and tell everyone. "Jamie! Jamie! Can you understand what we are saying?" He stressed the question and Jamie's hand moved once more in answer.

"I think that you had better ride for Dr Jessup, Daniel. He said to call him if there was any change in his condition. I don't think he will expect this change, but please ride and fetch him for me. And ask Mary to bring some fresh warm water and cloths and some of the fresh spring water for him to drink."

"I will, I will." Daniel left the room almost at a run, so eager was he to pass on the news to the family.

By the time Dr Jessup was tracked down and arrived at Penhallow Jamie could not only move his hand but had opened his eyes. As yet he hadn't said a word but he had indicated that he could see them as well as hear.

Ginifur was correct in her belief that Dr Jessup would be surprised. He was astonished. Shaking his head in disbelief he declared. “Well, Captain Tremayne, I have to admit that I truly thought that your days were numbered. But your mother never gave up. I am sure that it is only her determination that you should come through this, that has made it so. It will still take some time before you will be able to ride again, first you have to find your feet and walk. But I am sure that you will, in time. I would like to give you an examination if I may, check your reflexes and look into your eyes, the usual sort of stuff. Then if I am happy perhaps I could call every other day instead of daily.”

Ginifur left the room whilst Dr Jessup made his examination and she waited with Daniel in the drawing room, she had just seated herself when Mary knocked on the door and asked if she would be kind enough to see Davey. “Of course, Mary. Send him in.”

Davey Rawe came into the room, his hat in his hand. “Mornin’ Mrs Tremayne, Mr Franks.”

“Hello Davey, how are your mother and father, and John’s widow of course, Grace isn’t it? I am so sorry I wasn’t at the funeral, I do hope that you will forgive me.” Ginifur apologised.

“Nothin’ t’ forgive, Mrs Tremayne. It was good of Miss Tremayne and the Captains friends t’ find the time t’ come. T’was much appreciated by Mother, and the gift t’ ’elp Grace through the next few months was very generous of ’ee.”

“Not at all. Did you have a special reason to ask to see me Davey?”

“Yes. . . ’n I’m glad that Mr Franks be ’ere too. It’s about this meetin’ of the shareholders, y’see. It ’ave got the men at Wheal Jenny real worried about what’s goin’ on. What’s the meetin’ about? I realise that Mr Tremayne is very ill but the mine is still workin’, ’n our order books are full. The rumours runnin’ around are unsettlin’ the men ’n I’m afraid that some of the best of ’em might look for new jobs.”

“What rumours?” Daniel asked.

“Well. . . of course the one that be doin’ the worse damage is the one that says Captain Tremayne is only just hanging on to life, ’n tis just a matter of time afore ’ee goes. I’m sorry Mrs Tremayne, tis what they say though.”

“That’s alright Davey, carry on.”

“Then o’ course that Mr Fry says the mine will ’ave t’ fold, that I’m no use as a mine captain and should never ’ave been given the job in the first place. Then there’s rumours that ’enry Bishop, of the Magdalene Mine, is still nosing about, and making offers to the smaller shareholders and tellin' 'em that 'ee will be able t' put things right. His mine 'as a safety record next t' none, I c'n tell 'ee. Ask 'im 'ow many men 'ave died in the Magdalen this last twelve month. And there's somethin' else too. . . if Cap'n Tremayne was. . . but ee's not. . ."

"If you can't tell Jamie, Davey, I'm sure that you can tell Mr Franks. After all, it was to him and his father you went when the Wheal Jenny was in trouble before."

Davey fiddled with his hat as he thought about it. "Well. . . 'ard as I've tried I can't find they men that ye saw at the mine that day, Mr Franks. I'm not sayin' they wasn't there, just that no one else saw them. But there is someone else who's turned up."

"Who's that Davey?"

"Mr Hawes."

"Walter Hawes is back in St Austell?" Daniel repeated.

"No, ee's not at 'is 'ome, but I've been told 'ee be back in the area, 'n hidin' up on Bodmin moor. I've also been told that 'ee is expectin' t' get 'is old job back."

"Well, well." Daniel's mind started to work quickly. "Can you find out where he is?"

"I've done that already. Just kept it t' meself that's all." Davey glanced at the door, then at Ginny. "I'm sorry, Mrs Tremayne, I've been so took up with the mine I 'aven't asked how Captain Tremayne is."

Ginifur glanced at Daniel before saying. "Dr Jessup is with him now Davey. Daniel, what do you think about this news?"

"I think that we should put Davey's mind at rest and tell him that Jamie has actually regained consciousness." Davey let out a gasp of surprise. "But in view of what you have just told us Davey, I suggest that this news is kept between these four walls for the time being."

"Is Captain Tremayne going to recover after all? Mary said ye was convinced ee'd get better. Tis wonderful news, I'm that glad I really am. Is it really true, Mrs Tremayne?"

Ginifur smiled at the eagerness on Davey Rawe's face. "I truly believe that he will recover completely Davey, but I fear that it might take some time before he is back in harness at the mine."

"Don' 'ee worry 'bout that; us'll make sure everythin' is kept runnin' just as the Cap'n would want it to. Y'know. . . Mother and Father will be that pleased; s'pose I can't tell them either, just yet awhile like?"

"Better to keep it just to ourselves for a while." Daniel agreed. "Till we know which way the wind is going to blow. If Robert Fry and Henry Bishop want to continue to believe that Jamie will not recover, let them. We have a lot of work to do before the shareholders meeting, and the first thing that I want to do is speak to Walter Hawes."

* * *

Davey Rawe agreed to keep the news of Jamie's recovery to himself, as too did Dr Jessup. Daniel stayed on at Penhallow and he and Davey were often to be found at the mine office. They also paid a visit to the isolated, damp dwelling on Bodmin Moor where Davey had tracked down Walter Hawes. On the verge of starvation, having found no work out of the county for a tin mine captain, he had crawled back to Cornwall and approached Henry Bishop for a job. It transpired that Henry Bishop had sought Walter out and bribed him to bypass any signs of copper or tin at the Wheal Jenny in an attempt to devalue the mine. If Henry Bishop was successful in taking the mine over, then Walter would, of course, return to his position as mine captain. But the plan had backfired and, when it failed, Walter Hawes was forced to flee and leave his family to struggle. In desperation he had now returned to find that the Magdalene Mine was in a bad way and Henry Bishop even more determined to get his hands on the Wheal Jenny. Bishop said if Walter helped him to recruit some men to do a job for him and the Wheal Jenny was joined with the Magdalene then Walter's position would once more be secure. Walter had been told to hide up in the hovel on the moor, keep hidden until after the shareholders meeting and food would be sent up to him.

When Walter recruited the miners he didn't know any of the details of what was expected of them, he said, and when he found that there was to be a fall at the Wheal Jenny he wasn't over concerned until one of the recruits told him that the plan was to involve Captain Tremayne. Walter had tackled Henry Bishop on the subject and had been told to keep out of sight and hold his tongue if he knew what was good for him. The food had run out over a week ago and Walter was now trying to survive on water from the stream and a few stale crusts of bread that were left.

It wasn't difficult to persuade Walter to agree to give evidence when Jamie was well enough to go to the sheriff and press charges.

Hour by hour and day by day Jamie's health improved and within a few days he managed to speak again. When Daniel was not at the mine with Davey he was to be found in Jamie's bedroom keeping him up to date with all that was going on.

Davey had made a thorough examination of the levels eight and nine. His suspicions had been raised by the scale of the fall, far greater than he would have imagined from a natural fall. He wasn't entirely surprised to find evidence that gun powder had been involved. After consulting with Ginifur it was decided that Daniel and Davey would tell Jamie about Walter Hawes and the plot hatched up by Henry Bishop. Davey made another trip out to the hovel on the moor with food for Walter Hawes who insisted he was anxious to make amends.

Dr Jessup continued to make regular calls at the house, telling everyone that Jamie was still clinging on to life, which of course was true.

On the day of the shareholders meeting in St Austell, the street outside the meeting hall was crowded with miners from the Wheal Jenny Mine. When Robert Fry demanded that the constables clear the street he was told that their orders were to insure that there was no trouble, otherwise they were not to interfere with a peaceful protest. The shareholders had to brave their way through the crowd as the miners heckled and pleaded with them to stand by the Wheal Jenny Mine and wait for Captain Tremayne to get better.

Liam had returned to Tremanyon to bring Ben Nancekivel to St Austell and Daniel met him inside the hall. More than a little flustered by the effort, Ben took the offered chair and asked. "What on earth is all this about?"

Daniel feigned ignorance. "Your guess is as good as mine, Sir. We'll just have to wait and see what develops."

When everyone was settled Robert Fry took the stage. "It is my sad duty to inform you that Mr James Tremayne, Chairman of the Wheal Jenny, is still indisposed. There is no need for me to tell you that he is suffering from fatal injuries incurred in the unfortunate accident at the mine."

"Fatal?" Someone picked up on the word. "Is he going to die?"

"He is unconscious, can neither speak, see nor hear. After three weeks he has no chance of recovery." Robert Fry assumed concern. "I am sure that you will all join me in offering our sympathies to his family at this dreadful time." A rumble of sympathetic wishes came from the floor. "As you all know, Mr Tremayne has played a major part in the running of the Wheal Jenny over the last few years; without him to continue there is little hope of success in the future. The mine collapse has left the company in a very bad way and we need to consider a way forward. A few years ago Mr Bishop made an offer for the Wheal Jenny and I have been in contact with him to see if he is still interested; with the Magdalene being the adjacent mine it would be advantageous for all. Following talks with him and his legal advisors I have pleasure in introducing him to you. I give you Mr Henry Bishop of the Magdalene Mine."

Henry Bishop took centre stage. "I was so sorry to hear the sad news about Jamie Tremayne. He has worked hard for the Wheal Jenny mine, but safety issues were compromised by the slack leadership of the man he elevated to mine captain. Davey Rawe did not have the experience to be a mine captain, and the result was that the eighth level was left insecure, a danger to anyone who ventured on to either the eighth or ninth level. Mr Fry approached me, as there would appear to be no one to replace Mr Tremayne and I reconsidered my original proposal to combine the Wheal Jenny with the Magdalene Mine. Contrary to what you may have heard the Magdalene is doing very well indeed and I am offering not only payment for any shares purchased in the Wheal Jenny, but shares in the Magdalene too."

"Why would you offer to buy our shares and give us Magdalene shares as well?" one voice asked.

"What price do you put on your own shares Mr Bishop?" another added.

Ben Nancekivel had been temporarily stunned by Henry Bishop's appearance, suddenly found his feet. "Mr Bishop, whatever your proposal, I judge it to be seriously mistimed. We should wait until Jamie Tremayne's future is decided. . . one way or the other."

Questions were raised from the floor, each answered by Robert Fry or Henry Bishop. Martin Petherick asked why Davey Rawe had not been asked to attend to explain why the accident had occurred; Robert Fry informed them that there was no need for explanation, the result was the same and Jamie Tremayne would likely die as a consequence.

The rumble of voices continued outside on the streets as the shareholders asked each other what was going on but now the voices of the miners increased in volume until finally the sound of a loud cheer filled the room. The noise of the crowd escalated in intensity, so much so that it now almost over rode the meeting inside but, when there was a sudden silence, Robert Fry banged the gavel on the table and demanded a vote on the merging of the Wheal Jenny with the Magdalene Mine, declaring that as Jamie Tremayne was too ill to vote his shares did not count.

Thus there were seventeen percent of independent shareholder votes, four percent for Henry Bishop who had purchased these from Robert Fry. Robert Fry still held ten percent, Martin Petherick ten, Charles Bolitho eight and Ben Nancekivel twenty percent. It was essential for Martin Petherick and Charles Bolitho to vote for the proposal and Robert Fry had been working on them over the last week. Nevertheless they hesitated, looking shamefaced at Ben. A commotion at the door drew all eyes to the back of the hall as it burst open and Ben somehow managed to make himself heard above the noise. "Vote as you see fit Martin, me I say no; I do not believe that Davey Rawe is responsible for this accident at the Wheal Jenny and I also believe that this meeting is most ill-conceived and that Jamie Tremayne will indeed recover from his injuries."

A gasp of surprise went up from the hall as Jamie Tremayne was helped inside. Supported on one side by Davey Rawe and on the other by Jean-Louis; and followed by Liam, who made sure that Jamie was in no danger of being knocked over in the melee, as they made a slow progress towards the platform where he came to a halt and turned to address the room.

Jamie was a shadow of himself but in spite of the effort it had taken him to attend the meeting, he stood tall. "Well said Ben; I'm glad that someone hasn't given me up for dead. As for the accident at the Wheal Jenny. . . it was no accident. The rock fall was caused by a charge laid at the fault line on the eighth level. The man involved was recruited by Walter Hawes, as was the other who was sent with the message to me at Tremanyon and the others who directed me to go below. This was not an accident; it was an attempt on my life and has caused the death of a fine young man. I will be going to the police to ask for a criminal investigation into the affair." He paused in the stunned silence. "With regard to the meeting here today, I would like to make an alternative proposal. I propose that the Wheal Jenny remains an independent mine and I declare my complete confidence in its mine captain, Davey Rawe."

It had been a long speech for someone who had been, for a while, at deaths door and Davey helped him to a chair that Ben Nancekivel had vacated.

Jamie turned his attention to Henry Bishop and Robert Fry. "Is there anything else that either of you two gentlemen would like to add?"

Henry Bishop glared malevolently at him, whilst Robert Fry looked as if he had seen a ghost, and a troublesome one at that.

"Why is it that you don't seem over enthralled by my recovery, Robert?"

Ben Nancekivel had tears in his eyes as he looked at his son-in-law. "I'll have words to say to you in private my lad, but my. . . I can tell you, there was never a better sight for these old eyes than to see you walk in." Turning to the floor he raised his voice. "My vote is for Jamie Tremayne."

"And mine," added Martin Petherick.

One by one the shouted support of all the other shareholders came from the floor, along with well wishes for a speedy recovery for Jamie Tremayne.

Jamie smiled. "Robert! Mr Bishop!" Both gentlemen answered with a glare as Daniel took up the gavel in his hand and brought it down with a resounding crash upon the table. "Carried by a majority vote." he declared as cheers rose first from the floor and then echoed along the streets of St Austell as the news spread and Jamie was assisted back to the carriage.

Jamie was indeed on his way to recovery, but the events of the day had taken its toll on him. By the time they had arrived back at Penhallow he was on the point of exhaustion. It had been the intention to go to the police after the meeting but it had taken too much out of him and within minutes he was fast asleep.

The day after the meeting Jamie made his statement to the sheriff, Davey and Daniel accompanied the constables to Walter Hawes dwelling on the moors to find it abandoned, with no evidence that it had been recently occupied. Without Walter's corroboration there was no evidence for either the murder of John Rawe or the attempt to murder Jamie. Jamie had to withdraw his charges that Walter Hawes and three others had enticed Jamie to Wheal Jenny, laid a charge and caused the rock fall. Davey's evidence of a charge being laid at the fault line was not enough in itself.

Davey was initially angry that it appeared that Walter had reneged on their agreement, but on reflection he realised that it wasn't surprising. No doubt he had been bought off by an offer from Henry Bishop.

As a result of these events, Jamie's birthday passed quietly, and there was a simple celebration at Tremanyon with the members of the Tremayne family and the *'de Varrons'*. Of course Liam and Kate's family joined in and Kate and her daughters put on a wonderful spread. Although Jamie still tired easily, he enjoyed every minute.

Once again Beau refused to attend the family celebrations at Tremanyon and, although the take over bid for Wheal Jenny had failed, it still did bother Jamie that there could be a possibility that his brother may have been involved in an attempt on his life.

* * *

Jamie's *'accident'* and his recovery period had brought Jean-Louis and Sara into closer contact with each other. Sara had been distraught at the possibility that she might lose her much loved brother and had turned to Jean-Louis for comfort.

Rebecca had married late in life, and Ginifur had almost thought that Sara was fated to do the same. She blamed herself for the fact that they had attended very few social events in recent years which would have brought Sara into contact with eligible members of the opposite sex. Like Rebecca, Sara appeared to reap enjoyment from teaching the children in the village. But here she was, just radiating happiness beside the son of Richard's friend, Jean-Louis de Varron.

Jamie had just returned from a walk to the quay and was enjoying a few quiet moments with his mother and hid a smile.

Jean-Louis fingered his shirt collar. "To be honest Mrs Tremayne, I am not quite certain whether I should be asking you or Jamie. So Sara suggested that I ask both of you," he glanced uncomfortably from one to the other.

The sight of the happiness on her daughter's face brought a smile to Ginifur's lips. "And just what would you like to ask of me. . . and Jamie of course?"

Jean-Louis took Sara's hand for encouragement. "I would like to ask for your daughter's hand in marriage, Madam."

Ginifur's smile broadened. It really wasn't any more than she had expected. Indeed, for weeks everyone had been waiting for this moment. The growing relationship between her daughter and Jean-Paul's son had been the subject of many a conversation at Tremanyon. "That is very formal, Jean-Louis."

"It is a serious business, Mrs Tremayne. I have spoken to my father and, as you are aware, we have considerable properties in

Canada. Those in France have been confiscated, but my father will make a settlement that will allow me to give Sara a comfortable life."

"But. . ." Ginifur pulled a wry face.

"But?" Repeated Jean-Louis, a little flummoxed by the question.

In spite of her innermost fear Ginifur managed to continue to smile. "Somehow I feel that a 'but' is about to be included. . . "

Jean-Louis looked uncertainly at Sara for her acknowledgement that he should continue. "We. . . that is I would like to return to my home and life in the New World, and Sara has agreed to come with me. . . of course, that is. . . should you give approval to our marriage."

Ginifur considered her answer. "Richard always said that there was a great future to be had in the New World. Indeed if Rachel, Rebecca and I had not been back here at Tremanyon, I think that he could easily have stayed there." She took her daughter's hand. "My only wish is for your happiness Sara, and if you choose Jean-Louis as your partner in life, I am delighted. . . and I am sure that Jamie is too."

Jamie was beaming from ear to ear. "This is wonderful news. Congratulations to you both." He kissed his sister on both cheeks and then repeated it with Jean-Louis.

* * *

It took a while for Jamie to recover completely from his injuries incurred at the incident at the mine and it wasn't until October that he began to ride again. Jamie's first visit was to the cottage on the far side of the village. Liam and Kate had kept Betsy informed of Jamie's return to health and delivered regular supplies of food and wood, but she was delighted to see him when he rode up to her door. Betsy had heard the horse approaching and was at the door when Jamie dismounted. "Oh Jamie. . . ! The sight of 'ee 'as made an ol' woman 'appy." Betsy was now frail, stooped and needing the stick that she carried to help her walk but she didn't let this stop her greeting Jamie at the door. "Come on in me 'andsome and bide awhile wi' ol' Betsy."

Jamie stooped to enter the low doorway and settled himself in Betsy's visitors' chair, where he passed an hour telling Betsy of the news at Tremanyon and Wheal Jenny. But the incident that had befallen Jamie could not be ignored and Betsy told him that although she had the vision of him in danger, this time she could not be sure that he would survive. "The visions be gettin' weaker Jamie, tis only t' be expected as ye get old. No one t' pass the learnin' to either. T'would 'ave been nice t' 'ave a daughter t' carry on after me. There be no one t' morn my parting."

Jamie was justifiably indignant. "You ingratiate," he chided. "You know full well that isn't true." Nevetheless he smiled at the frail form opposite him.

"Yes. . . Yes. . . I knows. Miss Ginny and the Cap'n, you young Jamie 'n that sister of your'n, young Sara. . . 'n Liam 'n Kate 'n that brood of theirs. . . yes, yes. Tis the nearest I ever got t' 'aving a family of me own."

"Rachel and Rebecca too," he added defensively.

" Yes. . . y'ur sisters, but I notice ye don' mention y'ur father's namesake though." Betsy scowled, but relented and added. "I'm sorry Jamie, ee's a wrong 'n for sure, 'n if ye don' know it now, ye will in time."

Jamie looked shocked. Beau hated Betsy with a malevolence that Jamie could not understand, but Betsy had never spoken of him before, he now realised. "What do you mean?" He was filled with unease at his question.

Betsy leaned across the short gap between them and patted his hand. "In time, Jamie, in time. Now is not the time. I want t' 'ear 'appy things. What's this news I be 'earing about that sister of your'n?"

Jamie knew that there was no point in pressing Betsy further at this moment, so he went on to tell her of the engagement between Sara and Jean-Louis, the forthcoming marriage and their plan to live in Canada.

The afternoon flew by and it was time for Jamie to take his leave. "Oh, I forgot. Kate sent over a seed cake and a rabbit pie for you." He went to fetch the package that had been strapped behind the saddle and returned to find Betsy shaking more than was usual. "Betsy, what is it? Are you alright, what can I do for you?"

Betsy raised a tear washed face. "Just me bein' maudlin' young Jamie. That comes with age too. Just remember one thing when I'm gone. If I could 'ave chosen a family for me own it would 'ave been Miss Ginny and 'er own, yes it would. Don' know as I rightly know what love is, but I s'pose it must be somethin' like what I feel for ye all."

Jamie was alarmed. "Betsy, what has brought this about, are you ill? If so Mother must be told."

"No I'm not ill, don' 'ee be botherin' 'er mind. Just wanted t'let 'ee know." She shushed her hands at him. "Now be away with 'ee, but not afore ye fills the log basket mind."

Jamie was still concerned, but Betsy had appeared to recover from whatever had troubled her and after filling the basket with logs he took his leave, promising to return soon.

Visits to Wheal Jenny also had to be put on hold with Daniel left to liaise between Jamie and his mine captain. Jamie was eager to get back to the mine to see the results of the fall on the ninth level for himself.

* * *

It was Ben and Ginifur who instigated the visit to Penhallow at the end of October. It had been an unusually warm end to September and beginning of October and Ben was keen to bring his horse over to the Tremanyon stables. Ginifur, knowing that Jamie was keen to visit the mine, thought that it would be good for the family to have a few days there together. Dickon and Robyn had understandably been disturbed by the incident at the mine and Ginifur thought that they should pay another visit when everything would be running normally with the miners happily going underground and returning safely at the end of their shifts. Sara and Jean-Louis were busy with preparations for the wedding and it was Dickon who suggested that Marie-Claire went with them.

Jean-Paul had decided not to return to Canada, he was in no hurry to leave Cornwall; and of course he wanted to celebrate his son's wedding and he was enjoying his quiet life on his estate here. There was no reason for Marie-Claire to return to France either, even if the political situation was to make this possible; she had received confirmation that her husband had indeed been executed.

Marie-Claire had become very much a part of life at Tremanyon with both Dickon and Robyn urging her to take them along when she rode around the headland. The daring rescue by Jamie, Jean-Paul and Aidan and the crew from Tremanyon had captured the villagers' imagination, and there was heartfelt sympathy for the beautiful young French woman who had so tragically lost her husband in the revolution across the water. Marie-Claire's warm smile and happy nature ensured her complete acceptance.

The visit to Penhallow was made in the Tremanyon carriage; there were plenty of horses in the stables at Penhallow for them all to ride. Mary Rawe had been informed of their impending arrival and had taken on extra staff; everything was ready for them.

Penhallow was alive with laughter and people and although it could have brought unhappy thoughts to Ben's mind he delighted in having them all around him. Ben had become very fond of Ginifur, and she him. Jamie, of course, was the son he would have chosen for himself and he loved his grandson unconditionally. In truth he also loved young Robyn as a grand-daughter too, and since the incident at Wheal Jenny had become very fond of Marie-Claire. If he was honest with himself, he would have agreed that in the beginning he had resented her arrival in Cornwall and her acceptance by the Tremaynes. But time was the only healer and it wasn't Marie-Claire's fault that Ellen had died. Marie-Claire was sensitive to these feelings and careful to try to ensure that her words and actions were not misconstrued as interference or a wish to remove memories of Jamie's wife or Dickon's mother.

On the morning following their arrival at Penhallow, Ben found Marie-Claire placing a small posy of flowers beneath a portrait of Ellen. She turned round to find him standing behind her.

"Ellen was very beautiful; you must miss her very much."

"Yes, we all do. But Ellen would not want us to dwell in the past. She was always for moving forward, not looking back at what could have been." He smiled at his daughter's face which was smiling back at him and then he looked into Marie-Claire's eyes. "She would have liked you and I am sure that you would have become great friends."

"Thank you. I wish that it could have been so," it was her honest reply. "I really do."

Ben lifted the posy of flowers to his nose. "She loved flowers, did Ellen." He replaced them in front of the portrait. "You're a thoughtful girl, Marie-Claire, and you've had your share of heartache too. No one should have to go through what you have."

It was a turning point in their relationship, they both knew it, and during the next few days Ginifur would smile to herself as she watched them forging a friendship as they wandered around the stables and grounds.

Marie-Claire had been brought up with horses and could discuss equine breeding and lines with the best of them. Jamie came upon the pair of them leaning upon a fence as they studied a new filly foal on its first outing into the field. The filly, at first hesitant to leave her mother's side, twitched nervously, then gaining courage she inched further away until she was kicking her legs with frisky pleasure.

Ben turned to greet him "Hello Jamie, how are things at the mine?"

"Good. I went down to see how they are getting on clearing the ninth level. Davey didn't want to start until I had seen it for myself."

"A bit nerve wracking wasn't it? Don't know I could do it after what you'd been through."

"It wasn't as bad as I thought it would be, actually. Probably because I don't remember anything after taking that first step on the ladder at the top of the shaft." Jamie admitted as he too leaned on the fence. "Nice foal, Ben."

"So. . . What did you see? Help to clear your thoughts did it?"

Jamie turned his back on the field and looked back at the mine buildings standing on the top of the hill. "No doubt about it, the fall wasn't natural. It was caused by a charge laid on the eighth level and, in my opinion, intended to kill me." Marie-Claire shivered at the thought, as Jamie continued. "No way of proving it of course, not without Walter Hawes or one of his companions. At least now Davey can set about following the new lode. It should be a good one Ben. You'll be able to make another trip to Ireland and look for new breeding stock."

"Don't you wonder where it will all end Jamie, lad? Luck's been with you and the Wheal Jenny when others are failing. How long can your luck hold out."

Jamie gave a wry grin. "I'll agree with you Ben. I have been lucky with Wheal Jenny, we all have. Whoever made the first assessments founded a fine mine. Yes there have been closures but look at how the North Downs Consolidated have grown in the last few years and Wheal Vanity and Poldice Mines. Our greatest problem will be the smelting works in Swansea. I am convinced, as others are too I might say, that Anglesey copper supplies will dwindle and that we can, and will, fill that gap. But it is in the smelting that we are falling behind. I am not alone in this thinking. Pascoe Grenfell agrees with me and we have discussed the possibility of a joint venture. As for Wheal Jenny, we must always remember to invest wisely and not take our 'luck' for granted. Our profit this year should keep our shareholders very happy for yet another year."

"Even Robert Fry?"

"Yes, even Mr Robert Fry." Jamie agreed. "I'm not so sure about my brother Beau though."

"I hear that he is short of cash again."

"I'm not surprised. Alf Angrove, the bailiff at Kylyn Farm approached me for a job last week. The farm is falling down around his ears and Beau has just sold the last of the live stock. There's not an animal left on the farm except Alf's chickens. Beau has not paid the mens' wages for weeks and Mother's been helping out. . . but she can't continue."

"Do you think that he would sell the farm?" Ben asked.

Jamie considered the question. It had crossed his mind to ask Beau if he would sell it to him. "It's possible. But I don't know how one would broach the subject."

"It seems a shame to see it getting into such a state. Perhaps Ginifur could suggest she buy it from him if she is already propping the farm up by paying the men."

"It's possible." In fact Jamie thought it a very good idea. "I would be quite happy to buy it for her." Jamie turned to Marie-Claire and changed the subject for the moment. "Are you enjoying this visit to Penhallow?"

"Oh yes. It's wonderful to be able to explore the area on horseback; it is so wild above the mines on the moor."

Jamie laughed. "Your last visit was somewhat taken up with helping Mother with nursing duties and childminding."

"I didn't mind in the least, it was a pleasure to help." Marie-Claire assured him as they moved away from the field and headed towards the house.

Chapter Seven
1795

SARA AND JEAN-LOUIS had a short engagement and were married at the end of February in the Church in Porthcarrow. It was a fine and sunny spring day and the whole village turned out to wish the happy couple well. A reception was held at Tremanyon for those friends and relatives of the families and the following day Sara bid a tearful farewell to her mother with promises to write. The happy couple's honeymoon would be spent at sea on their voyage to Sara's new home.

Ginifur spent a restless few months until she received a letter to say that they had safely arrived in Canada. From here they were to make the journey across the country to the land that Jean-Paul had staked a claim to and built the home that would now be Jean-Louis and Sara's. Sara, like Rebecca, was an adept artist and had spent many hours doing drawings and paintings of their journey, promising to send more when she reached her new home. She also attempted to put Ginifur's mind at rest by telling her that they were at peace with the native Indians, and they had all been delighted to hear that Running Bear had somehow learned of their arrival. He had journeyed to meet them and would travel with them to their new home where he said that he would like to set up his Tepee on the edge of the farm and stay for the summer. The last drawing was one that Sara had sketched of Running Bear; it had been captured during moments whilst he was unawares.

After all this time Ginifur could finally see the face of the man who had saved Richard's life all those years ago and she felt compelled to visit Old Betsy to show her Sara's pictures. Jamie's fear for Betsy's health were not groundless, her health was failing, she now relied on the help she received from the family at Tremanyon and as the year grew to a close Ginifur realised that she had not long to live.

When Betsy could no longer look after herself she finally agreed to be moved to the small dwelling where Liam and Kate started their life at Tremanyon, beside the dog kennels. Ginifur had been of a mind to demolish it but was glad that she had not made the final decision, for Betsy would not have moved in to any other accommodation at Tremanyon.

It was here, with Ginifur and Jamie by her side, that Betsy passed away quietly at three in the morning on the first day of the year in 1796.

Chapter Eight
1796

IT WAS BEAU himself who brought up the subject of Kylyn Farm. Jamie had arrived at Tremanyon to hear raised voices coming from the drawing room. As much as he was tempted to go to his mother's aid, Jamie held back. Ginifur had always been able to fight her own corner, and this skill had not diminished with the passing years. He entered the library and took a seat at the desk, leaving the door ajar, if he felt that she needed his support he would be able to step in quickly.

"You have no idea how expensive it is to maintain a wife and family, Mother. You don't live in the real world at all." Beau stood up defiantly to Ginifur.

"Let me tell you Beau, I have lived in the real world all my life. I have known a life without the benefit of money in my family, when I only had a pair of shoes for Sundays and clothes made from my mother's dresses and, yes, I have also been lucky to live a life where money was never a worry, but I have never taken it for granted and always been aware of how and where it was spent. I have brought up a family of five children Beau, not one; and I have organised the household accounts all my working life and run the estate in your father's absence and since his death. I think that I have a very real understanding of the costs of bringing up a family." Ginifur rounded on him. "Your father left you a very generous allowance to live on and a farm that should generate a good income if run properly. You have a good bailiff at Kylyn, Beau, why are you so short of money? I will not pay the wages or debts at Kylyn any more. I told you last month that it was the last time I would help you. Now you are on your own."

Beau's face turned white as he realised that Ginifur indeed did mean what she said. Then as it sunk in that he was not going to get any financial assistance the colour returned with his anger. "If I had been left my due this wouldn't have occurred. Instead Jamie receives more than he should and beggars me, and you still sit on the bulk of the estate denying me my rights."

"Enough Beau." Ginifur felt her own anger rising to match her sons. "Jamie was left no more than you. In fact less, for he receives no allowance from his father's estate. He has benefited from Adam's will it is true, but he has worked hard to improve upon it. He has worked at Rhosinnis too and continues to help me here at Tremanyon. What Jamie has is well deserved." Ginifur was not seated, preferring to stand as she faced up to her son. "When did you put any effort into Kylyn or the Mill?"

"Effort? Are you suggesting that I actually work?" Beau was stunned by the thought that Ginifur might suggest that he actually participate in physical labour.

"There is no shame in physical labour, Beau. Your own father went out with the fishing boats and unloaded the catch on many an occasion. He also helped with the hay making and at harvest time too, he carried sacks of grain from the threshing floor and helped to build ricks in the mowie. He even helped Ed, at the Mill, carrying sacks of flour. Your father believed that it was essential to really know what effort was put in by those on his estate for his families benefit. Jamie believes the same and you should do so too." But now she came to the major point he had made. "As for Tremanyon. How dare you question your father's decision to leave Tremanyon to me and allow me to decide to whom I shall bequeath it. I might add that I hope that I will have a few more years ahead of me to enjoy my life here and believe me, I will use those years wisely."

Beau decided not to push this point but returned to the previous conversation. "Kylyn will never yield a decent living. Father should have known it; I don't know why he bothered leaving it to me anyway."

Ginifur refrained from pointing out that Rhosinnis had showed a healthy profit since Jamie had returned home, instead continued. "In that case why don't I buy it back?"

That stopped Beau in his tracks, wondering what the catch was. He looked uncertain. He couldn't pay the bills at Kylyn, he had sold off all the livestock, and the grass fields as well as the cornfields were full of weeds. In truth he was looking disaster in the face. "What do you want it for? Don't you have enough to get on with?"

Ginifur sighed. "I don't want Kylyn Farm, Beau, but neither can I stand aside and risk it being lost to the estate."

Beau considered the suggestion. Why shouldn't he take up the offer? Kylyn would be joined on to Tremanyon once more. . . and of course Tremanyon would one day be passed on to him and his son Richard. He really would be able to have his cake and eat it too. "What are you suggesting is a fair offer?" he tentatively asked.

"I don't know, Beau, I haven't given it any thought. If you will consider it then I will ask Daniel to suggest a reputable valuer to advise me. You may wish to do the same."

Beau found himself thinking that things were looking up, but didn't want to look too eager. "I'll think on it."

Ginifur was relieved that her son's anger had diminished. "You should Beau; it's not a decision to make lightly." Beau's heckles were rising again, he was about to snap at her for the continued use of the name Beau, but checked himself in time. "Think it over, Beau, and we'll talk again if you want to take it further."

Beau nodded, hiding his elation. "I'll give it consideration and let you know my decision." Of course there was no decision to make; Beau had already decided to accept her offer.

Ginifur smiled in relief, Beau's anger had subsided. Of course she knew what his answer would be but she was happy for him to save face by allegedly thinking the matter over. "Why don't I get Liam to bring us refreshment?"

Beau's expression gave his feelings away before he masked them with a smile. "No, I must make haste. I promised Richard that we would spend the afternoon together and it is well after noon already." He made for the hall and Ginifur followed him to the front door where he turned to say. "We'll speak again. Goodbye for now, Mother."

Ginifur smiled and with the simple acknowledgement of "Beau," she watched her younger son run down the front steps and waited until he had vanished round the side of the house before turning back into the hall. "And what did you make of that then?" Ginifur gave the library door a light push to reveal Jamie sitting at her desk.

Jamie grinned back at her. "Does nothing escape your notice Ma?"

Ginifur laughed. "I am sure there is much that I miss, but I knew I had left this door firmly closed and I can always tell when you are in the house."

"How?"

"I don't know. I always knew when your father was in the house, I could feel Richard's presence close to me, and I can tell when you are here too." She settled herself in one of the comfortable chairs that Richard had placed in the room. "So. . . what do you make of that conversation? For I am sure that you heard most of it."

"Of course he is going to agree." Jamie paused before continuing. "But you do realise that he believes that it will come back to him in the end, with the rest of Tremanyon."

There was no bitterness in his voice and Ginifur answered. "I notice that you don't ask me if I will indeed leave Tremanyon to Beau."

Jamie's smile was genuine. "Ma, what you will ultimately do with Tremanyon, or who you may bequeath it to, that is your decision alone. And I will accept your judgement when the time comes, knowing that you will have thought it through very carefully. In the meantime, I hope that time is many years hence."

Ginifur shook her head as she fought back a tear. "Oh Jamie! What did I do to be so blessed by two wonderful men in my life? You are so like your father it is almost as if you are one."

"The big question is, if he accepts your suggestion just how long do you think the money will last?"

"I would like to think that he would use some of it to set up in a home of their own. It really isn't good for any of them continuing to live under the influence of Robert and Margery Fry."

"I agree, but I expect that suggestion will be met with objections."

The sound of running feet coming down the stairs attracted their attention and as Dickon flew in to see his father, followed closely by Robyn, and their conversation was brought to a close.

* * *

Beau did indeed accept Ginifur's proposal to bring Kylyn Farm back into the Tremanyon Estate, together with The Mill. Advice was sought and a generous figure, which satisfied Beau, was agreed upon. No one mentioned that it was Jamie who supplied the money, for Ginifur could not raise it on her own and Jamie insisted that it was a gift to her with no ties. Some months later she was relieved to hear that Beau and Clara, with young Richard, had moved out of Killow Barton to a house Beau had purchased in Truro. Beau rode over to give her the news himself. She didn't raise the question as to what he was going to do with his life knowing that this was a subject best not discussed. Daniel brought home news of the entertaining that Beau and Clara gave and it seemed that they were gaining a new circle of friends. Ginifur sincerely hoped that they would at last find some true happiness.

It was this summer that Dickon sailed into Kylyn Cove on his own.

Sandpiper was now kept permanently at Kylyn. After Ginifur's father, Simon, had left Quay Cottage to live at Well Cottage they had sailed the boat round to Kylyn and for a few more years they had regularly sailed together from the cove to go fishing either in Falmouth Bay or Dingerien Bay. Ginifur missed these times that she had shared with her father and for a time the boat was left high and dry until Jamie one day suggested that they went out together. "I think the time has come to pass on your knowledge to Dickon," he suggested, "for I don't think that young Richard will ever set sail in a boat."

Ginifur laughed. "I think that is a safe supposition," she agreed.

The entrance to Kylyn Cove was protected by rocks which ran from The Point, a promontory of land that jutted out into the sea, to the cliff edge. Long ago smugglers had navigated the uncharted entrance to the cove and in each family the secret had been handed down to one person in each generation. In most cases this had been from father to son but Simon, who had learned the secret from his father John, did not have a son and against all objections he had passed on this knowledge to Ginifur. Ginifur had passed it on to Jamie and now he felt that it was time to start teaching Dickon the route through the rocks. Ginifur's grandfather, John Retallick, and his father before him had been the last to be involved in smuggling into Kylyn Cove, until Adam Sawle stumbled on the disused cave and tunnels back in 1756. Adam had been mortally wounded by rifle fire on Kylyn beach, by soldiers sent to arrest them. Ginifur had learned that Adam and his friends were in danger and had gone to warn him. With Richard Tremayne and Liam's help they had managed to get him back to Tremanyon where he died from his wounds.

Ginifur, Jamie and Dickon had enjoyed many hours in *Sandpiper*, but on this particular day Ginifur and Dickon were out alone. Dickon had asked if they could sail into Falmouth Bay and with a good breeze they were there in no time at all. As they rounded the headland with Dickon at the tiller he indicated that he wanted to sail into the Carrick Roads. The Roads were the large body of sheltered water between Falmouth point and Rhosinnis headland. It had been some while since Ginifur had sailed in towards Falmouth and she readily agreed.

Looking upriver to Penryn Ginifur espied a Frigate being towed into mid stream. It was a ship of His Majesty's Navy, and

Ginifur's mind flew back to the day she had sailed out here to see Richard and Liam set off on their voyage to the New World with Jean-Paul de Varron on Admiral Edward Boscawen's ship *The White Rose*.

Dickon had first set sail up the Fal towards Truro but came about as the frigate headed out to the bay and they hove to so that they could sit and watch. His face lit up as he watched the crew scrambling about on the yards, listening to the sails fill with a snap and the ship keel over as she picked up speed as it sailed past them, leaving *Sandpiper* bobbing about in its wake. "Did you see that, Grand-mama? Don't you think that it is a wonderful sight?"

It was indeed an impressive sight and one to kindle an interest in a young boy of Dickon's age. Ginifur's attention was drawn to her grandson. The boy was fast growing into a young man, indeed he was the same age as Jamie had been when he first went to sea. In her minds eyes she could see him now dressed in his midshipman's clothes as she and Richard saw him set sail from Plymouth. Could it be that Dickon too had his mind turned to a career in the Navy? For the first time she realised that she hadn't considered a future for Dickon, assuming that he would go on to Cambridge and she wondered whether Jamie had made the same assumption. They had never talked about Dickon's future and she realised that they should have considered it before now.

"Father sailed to many places during his time in the navy, didn't he? He must have had an exciting life."

Ginifur pulled a wry grin. "A dangerous one too, at times," she reminded him. "It is a dangerous life now as well, I am sure that you have heard us discussing it at home."

But Dickon was too busy concentrating on the ship leaving the estuary to hear Ginifur's remarks and when it had finally broken free into Falmouth Bay he turned their small craft in its wake and headed back around the headland. This time, as at others, Ginifur took the helm to take the boat through the unmarked channel into Kylyn Cove. Dickon handed over the helm readily but, having changed places asked. "When will I be able to bring *Sandpiper* in on my own Grandmother?"

"I should think that you won't have to wait long; actually Jamie was a little younger than you when he first sailed in here unaided. We'll ask your father, shall we?"

Robyn was curled up on the window seat with a book when Ginifur and Jamie entered the drawing room, and they had already begun their conversation before realising it.

"Were you aware that Dickon is showing an interest in a naval career?" Ginifur asked.

"When did this come up?"

"When we sailed out to Falmouth Bay the other day. We watched as one of the ships set sail and it came up. He also wanted to know if he was old enough to sail into Kylyn Cove on his own, I said I would ask you."

Robyn stirred and closed her book. "He is always riding out to the headland to watch the ships coming and going. I'm surprised he hasn't said something before now."

"Has he mentioned joining the Navy to you Robyn?" Jamie obviously was not aware of his son's interest in a career at sea.

"Not directly. I think that he is unsure of your reaction to the suggestion."

"Why?" Jamie was mystified. "I have never thought of myself as unapproachable, he's always come to me on other occasions."

"It's possible that he thinks that you want him to go up to Cambridge. . . or even take over the mine. Personally I wouldn't like him to be in the Navy right now with this war going on, I would rather he was safe home here at Tremanyon. But then I am a woman, I don't think that I crave for adventure or danger."

Ginifur studied her grand-daughter. Robyn too was growing up fast, far more mature than her years too for she had been brought up surrounded by adults and adult conversation and she watched Jamie's face as he tried to take in this new information. "I think that you should take him aside and discuss his future, Jamie. Perhaps it should have been discussed before but I understand how these things can drift on. I remember when you first told us you wanted to join the Navy. Your father and I were understandably nervous for you too and there were times when we feared for your safety. But it was your life, and you had to live it as you wished. However, I am glad that you are now at home in this time of trouble."

Jamie just nodded. "Thank you Mother, and you Robyn, I will have a talk with Dickon, soon, I promise."

After a long talk it was decided that they would look further into a career for him in His Majesty's Royal Navy and Jamie and Ginifur concentrated on revealing the secret passage through the rocks at Kylyn Cove.

* * *

It was to be a summer and autumn of revelations for Jamie; and it was Ginifur who also gave him the news that Jean-Paul was returning to Canada, and that Marie-Claire was planning to go with him.

"That's ridiculous! You've read Sara's letters." Jamie exploded. "Yes, I agree that she seems very happy out there, but she has her husband with her, and a daughter to care for and a babe on the way. There is little or no social life out there, what on earth will Marie-Claire do to occupy herself?"

Ginifur smiled. "I don't know Jamie, but she is a very loyal daughter. . . she will go with Jean-Paul I have no doubt. There really is nothing in Cornwall for her to stay for if Jean-Paul leaves, Jamie, just a large empty house to live in on her own. I can see that returning to their home in Canada to be with her family could easily seem the best option."

With a grunt of disapproval Jamie turned on his heels and strode from the room, leaving Ginifur smiling at the empty space where her son had just stood.

Jamie searched high and low for Marie-Claire, knowing full well that she was still at Tremanyon for her horse was still tethered at the stable. Finally he tracked her down at the bottom of the orchard; he found her standing beside the hedge overlooking the valley towards Rosvarron and the sea. She was watching the mares and their foals enjoying the warmth of the day.

"What is this rubbish I've been hearing about you leaving Rosvarron?" Jamie demanded.

Marie-Claire turned away from her study of the latest additions to the stables. "Father wants to go home, to see Jean-Louis, Sara and Charlotte. I have decided to go home with him."

"It is not your home any longer. You belong here; your home is Rosvarron and Cornwall." Jamie declared.

Marie recovered from her surprise at Jamie's sudden arrival. "I am going home. You forget, I was raised there."

"You were born here." Was the abrupt retort.

"My place is with my family. I owe my father that much at least." Marie struggled to conceal the distress caused by the conversation.

Jamie ignored the flashing eyes; it wasn't the first time that they had a difference of opinion. "Loyalty is an admirable quality, but you are taking this too far Marie-Claire," he raised his voice, startled by the anger he felt towards Jean-Paul. "You are making yourself a prisoner to your feelings of loyalty to Jean-Paul. What on earth is he thinking of, making you go with him?"

Marie-Claire stamped her feet, raising her voice as she rounded on him. "Damn you Jamie. He is not making me do anything. . . can you not see beyond the end of your nose. Yes, I have loyalties to my father. . . I will go with him if I must. But my heart and true loyalties lie elsewhere, were you but to open your eyes to see."

Jamie's anger vanished as if by magic, as he studied Marie-Claire's indignant stance. Raven black ringlets cascaded over her shoulders, the bright glitter of unshed tears in her dark brown eyes and her pink flushed cheeks and even rosier lips. Unexpectedly he realised just how desirable she was and how foolish he had been to attempt to deceive himself into believing that no one else would be able to arouse the feelings that were once more struggling to the surface. As Marie-Claire turned to walk away Jamie reached out to grab her wrist and when she struggled ineffectively, finding it difficult to breath, Jamie pulled her closer. The rapid rise and fall of her breasts drew his attention away from her face, causing her even more discomfort as she recognised the undisguised longing in his eyes.

Jamie felt Marie-Claire's pulse race beneath his fingers wrapped tightly around her wrist, and he raised his eyes to her face. Their eyes met. . . and locked as Jamie reached for her other hand, drawing her ever closer until she could almost feel the emotional charge that existed between them. She felt his hands slowly release their grip, slip about her waist and draw her ever closer as the look of wonder spread across Jamie's face.

Jamie's first kiss was a tentative exploration; Marie-Claire's lips parted in response, her body melting into his embrace. She had waited so long for this moment and as she felt Jamie's tongue flicker across her lips, she also felt a tear escape her eye and tremble briefly on her lashes before running down her cheek. Jamie felt its saltiness and drew away. The look of wonder turning to one of confusion, yet he didn't release her. "I thought. . ."

"You thought what, Jamie?"

Jamie hesitated; he felt her trembling in his arms and knew that he did not want to lose her. He brushed a second tear away as it slowly slid towards her beautiful mouth. "I thought that you. . . that we. . ." He lifted his hand and ran a finger gently across her lower lip and Marie-Claire struggled to maintain her outward calm, wanting Jamie to be sure of himself and his own feelings. Marie-Claire had no such doubts; she had waited for so long for this moment. She had thought that she would be happy to wait and give Jamie the time he needed to grieve for the wife he had loved and so tragically lost; but she couldn't wait any longer. Being so near to Jamie on occasions, but not closer than that, was becoming unbearable. The time had come when she would have to leave. . . unless. . . Marie-Claire looked up into the blue eyes that she loved so much; deep blue eyes set above a straight nose and well defined mouth. The lips that had only a moment ago kissed her lovingly. He was a head and shoulders taller than her, wide at his shoulders and slim waisted with a well-muscled torso. He was a handsome man, as his father was before him, but it was his eyes that captured your attention, showing his every mood; at one moment they would sparkle with happiness but they could equally display his scorn, sadness or simply. . . just kindness. But at this moment Marie-Claire wasn't quite sure what she could see in his eyes. She wanted it to be love. . . "Oh Jamie. . ." she whispered as another tear escaped and she feared that he would turn away. But Jamie took her face in his hands and kissed the tear away before kissing both her eyes, the tip of her nose, then her mouth. When they finally drew apart Jamie placed his hands on her shoulders and held her at arms length. "You cannot go away Marie-Claire."

"Why Jamie? Why?"

His voice was rough, as though he struggled to find the words. "Because you belong here." He felt her stiffen in his hold. "You belong here, Marie-Claire. . . with me." Jamie took in the angle of her head, the sparkle of defiance in her eyes and knew the moment had come. "Because I love you Marie-Claire, and I want to spend the rest of my life with you." His eyes searched her face for a response, and the next moment she was once more in his arms and he could feel the answer in their next kiss.

Ginifur was naturally delighted, and had only been waiting for Jamie to realise how much Marie-Claire meant to him. Dickon too was delighted, as was everyone at Tremanyon, Rosvarron, Porthcarrow and the whole peninsula and they all waited for the news of when the wedding would be held. Jean-Paul put his return to Canada on hold, declaring that he would not allow anyone else to stand in his place to give his daughter away in marriage and the news that Jamie and Marie-Claire were to wed was immediately sent to Jean-Louis and Sara. Of course they all knew that they would not be at the wedding, but the reply was full of congratulations and good wishes for their future.

But the biggest revelation was still to come.

Chapter Nine
1797

JAMIE AND MARIE-CLAIRE Marie-Claire were married on 26th June 1797, Jamie's birthday.

Never was there a wedding at Porthcarrow Church such as that of Jamie Tremayne and Marie-Claire de Varron; not in the years before nor in all the years to come. It would be safe to say that anyone who could walk or ride a donkey or pony came from miles around to witness the celebration. Outlying farmers offered free rides on their carts to those who could not walk and many left their homes early to ensure a good viewing point along the street outside of the Church. Some set themselves up along the routes to and from Tremanyon and others waited patiently along the road from Rosvarron to get a glimpse of the bride on her way to the Church.

John-Paul had converted to the English Church when he married his wife Lady Caroline, Jean-Louis and Marie-Claire had been brought up in this faith and although Marie-Claire had been considering converting to the Catholic Church since her marriage to Pierre, her life had been turned upside down by the revolution in France and she had not gone through with it.

Jamie was the first to arrive at the Church with Daniel as his support. A great cheer rose from the crowd as he arrived in the open carriage decorated for the occasion and as he alighted another cheer caused him to pause and acknowledge it with a bow and a wave. He looked splendid in his formal attire. The blue short fronted coat with long tails was embroidered at the front under which he wore a ruffled shirt. His breeches were a lighter blue and. tucked into his long boots. Alighting from the carriage Jamie paused long enough to accept the good wishes of those nearest him, whilst waiting for the next carriage to arrive. Ginifur followed in the enclosed Great Coach with Ben Nancekivel, Dickon and Robyn. Robyn looked delightful in her dress for the occasion, the deep rose gown embellished with beads and embroidery had been a gift from Marie-Claire. Dickon wore a miniature outfit of his father's but without the embellishment. Ginifur was at her elegant best, once more favouring green. The tightly fitting emerald green bodice fitted over a full skirt with an over mantle to match. The long sleeves fitted to her elbows and then flared beautifully to show off her long fingered hands. The bodice and skirt were embroidered in matching thread and beads. If Jamie was a splendid sight it would be true to say that Ginifur looked radiant and it was remarked that she didn't look anywhere near her age. "She couldn't have looked more radiant if she had been the bride herself." Someone was heard to say. To see Jamie so happy was enough for Ginifur and she smiled at the well-wishers who were waiting at the Church gate. Jamie moved forward to assist his mother as she stepped down from the carriage, accepting the compliments from the crowd gracefully before he offered her his arm, gave another wave to the delighted crowd and led his family into the Church.

Rachel and Rebecca, with many willing hands, had decorated the Church with flowers and their fresh summer scent filled the Church. All the seating had been allocated for the guests and Toby and Aidan had been given the responsibility of directing the guests to their seats. Jamie had asked Beau if he would like to take a part in his marriage service but Beau declined. His refusal was given with good grace, but a refusal it was and Jamie wished that he had accepted. However Beau did accept the invitation to the wedding on behalf of himself, Clara and young Richard, and this pleased Ginifur who thought that he would even refuse this.

Rachel and Rebecca and their children were the next to arrive in Daniel's coach and they too received a welcome from the crowd. Both the young women were well respected in the district and Rebecca especially for all her work teaching the young children. Rebecca raised her hand as pupils past and present called out to her. Dressed in the latest fashion the sisters complimented each other well, Rachel with her dark hair and striking features and Rebecca with her pale blonde curls and pink and white complexion. In the Church they spoke briefly to their husbands, Toby and Daniel, before taking their seats near the front of the Church and settling the children.

One by one and two by two the Church began to fill; the two most notable guests being Fanny Boscawen, Jamie's self-elected God Mother still known as Lady Falmouth although their son George had now inherited the title of Viscount Falmouth, and Martin Harris with his wife: Martin was still the standing member of parliament for Tregony.

The sound of cheering outside announced the fact that the bride was arriving from Rosvarron. Marie-Claire also arrived in an open carriage, sitting next to her father Jean-Paul de Varron. It took some minutes for them to make the last few hundred yards as the well wishers crowded so near that she was fearful someone would be hurt. Marie-Claire's face clearly displayed her happiness and her cheeks had a natural rosy glow without the aid of artificial colour; she wore just a touch of pink on her lips. Her neatly shaped eyebrows and long dark lashes framed a pair of dark brown eyes above a small straight nose which she must have inherited from her mother for Jean-Paul and Jean-Louis had very aquiline noses. Her mouth was wide and her lips full and generous; they were well shaped and always looked as though she was going to burst out laughing. Marie-Claire was laughing now; this was the happiest day of her life.

Robyn was waiting for Marie-Claire in the Church entrance, it was the first time that she had seen the wedding dress and let out a gasp as she first saw it. Unusually for the time Marie-Claire had chosen very simple lines for the dress which showed her figure to its best advantage. It was made of the finest pale pink silk, but the whole dress had been embroidered with silver and gold thread and from the shoulders fell a long train of the best Flemish lace. Robyn teased out any obvious folds in the lace and then took her place a few steps behind Marie-Claire and Jean-Louis as they made their way between the pews filled with family and friends towards the front of the Church where Jamie waited patiently with Daniel and the Reverend White.

Jamie curbed his desire to turn around to see his bride make her way towards him and when she finally stood beside him and he looked down into her eyes, which sparkled with happiness, he smiled. To Marie-Claire, Jamie's smile said more that a thousand words could have ever done and she answered him like for like.

The wedding service was all that could be desired and when they gave their solemn vows there was not a dry eye in the Church. The honourable Reverend White, being so well acquainted with the couple was happy to perform the marriage service, and it showed; even Beau's late arrival with his wife and son did not disturb the flow of the proceedings.

Accompanied by a peel of bells Jamie and Marie-Claire left the Church as man and wife to a tumultuous reception in the street outside. It seemed that everyone wanted to wish the couple well. As Annie Driscoll was overheard saying. "It is a fairytale wedding to end a fairytale story of a handsome sea captain rescuing a beautiful maiden in distress."

To enable the villagers to celebrate the day Ginifur and Jean-Paul had arranged for an ox to be roasted over a fire pit on the green and tables filled with simple foods and deserts to accompany it. The local inn keepers had been paid enough to keep the beer flowing for everyone to have a good time and there was ginger beer and herb and fruit cordials for the young ones.

At Rosvarron the food and drink was more elaborate. Gourmet creations were accompanied by Champagne and fine French wines. The weather, being kind, allowed guests to wander about both inside and out but Rosvarron was a larger house than Tremanyon and there was seating for all in the Great Hall when the time arrived for them to dine.

As Ellen before her, Marie-Claire resisted Jamie's suggestion of a honeymoon, insisting that it was not safe to travel on the continent and all she wanted was to spend a few days, without interference from Wheal Jenny, at Rhosinnis. . . their new home.

This was easily accomplished as Ben Nancekivel had not returned to Rhosinnis since Ellen's death. He now lived permanently at Tremanyon where he and Ginifur had found companionship after the loss of their loved ones. Dickon too, had not yet returned to Rhosinnis. The tutor that Jamie had hired to continue on from the teaching by Ginifur and Rebecca also lived at Tremanyon and tutored both Dickon and Robyn in the room set aside for their studies.

When interviewed Josiah Roach had made it quite clear that he did not believe that a girl should be given as much education as a boy and that, although he was happy to tutor Dickon to a standard that would be necessary for entry to Cambridge, he wasn't happy to give this amount of knowledge to Robyn. But Josiah had not come across any family like the Tremaynes and particularly Ginifur. She made it clear that Robyn was to have as much education as she desired and Jamie was quite blunt about it. . . Josiah would teach both children or none. The decision was his.

With no other offers of employment available to him at that time, certainly not with the remuneration on offer at Tremanyon, Josiah accepted the position and was surprised to find what an adept pupil and quick learner Robyn was.

The celebration at Rosvarron would go on well into the night, but after the wedding feast Aidan and Prue collected the two 'live in' girls from the village celebrations and returned to Rhosinnis to ensure that everything was ready for the master to return with his bride.

Jamie had asked Ginifur if she would like to supervise the decorating of the master bedroom, as a surprise for Marie-Claire. Previously it had been furnished to Ellen's requirements and Jamie felt that they needed to start 'a new page'.

Ellen's choice of furniture had been influenced by the Nancekivel family home where the furniture was large, dark and heavy. Although Marie-Claire had made no comment on the existing furnishings Ginifur felt quite sure that her taste for interior design would be quite different.

Ginifur had studied France in her lessons with her Grandmother. Indeed she had been extremely well educated in her youth and one of the many surprises that Richard was to experience as he grew to know and love the girl who would become his second wife. It was Ginifur who had given Rachel and Rebecca their early learning, Jamie, Beau and Sara too and finally she had begun to teach Dickon and Robyn as well. Ginifur not only spoke French she had studied French customs, architecture and history. She was aware that French furniture was not as heavy as the current trend for English furnishings. Table and chair legs were much finer, colours lighter and bedroom furniture often even painted. . . and they loved the use of mirrors.

Ginifur delighted in her task and learned that it was even possible to pick up some articles of French furniture from aristocrats who had managed to ship furniture out of the country in the early months of the revolution; when it was easier to make an exit from the country and before the ransacking of their large and wealthy dwellings. Some of these exiles were now being forced to sell their possessions in order to live, for they had not reckoned on such a lengthy stay and were rapidly running out of money due to their assets in France having been confiscated by the New Order.

With Daniels help, Ginifur had managed to purchase an elegant painted bedroom suite. It was painted cream and was gilded with gold leaf, in the current Louis style. The size of the wardrobe was lightened by the fact that the whole centre section was mirrored. There was a matching triple mirrored dressing table on finely carved legs, a matching dressing stool, a large bed with carving to the bed head and bed end, and to complete it two matching bedside tables. Ginifur's final purchase, to complete the picture, was a comfortable boudoir chair upholstered in rose pink damask. The decoration of the room Ginifur kept simple, using a mixture of creams and greens and using a deep pink as an accent. Naturally she kept Jamie fully informed of her suggestions for furnishing and decoration but he was adamant that it should be a bedroom that would surprise and delight Marie-Claire.

Indeed it did just that.

Having arrived at Rhosinnis Barton to be welcomed by Jamie's staff members, they enjoyed a comfortable hour in the drawing room whilst they discussed the events of the day before Jamie instructed Prue that they would retire.

Making their way up the central staircase, not as wide as the one at Tremanyon where two crinoline dresses could easily pass, but wide enough for them to climb together, Jamie indicated the door to the bedroom that was to be his and Marie-Claire's. Ginifur had suggested that it should be the seaward facing room, with light flooding the room from the south, Jamie and Ellen's room had faced west.

Of course, Jamie had seen the completed room before, but that was in daylight. Even he wasn't prepared for the impact it would have when lit with candles and lamps, with the scent from bowls of summer flowers filling the room as they had done at the Church.

It was a large room and the effect was stunning, even Jamie had to admit that, but Marie-Claire just stood there with her hand to her mouth and Jamie began to have doubts.

"Do you not like it? You can change it you know."

Marie-Claire found her voice. "Change it! Never. How on earth did you manage to accomplish this?"

Jamie grinned as he admitted. "I didn't. It is entirely Mother's idea, I just gave her the brief to make a special bedroom for us to start our married life in. This is the result of her efforts. She has scoured far and wide for everything that you see in this room." Jamie was rightly proud of his mother.

Marie-Claire walked to the centre of the room and slowly turned full circle. "You don't have to tell me, I can see," she whispered in awe as she took in the blue and gold Sevres vases on the gilt shelves, the porcelain oil lamps on the side tables, the French watercolours of the French countryside on the walls. There was French lace to decorate the windows and the bed was covered with imported silks and satin. She turned to Jamie.

"Does it please you?" he asked.

"Oh Jamie. . . It is just perfect. Your mother has accomplished something that I would never believe possible here in England."

She spread her arms wide as she twirled around and pronounced, with a twinkle in her eye. "It is truly a room to make love in."

Jamie feigned astonishment at her brazen declaration then, laughing, he took her in his arms saying. "Then, come here you brazen hussy and let us see if Mother has managed to weave enough magic into it."

Later as they lay satiated by their lovemaking, Marie-Claire lay with her head settled into the curve of Jamie's shoulder and ran her fingers through the dark curls of hair on his chest. Gradually her fingers worked their way downwards over his flat belly until she felt him stir again, turn towards her and once again take her in his arms.

"Does it worry you?" she suddenly asked.

He pulled far enough away to be able to look deep into her eyes. "Does what worry me?"

Marie-Claire lowered her eyes, afraid to see the answer. "That there was someone else in my life. . . before you?"

Jamie raised her chin, forcing her to look back at him. "Does it worry you, that there was someone else in my life. . . before you?"

"Oh no Jamie. We wouldn't have Dickon if there wasn't. Oh no, not for a moment."

He smiled. "Then you have your answer don't you; but to answer your question, no Marie-Claire, it doesn't worry me." He took her face in his hands and kissed her lightly on her full mouth. "What came before, as you put it, is in the past. The happiness we will share together in the years to come is what we must look to, for I believe that we were brought together by destiny." Marie-Claire was suddenly still. "What's the matter now?" he asked as he moved away from her raising himself on one arm to look at her with her dark ringlets spread across the pillow.

"I was remembering the time when we were children. You didn't know it back then, but I adored you as a child and my dreams were that I would marry you when I was old enough. When Mother died and Father took us to Canada I believed that my heart had been broken and that I would never marry. I think that I have Pierre to thank for bringing me home to you."

Jamie was inclined to agree and running his fingers between the fullness of her breasts he felt a quiver of anticipation rising in her once more. Jamie moved over her prostate body, taking a nipple between his lips he teased it gently with his tongue until he felt her body squirm beneath him and her legs twined about his buttocks increasing his desire for her once more. Jamie had loved Ellen but, although she had attempted to participate in their love making, her attempts were hampered by her disability and her natural reserve.

Marie-Claire had no inhibitions and her love for Jamie had been kept hidden since the moment she realised that the love she had had for her childhood companion had never died, just lay hidden. Looking back at the moment that Jamie had arrived at the convent at la Croix, it had seemed that it was only to be expected that Jamie, her childhood knight in shining armour, had turned up to rescue her. It had taken much longer for Jamie to realise that he loved her in return, but the wait had been worth it even though she had to keep her feelings hidden.

Now on the night of her marriage, all the love that she had kept bottled up was released and she gave herself to him with abandon. Once more he could feel the passion rising in her as her body rose to join with his and he felt that his life was now complete.

The honeymoon period for Jamie and Marie-Claire Tremayne lasted three glorious days as they enjoyed uninterrupted solitude. Their only contact with people was the staff at Rhosinnis and even there Prue ensured that these meetings were kept to a minimum. Prudence not only prepared all their meals, with the assistance of the kitchen girls, she served them too and Aidan now in charge of the stables made sure that the horses were always ready when required but quietly slipped away before they had realised that he was around.

It was idyllic June weather and Jamie and Marie-Claire discovered afresh this unique peninsula of land betwixt river and sea with it's mixture of valleys and fertile land, winding creeks beside mysterious woods, beautiful coastal scenery and enchanting coves and beaches. On horseback and foot they began to see it as if for the first time, and at night they found new delights to share in the room that Ginifur had prepared for her son and daughter-in-law.

But this idyllic period in Jamie's life was about to come to an end.

On the first day of July three men rode in to Tremanyon.

* * *

Ginifur had risen earlier than usual and completed her tour of the house. Even after she had married Richard she never relinquished her duties as housekeeper. She gained great satisfaction from ensuring that everything ran smoothly in the house; from the linen room on the first floor to the still room in the basement Ginifur knew every room in Tremanyon, every nook and cranny, even the staff rooms at the top of the house. She still kept the household records too, of course, but had handed over those of the estate to Jamie.

Of all the household duties, the one that gave her the most pleasure was to pick and arrange the flowers in the rooms of this beautiful manor house. The Georgian Manor had been built by Richard in 1750 after the fire had burned the original one to the ground and Ginifur had been employed to help with Richard and Annabelle's daughters.

The last task of her tour of the house was to make a note of the flower arrangements that needed replacing and, with these in mind, Ginifur picked up a light shawl, pushed her feet into a pair of sensible shoes kept under the coat pegs in the side hall for this purpose, and made her way to the walled garden.

She paused for a moment by the steps at the front door and looked out to sea. On first impressions she had thought that the beautiful weather they had enjoyed of late was set to last. The sky was blue, as it had been for many days now, and the light fluffy clouds not an unusual sight on a fine day. But the sea had changed hue. It had lost its sparkle and colour. Gone were the cobalt and jade and today the sea was tinged with grey and speckled with white as the white horses blew across it in the stiff breeze; along the horizon ran a thick dark line, as if an artist had run a stick of charcoal along its length and Ginifur knew that the weather was about to change.

She looked up at the beech trees, sunlight filtered through the delicate canopy of leaves. Old Tom always said that the leaves turned upside down in the wind if it was going to rain, but the breeze as yet wasn't strong enough to cause them to stir. Old Tom had retired long ago, he and Netty, their old cook, had lived out their last years in Primrose Cottage, in the copse just below Tremanyon's lower lawn.

Passing along the drive Ginifur noticed that the small door in the centre of the large wooden gates was open. She knew that at least Mark Sawle had arrived and was already at work.

Mark was the younger son of Samuel Sawle, Adam's father. When Sam had become too old to continue running the stables Ginifur had given him the cottage that Adam had left to her. Sam too had passed away in the last twelve months and this had added to Ginifur's feelings of bereavement; now Mark lived there with his wife and his son' Luke and Seth, and Seth's wife.

Of course, she realised that if Richard had not died so tragically things would have been different; in him she had lost her greatest friend, her lover and her soul mate. In spite of being surrounded by a loving family there were times when she felt very alone and feared this loneliness would grow with the passing of the years into old age. She smiled to herself; some people thought that she was old already. Maybe she was, but in her heart she was still young and her mind as quick and agile as it had ever been.

Ginifur stepped through the gate and stood for a moment admiring the gardens. The kitchen gardens had never failed to fill her heart with joy. Neat paths edged with box ran vertically and horizontally across the garden dividing it into segments that were regularly rotated to ensure that the crops were always grown on fresh ground. In the far corner, protected by the wall from the south easterly winds, were old Tom's beehives. Mark's son, Seth, now looked after the bees as part of his garden duties; she could see him now with his smoker as he puffed it gently into the hive to settle the bees before he checked them.

Along the wall at the top of the garden ran the south facing glass houses and in the corner the potting shed. To her left the large fig tree filled the corner spreading its glossy leaves and ripening fruit.

This year the cutting flowers were grown on the far side of the garden, near the door that led out to the orchard, and Ginifur made her way down the shingle path between the flower covered arches that spanned it. Half way across she paused where Mark was hoeing between the plants. "Good morning Mark." Ginifur greeted him as he turned and touched his cap. "Everything is beautiful as usual."

"Thank you Ma'am. What is it today? Flowers or an order from the kitchen?"

"A bit of both Mark. Lorna will need some potatoes and a selection of vegetables for dinner please, and I could do with some honey to make a salve. I will pick the herbs I need for that myself then cut a selection of flowers for the house."

"There be plenty there." Mark smiled broadly. "I knows how you love 'em so."

"I know you do, Mark. Thank you."

"S'pleasure Ma'am." He glanced up at the sky. "Weather's 'bout t' change I'm thinkin'."

Ginifur answered him with a smile, agreeing that she felt that he was correct and passed on to pick her flowers and herbs.

It was as she made her way back through the small door that she first heard the horses and carriage, and she shivered at the memory of hearing another carriage hurrying home with Richard from the New World. She had been on this very spot when she heard it. Well, this time she wasn't waiting for any one special and she didn't hasten her return. Nevertheless she was nearing the front door when she was surprised to see Daniel's coach draw around the bend in the drive.

As Daniel opened the door and stepped down Ginifur gave him a wide smile. "This is a surprise, it's an early call for you Daniel." The smile left her face as she spied Davey Rawe and a stranger in the carriage. "It's not trouble at the mine is it?"

Daniel Franks had a grim expression. "Not exactly, but I am afraid that we will have to disturb Jamie's few days of peace and quiet."

"Is it absolutely necessary Dan?

"I am afraid it is." A lawyer, Daniel's face usually gave no hint of his emotions, thus his facial expression now gave Ginifur cause for alarm.

"Can you not tell me?" she asked.

"I would rather wait till Jamie is here. Can Joe ride out to Rhosinnis for him do you think?"

Liam had appeared at the door and heard the last part of the conversation. "I'll go," he said as he took the last step. He looked at Ginny, gripped her arm and added. "I won't be long. See t' y'ur visitors, looks like one of 'em needs y'ur attention," and he headed towards the stables.

Liam's comment drew her attention to the occupants in the carriage and looking past Davey Rawe, who looked grim but otherwise his usual robust self, she studied the other man slumped back in the seat with little colour in his face. He was very thin and indeed did not look well. "I think that you had all better come inside Daniel." Taking her basket of flowers and herbs with her Ginifur led the way up the steps. In the hall she made her way through the house to the room where she mixed her potions and tonics.

Daniel and Davey helped the young man from the carriage and through the house as they followed Ginifur to her room where she placed the basket on the floor and turned to view her patient. "What is the matter with him?" she glanced from Daniel to Davey.

"I would think, for the most part, it has been caused by exposure from living rough on the moor. . . and starvation," was Daniel's observation. "Of course I could be completely wrong, but I don't think so."

"When he turned up at Penhallow, Mary took pity on him. She boiled some water for un t' 'ave a bath and gave 'im some broth while I rode t' Truro for Mr Franks." Davey added. "His clothes were naught but rags 'n she found some of mine. They'm a bit baggy on 'im mind."

They were indeed too large and served to exaggerate his thinness. But thin he really was and Ginifur could see the bones in his arms, which gave an indication of the rest of his body condition. "How long has he been living rough?"

"For the last three years. Since the collapse at the mine." Dan informed her and Ginifur glanced uneasily at his face but he didn't further the subject.

"And he's been hunting and scavenging for food since then?" she looked to Davey for an answer.

"As I understand it, aye."

The young man had slumped in the chair, seemingly uninterested in what was going on around him. Ginifur put a hand to his shoulder. "What is your name?"

Slowly he raised his head to look up at Ginifur. Hazel eyes looked blankly at her from deep hollow sockets. His cheeks were sunken and his pallor unhealthy. He was starving, but he must be fed carefully and slowly if he was to recover. "Daniel. . . Poppy should be in the kitchen, please go and ask her to prepare some warm oats will you? And ask her to add some honey and milk, not water. We must keep his food simple at the beginning, nothing too rich. It will take time to build him up, I fear." Daniel left the room to do her bidding. "Do you know his name, Davey?" she asked when he had gone.

"He said 'is name was Fred when 'ee came t' the 'ouse. Didn' give a surname, just Fred. Will 'ee be alright d'ye think?"

"It's difficult to say, Davey. It depends on how it is affecting his organs; they can fail due to starvation." Ginifur turned to Fred. "I would like to examine your eyes, is that alright?" and she received a slight nod of the head, no more.

Ginifur studied his nails; brittle and broken, whilst flecks of white suggested he was short of calcium. She felt his pulse, timing it with the watch that she had received from Annabelle and Richard on her eighteenth birthday, always pinned to her dress. His pulse was both weak and erratic. She lifted his eyelid to see his eyes; they lacked lustre, the whites tinged with yellow showing signs of jaundice. Fred was a very sick young man. "He needs lots of rest and good food. But if you don't know him, why did he come to you for help?"

Davey looked uneasy. "Well. . . 'ee did'n. Not for food or 'elp. . . that is."

Ginifur was puzzled. "Then why come to you?"

Davey looked down at Fred before answering. "I'd like t' answer ye Mrs Tremayne, really I would. But I reckon as 'ow we should wait fur Captain Tremayne t'get 'ere. Mr Franks. . . well 'ee said Cap'n should be the first t'be told."

Of course Ginifur was concerned. She just knew there was something seriously wrong, but attempted to put Davey at ease by assuring him that it was alright, she quite understood.

Daniel chose this moment to return with the bowl of warm oats and honey, which he placed on the table with a spoon. Fred looked at it but couldn't raise the energy to pick up the spoon let alone feed himself. Ginifur took pity on him. "Would you like me to help you?" Fred extended his hand towards the bowl briefly before nodding his head. It was a slow job; Fred was starving but had little energy to eat. Luckily the oats were warm, smooth and sweet and slid down without him having to chew but, nevertheless, Liam had returned with Jamie as he took his last mouthful. When he had finished the last spoonful he lent back in the chair and smiled his thanks.

Jamie took a look at the stranger then turned to Daniel. "What's all this about, Dan?"

Daniel didn't answer immediately, forcing Jamie to look again at the man in the chair, thinking to himself that the poor man was in a dire way. "Dear God, he is thin. Where on earth has he been living?" Daniel and Davey still said nothing but were looking down on the young man. Well Jamie supposed that he was young. In truth at this moment he didn't look particularly young. But if he did. . . Jamie looked at him again. If he did. . . he would look like. . . who?

"Do I know you?" The man looked back at him and nodded.

"Do you work at the Wheal Jenny?" Fred shook his head, the effort was too much and he slumped back into the chair. Jamie glanced at Daniel, "Dan this is ridiculous. Who is he?"

"No Jamie, I want you to remember yourself."

Frustrated Jamie studied Fred again. Yes he was sure he had met him before. . . but he hadn't looked like this then. Jamie struggled until a moment flashed before his eyes. . . Yes. . . he had ridden into Tremanyon on a hired hack, and he had worn a hat pulled well down on his head. "You are the man who brought me the message that Davey Rawe wanted me to go to the Wheal Jenny," he said in astonishment before turning to Daniel and Davey. "What on earth is he doing here now, and in this condition?"

Daniel looked down at the young man. "Fred, we are going to tell your story to Captain Tremayne. I want you to rest here for a while." Fred nodded. Dan turned to Ginifur. "Is that alright with you?"

"Of course, I'll get a blanket to cover him. The more rest he can get the better," she opened the door. "Go on, you can go into the library with Jamie. I'll see you in a little while."

Jamie led the way to the library where he indicated the two easy chairs to Daniel and Davey and took the chair behind the desk for himself. "Come on you two; tell me what all this is about."

Daniel took a deep breath. "He says his name is Fred. . . it might be, it might not, but he turned up at Penhallow three days ago asking for you by name; Captain Tremayne. He became quite distraught when he learned that you were not there. Mary took pity on him and called Davey back from the mine and he persuaded him to tell him his tale. Then, whilst Davey set off to fetch me Mary produced a bath, clean clothes and some food followed by a long sleep on their bed. When I arrived he felt strong enough to tell me why he had come. His story is that he needed work and approached Henry Bishop for a job at the Magdalene. He was first turned away, but then he ran into Walter Hawes who said that he was recruiting a few men for a job and when it was finished he would be made the new mine captain for Wheal Jenny and then he would be able to give him a job there. It couldn't be simpler; all he had to do was to deliver a message to Captain Tremayne." Daniel paused to see that Jamie was following him. "This done, his job was over, and he only met the other men once and not told what their particular job was to be. Walter Hawes recruited them with the promise of work too. Walter was to stay hidden on the moors until everything was carried out, and it was here that Fred went the day after the mine collapsed and learned of the blast and attempt on your life. Some days later Davey found Walter and learned the truth of what had happened and when we arrived Fred had hidden outside and Walter told him that he had made a deal with us and would give evidence against Henry Bishop. One night, in the hovel on Bodmin moor, Fred heard horses approaching. Quickly he picked up anything that was his and left, keeping close to the walls where he was in the dark he hid in the scrub at the back of the abandoned herdsman's hut. Hiding among some furze bushes he saw Henry

Bishop arrive with the other two recruits and heard raised voices followed by arguing and shouting. From the noise it was obvious that a fight had broken out and the next thing he saw was the two thugs carry Walter Hawes from the hut followed by Henry Bishop. Keeping enough distance not to be seen, but enough to see what they were up to, Fred watched as they dropped the unfortunate man into an abandoned shaft. Returning to the hut, having first taken everything out of the dwelling to make it appear that no one had been sheltering there recently, they left." Jamie was listening intently, shaking his head now and then when some detail disturbed him, and Daniel ploughed on. "Fred hid all night and in the dawn went back to the shaft and called down hoping that Walter was not dead. He had no reply but wasn't satisfied with that and when it was dark 'borrowed' a length of rope from the Magdalene mine. He had dropped a rock down the shaft and was sure that it didn't go very deep, probably just a testing shaft. The following day he climbed down and confirmed to himself that Walter Hawes was indeed dead. Shortly after this he heard that the two thugs had died in a drunken brawl and Fred decided that his own days were numbered. He moved further onto the moor and found shelter in the rocks and since then he has been living on anything that he could catch or pick." Daniel paused again.

"So what brought him to your door, Davey?" Jamie turned to his mine captain who till now had not spoken.

"T' tell the truth 'ee was quite delirious and come t' Penhallow thinkin' 'ee might find you there. He thought that 'ee was dyin' 'n did'n 'ave long t' live. Got in quite a state when Mary said you was at Tremanyon 'cos 'ee would never 'ave made it that far on foot. Then it all comes out. We put un up for the night while Hal saddled a horse for me 'n 'im 'n we rode t' Truro to fetch Mr Franks. Mr Franks brought the carriage to Panhallow, then us came on 'ere."

"Did this young man speak to you Dan?"

Daniel took up the story again. "Yes, he confirmed everything that Davey told me. As far fetched as it sounds, I believe him. He had described how to find the shaft where Walter Hawes body lies, got Davey to draw a map as he directed him. I think that he really believes that he will die; he is indeed a very sick young man. He wants to make a statement of the facts behind the collapse and the names of those involved, even if it does implicate himself in the charges. He has lost everything, he has nothing more to lose and he feels that his days are numbered anyway.

Jamie pushed his chair away from the desk. "Has he mentioned anyone else?"
Daniel thought about his answer. "Walter Hawes told him that Robert Fry was with Henry Bishop when he was promised his reinstatement as mine captain at Wheal Jenny."
Jamie stared out of the window. The wind was getting up and rain beginning to roll in from the west. "Beau? My brother?"
Daniel was quick to reassure him. "No Jamie. There has been no mention of your brother."
"How could he have not known?" Jamie's voice was low, his tone subdued as he tried to dismiss the thought that his brother might be implicated in an attempt on his life.
"You must put it out of your mind, Jamie. As far as I know there is no evidence to suggest that Beau might be involved."
"And if he was?"
"Then we will have to cross that bridge when and if we get to it."
"So what is the next step?"
"On your instructions, I will take a statement from Fred and present it to the High Sheriff. I expect that he will order Fred to be placed under arrest but I will argue that he is the only witness to the crime and in his present state of health he would die in days if he was imprisoned in Bodmin. It is possible that we might be able to come to an agreement." Daniel explained.
Jamie indicated that he agreed and followed up. "And if you can keep him out of prison, where would he live?"
"'ee can live with we." Davey interrupted.
Jamie was surprised by the strength of Davey's answer. "You would do this? Why?"
"T' tell the truth Cap'n, I don' believe 'ee knew what he was getting into, just desperate for work. Now 'ee 'ave lost everythin', 'is family included. His cheeld died of a fever 'n 'is wife was found dead in the 'arbour at Mevagissey."
As Jamie paced the room Daniel and Davey kept their silence. They had had time to consider and talk over the information that Fred had given them. Jamie needed time to reflect on this himself. Once again Jamie paused at the window as he stared out at the steadily worsening weather. "Alright Daniel; do what you have to do. However, if they agree to bail and allow him to live at Penhallow with Davey, I insist that guards are placed on the property day and night. Not to keep him in, you understand, but to keep others out. If his life is in danger now, how much greater

is that risk once he has made a statement and these allegations are public knowledge."

Daniel agreed that this would probably be a necessary precaution and asked if Jamie wished to be present when he took Fred's statement.

"Yes I would. I hope I would be able to recognise if his story is true or false. Where do you propose to take the statement?"

"If it's acceptable to you and your mother, we could do it here. I would like him to have a good sleep, he is exhausted. That and a little more food will help and by tomorrow I hope that he can go through it again." Daniel suggested.

"I'll have a word with Mother. But I don't anticipate a refusal. Will you stay with him Davey?"

"If ye'll let me, yes I will." Davey declared without hesitation.

"In that case I'll ask her to come in here and we will repeat your story for her. The ultimate decision must be hers alone."

Ginifur was, of course, stunned by the news and agreed that her initial impression of the man was not that he was a danger to them. She was naturally disturbed at the information that Robert Fry was involved and that there could be even a slightest possibility that Beau might be implicated. She suggested that the old school room in the basement be equipped for Davey and Fred to sleep in; the staff sitting room was next door to it. It was quiet in the basement and the fewer people who knew that he was here the better.

Liam and Aidan, with Davey's help, soon fixed up something for them both to sleep on whilst Ginifur organised some more food for their guest. After Ginifur had fed Fred, as before, Liam and Davey helped him down to the bed that was made up with clean sheets and warm blankets. They helped him to remove his outer clothing, leaving him to sleep in his shirt. Fred's head had hardly touched the pillow and he was fast asleep.

Liam looked down at the man who could have sent Jamie to a certain death and shook his head, then turned to Jamie's mine captain. "Come Davey, let's get Lorna and Poppy to give you some food whilst I go and find Jamie and Mrs Tremayne."

A good night's sleep and a little good food had already improved Fred's condition. He managed to spoon some of the oats and honey for himself and hold a cup of warm tea. He clutched on to Davey's arm for support as they made their way to the library where Daniel and Jamie were waiting for them and then Davey left the room. Ginifur had been briefed about the events which had brought about

Fred's present circumstances the previous night, now she sat in with Jamie whilst Daniel took Fred's statement which implicated Henry Bishop and Robert Fry in what they now believed to be an attempt on Jamie's life, the murder of young John Rawe and ultimately that of Walter Hawes. It was also quite conceivable that he was connected to the death of the two thugs who had died in the drunken brawl; but there was no evidence to prove that.

Ginifur voiced her concern that, however slim it may be, Beau could have known of the plans for the Wheal Jenny mine and Jamie without warning him. But there was nothing in Fred's statement to suggest that Beau was aware of his father-in-laws connection with the events at Wheal Jenny. However with the best will in the world it was difficult to believe that Beau had no knowledge at all.

Daniel was very patient with Fred whilst taking his statement, giving him plenty of time to consider what he was saying and reading it back to him frequently to ensure that he knew exactly what was being recorded. When they finished Fred was exhausted and helped back to his bed in the basement where he fell fast asleep. It was later in the afternoon, after he had woken again, that Daniel re-read Fred's statement to him again and when he agreed that all was correct made his mark, witnessed by Jamie and Liam.

"What now Mr Franks?" Fred glanced anxiously about him.

"In the morning I will ride to Truro to make a call on the High Sheriff. I will try to get him to agree to a proposition to keep you out of jail for the time being on the grounds of your current state of health and the fact that I want you protected, for I fear that your life may be in real danger once this news becomes common knowledge.

"Do you think he will? Agree. . . that is?" Jamie voiced all their thoughts.

"I think that there is strong enough reason to keep him under supervision and to ensure the protection of our main witness."

"Can I come with you? Will I be of any assistance, or in the way?" Jamie asked.

Daniel laughed. "Certainly not in the way, Jamie. But it might be helpful to have you put weight behind the argument to keep him out of jail. After all, by his own admission he is implicated in the conspiracy to cause an explosion at Wheal Jenny and therefore in the murder of John Rawe also."

* * *

Ginifur and Jamie sat up into the early hours of the morning, neither of them would get much sleep, the mere thought that Beau was implicated, even if only by marriage, was enough to distress her. No matter how many assurances Jamie could contrive made her rest any easier and it was as the sun clawed its way above the horizon beyond Dingerien Bay when Ginifur finally climbed the stairs to her bedroom, and Jamie and Daniel saddled their horses for the ride into Truro.

In the early dawn they kept up a steady pace, keen to cover the distance. There was little call for the ferryman this early so the ride to Truro involved riding to Tregony, by-passing Probus and travelling through Tresillian. As Jamie and Daniel rode through the woods in the steep sided valley at Trewarthinick they slowed to an easy pace which made conversation possible.

"Your mother is understandably worried." Daniel opened the conversation.

Jamie didn't answer immediately, even when they had been riding hard his mind had been fully occupied, his assurances to Ginifur had not been given with any great conviction and he was conscious that she was aware of this. "What do you think? Honestly?"

"About Beau?"

"Yes. . . Beau."

"In truth, I don't know. It is hard to believe that, if Robert Fry is truly involved, that he could be in total ignorance. . . but equally I cannot believe that he could know and be a party to the conspiracy that would result in the death of his brother." Daniel attempted to re-assure him. "There would need to be compelling evidence to implicate him."

"Are you acquainted with the High Sheriff?" Jamie turned the conversation. "What's he like?"

"We have met on occasions, both socially and on official occasions. An honest man, with a sense of public duty."

"But is he going to believe Fred's statement?" Jamie voiced his doubts.

"Well. . . I do. It remains for me to convince him to do so also." Daniel said with conviction. "The first thing we must do is to ask for constables to accompany us to the moor and investigate the alleged murder of Walter Hawes. Fred will have to lead us to the shaft to recover the body for I doubt we will find the shaft without his assistance. Finding Walters remains should be enough to call for an investigation into the allegations. From that point on it will be up to the prosecution and the defence to find or disprove any evidence that can be accumulated."

Jamie considered the problems facing them as they picked up their pace and continued their journey towards Truro.

Truro had been developed in the last few years. New buildings had sprung up along Boscawen Street and Lemon Hill. In 1794 buildings had been demolished to make way for improvements to Boscawen Street and the construction of Lemon Street and Lemon Quay, named after William and Charles Lemon. William Lemon was born into a poor mining family in the 1690's and went from a 'balboy' paid in pence for watching the stamps, to control one of the most important copper mines in Cornwall in his twenties. He was known as the Great Mr Lemon and became the wealthiest man in Cornwall: businessman, banker, landowner and mine owner and his grandson represented Cornwall in Parliament. Now, large houses were being built along the upper part of Lemon Hill for their wealthy owners and Daniel led the way to the top and the large house which was the residence of the High Sheriff of Cornwall.

It was mid morning when the butler led Daniel and Jamie to the morning room where they were greeted warmly.

"Daniel Franks! What on earth brings you here at this hour? And who is this you bring with you?" He shook hands with Daniel and turned to the newcomer. "I feel that I should know you," he remarked.

"May I present Captain Tremayne?" Daniel introduced him.

"Captain Tremayne? Of Tremanyon. . . Richard Tremayne. . . but surely. . . !"

Jamie laughed. "No, Jamie. I am Jamie Tremayne, Richard's son."

The Sheriff joined in the laughter. "Of course, but you are so like him. I remember meeting him at the Assembly Rooms. Bad business, a riding accident I believe."

"So they tell me." Jamie appeared to agree.

"So what is it that brings you both to my door?"

Jamie indicated that Daniel should present their story.

"You may remember hearing of an accident at the Wheal Jenny Mine in 1794, in which a man died and Captain Tremayne was quite seriously injured."

"I do; a fault line was the cause wasn't it?"

"That is what some people would like to believe. However, information has come to light which proves that our original suspicions that it was caused by an explosion accomplished by persons' unknown, could indeed be correct."

"This sounds interesting. . . let us go through to my study where you can illuminate me of your findings." He led the way across the imposing hall to his study at the front of the house and, forsaking the chair behind the desk, ushered them to the group of informal chairs, settled himself comfortably and signalled that they should do the same. He reached out to pull the bell-cord beside the fireplace. "Have you ridden in this morning, did you stop for refreshments?"

"Yes on both counts John. We left at dawn but stopped for sustenance at the Red Lion before calling on you here.

"Splendid, splendid." As the door opened John Carr turned to his butler. "No one is to disturb us, Hutton."

"Indeed, Sir." His manservant assured him. "Is there anything else you require?"

"Not for the moment, I will call for you if needs be."

"Sir." With a bow Hutton closed the door quietly behind him.

"Well Daniel, pray continue." John Carr, High Sheriff for Cornwall, settled himself back in the chair to listen.

It was some while later before the whole of the story was presented to the interested listener. The Sheriff asked many pertinent questions of Daniel and Jamie as they went along, and it was soon well after noon before they came to the end of the tale. Daniel lent back in his chair, slapped his knees and declared. "And now you know it all."

John Carr ran a hand across his mouth and fingered his neat moustache as he mulled over the story that had unfolded. "Believe me Daniel, you too Jamie, it is not that I doubt you; please do not misunderstand me, but these are extraordinary allegations and I am wondering how difficult they will be to prove. Henry Bishop and Robert Fry are both well known individuals in respectable circles. Will it be possible to find anyone else who could corroborate these allegations?"

"Our first move must be to retrieve Walter Hawes remains from the shaft on the moor." Daniel insisted. "Constables should be in attendance and his recovery recorded. I would like to be present and also I wish to visit his family to see if there is anything that they can add."

"I will arrange that, of course, we will need your accuser to guide them. Needless to say he has opened himself up for arrest on the count of the incident at the mine which culminated in one death and James Tremayne's injuries."

"He is aware of that, as Jamie and I are also. However, he is a very sick man and it is quite likely that he could easily die in custody in his present condition; also when this gets out, these allegations could place his life in danger from other sources. I believe our best chances are to keep him safe, under supervision, on our assurance that he will appear as prosecution witness at any future trial."

John Carr gave this suggestion consideration before answering. "He is at present at Tremanyon. . . yes?" Jamie acknowledged this point. "Then I suggest he should stay in your care whilst we look further into these accusations. How would you and your good mother feel about that?"

Jamie agreed, with reservations. "I would have to speak with her, of course, but I feel that she would agree. My family and I will move back to Tremanyon as well, to put some security measures in place. He is a sick man and won't be moving far for some time. I am hopeful that we can keep his presence quiet for a while yet."

Consulting the clock John Carr called for food and drink to be prepared and conversation moved back and forth until the man-servant announced that the dining room was prepared for them.

It was late before they left the house at the top of Lemon Hill, but their horses were refreshed and there were some hours of light still ahead of them. They decided that if they could catch the ferryman they would be able to cross the River Fal at Tolverne and it would be possible to reach Daniel and Rebecca's house, near Philleigh, by nightfall.

* * *

Ginifur accepted the need for Fred to be kept safely hidden away, agreeing that she thought that he wouldn't survive long in jail conditions such as there were at Bodmin or even the lock up at Truro.

Jamie reluctantly told Davey that he needed him to return to the mine to keep an eye on things for him while he dealt with this current problem. Davey was unhappy to leave Fred, but was assured by Jamie that he would be taken good care of and was placated when Jamie told him that he could ride over in a week to see for himself. Meanwhile arrangements were being made to go to the moor and retrieve Walter Hawes remains. The constables, together with Daniel and Jamie, would be making further enquiries. Davey Rawe was to be kept informed of the progress of the investigations and, his mind put at rest, he rode back to Penhallow and the Wheal Jenny Mine the following morning.

It was a few days before the news reached Tremanyon to inform them that a time and date had been agreed for Daniel, Jamie and Fred to meet up with the constables. They were to meet at Penhallow and although the constables had been informed that they would probably recover the remains of a human being no further information had been divulged.

They travelled by coach; although recovered a great deal Fred was by no means well enough to do the journey on horseback. How he had made the journey to Tremanyon in the first place was a miracle, according to Ginifur. With the constables, awaiting their arrival, was a doctor and, to their surprise. . . John Carr, the High Sheriff of Cornwall.

It was a miserable day; the mist encompassing the moor making it appear both bleak and uninviting. They first visited the abandoned hovel to search for any missed evidence of the unfortunate Hawes occupation, but it had been swept clean three years ago and there was only the amount of rubbish that you would expect to accumulate in this time, no more. "Too clean." Jamie commented. "This is not a dwelling that has been abandoned for many years. The dust and cobwebs here are relatively recent."

John Carr and the constables had Fred go over his story again; there was no alteration to his story and everything was just as he had detailed to Daniel. He showed them where he had hidden outside, described how they had carried Walter from the hut and then led them over the uneven ground to the shaft high up on the desolate moorland.

If Fred had not known where the shaft was they would never have found it. Heather and gorse had grown right up to the very edge. Anyone wandering over the moors would have fallen in before they had even been aware that it was there.

They were there on a wretched mission and, in spite of the oilskin cloaks they wore, they were already wet and miserable. At

Fred's suggestion, Jamie had brought two lengths of strong rope with him and a bundle of sacking. Casting around Jamie spied a large rock nearby and securing one end of a length of rope around it he dropped the other down the dark opening into the ground below before, reluctantly, suggesting that he went down first. As a midshipman Jamie had spent many hours clambering up and sliding down the sheets, the naval term for ropes, for he, as with all sailors, had to be familiar with the rigging of a ship. He had climbed aloft in fair weather and foul, sun and rain, both in day and night. Luckily he was also familiar with a miner's life underground; otherwise he doubted whether he would have offered to go first. What is more he doubted if either of the constables had been warned about what their task might involve. Removing his oilskin cape Jamie picked up the other length of rope and formed a loop at one end and carefully knotting it, to ensure that it would not slip and tighten, he passed the loop over his head and under his arms before securing the other end to the rock as before. Turning to Daniel he held out the surplus rope. "I will climb down to the ledge that Fred has described; if I fall or get into difficulty you will be able to haul me up. Let the slack out slowly as I descend." Daniel accepted the rope. "Don't look so worried Dan, I'm not going fathoms deep. Fred says that the ledge Hawes' body fell on is not too far down. I expect this was only an exploratory shaft for there is no evidence that it was ever used to extract tin ore." To Fred, he added. "You are sure I have enough rope Fred?"

"Oh, 'es, Sir. The one I took from the mine weren't as long, 'n I 'ad more'n enough. Tid'n that deep, but it's a mite dark mind."

Jamie had brought one of Davey Rawe's candle lamps with him. He lit the candle and secured the lamp to his waist, then he sat down at the edge of the shaft and took a firm grip on the rope before giving a firm tug to check that it was securely fastened to the rock. With a "Here we go then." Jamie began to lower himself down the shaft. Inch by inch Jamie climbed down the rope. It had been some time since it had been necessary for him to climb up or down a rope but it was a skill well learned and he soon fell into an easy routine. The dim interior at the opening of the shaft gradually darkened as he climbed ever lower, but as he went deeper his eyes became accustomed to the gloom and the little light that was shed by the candle aided him. It seemed longer, but it could have only been minutes before his feet contacted the ledge, just as Fred had described. Climbing down a little further, still holding firmly to the rope, Jamie balanced himself on the ledge, removed the candle lamp from his waist and, holding it up, looked about him. If he hadn't been prepared for what he might find he may have stepped back and fallen. There, only inches from his feet lay the remains of Walter Hawes. At this depth Jamie was surprised to find just how dry it was. There was nothing left of Walter's earthly body, now only his skeleton remained. It didn't look as though it had been disturbed by animals; the flesh had all rotted away, there was still a little skin and hair left on the skull where the bones lay undisturbed on the ledge and a large amount of his clothing appeared to be intact. Jamie wondered if his jacket concealed any evidence of his identity.

In the miserable atmosphere on the moor above, Daniel and the constables had slowly released the slack as they had been instructed, ever ready to tighten their grip if Jamie should fall. For Daniel it seemed an eternity before they stopped releasing more rope for Jamie to descend. Ensuring that the constables kept a tight grip on the rope Daniel knelt down at the dark opening and called down. "Jamie! Jamie, can you hear me?" For a moment there was no answer and Daniel felt a moment of panic. "Jamie!! Jamie, can you hear me?" he called again into the darkness.

"Yes Dan." Jamie's voice echoed up the shaft. "I have found the ledge."

Daniel gave a sigh of relief. "What else have you found?"

"I'm coming back up Dan, I'll tell you when I get there."

Once more Daniel and the constables took up the rope, this time taking up the slack as Jamie climbed towards the surface. Scrambling up onto the heather Jamie ran a hand over his face to brush away the dust and dirt. Turning to John Carr he took a deep breath to clear his lungs and reported. "Well, he is down there alright. Perhaps it would be better to say that the remains of someone are down there. There is little left now but bones and a few scraps of clothing and leather. What evidence there is that it is the body of Walter Hawes I do not know? One of the constables can come back down with me to verify where the body is lying and we could bring all the remains to the surface for investigation if you wish?"

John Carr also took a deep breath before he spoke, he hadn't realised that he had been holding his breath for long periods during Jamie's descent down and his ascent up the shaft. "Yes, it is imperative that we must recover the remains. You will be surprised what can be discovered, am I not correct Doctor?" The doctor agreed that this was so. "Anyway, his family deserve the right to give the man a decent burial, whatever he may have been involved in. They will need to know what has happened to him; have you been in touch with them yet, Daniel?"

"No John. . . I was waiting until I had some more definite information to give them."

"Good. Alright then Jamie, if you don't mind going below again to assist the constable I would be grateful." Turning to the constables he asked, "Which of you is going to retrieve the remains?"

The two men exchanged fearful looks, both reluctant to be lowered below ground. Jamie's suspicions that they had been given no warning about what their task might entail was quite correct.

"Come on. . . come on. Which of you will help Captain Tremayne?" Snapped an angry Sheriff.

The younger of the constables gave in hesitantly. "If tiz necessary, I reckon as 'ow it'l 'ave t'be me."

"Of course it's necessary," blustered the Sheriff. "You represent the law, man! We can't have Captain Tremayne doing all the work for us, can we?"

"No Sir." Agreed the young man, without conviction, as he viewed the means for his proposed trip below ground to retrieve the collection of bones and rags from the dark hole in the ground with trepidation.

Jamie, recognising the man's reluctance, attempted to re-assure him. "It's not so bad really. A little dark, but in truth not as cold as it is up here. Can you climb a rope?"

"Never really tried, Sir," the young man grasped at the vague chance that this would rescue him from this unwelcome duty.

"Don't worry, I'll go down first then send back the safety rope and your companion and Mr Franks will lower you slowly. There will be enough light from the candle to see what we must do. Do you have any special requests, Sheriff?"

John Carr fingered his moustache. "Yes. . . I will need you both to agree on a description of how you find the remains. Make sure that you do before starting a collection of his remains."

The young constable's face visibly blanched and Jamie quickly added. "There is nothing to fear, it is all quite dry now, just a collection of bones." He attempted to lessen the gruesome aspect of their task and he was rewarded by a weak smile. "Are you ready?"

"Yes, Sir"

"What's your name constable?"

"Johnny, Sir."

"Alright Johnny. I'm going down now, when the rope comes back slip it under your arms as I am now. As Dan and your constable lowers you, use your feet to stop yourself bumping the sides of the shaft. Don't worry, you are no great weight, they won't drop you."

John Carr and the good doctor surprised him by adding that they would add their assistance to help lower the constable below and bring him back up.

"We will send up the remains in two collections before coming up ourselves." Jamie explained as he began his second descent.

Although Johnny began his voyage underground with great trepidation, once on the ledge with Jamie they quickly agreed on a description of how the body had come to rest and efficiently collected the remains into two piles secured in the pieces of hessian that Jamie had brought with him. These were secured to the rope, one at a time, and carefully lifted up the shaft before, first the constable making the return to the surface followed by Jamie.

Carefully transporting the human remains back over the moors to the coach Jamie and Billy carefully described the site where Walter Hawes remains had been found. At Penhallow Jamie gently placed the gruesome find in the Sheriff's coach and John Carr, along with the constables and doctor, proceeded to Bodmin.

Jamie, Daniel and Fred returned to Tremanyon. The Sheriff had agreed that Fred could stay at Tremanyon with Jamie's guarantee that he would ensure his appearance at Bodmin should the need arise. John Carr also promised to keep Jamie informed of any and all developments regarding the case and a week later a letter arrived telling him that Henry Bishop and Robert Fry had been requested to present themselves to the Sheriff to assist with some enquiries. It was a few days later that Beau made another visit to Tremanyon.

* * *

Ginifur heard the side door close with a violent crash which caused the picture to vibrate on the wall and the china vase shake and shudder precariously upon the highly polished rosewood table where it stood in the side hall.

Beckoning Liam to follow her, Ginifur left Kate and Poppy in the kitchen and met Beau at the bottom of the stairs.

"Where is he? Where is that damned brother of mine?" Beau demanded in a raised voice that trembled with anger.

Ginifur remained calm. "Jamie is not here Beau."

"Where is he?" he repeated. "God damn the bastard, what is he playing at?"

The blood drained from Ginifur's face and Liam feared for her, thinking briefly that she may pass out; but he should have known better. As fast as her face drained of all colour, the blood returned again with repressed anger. Once before someone had referred to Jamie as a bastard; Ginifur clearly remembered Adam shouting abuse at her on the beach at Kylyn Cove, and her reaction to it then. Her body stiffened with fury as she faced up to her younger son. "Don't you ever dare to use that term for your brother again, Beau. Or, believe me, I will cut you out of all or any of the inheritance that you believe might come your way. I will not, I repeat not have you refer to your brother in this way and neither will I have you talk to me in this fashion. . . nor take the Lord's name in vain." She turned on her heals and made her way to the library door, saying over her shoulder. "If you wish to discuss your problem in a reasonable manner then we will discuss it in here, if not. . . then please leave my house and my home." Liam made to follow her.

"Do you expect me to discuss family business in front of your Irish lackey?" Beau retorted.

Ginifur turned slowly to face him. "You will show respect to Liam, Beau. Liam has been both your father's and my confidante over the years and his concern is for my welfare, his integrity in no doubt. If you think that I am prepared to deal with you alone in the state of mind that you are in, you are much mistaken. It is up to you, but I insist that Liam is on hand for my protection."

"Protection!" Beau shouted back "Protection! Just what do you think that I would attempt to do, whilst you are in your own home?"

Ginifur paused to study her son carefully, her expression cold and hard, almost despising herself as her reply formulated in her mind; a look that Beau had never seen on his mother's face before. "Perhaps. . . not a lot; but your answer raises the question of what you might consider doing when I am not."

This time it was the blood that drained from Beau's face, his eyes taking on a fearful look as they flitted between Ginifur and

Liam's watchful gaze. Unlike Ginifur, the blood did not flood back into his face but instead it took on an anxious, almost scared expression. Beau fidgeted uncomfortably under his mother's unflinching examination, as both she and Liam wondered what lay beneath his fearfulness. Everything about Beau's guardedness worried Ginifur. Just what was he hiding?

Liam also studied Beau carefully. In his mind there was no doubt that Beau had something to hide. Beau would not hold his gaze; his eyes wandered between Ginifur and the door.

Ginifur made the decision for Beau "Well, you make up your mind," she said as she turned and entered the Library with Liam close behind her. Ginifur made for the chair behind the desk and gratefully lowered herself down, only Liam was aware of the slight tremble in her hands as she sorted through some papers on the desk. Liam moved to the far window and settled himself on the window seat.

In the hall Beau remained stiffly at the foot of the stairs, studying the door. He waited there for some minutes whilst he deliberated as to what his next move should be. Ginifur had caught him off balance, she now had the advantage. He didn't like the look in Liam's eyes, nor his mother's for that matter, what did they suspect? What had he given away? When news of the Robert Fry's summons to the Sheriff's office had arrived, Beau had reacted rashly. . . without thought to the consequences. Now. . . how did he extricate himself from the situation that he had unwittingly put himself in?

Ginifur listened for any sound in the hall. As far as she was aware Beau still remained there, for she had not heard the side door open or close and, in his mood, she felt sure that he would have closed it with force if he had left. No. . . Beau was fighting some demon inside him, she decided, taking a breath to settle her own nerves as she waited for him to make the next move.

Beau finally submitted, crossed the hall and entered Ginifur's room. He ignored the fact that Liam sat comfortably in the window and studied his mother's expression. "Mother! I am sorry that my anger got the better of me." He attempted to placate her but Ginifur's expression did not change. "I hope that you will forgive me," he added insincerely.

"I am sorry Beau, but at this very moment I cannot do that. Maybe in time. . ." her voice was cold, as was her manner; not at all herself in this moment.

Beau flinched. How was he to extricate himself from his current position? Would she really cut him out of any inheritance that she might have made? It didn't bear thinking about. Tremanyon should be his to pass on to Richard. He felt the anger rising once more within him and struggled to contain it. Ginifur unwittingly gave him a moment's reprieve.

"What is the cause of all your anger, Beau?"

Ginifur's young son controlled himself with difficulty. "My father-in-law has been asked to report to the Sheriff's office on some trumped up charges. Clara is beside herself with worry, her mother also."

"What has that got to do with Jamie?"

Ginifur had a puzzled look upon her face and Beau began to have misgivings. Perhaps Jamie wasn't involved in this investigation, maybe he had acted too hastily. He decided to brazen it out. "Well he is isn't he?"

"I don't know Beau. Has he brought a charge against your father-in-law?" Beau had to admit he didn't know and shrugged his shoulders by way of an answer. "Then why should you think that he should be the cause of an investigation into some claim or other? Has the Sheriff suggested that he is to be arrested on some charge?"

"No. . . not exactly," he was forced to admit.

"Then if Robert Fry is not guilty of anything, neither he, nor you, Clara or her mother have anything to fear." Ginifur suggested but she could see that Beau wasn't any happier. "What is the investigation about?" she asked innocently.

Beau felt that he was being pushed into a corner. "Apparently there has been a body found on the moor and Clara's father has been summoned to the High Sheriff's office to answer questions," he admitted.

"Well I am sure that you all have nothing to fear, for what on earth could Robert Fry have to do with a body being found on the moor? And how you have come to the conclusion that Jamie has made a claim to that effect, I cannot imagine. Has he?" Beau had to admit to himself that he had no evidence that this was so and shrugged non-committedly. Ginifur continued the study of her son and relented. "In that case I think that you should return to Killow Barton and put your wife's mind to rest."

Beau was grateful of the excuse to escape. "I will, thank you mother for your understanding." Ginifur inclined her head and Beau took a faltering step towards her but, having correctly read the expression on her face, he changed his mind and turned to the window. "Good day Liam." Beau finally acknowledged his father's faithful servant and turned towards the door. "Mother." he added briefly before he left the room and this time the side door opened and closed quietly as he departed from the manor.

Ginifur waited whilst Liam checked that they were truly alone and settled herself more comfortably in her chair. The whole episode had un-nerved her, it had affected her more than she was prepared to admit.

Liam returned and sank into the comfortable chair in front of Ginifur's desk. "And what will ye be makin' of that, mavourneen?"

Ginifur smiled briefly, Liam rarely used this form of endearment for her though frequently he did when talking to Kate. She remembered their first meeting in the cold dark hovel they called their home. The children undernourished and inadequately clothed. Ginifur's family Richard had named them. When Richard met them he too was horrified by their situation and offered them work and a home at Tremanyon where in the years that followed Liam had become a close confidante.

Ginifur gave an involuntary shudder. Just what did she make of it? Beau's attitude had so quickly turned from anger to fear; what should he have to fear? Why such a rapid change in his attitude? Ginifur attempted to push her feelings of sentiment and emotion aside. Intuition and prescience had served her well in the past, never letting her down. No. . . Beau was afraid, but afraid of what? Richard's letter to Jamie flashed before her eyes and she flinched at the thought of the contents within. Had Richard really feared for his life. . . and hers? Who on earth would he suspect of proposing to inflict harm upon either of them? Not Beau, surely? Not their own son? Liam waited silently while she considered his question. He hated to see her so troubled and torn, her life devastated by the loss of her husband and her peace destroyed by constant conflict with Beau.

Finally Ginifur voiced her concerns. "What is it that he fears so, Liam? What was it that caused Richard to write that letter to Jamie? What were his fears? Of all the people in Richard's life he took you into his confidence on more than one occasion. What is it that you know, and I don't?"

In his heart Liam knew that this day would one day arrive. Richard had no real proof in his lifetime that anyone bore him ill will, but he had become uneasy. There had been a number of small incidents that had caused him alarm. The riding accident that had caused the death of Richard Tremayne was not the first accident that had occurred in his last months. Even when Joe had brought him the evidence he had to admit that the proof was not compelling, but the second time!! Jamie had refused to listen to Joe... perhaps he should have gone to Ginifur then!! Should he even bring up his fears now? How would Ginifur react to even the slightest suggestion that there was a genuine possibility that someone meant them very real harm? Surely the death of Ellen and Jamie's 'accident' in the mine pointed to that fact.

"Liam! I know in my heart that Richard confided in you. Only you know what his fears were. You have to tell me Liam."

Liam took a deep breath before answering. There would be no way back from this point, it could even result in a rift between himself and his family with that of Ginifur, Jamie and the rest of her family. Whatever the outcome, there had now been too many incidents to ignore and he owed it to Richard to tell Ginifur all that he knew. "Dickon did truly fear that someone might wish him harm, his greatest fear was that they might wish you harm also." Ginifur let out a gasp of surprise. "In the last couple of months of Richard's life there had been a few careless accidents. A wheel came off the gig when he was travelling a little fast, on another occasion the brakes failed as he travelled down the hill at Tregony. None of them caused him any great harm and he insisted that you were not told. Joe was distraught and insisted that he kept all the carriages in top condition. Wheels and brakes were of special concern and were regularly inspected for wear and tear; renewed at the first sign of damage. In fact Joe keeps a record of all repairs and showed it to Dickon at the time. Dickon believed him and did not hold him responsible."

Ginifur's unease increased with each word uttered from Liam's mouth. "How can any of these incidents involve Beau?" She wished that she could halt this conversation before it went any further yet she knew the time had come to perhaps face up to some unwelcome truths.

"T'be sure Ginny, there be nothin' to dreckly link Beau to any of them. But Dickon was unhappy with Beau's obsession with being his legitimate heir to Tremanyon, the lad's irresponsible attitude to money and contempt for the people who work on the estate, or as 'e puts it so nicely, 'the peasants of the lower classes'.

Dickon never brought the subject up in front of ye. Well. . . Dickon wasn't wantin' ye t'be worrit, y'see."

"And then, the riding accident. But it was just an accident, that's all." Ginifur clung to the only explanation that she could accept.

Liam didn't answer. He just stared, unseeing, out of the window.

"Liam! It was an accident, wasn't it?" Ginifur desperately wanted to hear him say yes, but still he didn't answer and she waited with bated breath.

Finally Liam looked her right in the eye. "Ye know how meticulous Joe is with the horses and the harness."

"Of course Liam, there has been no questioning his loyalty or competence. He learned well under Sam Sawle and I know that he keeps all the harness as good as new. I know that, so what are you getting at? Come to the point."

There was no easy way to tell her, Liam finally decided. "Casper must have been spooked, there was no reason for Dickon t' take a fall. T'was the girth strap that broke, Joe brought it t' me y'see. They called it an accident. . ."

"Well it was, wasn't it?"

" 'n who am I t' argue with that then? Tis they that are s'posed to know better than the likes o' we?"

Ginifur wished that she could leave it there, but she couldn't. "Why do you think otherwise Liam?"

"Cos it 'ave 'appened twice, 'n nearly in the same place too."

Ginifur took a sharp intake of breath. "Ellen! You think that Ellen. . .?"

"I'm thinkin' that Miss Ellen's accident was no accident at all, yes."

"No Liam! No!" she exclaimed. "Jamie would not have let it go at that if he believed otherwise. You know that he wouldn't."

"Joe came t' the house 'n asked t'see'im. . . Jamie wouldn't even entertain the thought of Joe bein' in the same room as 'im."

"But what did Joe want?"

"Well. . . 'e kept the 'arness y'see, the both of 'em. They was both tampered with, that's why they broke. Same place, just by the buckles. Difficult t'see if ye didn' know what ye was lookin' for. But Joe knew the 'arness should not 'ave broke, so 'ee wanted t'know why they 'ad."

"But how does this affect Beau?" Ginifur was troubled by the connection in Liam's mind.

"I don' know 'n I certainly can't prove that 'ee is."

"Then why suggest it Liam? Surely that is grossly unfair?" Ginifur was showing the first signs of protection towards her son.

"If it 'adn't been for Dickon, I probably wouldn'."

"What about Richard?"

"Tis 'ard Ginny, some 'ard, believe me, but Dickon had been thinkin' that young Beau actually meant 'im 'arm, 'n ye too."

Ginifur clung to whatever remained of her sanity. "I don't believe that. . . No, not his own son."

"Tis true, 'ee found it 'ard, very 'ard. But young Beau was fond of the drink ye'll mind. . . too often 'ee kept bad company 'n Dickon would 'aul 'im out o' some inn or other, shootin' off 'is mouth. Tis 'ard t'keep a secret anywhere. . . Y'see, word got back t' Dickon of the things he threatened whilst the drink was on 'im."

"He threatened to kill his Father? Beau actually threatened that?" Ginifur was aghast. It was incredulous, surely it could never be.

"I'm afraid 'ee threatened ye too. T'was 'is mother that really stood in 'is way, y'see."

"No I don't see."

"I c'n understand that. But y'see Jamie was your first born, 'n Beau believed that ye loved 'im the most and would make sure that Dickon treated 'im better in the long run o' things."

"I can't believe it. I won't believe it. Not his son. . . No, not Richard's own son. . . my own son. . . No. . . Never."

"I understand. I'm sorry Ginny, real sorry. I should've kept things t'myself. If'n I've said too much, Kate 'n me 'n the girls will leave. Right now if ye wish it."

Ginifur was stunned by Liam's revelations. How could this be happening to her? Her first instinct was to dismiss Liam from the room, from her life. He had been Richard's closest companion, their loyal servant, how could he bring himself to make these accusations? Somehow she managed to drag herself out of the chair and turn to the high window which overlooked the lawns. Without Richard she was like a ship lost at sea, there was no one to turn to, no one to advise her. Suddenly she remembered the letter that Richard had written to Jamie. *'Just a whim'* he had said *'on the spur of the moment'*. But in the letter he had voiced his fears for Tremanyon; he had *senseless fears caused by incidents that might have been exaggerated*. What incidents? The incidents with the gig, the wheel and the brakes? And then Richard had gone on to beg Jamie to watch over his mother. . . why?

Liam had risen from the chair, dejected. . . crestfallen. He believed that he was facing a bleak future. . . far away from the family he loved. He had taken a risk, and had lost. With his back stooped and his head lowered Ginifur, glancing out of the corner of her eye, realised that he like her was now in his latter years. He was older than Ginifur, not by many years it was true, but at this moment he certainly looked it.

Ginifur turned from the window, a sad figure facing a heart-rending decision alone. Liam had been her stalwart since Richard's death and he had given her his steadfast support throughout her life here at Tremanyon. It was Liam who had helped her nurse Richard back to health when he was almost at deaths door following his return from the New World, and it was with Betsy's herbs and help that made this possible. It was Liam who had brought her the news that the militia were lying in wait for Adam to return from one of his smuggling trips and it was Liam, with Richard, who had carried him back wounded to Tremanyon. And what would she have done without him these past years since Richard's death and before Jamie's return home from the sea? Liam was about to close the door behind him. "Wait, Liam. Please come back." The door slowly re-opened to reveal the sad figure of Liam. "Please, Liam, come back in. I am sorry. . . Please. . . Forgive me for hurting you." Liam paused and glanced over his shoulder to assure himself that she truly did not consider that he had slighted either her or her family. "Liam. . . I am sorry. Please come back and sit down." She moved towards him and seated herself in one of the chairs indicating that Liam should return to the one he had just vacated. "Liam, you have been a loyal friend for too many years and we have been through so much together. You helped me to nurse Richard back to health and he never doubted your loyalty in all the following years. He confided in you, I know. Who am I to doubt you now?" She paused for a moment, closed her eyes and buried her head in her hands. Straightening herself up, she looked at Liam. "I am a mother. It is the mother in me that finds it hard to accept that one of her own could turn against her and the family, just as it must have been hard for Richard to harbour doubts. It is this that will make me continue to have doubts until I have firm evidence to the contrary. I am not saying that you are lying, Liam. . . but I need hard evidence that this is so. Can you understand that?"

"Be Jesus. . .I understand too well. T'was 'ard fer Dickon 'n all, ye must know that. But then 'ee couldn' see the girth straps."

"You mean that you have?" Ginifur's eyes widened as her interest increased in intensity.

"Yes. . . Joe showed me Dickon's after the fall. . . but what was I t'do? Then t'other one when Miss Ellen fell. . . both similar. . . 'n both with new tack. Joe came to show Jamie. . . but 'ee just wouldn' listen. I don' blame 'im mind, he was distraught at loosin' 'is wife."

"Does Joe still have the harness?"

"Aye. . . said 'ee was keepin' 'em, cos one day 'ee 'oped someone would listen to 'im."

"Jamie's in Truro, he won't be home until late, bring Joe to see me Liam. . . and ask him to bring the harness with him."

Liam pushed himself wearily from the chair, leaving Ginifur gazing out at the lawns and the distant view. He wondered if her eyes were actually seeing anything for her mind was quite clearly elsewhere.

It was a little while later that Liam returned with Joe, Ginifur had hardly moved in all that time and was still in the same position when Liam knocked on the door and entered. She turned and smiled. "Hello Joe."

Joe anxiously fingered the harness he carried in his hand. "Good mornin' Mrs Tremayne." Joe felt that it was anything but a good morning. Over the years he had managed to put the accidents behind him, the fears were still there but he had managed to move on from those two dreadful days in his life. What would happen now if his employer believed that it was his negligence and not interference and damage caused by someone unknown that had caused the accident?

"Come in Joe, you too Liam." Liam took a seat in the window as Joe came forward to Ginifur. "Liam tells me that you tried to show the harness to Jamie after Ellen had her fall from Willow, is that correct?"

"Yes M'am." Poor Joe looked extremely anxious.

"Would you like to explain to me why you came to see Jamie? Believe me Joe, I am not going to get angry with you. I would just like you to go over the incidents that surrounded my husband's and my daughter-in-law's riding accidents.

"Well, y'see M'am both accidents was similar, in that Casper's 'arness 'n that o' Willow's was virtually new. Ye'll mind that the Captain insisted that Sam kept a book on all repairs to the carriages 'n the 'arness. Well 'ee taught me t'do the same. . . never was much at learnin' but I 'ad t'do it. When Sam left t'live in Adam's cottage 'ee made me promise t'keep it up. I'm right glad 'ee did 'n all."

"It's not that I doubt you, Joe, but do you have that book?"

Joe nodded towards Liam. "I give it t' Liam for safe keepin'. They was both in the one book y'see, 'n I started a new one."

Ginifur glanced at Liam. "It's in my room, Ginny. . . I'll get it shall I?"

"Please, Liam." Liam left the room. "We'll wait until Liam gets back Joe, please do not look so nervous, it is just that it is high time that any doubts over Captain Tremayne's and Ellen's death were put to rest. What you are telling me is all new and I need to get it clear before we can move forward. Do you see?"

At this moment Joe didn't see anything very clearly. He just hoped that what he had told Liam was enough to get him proven above suspicion for neglect in his work.

It did not take Liam long to return with the book which he handed to Ginifur before returning to his seat in the window.

Taking the book from him Ginifur returned to her chair behind the desk, opened the book in front of her and slowly turned the pages until she came to the entries close to the date of Jamie's accident. Sure enough, less than a fortnight before Jamie fell from Casper there was an entry, in Joe's laboured handwriting, which showed that Casper's harness was checked for wear and tear and minor adjustments to his bridle were made. Added to this there was mention that the girth strap needed attention and that Joe had deemed it necessary to make up a new one. Three days before Jamie's fall another entry showed that the old girth strap had been discarded and the new one was now in place. Ginifur sighed and turned the pages forwards until nearing the date of Ellen's fall. Once more an entry showed that Joe had made a full investigation of Willow's riding tack. The bridle, although good, was needing a little attention and the girth strap also showing little wear, but Joe had replaced and strengthened some of the buckles. "Are those the straps in question?" Ginifur indicated the harness in Joe's hands.

"Yes M'am."

Ginifur held out her hands and Joe carefully handed them to her. "This be Casper's, 'n this'n Willow's." Joe informed her.

Reluctantly Ginifur placed them side by side on the desk. "You have kept them polished!" she commented.

"Yes M'am."

"Why?"

"I didn' want them t' deteriorate. Reckoned as 'ow someone might one day take a look at 'em, 'n see the truth."

"You have done nothing else to them?"

"No M'am."

Ginifur turned Casper's strap over in her hands. It was quite obvious that it was all in good order until she handled the buckles. It was here that a weakness in the leather had caused it to rip apart, first one and then another. Once it had started it would have happened very quickly and the saddle would have slipped with Jamie upon it. Ginifur felt a moment of unease; for Jamie had not been a novice rider. . . he was a more than competent rider and should have been aware that something odd was occurring. Ginifur took a closer inspection of the leather. "Is there a weakness in the leather, here at the buckles?"

Joe looked at Liam for acknowledgement before leaning over the desk. "No M'am. I always check the leather I use. Cap'n insisted on the best. Y'see this rip, jest 'ere by the buckle. Now look 'ee 'ere, where it starts. It's not jagged and torn as weak leather would, There is a sharp. . . cut. Small mind, but it's definitely a cut with a very sharp knife, 'n tis not the only one. See. . . 'ere 'n 'ere," he indicated the remaining buckles. "'course, when one went the rest followed quick like. But Cap'n should ave felt it comin' 'n thrown 'isself clear."

"Was that all?" Ginifur asked.

"No." Ginifur's eyes widened. "When I got Casper back in the stable 'ee was in quite a state, all lathered up like. So I gives 'im a good rub down, 'n it was then I noticed a nasty scratch on 'is back where the saddle should've been."

"A scratch! How bad?"

"Bad 'nough t' make 'im tetchy with a saddle on. So I takes the saddle into the 'arness room t' take a closer look."

"And?"

"Sure 'nough. Would ye believe. . . a sharp stone was buried underneath, in the panel? Cap'n never used extra paddin', claimed that a good saddle didn' need none. Cut a good 'ole in it too, it did. I can't think of no way it could 'ave got there."

"That would have unsettled Casper." Ginifur agreed. "I don't suppose you kept the stone!" Joe pushed his hand into a pocket and withdrew the sharp stone. "Kept the saddle 'n all, 'ad a new one made for Casper. It's still over in the tack room, M'am."

"I will come over and see it later. And Ellen's, young Mrs Tremayne, this is Willow's?"

"Yes M'am, ye'll see the similarity."

Ginifur gave close inspection to Willow's girth strap, and sure enough it was an almost identical occurrence. The ripped straps started by precise sharp incisions. Ellen would have had no chance and fallen head first to the floor unable to save herself. She looked up at Liam. "This is dreadful!" she exclaimed. "It does really look as though this has been caused by wilful damage. . . but by whom?"

"Truth is Ginifur, it wasn't meant to 'arm Miss Ellen. . ." Liam left the rest of the sentence hanging in mid air.

For a second Ginifur was mystified, then she put her hand up to her mouth with an astonished "Oh!" and Liam nodded his head. "Me! You mean someone intended for me to take a fall? You are telling me that someone engineered events to make me take a fall from Willow?" Ginifur's mind returned to the day that Kate had fallen in the east wing just as she was about to go out riding with Robin and Dickon. She had called off the ride and sent a message to the children to stable the horses. But Ellen had arrived in her little trap and said that she would take them. Ellen was a fine horsewoman, although disabled. In a well maintained saddle she would have no trouble riding on Willow. She returned to the suggestion that an accident was supposed to befall her. "I am not being boastful here Liam, but it is hardly likely for me to take a fall that would kill me".

"One would say the same for Dickon." Liam reminded her.

Ginifur searched her mind for any clue as to who would wish them harm, and came up with no one. "But Beau doesn't live here, Liam. How would he know when we were about to ride out and it would have to be after Joe had checked the horses, for I have to admit I have noticed how thorough he is." She smiled at Joe for the first time. "Have you any suggestions, Joe?"

"The Squire!" Joe was all but open mouthed. "What 'ould 'ee want t' do that for?"

"Joe, anything that you have heard here this afternoon must be kept very quiet. We cannot go around making accusations that may be untrue. Of course, it can't be Beau." Ginifur assured him with a sinking feeling in her stomach. "We are just crossing out those who wouldn't wish either the captain or me harm."

"Well ye c'n cross out anyone 'ere on Tremanyon, 'n all them in Porthcarrow 'n all in my opinion. Wish both of ye any 'arm. . . no. Not 'ere. . . not on the peninsula."

"I understand your concern Joe, just keep this to yourself for now. But continue to keep a close eye on the tack, won't you?" Joe agreed that he would do so and Ginifur dismissed him for the time being, saying that she would come over to the stables one day to see Casper's old saddle.

When Joe had left the room Ginifur and Liam sat in silence for some time before Ginifur suggested that perhaps the time had come to discuss it with Jamie. He had remarried now and the loss of Ellen did not lay so heavy on his heart. Liam agreed that it should all come out in the open and hoped that they would come to a sensible conclusion.

* * *

It was to be a while before Ginifur and Liam could bring the subject up with Jamie, for he arrived home from his visit to Truro with the news that an epidemic of smallpox had broken out in the town. What was more it was not confined to the poorer sector of the town; there had been a reported case of smallpox in one of the large houses in Falmouth road, not far from where Beau and Clara lived.

"Beau was here earlier." Ginifur exclaimed. "He didn't mention it at all."

"Maybe he hadn't heard of it. If he has gone back there now, he will soon be aware of it for the news is spreading like wild fire."

Ginifur, like all mothers, feared for her family. "I wish you hadn't gone to Truro," she voiced her fear, forgetting all about Joe, and the harness.

"Don't worry Mother, I am quite sure I had no converse with anyone who had come into contact with the disease. But, for all that, I wouldn't like to be living in Truro just now." He threw off his cape and added. "I am just going up to wash and change but I'll see you in the drawing room in a few moments, I have further news to impart." With this he ran up the stairs two at a time and Liam went to make ready a tray of drinks to take to the drawing room.

The news that smallpox was back was greeted with fear by the local community, even though Porthcarrow was some distance from Truro. Most of the recent outbreaks had been way down in the west of the county, although there had been an outbreak in recent years in Polperro some distance to the east. In the next few days reports of new cases of the disease soon travelled to Tremanyon. The most severe cases ending in death and quite a number of these were in the wealthy houses on the outskirts of the town. Ginifur prayed that the disease would soon die out and hoped that it would spare her dear friends living in Truro. Silently she thanked God that Daniel had not spent any time at the office in Truro of late, due to the fact that Rebecca was near to her time again, and that he, Rebecca and the children lived at Philleigh and not in Truro.

Nevertheless, it was to be a shock when a horseman rode up the drive to Tremanyon and pulled up at the bottom of the steps. Liam opened the front door to receive a hand written letter to be given immediately to Ginifur; the rider said that he would await a reply. Liam directed him to the servant's kitchen for refreshment but he declined, saying that he would wait at the door with his horse.

It didn't take long to find Ginifur, she had heard the sound of the horse on the drive, as had Jamie, and they converged in the hall. Ginifur accepted the letter from Liam and entered the drawing room with Jamie and Liam behind her. Briefly glancing at the seal Ginifur opened the letter and the blood drained from her face as she reached out to the nearest chair for support.

"It is young Richard. . . and Clara! They have both been diagnosed with the first stages of smallpox!"

"Sit down Mother." Jamie helped her to a chair. "When was this?"

"Just two days ago. Beau has brought them out to Killow Barton."

"Best they had stayed where they were, damn him. Now it will spread to this district too. . . the fool! I'm sorry Mother, but you know it to be true."

"Apparently Beau had forbidden the servants to mix with the staff of other households until the epidemic had cleared. But you know how hard it is to enforce. Anyway, one of the upstairs maids must have had contact with it for she went down with it first and must have passed it on to Beau's household. Richard and Clara being the last of them."

"And Beau?" asked Liam.

"As yet he is clear of infection and helping to nurse both Clara and Richard."

A dark scowl appeared on Jamie's face. "Just what is he expecting of you?" he ventured as Ginifur's face formed a grimace. "Oh no! You are not going over there to nurse them. No Mother, I will not let you put your own life in danger for them, I just won't," he exploded.

Ginifur smiled at his concern. "You may not like it Jamie, but you will not stop me. You see. . . Beau is my son, as you are. . . and Richard is my grandson too," she explained quietly.

"You would not know it for the time they care to spend with you." Jamie growled. "When did they last call on you to see how you were or just pass the time of the day? You cannot even remember when Clara last entered this house."

"But I can, Jamie, I can, but that is no matter. Beau needs me and has asked me for help, I cannot deny him."

"Good God Mother!! Have you lost your senses? You will only catch it yourself and probably give it to the rest of the family too. Please. . . think of Robin and Dickon if you give no thought to anyone else."

"Believe me Jamie, I am. But I know where my duty lies and I cannot deny Beau now. I have nursed people through smallpox in the past, with Betsy's help, and I will do it again on my own. I may or may not be able to help to save them, but I must try. I will not return to Tremanyon until I am sure that I am not carrying the disease back to you all here."

Jamie slumped into a chair by the fireplace, his head buried in his hands with tears upon his cheeks. He knew that he had lost the argument and that Ginifur would go to Killow Barton with or without his blessing.

"Liam, I will write Beau a note. Give it to the rider to take back with him please. Will you also get Kate to pack a trunk for me? Two serviceable dresses and three of her aprons please. . . and an old sheet or two that I can tear up to use as masks and washing cloths. I will get some herbs and potions from my medical room." Ginifur rose to make her way to the library to write the letter and handed it to Liam before going to her tiny medical room to select the herbs and potions that she thought that she might need. Reaching for a bottle of rosewater she added that to the leather bag carefully wrapped and kept separate from her pestle and mortar. By the time she had made her careful selection Kate had made her up a small trunk of clothes and Liam had brought it to the door. He knew that there would be no stopping Ginifur on the course that she was taking, as much as his heart went out to Jamie.

"I have told Joe to bring the carriage to the door." Liam informed her. "I'll drive ye myself."

"Thank you Liam. I am sorry to have to leave you to keep young Fred safe."

“Don’ ’ee be worryin’ none. Fred’s no trouble ’ee still sleeps more’n ’ee be awake ’n seems quite ’appy t’stay in the old school room. If ’ee gets fidgety like, I’ll set ’im some jobs t’be doin’, never fear.”

“I have no fears Liam, but hope that Jamie will understand. I will go and see Marie-Claire and Ben before I go.”

“I’ll wait in the kitchen then.” Liam assured her. “Ye just ring the bell when ye’re ready.”

Marie-Claire, though anxious, understood that Ginifur could not ignore a plea for help from her son. Ginifur explained that it would not be the first time for her to come into contact with smallpox. She had lived through it before and was convinced that she could again if simple precautions were taken. Marie-Claire told her not to worry about Jamie and the children, or Ben Nancekivel, for she would ensure that they were always kept busy and didn’t fret for her welfare. Ben and Marie-Claire joined Jamie to see Liam drive her off to the Fry’s house at Killow Barton and her younger son’s family.

* * *

Killow Barton had an abandoned air about it as Liam drove up the drive. The Dower House, where Beau and Clara had lived was now closed up; the main house had all the drapes drawn across the windows. There was no sign of outdoor staff in the grounds and no one came from the stables as they drew to a halt at the front door. It looked for all the world, as though the house had been ‘shut up’ and the family gone away.

Liam helped Ginifur down from the carriage and lifted the iron knocker upon the sturdy door. It was some moments before the door was opened by the elderly footman employed by Robert Fry.

Gerald Truscott’s eyes widened at the sight of Ginifur Tremayne standing on the doorstep with a trunk and bag beside her, it looked as if she was coming to stay. “Mrs Tremayne! Surely. . . Forgive me, but have you not heard?” Gerald ventured.

“Mr Truscott, you remember me?” Ginifur smiled at the weary figure.

“Who could forget you Ma’am?” Over the years Gerald had worked for a number of well to do families in the area and had met Ginifur on a number of occasions. “But. . .”

“I know, Mr Truscott. My grandson and daughter-in-law are ill, and I have come in answer to a plea from my son, Beau.”

Gerald Truscott recovered from his surprise. “Of course Ma’am, Mr Fry and Mr Tremayne are in the drawing room. Would you care to follow me?”

Ginifur turned to Liam. “Thank you Liam, don’t come any further please. Leave the bags, Mr Truscott will get someone to see to them for me. Please return home and I will send news when I have some. Please don’t worry I will take precautions, I promise.

Liam forced a smile to his face. “Ye jest make sure ye do ’n all.” With a heavy heart he turned to leave.

Ginifur watched the carriage drive away before turning back to the entrance hall at Killow Barton. Dim and dreary, with dark paint to the woodwork and walls, the house was not as welcoming as Tremanyon. A young man appeared to take her things inside and was instructed to leave them at the bottom of the stairs for the moment, and then Gerald Truscott led Ginifur to the drawing room where he knocked on the door. Having received a curt “Enter.” Gerald opened the door and, before they could do so, it was followed by. “Who the hell was that, Truscott? What did they want?”

“Mrs Tremayne, Sir. . . It is Mrs Tremayne of Tremanyon.” Gerald introduced.

Beau had been slumped in one of the chairs, his clothes and hair dishevelled and at least four days of growth on his chin. This was a shock to Ginifur, for Beau was always so particular about his appearance. But at the sound of her name he leapt from the chair and all but ran to the door.

“Mother! You came!” he grasped both her hands so tightly that Ginifur feared that he was convinced they were truly a life line.

“You doubted it Beau? You shouldn’t have. . . I am your mother,” she explained as if this should be enough.

“Clara. . . and Richard. . . they are both ill. I don’t know what to do. The doctor has been no help, says we shouldn’t leave the house, that we should bathe them when they are hot and try to reduce the fever.”

Ginifur’s steady gaze encompassed both Beau and Robert Fry. “In all honesty Beau, there is very little that can be done. There is no medication to cure smallpox yet, only alleviate the symptoms. Although, I hear that Jenner believes that he has managed to derive a means of vaccinating against it. The best that can be done at the moment is to ease their suffering, and bathing them to reduce their temperature is one of them and an infusion of willow bark may help the pain. I am afraid that it is only the strongest who will survive." She turned to Robert Fry. "Have you or Margery ever had any contact with smallpox before Robert?"

"No. . . no. Will they die?" He looked a truly frightened man. "Margery is nursing them. The servants refused to go near them, so I told them to clear off. Insolent, ungrateful peasants."

"That is unfortunate." Ginifur uttered sadly. "Does that mean that you have no female staff?" Her eyes darted from one to the other.

It was Beau who gave the begrudging answer. "Yes."

"Yes. . . you have no staff?" Beau nodded. "Most unfortunate for your poor wife Robert. Who is fetching and carrying for her? Who is doing the laundry?"

Both gentlemen looked uncertainly at one another before Beau added. "I've been doing what I can to help, and Gerald and the boy are doing what they can too. Cook has stayed on but she won't leave the kitchen and refuses to do the laundry."

Ginifur shook her head in exasperation "Oh dear. . . you really haven't handled things very well have you?"

Robert Fry exploded. "Don't take that attitude with me Madam. This is my house and not for you to tell me how to run it. . . you. . . you. . . upstart."

"In that case, if that is how you feel, perhaps I had better leave. You obviously do not need my help." Ginifur turned towards the door.

"No. . . Mother! No. Please don't leave." Beau turned to his father-in-law. "Don't be foolish, this is your daughter and grandson's lives you are playing with."

Robert Fry's face crumpled in despair. "Alright. . . alright. Tell her to do what she must, but keep her away from me." With these parting words he strode from the room.

Ginifur studied her son carefully before asking him to take her to the kitchen. "And for goodness sake Beau, pull back the curtains and let us have some light and air in the house. We are not in mourning yet."

At the rear of the house the dingy kitchen was a vast contrast to the one at Tremanyon. Gladys Dyer was peeling vegetables when Beau and Ginifur entered. With a look of surprise she bobbed a curtsy as she recognised Beau's mother. "Mrs Tremayne, Ma'm. What be 'ee doin' 'ere?"

"Well, in truth, Mrs Dyer I have come to ask for your help."

"I baint leavin' me kitchen, I tol' 'im I'd stay 'n cook, but I'm not goin' outa this room. I'd rather loose me job than that." She was adamant.

"I'm not going to ask you to." Ginifur assured her. "I would just like to ask if you remember the smallpox epidemic in sixty three?"

"Oh 'es, Ma'm. Twas a bad'n in Treg'ny, so many folk died, young 'n old alike." Beau groaned with despair. "I'm sorry Sir, didn' mean no 'arm."

Ginifur smiled. "That's alright Mrs Dyer. But can you remember anyone who actually had smallpox and recovered?" She wanted to know.

"Well now. . . I were in Treg'ny then and was lucky t' live through it. Did'n get it mind. . . none o' we did." Gladys put her hands on her hips as she put her mind to the question. "Oh 'es. . . there were a few. Madge Weaver nursed all 'er family before getting' it 'erself. She lived. . . the rest died. And little Eva, the constables daughter, she 'ad it 'n lived too. There must be others but I can't call them t' mind just now. Why?"

"It is possible that you have a natural immunity to the disease Gladys, it appears that some people do, but I wouldn't take it for granted if I were you. However, two will do. Do they still live in Tregony, Gladys?"

"Madge do, getting' on a bit now, but Eva married Sid Rush 'n lives right 'ere in Ruan. But why are 'ee askin' after them?"

"Because having had smallpox they cannot catch it again. Now who is the boy I saw with Gerald Truscott?"

"He's Truscott's grandson." Beau informed her.

"Can he ride, and does he know where these women can be found?" Gladys agreed that he could and Ginifur addressed her request to Beau.

"Then I want him to guide you to their homes Beau. Explain that I promise that because they have had smallpox they are immune. They cannot catch it twice; believe me it just doesn't happen. Offer them as much as it takes for them to come here to help me nurse your wife and son, Beau. Now get gone with you, and don't come back without them." She dismissed her son who, giving her a second glance, left the kitchen. "Now Mrs Dyer, do you have any hot water on the range"

"Yes m'am. . . do 'ee want it upstairs. Young Kev can take it up for 'ee."

"That would be good, but young Kev is otherwise engaged. Just direct me to Clara's room please."

Following Gladys's directions Ginifur climbed the stairs towards the bedrooms. On the landing the smell of sickness was hard to ignore.

The smell of fever was mixed with that of bodies unable to control normal bodily functions. In the hall she had picked up the bag with her potions and equipment and by the time she had discovered the door to Clara's bedroom she was pleased to find that young Kev was behind her with the kettle of hot water. Gladys had sent him up with it before he left with Beau.

Ginifur turned the door handle. "Just leave the kettle here Kev, I will pour it into a jug and basin and then if you will, please ask Mrs Dyer to put it on to boil again before you leave with my son. Tell her that it must be brought to a rapid boil."

"Yes M'am." Ginifur gave him a grateful smile and entered the room.

A startled Margery Fry turned away from the bed. Her face displayed her tiredness and concern for her sick daughter. "Mrs Tremayne... What are you doing here?"

"I thought that you could do with some help." Ginifur explained. "I would be pleased to stay if you wish."

Margery shook her head in bewilderment. "You would help me to nurse Clara and Charlie? We've no help you know, most of the staff have gone."

"So I hear. I have sent Beau to employ some more help." Looking around the room she spied a china bowl and jug on a dresser and taking the kettle she filled the jug and returned the kettle to young Kev. Now Ginifur opened her bag, took out the old sheet and tore it into pieces. These she left in a pile on the dresser. She poured some of the water into the bowl and carefully washed her hands, letting them dry on their own. Taking a length of clean linen she tore it in half and then tied a piece over her mouth and nose before moving nearer to the bed.

"What's that for?" Margery stared at her in astonishment.

Ginifur explained that when the smallpox hit the area in 1763 she had been told that this simple precaution could help to stop the wearer picking up the infection from anyone they were nursing. She didn't add that it was Old Betsy who had told her this, thinking that Margery would probably dismiss the advice of a simple healing woman who some called a witch. But between them Ginifur and Betsy had nursed a large number of victims of whom, sadly, only a few survived. She added that they also believed that washing their hands frequently, especially before and after handling each patient, stopped them passing the sickness to others. At Clara's bedside Margery moved aside for Ginifur to look at Clara's restless form as she struggled with a high temperature and raging fever. Her night clothes and bedding were soiled, her body running with perspiration and her hair damp and matted with all the tossing and turning. "Do you have any clean linen left, Mrs Fry?"

Margery nodded. "Not a lot, shall I fetch some?"

"Please. . . we must wash Clara's body and change her bedding. The bathing will ease her fever as her body dries in the air. Bring her a loose chemise which will let her move more easily."

"She'll catch cold and die," objected Margery.

"I'm afraid she will die more quickly of fever if we don't bring her temperature down."

Resignedly Margery made to leave the room but Ginifur halted her. "Your hands, Mrs Fry. . . for your husband's sake if not for yourself, please wash your hands before you leave the room. . . and every time you leave the room." She stressed the importance for this. Reluctantly Margery complied with her request and left Ginifur to start removing Clara's soiled attire.

Stripping back the heavy bedding Ginifur removed the wet and soiled top sheet. There were too many blankets and coverlets and Clara's fever was exacerbated by too much wool and duck down. The covers removed Clara's restlessness was eased a little as her body was exposed to the air, making it easier for Ginifur to remove her high necked and long sleeved gown. Now she could see the extent of the damage to Clara's skin. The spots were classically distributed on her face and extremities and had passed into the second stage where the pustules were broken and weeping. Ginifur brought the bowl nearer the bed and using the torn linen she began to bathe Clara's body from head to toe. By allowing her body to dry in the air her temperature was reduced yet again and for a moment Clara was at peace. Looking around Ginifur spied another bowl and dropped the dirty linen strips into it to be taken away and boiled. Ginifur had just finished cleaning Clara's body when her mother arrived with the clean chemise and sheets. Helping to re-dress Clara, she told Margery to cover her with only half of the bedding. She poured a little rose water into a dish and, diluting it with the boiled water, she instructed Margery to bathe Clara's forehead with it if she became distressed again, and then asked where her grandson lay.

Ginifur fetched the freshly boiled kettle from the kitchen and returned to the first floor. Young Richard Tremayne had thrown all his bedding onto the floor and lay in the middle of the large bed, delirious and restless with his night shirt uncomfortably twisted and rucked up under his armpits. Like his mother his symptoms were classic. The distribution and progress of the disease identical. Mother and son must have caught it from the same source, and at the same time.

Ginifur attended to her grandson in the same way she had his mother, asking Margery to fetch him a clean nightshirt and some bed linen. She had just settled the young Richard when Beau burst into the room.

"Is he alright? Mother. . . is he going to get better?" Beau pleaded.

"Beau I cannot promise that. He and Clara are a little more comfortable and clean. I am just going to prepare an infusion to help to bring their fever down."

"One of that old witches concoctions!" Beau's hatred of Old Betsy ran deep and Ginifur was aware of it.

"It is a tried and tested herbal remedy used by my grandmother and in many households Beau. Do you want me to help or not?" Ginifur's voice had a sharp edge to it.

"Yes. . . yes. . . of course," he turned from the bed in alarm.

"Then you must trust my judgement. Both Clara and your son are already showing advanced stages of the disease. I can't promise anything Beau, but I can promise that I will do my best for them both." Ginifur assured him as he slumped into the chair beside his son, laid his head on the bed and wept.

* * *

Beau had been successful in recruiting Madge and Eva; both arrived early the following morning when Beau ordered the trap to collect them. Both were keen and eager to help and Ginifur smiled to herself thinking that Beau must have been generous with his offer for them to be so willing. Immediately Ginifur set Madge to boil all the soiled linen, including the strips that she had used for washing Clara and Richard, or Charlie as Margery insisted on calling him. Eva was set the task of helping Ginifur and Margery to administer the herbal concoction in between bathing their faces and arms with rosewater diluted with a little water.

Their fever remained high and over the next days the bed linen had to be changed often and their bodies washed regularly in an attempt to break their high temperature.

Regardless of the fact that Eva could not catch smallpox Ginifur still insisted that the young woman wore a strip of sheeting over her mouth and nose and washed her hands regularly to stop the spread of infection throughout the house. She also suggested that Margery Fry should get a little rest, for the woman was worn out, reluctantly she agreed as long as Ginifur called her if there was a change for the worst.

Beau, in the first instance, refused to take the simple precautions until Ginifur told him that he would most certainly be the next person to succumb if he didn't, and then what use would he be to his son.

In between her tasks to make her patients comfortable, Ginifur took short periods of rest in a chair in one of their rooms. After a while she couldn't be sure whether it was night or day as one day ran into the other.

Surprisingly it was Clara whose resistance failed first. Ginifur had woken in the chair beside her bed to see a trickle of blood at the corner of her lips. Taking a piece of clean linen she wiped it away as Clara opened her eyes. For the first time in days Clara's eyes focussed on Ginifur's face and she lifted her hand a few inches from the bed as Ginifur took it in her own. "Hello Clara."

As Eva opened the door Ginifur turned and indicated that she should call the family.

Beau's wife tried to move her head, but the effort was too great. "Charlie!!" The word was barely above a whisper.

"Beau is with him now, Clara."

"He is alive?" Clara's eyes searched for the truth.

"He is still a sick little boy, my dear, but he lives." Although Ginifur found herself adding, silently to herself, 'for now. . .'

A tear formed at the corner of Clara's eye as her grip tightened on Ginifur's hand. "Thank you," she whispered as the door opened to admit Beau and Margery Fry. Clara's attention was drawn away from Ginifur's face towards her husband. . . she smiled briefly and then her eyes closed.

"No. . ." Beau let out a painful groan and he sank down beside the bed as Margery wept. Ginifur moved away from the bed and left them to grieve alone.

Ginifur now centred her efforts on trying to save her grandsons life. She had believed that children had the least resistance, but she had been wrong. She had to leave Madge and Eva to lay out Clara's body for burial.

Richard Charles Tremayne past away three long days after his mother and just one day before his father succumbed to the disease.

Ginifur sent word to Tremanyon that her daughter-in-law and grandson had passed away but that she would be staying at Killow Barton to nurse her son.

Having lost his wife and adored son, Beau's resistance was low and Ginifur believed that there was little chance of his surviving. Exhausted as she was she doubled her efforts and, with the help of Madge and Eva, Beau finally pulled through.

In spite of her helping to nurse her daughter and grandson, Margery Fry managed to stay free of smallpox as did Ginifur and, as she had promised, so did Madge and Eva. But Clara's and young Richard Tremayne's death due to the disease was to be followed by that of Clara's father, Robert Fry. Ginifur stayed on at the Fry home to nurse him to the end, and giving him as much care as she had to Beau and his wife and son.

Needless to say Margery Fry was devastated by the death of all her family, claiming that she wished the smallpox had taken her also, for she had nothing to live for. Ginifur tried to reason with her, but knowing how she herself had felt when Richard had died, she could quite understand her feelings.

Remarkably, possibly due to Ginifur's insistence that the few staff who remained at Killow Barton kept themselves in isolation, away from friends and families, there were no other instances of smallpox on the Rhosinnis Peninsula.

Ginifur remained at Killow Barton until she was firmly convinced that she was no longer able to spread the smallpox virus further and her return to Tremanyon was greeted with both smiles and tears of joy in equal measure, by her relieved family.

* * *

Daniel and Jamie had been busy during Ginifur's absence, in an attempt to build up evidence that would convince a jury that Henry Bishop had conceived and arranged an attempt to murder Jamie.

Once confirmation had been received that the body they had retrieved was almost certainly that of Walter Hawes, Daniel and Dickon set off for Bodmin to collect the few personal items that had survived the incarceration in the mine shaft.

They studied the meagre collection on the table. The remains of a jacket and a pair of boots which had seen better days, but Daniel was hopeful that Walter's family would be able to identify something. From one of his pockets they had found a small plated tin which would probably have contained tobacco, and a briar pipe. Surprisingly there was also a gold chain and a three stoned garnet ring. The constables informed them that neither fitted any description of stolen goods and as they had been recorded as his personal effects by the Sheriff John Carr they were under an obligation to return them to his nearest kin.

"Bet they'd 'ave took 'em if'n the Sheriff adn't signed they papers." Davey remarked , when they stopped at Penhallow for the night on the way back to St Austell.

"Not much to show for a hard life spent under ground." Daniel mused. "We'll set of tomorrow and see if we can find his wife and family. Of course it's possible that they are no longer at the address that I have been given."

They had to stop and ask for directions a number of times before they finally arrived at the low door of a ramshackled dwelling set in the middle of a row of cottages in a damp valley called Holmbush. It looked for all the world as if it were empty and when Jamie slipped from his horse and approached the cottage no one answered the knock on the door.

Glancing around he realised that they were being watched surreptitiously. Two doors down a young man leaned nonchalantly against a door post as he attempted to light a clay pipe, taking deep puffs until it caught alight. Across the way a woman sat in her doorway as she slowly peeled potatoes letting them fall one by one into the iron pot at her feet whilst she waited for their next move and a curtain twitched in the window of the dwelling next door. People were sauntering past, seemingly going nowhere for they returned a few moments later with nothing in their hands to explain where they had been.

Jamie looked again at the cottage; the curtains were drawn across the small window at the front of the house. Surely, he thought, no one would leave their curtains if they were to leave home, and anyway where would they go?

Jamie decided to approach the young man. "Do you know where I might find Mrs Hawes?" he asked politely.

The young man looked up. "Who's askin'?"

"Well. . . I am to start with." Jamie understood the resistance to give information.

"What for? 'n who are 'ee?"

"I am Jamie Tremayne of Rhosinnis."

"Ah. . . Cap'n Tremayne's other son. The one what's give new life t' Wheal Jenny."

"Do you work at Wheal Jenny?" Jamie enquired. "I don't think I recognise you."

"No reason why 'ee should. I did 'ave work at the Magdalen till we was put off. Anyways, what are 'ee wantin' of Peg Hawes?"

"To tell the truth we have news for her regarding her husband, Walter." Jamie glanced again at the cottage. "I'm sorry to have found her out." He turned away. "It looks as though we have made a wasted journey Dan. I guess we might as well return home," and gathered the reins in his hand as he made to put his foot in the stirrup.

"'old on!" The young man pushed himself away from the door. "Are 'ee sure you'm not from the Magdalen mine, come t' put even more pressure on the poor woman?"

Jamie turned. "I tell you I am Captain Jamie Tremayne. . . yes. This is my brother-in-law and friend, Mr Daniel Franks."

"The lawyer man from Truro. I've 'eard of 'ee."

"And who may you be, might I enquire?" Jamie asked civilly, for he was aware that this young man knew more about the whereabouts of Peg Hawes and her family than he was letting on.

"Names Denzil." He answered after giving it a little thought and then looked Jamie and Daniel over a bit more before adding. "Peg and Walter's daughter, Maisie, be me wife."

Jamie considered this information "Peg Hawes has been having trouble, is that it?"

"Ye could say so."

"Well believe me I mean to inflict no harm on the poor woman; I have just come to give her some information about her missing husband."

"Ye mean 'ee can't come 'n give it 'er 'isself?"

Jamie shook his head. "I'm sorry, no."

Denzil looked about him. There was no one in the road now, except these two gentlemen and a man loitering at the end of the lane. Denzil let out a piercing whistle which caught the attention of the man who signalled back that all was clear before Denzil moved to the door of the cottage calling out. "Open the door Peg, ye 'ave vis'tors. They'm alright Peg, tis Cap'n Tremayne from Wheal Jenny 'n 'is lawyer friend from Truro. They bring news for 'ee Peg, news of Walter."

Jamie heard a bolt being drawn back from behind the low door. Slowly it opened to reveal the frightened face of Peg Hawes. "'ow does I knaw y'ur not from 'enry Bishop?" she asked refusing to open it further.

"Ye don' Peg, but I'm thinkin' 'ee be tellin' the truth. Let un in 'n I'll come too in case there be trouble." Denzil promised.

The door opened wider to reveal a dark, damp dwelling consisting of one room downstairs and probably one above. The hard dirt floor was covered in the middle with rush matting probably made by Peg herself. There was a small fire in the large grate with a cauldron suspended from a chain above, two handmade benches were either side of a roughly made table and a variety of utensils cluttered a side table near the window which gave the only light to the room. A crude ladder in the corner was the only means to reach the upper floor.

With Jamie, Dan, Denzil and Peg in the small room it would have been crowded but to this Jamie realised there were others already in the room. Denzil put a reassuring arm around a young woman who had been hiding behind the door, two younger children were hiding behind Peg's voluminous skirts and a teenage boy stood sullenly at the door to the outside back yard.

"So ye've news of Walter?" Peg came straight to the point, indicating the benches, and Jamie and Dan took a seat on the farthest one as Peg sat down opposite them. "Well. . . what news do 'ee 'ave? Is 'ee goin' t' come 'ome or is this what me life is t' be from now on?"

"I am sorry Mrs Hawes, I am not the bearer of good news I am afraid."

"Jest as well I be expectin' none then." Peg tried to brush it off. "So what's 'is excuse this time?"

Daniel actually gave her the news. "I am afraid, Mrs Hawes, that we believe that your husband's body has been found in a mine shaft on the moor."

Peg showed little emotion at this piece of news; she just sat very still twisting the fabric of her skirt in her fingers as she accepted her situation. Walter was not coming home; she was left alone to bring up their son. In her heart she had known that it would come to this. She had fallen so far since the days when Walter had been the mine captain at Wheal Jenny. Then they lived in a stone built house with a slate floor, a kitchen with a range, a living room with three bedrooms above and their own privy in the yard. Now she had been forced to beg her daughter for a roof over her head, and they all had to survive in the cob hovel with a dirt floor that someone had let them rent cheap because they had taken pity on a young woman with two toddlers and a babe on the way. Once upon a time they had furniture to call their own, long sold to pay for food. Walter had earned a good wage and the family were well fed and clothed, why couldn't he have been satisfied with his lot? Jamie didn't hurry her and waited until she finally looked up.

"What 'appened to un?"

"Well. . . we believe that Mr Bishop might have hired Walter to do a job for him. Walter agreed to hide out on the moor until it was finished, and then he was promised work."

"That man's promises come t' nought. We 'ad a good 'ome Cap'n, 'n Wally 'ad a good job. We was 'appy 'nough till that man come along with 'is promises."

"Did you hear him make those promises Mrs Hawes?" Jamie's hopes rose.

"Nah. . . 'ee kept me outa the way when Bishop come a callin', But 'ee tol' me after 'ee left, sure 'nough. The first time Walter was so feared 'ee run away 'n it were a long time afore 'ee returned.

"Did you know that your husband was on the moor?" Daniel wanted to know.

Peg Hawes glanced at her son-in-law before answering. Denzil gave her a brief nod and she continued. "We did. Mr Bishop told un not t' come down to' see we, but 'ee did, e'd writ a letter y'see. Didn' trust Mr Bishop no more. Walter was ejicated 'n 'ee could write just fine. Me I can't read nor write, but 'ee 'could."

"A letter?"

"Tha's right, 'n 'ee made me swear t' keep it safe. If'n the day come when I was t' 'ear that 'ee was dead then I was t' give it t' someone who 'ee 'oped would 'elp us."

"Who was that Mrs Hawes?"

"Said 'ee couldn' tell me, said I'd knaw when the time come."

"Have you read the letter Peg?" Jamie asked.

"I tol' 'ee, I can't read nor write."

"Well I am afraid that your husband is probably dead." Jamie lifted a bundle onto the table and untied the string to reveal all that remained of Walter's belongings. Peg reached out to touch the fabric of the jacket, pulling it gently towards her and clutching it to her breast. "You recognise this?" Peg's answer was the look on her face and the tears in her eyes. She fingered the pipe and tobacco tin lovingly and then took the chain and the ring that Jamie offered her.

“His mother’s,” she explained. “They was Walter’s mother’s, ’ee wore ’em round ’is neck always.”

“I would like to keep them for now, if you would agree?”

Peg Hawes looked puzzled. “Why?”

“To be honest with you we are hoping that Henry Bishop will stand trial at Bodmin and we will need these items as identification of your husband.”

Peg, Denzil and Maisie gasped in unison then Denzil turned to his mother-in-law. “Walter said ye’d know when the right person turned up Peg. I think ’ee ’ave. I think ye should give Walter’s letter t’ Cap’n Tremayne.”

Peg looked at her daughter and young teenage son before going to the fireplace. She removed a stone from the side and drew out a grubby piece of paper which she handed to Jamie. Jamie spread it out on the table in front of Daniel and himself as they studied it.

Walter’s letter was well written, though a little dirty. As Peg had so proudly stated Walter had been educated and he wrote a fair hand. As Jamie and Dan digested the contents of the letter they became more confident of a conviction. Walter’s letter gave time and dates of meetings and events, it was a very damning letter indeed, a very dangerous document for Peg Hawes to have kept hidden.

They explained the contents to Peg and her family and she insisted that they kept it, along with Walter’s belongings. Her only request was that they should avenge Walter’s death for her.

Jamie left enough money to see the family through the next few days and told Denzil and Peg’s teenage son Paul to present them selves at Wheal Jenny and he would get Davey Rawe to offer them a job and help to find them better accommodation.

The next bit of good news was that one of the thugs that Fred thought had died had in fact survived. They had not been fighting as was suspected but had been set upon by persons unknown and left for dead. His friend had indeed died but Saul Jacob had gone into hiding frightened for his life and for this reason his family had claimed that he too was dead. He backed up Fred’s story and Sheriff John Carr agreed that Henry Bishop should stand trial for the attempted murder of Jamie Tremayne and the actual murder of John Rawe together with that of Walter Hawes. Naturally both Fred and Saul would both have to stand trial too but he would recommend leniency for giving evidence. Due to his position as the owner of the Magdalen Mine, Henry Bishop was not required to be arrested and imprisoned and after his first hearing when he faced the charge and pleaded not guilty he was allowed to continue his life outside until the trial. Legal advisors for the defence and prosecution said that they would need time to collect their evidence and the date for the trial was set for March 1798.

The charges for Robert Fry were dropped as soon as it was declared that he had died of smallpox.

* * *

Ginifur had lost all track of time whilst nursing Beau's wife and family and she was surprised to find that another Christmas was fast approaching.

It seemed that her insistence that the Fry house should be put into voluntary isolation had saved smallpox from being spread on the Rhosinnis Peninsula. Beau had survived the disease and his face would continue to bare the scars of the pox marks. In truth he wasn't as badly marked as he might have been, Ginifur had remarked on the fact that he had not suffered as badly as Clara or young Richard. Their faces and arms had been covered with spots so thick you could hardly place a pinhead between them Beau had just seven spots on his face which had finally ruptured and left their scars, but he had lived where his wife and son had died.

When Ginifur made plans to return to Tremanyon she asked Beau if he would like to return with her. She was concerned about her son. Since the funeral at Ruan, Beau had been understandably quiet and withdrawn yet for once in his life he did not turn to drink to drown his woes. Occasionally he would ride out on his favourite horse, but more and more now he would set out on foot and spend hours striding round the peninsula, sometimes returning long after nightfall.

Ginifur and Beau were enjoying a coffee in the drawing room at Killow Barton when she asked him if he would like to return to Tremanyon with her.

Beau placed his cup in the saucer before his eyes rose to meet hers, and he shook his head. "No. . . not for the moment Mother. Thank you for the offer though." He had lost weight, his face thin and gaunt; his eyes lacked lustre and were sunken in the shadowed depth of their sockets. Beau had once been a very handsome young man, but there was no trace of that person in the face before Ginifur now, and it wasn't the few scars that had caused it, for most of them would be hidden by the blonde curls that normally fell over his forehead. Of course it was only natural for Beau to grieve for his wife and son, but Ginifur feared that his grief was going too deep. "Don't thank me, Beau. Tremanyon is your home and the door will always be open to you."

Beau gave her a weak smile. "No, I will stay here a while with Clara's mother, give her time to come to terms with her loss before I leave her totally alone in this large house." But this statement gave Ginifur cause for disquiet, for Beau was not normally concerned for the feelings and needs of others; however she accepted his reasons with a smile. "But perhaps, after Christmas, maybe I could join you for a few days. I have been invited to spend Christmas with Father's family as usual but I feel that I might even give this a miss." Beau suggested.

"Whatever you wish. I will have your bedroom prepared for whenever you wish to return home." Ginifur assured him. "Rachel and Rebecca and their families will stay over on Christmas Day and return to their own on Boxing Day, you will be welcome whenever you wish to join us."

"Jamie and his family are still with you?"

"Yes, for the moment." Naturally she didn't say that they would stay until the trial as Fred was still living in the basement.

"Mmm. I'll come home for a few days over Christmas. I'll let you know when. Don't worry Ma, I'll be fine."

But Ginifur did worry; there was a change in Beau. What had brought it about? The death of Clara and his young son? Ginifur returned to Tremanyon alone.

The past few weeks had been dull and overcast, but as Christmas approached they were treated to a spell of dry but crisp weather and Ginifur set out with Dickon and Robyn to collect holly and ivy for decorating the house for the festive season. Ginifur had picked and dried flowers and herbs during the summer to make a flower garland for the dining room and Lottie and Mabel had been busy making extra candles from the beeswax that had been brought in from the hives.

They set off for Lerryn Wood with Dickon leading the small donkey cart, and in a short time they had collected a good selection of holly, ivy and other evergreens and, before returning home, they continued down the lane to visit the orchard in the valley where Ginifur had been watching mistletoe flourish in an old gnarled apple tree. Ginifur had enjoyed the time outside in the fresh air and returned home feeling happy and refreshed. For the first time in weeks she had a smile on her face and rosy cheeks to go with it.

Lorna and Poppy had been busy for weeks. In the summer they had been preserving fruits, some in syrup and others in brandy and a selection had been preserved in sugar to make candied fruits. In the autumn they had carefully wrapped apples and pears to put into the store and, in recent weeks, they had been preparing menus and adding spices and brandy to dried fruits for puddings and pies.

Kate's health was failing. Since the day that she had fainted and fallen down the short flight of steps to the west wing, she had been plagued with headaches and fainting spells for which the doctor could find no cause nor cure. His only suggestion was rest. As far as Ginifur was concerned Kate could have as much rest as she needed, for she had given great service to Ginny and the Tremayne family since the day that Ginifur purchased some Christmas gifts from her stall on the quay at Truro. There, beneath the stall her two little girls had huddled to keep warm and Aidan snuggled beneath rabbit furs in a crude crib at his mother's feet. Kate had helped Ginifur in the house when she first came to Tremanyon but had expressed an interest in cooking. Netty Teague had taken her under her wing and suggested that she train her up to take her place when age got the better of her. It had worked well and Kate proved a quick learner and her skills equal to her tutor. Lorna had been a natural choice to continue when it became obvious that Kate would not be able to continue, for she had worked along side her mother in the kitchen since she was thirteen.

Kate had always had a trim figure, never prone to carrying extra weight in spite of the fine food that she prepared over the years. But now Kate's loss of weight concerned them all, she was just wasting away before their very eyes. Liam and Ginifur would try to tempt her to eat the light food that was beautifully prepared for her by Lorna; sometimes with success but at others she found it impossible to eat more that a mouthful or two.

Even so Kate brightened at the sight of Ginifur and Poppy bringing in arms full of bright green foliage with the red berries of the holly and the white of the mistletoe, and she took great pleasure in watching whilst Ginifur produced festive displays to decorate every room in the house. Kate even managed to join with the festivities in her own quiet way and it was yet another year without Beau joining them.

The day after Boxing Day Ben Nancekivel decided to ride over to the stables at Rhosinnis and suggested that Dickon ride out with him. Ginifur, Jamie and Liam walked over to the stables to see them off and afterwards made their way to the tack room to see Joe. Joe was busy making a new halter for Jamie's stallion. Joe kept the tack room as clean and tidy as Sam Sawle had, it smelt of leather and dubbin and Jamie wandered around the walls looking at the saddles and harness that hung in rows on the saddle racks when he paused before a hook on which hung two sets of harness and girth straps.

"Why are these two sets hanging here? Where are the saddles?"

Joe glanced uneasily at Ginifur before answering. "The saddles are on the spare racks, at the end, Captain Tremayne."

Jamie moved on to finger the saddles before turning to see three pairs of eyes watching him. "I think that someone has some explaining to do, don't you?" His question was to his mother and Ginifur nodded her head in agreement.

Whilst they settled themselves on the tack boxes Liam laid a reassuring hand on Joe's shoulder as he lifted the girth straps down. Between Ginifur, Liam and Joe they explained Joe's suspicions and, as they had thought, Jamie was now ready to listen. He fingered the straps thoughtfully. "You have kept them in good condition Joe."

"I always 'oped the day'd come when someone would 'ear me out." He hesitated. "Not that I blame anyone mind, for not listenin'."

Jamie stared at the floor. "Maybe you don't Joe. . . but, I should have listened. This is why you came to see me. . . back then. . . after Ellen died?"

"Yes, Sir."

Jamie shook his head in abject dismay. "I am sorry Joe; I should have given you a hearing."

Joe was appalled that Jamie Tremayne felt the need to apologise to him. "Oh no, Sir. There be no need to feel that way."

Jamie rewarded him with a brief smile as he rose from the tack box that had been his seat. Ginifur followed him as he made his way back through the stables whilst Liam paused awhile with Kate's young brother before making his way back to the house and caught up with Ginifur and Jamie in the front hall. "It's all very well Mother, I agree with you that the girth straps do indeed look as though they have been tampered with." Jamie opened the door to the drawing room and waited for Ginifur to lead the way into the room. "But there is no way that Beau could have been aware that you were taking the children for a ride on the day that Ellen died." Jamie swung round as he heard the rustle of the curtains, to see Robyn curled up on the window seat with a book and his eyes flashed a warning signal to Ginifur and Liam.

Robyn looked up thoughtfully as she remembered the day that her aunt Ellen had fallen from her horse whilst riding with her and Dickon, and the sight of her brother as he sat in the gig watching her father as he stroked her grandmother's horse, Willow. "I don't expect he did until he rode in." There was a deathly hush as Ginifur, Jamie and Liam exchanged worried looks. "Is there something wrong? Grandmother. . .?"

Ginfur pulled herself together, not really wanting an answer. "What do you mean, Robyn, when he rode in?"

Robyn put down her book and swung her legs to the floor so that she was in a sitting position with her hands gripping the cushion as she tried to recall the chain of events of that fateful day. "It was after you were called to see Kate, you remember she fainted and fell down the steps and you went to see how bad it was?"

"Yes I remember, we all do, but what has that got to do with it?"

"Well you told us you wouldn't be long and so we were waiting for you to return when my father rode in with. . . my brother." Robyn rarely used her brother's name; she rarely spoke at all about her natural family.

A dark look crossed Jamie's face. "What did he do, Robyn?"

"Do. . . ?" His niece looked puzzled. "What do you mean. . . do?"

"Did he remain in the gig, Robyn? Can you remember anything he said?" Jamie made an effort to keep his voice calm.

Robyn frowned in concentration before answering. "Dickon spoke to him. . . I don't usually have much to say. As I remember, Father asked where we were going and Dickon said we were going riding with you grandmother." She paused whilst she remembered her brother's dark looks, the hatred that burned behind those pale grey eyes of his. "Father got down from the gig and made a fuss of Willow I remember. He said that he remembered her being born."

"Was that all?"

"I can't remember, to be honest, I think that I was watching my. . . brother. Why did he hate me so?"

"I'm sure he didn't Robyn" Ginifur tried to re-assure her. "But what happened next?"

"Lorna came out and told us to either ride over Home Farm or stable the horses, as you couldn't leave Kate. Father got back in the gig and drove off."

Ginifur, Jamie and Liam had their backs to the door and although Robyn could see the door she wasn't aware that there was anyone behind it until it slowly swung open to reveal her father, white faced and with a sad expression on his face as he gave her a steady look.

A gasp escaped Robyn's lips, the colour drained from her face, and as Ginifur, Jamie and Liam slowly turned around she added "Have I said something wrong?" Her question hung on the air. "Grandmother. . . Uncle Jamie. . . Father. . . what is wrong? I'm sorry if I have said something to upset you all."

Beau found his voice first and smiled at his daughter. Robyn had never been favoured with a smile from him and was confused. He continued to look her in the eye as he addressed her. "No Roberta. You have not said anything that you should not have said. In truth I am grateful to you for bringing it out into the light." Beau glanced briefly at the three other people in the room before stepping towards his daughter and taking her hands lifted her from the window seat. "Perhaps you would be kind enough to leave us a while Roberta, there are things that need to be discussed with your Grandmother and Uncle." Leading her to the door he felt her hand tremble in his grasp and briefly wondered how he could have disowned this daughter of his, so nearly a woman now. Sadly he watched her walk away and closed the door behind her before turning towards the room.

Beau's eyes first fell on Liam, his father's faithful retainer, he believed that he would even have given his life for his master his devotion was so strong. Beau turned his attention to his mother. She was a strong woman, but the death of her husband had been a great shock to her. Beau realised now that his parents had shared a great love and wondered if this was unusual for, if he was truly honest, he had not loved Clara greatly. It had only started because he tried to thwart his brother Jamie. At the thought of his brother Beau finally turned to face Jamie and realised that he could not read the expression on his face. His eyes, normally the same bright blue of his father's eyes, were now so dark that you could not distinguish them from the black of the pupils. Why had he hated him so much? Why had he been so jealous of him? Jamie had never done anything intentionally to harm him in either word or deed. In fact he had always taken him under his wing when he had been a small boy.

Jamie was five years older than himself and at the age of eleven a competent rider. It was Jamie who had spent hours taking him for rides around the estate, it was Jamie who rescued him when his pony had bolted on the headland at Rhosinnis; by galloping dangerously close to the cliff edge Jamie had forced his pony to turn inland before catching hold of his reins and pulling him to a halt, and it was Jamie who had rescued him when he fell into the water tank whilst he had been watching the water boatmen skating across the surface of the water when he was just six years old. From that day to this Beau had hated water, refusing point blank to sail in a boat of any size.

Jamie's eyes slowly came into focus and took in the figure of his younger brother. Beau was thin and gaunt, was this a result of the smallpox? He was uncomfortably thin, his shoulders slumped as though he carried a heavy burden on his back, and his eyes held a haunted look.

Ginifur broke the silence. "Beau! We didn't expect you until New Year's Eve, is anything wrong?"

Beau took a step into the room as he answered his mother. "I wasn't comfortable. . . it was difficult for the others."

Liam had distanced himself from the family, leaving Jamie and Ginifur in the centre of the room he had taken up a position near one of the windows. Liam shared Ginifur's sorrow when Richard had died from a fall from his horse and he had helped her to come to terms with a life without him. He couldn't have loved this family more if it had been his own and now he watched Ginifur very carefully, readying himself to move if needed.

Jamie's dark eyes studied his brother's face before he spoke. "Willow's girth strap was tampered with on the day Ellen died. I blamed Joe for her death. . . but it wasn't his fault. . . was it?"

Beau ran his fingers through his untidy hair as he struggled to answer. He finally forced the word from his throat. "No."

Ginifur drew in a sharp breath and Liam moved a little closer as Jamie clenched his fists in anger.

Ginifur's eyes fastened on Beau's face. "Tell me it is not true, Beau. I. . . you couldn't wish harm to your father! Not Richard, who loved you so. . . I won't believe it, I just won't." All the remaining colour drained from her face as she was forced to confront the worst moment in her life. "Beau," she pleaded, "tell me. . . please. Tell me you didn't do it."

Jamie's voice was cold and hard, the words cut at her heart. "He can't Mother. . . his silence condemns him."

Ginifur concentrated on Beau's face as he struggled to answer her. Against her will the vision of Liam carrying the body of her beloved husband into the hall at Tremanyon flowed back into her mind and she blinked as the light appeared to dim. She was vaguely aware that Liam was moving towards her as a roaring sound filled her ears, like a high wind rushing through Tremanyon woods. The darkness began to envelop her in a warm blanket, slowly it crept upwards from her legs into her body then she heard someone give a plaintive cry as she gave herself up to the darkness and silence. . . and peace.

Ginifur had let out a cry of such pain that Liam leapt forward as she collapsed slowly towards the floor, catching her in his arms before her head reached the corner of the brass fender.

* * *

Ginifur had never fainted in her life, but she had been unconscious for a number of days after she had dived into the sea to rescue a child from a shipwreck. The result was similar this time. Ginifur stayed in a comatose state, nothing would raise her from her deep sleep and the doctor was called the following day.

"Has she had a shock?" Doctor Carlton asked when he had completed his examination. "I can find nothing wrong with her."

Marie-Claire was sitting beside the bed where she had spent her nights vigil. "She has, but she will recover won't she?"

Dr Carlton closed his bag as he studied his patient. "I could bleed her. . . " he suggested.

"No." Jamie entered the room as the doctor suggested this remedy." She doesn't believe in bleeding, you know that Doctor."

"Indeed I do. Ginifur and I have had many discussions on the efficacy of this treatment."

"Will she come round on her own?" Jamie wanted to know.

"In time, she should. It depends on how severe the shock. I can't tell Jamie. . . I'm sorry. Ginifur will need to feel ready to face the problem again I fear, before she recovers. Meanwhile, it is time. . . just time."

Ginifur lay in her sleep for three more nights and days and remembering that she had insisted on getting Jamie to take fluid, Marie-Claire persisted with Robyn's help. Jamie had to insist that they both had periods of rest themselves, for neither of them would leave her room without being urged to.

Jamie's initial anger at Beau's admission of guilt had eased a little on Liam's insistence that the priority at the moment was their mother's recovery. Beau, it seemed, was pleased that the truth was out for he was finding it impossible to bear the guilt any longer. It seemed that all the bad facets of his character had died along with his wife and son. He professed that he would make amends if he could, but nothing would bring his father back. He admitted his actions arose from his passion to own Tremanyon, a passion now extinguished and incomprehensible, even to Beau. Liam believed that he was being honest in what he said and persuaded the brothers to talk things through rationally for Ginifur's sake. Beau carried a great burden and wanted to make a clean breast of it. His final admission was that he had been aware of Henry Bishop's plan to involve Jamie in an accident at the mine and Robert Fry's active agreement - yet he had not attempted to warn him

Jamie was a realist, not a dreamer, his marriage to Marie-Claire had eased the pain of the loss of his first wife and he addressed the problem objectively. Of course he would never understand what could have driven his brother to cause an accident which would result in the death of his father, and then to attempt to repeat it with his mother. Jamie and Liam talked long into the night, wondering what action, if any, they should take. They agreed that nothing could happen until Ginifur made a recovery.

* * *

Ginifur had always known when Richard was in the house and even after his tragic death she had often felt his presence on occasions when she relaxed in his favourite chair in the library. Ginifur opened her eyes to find that she was surrounded by a white mist and felt his presence near her now. Was she dreaming? It wasn't like other dreams if so, they were usually quite vivid in detail. The thought crossed her mind that there was something that she should be attending to and struggled for a moment to recall what it was. Eventually she gave up the struggle for the effort was too great. No Matter! Jamie would deal with it. Yes, that would be for the best, Jamie would know what to do.

"You can't leave Jamie to deal with your problems alone." Richard's voice addressed her from somewhere in the mist.

Ginifur wasn't at all surprised; it seemed the most natural thing that she should hold a conversation with her dead husband. "Yes I can, Jamie is not a child now. He is a man and can deal with any problem."

"But this isn't only Jamie's problem, Ginny. It is yours too. In any case, it isn't your time Ginny, there are still things for you to do." It was as though Richard were sitting beside her.

"I don't think I want to." Even to Ginifur's ears the words seemed like the petty words of a truculent and spoiled child and she added. "I am so tired."

A grey form appeared in the mist, indistinct and without features but Ginifur knew who it was.

"What about Jamie, Dickon and Robyn? Are you ready to leave them. . . now, when they need you the most?" Ginifur willed him to come closer so that she could see his face once more. "No Ginny, heart of my heart, Robyn needs a mother still and her mother is you. . . and Jamie though grown to manhood still respects your thoughts and wishes. He and Dickon need you too. . . Beau also. I will be here when the time is right, you know I will. Go home Ginny, please. . . go home."

"Don't go Richard. Please don't go." Ginifur heard herself calling out as the shape shifted.

* * *

Doctor Carlton had warned them that he thought that Ginifur's time was drawing near, that her body was giving up the fight to live.

Beside her bed they gathered in silence. Jamie, Marie-Claire and Beau had been at her bedside for the last twelve hours, believing the worst. Dickon and Robyn had just entered the room with Liam and Kate; they had been asked if they wished to say farewell and Robyn ran to the side of her grandmother's bed and taking up her hand in hers she knelt beside Ginifur as Beau eased himself backwards to give her room. Dickon joined Jamie and Marie-Claire, and Liam and Kate took up a position at the foot of the bed.

Liam glanced around the room. Ginifur appeared to sleep peacefully in her bed and for the first time Liam noticed a strand or two of silver in amongst the dark curls. He smiled at the thought of all the times she had tried to hide the curls in a severe style; more suited to her position as a servant, she had said. Richard changed all that when he married her, loving to see Ginifur's hair flow free. Liam acknowledged the prickling sensation in his eyes, blinking rapidly to disperse the unshed tears he grasped Kate's hand and saw the sparkle in her own. Kate had aged in the last twelve months as her illness progressed and Liam feared that her days too were numbered. Her early years of hardship and poverty, living in damp dwellings, had left her lungs struggling to cope. If it hadn't been for Ginifur rescuing them from their hovel, poor Kate would have died long ago. Old Betsy, bless her, had concocted a remedy that eased the worst of her condition and Ginifur had continued to prepare it in recent years. He let out a long sigh; yes there would be a hole in all their lives on the day Ginny Tremayne passed away.

Beau looked up as he heard the sigh escape Liam's lips. The man was genuinely moved; he noticed the sparkle of unshed tears in his eyes, his wife's too. He had never understood the unusual relationship between the Fierneys' and his father and mother. Outwardly they behaved as any other member of the household staff, in company they addressed Richard and Ginifur respectfully as would have been expected of them and only in private were they on personal terms. Richard had had a great respect for this man and Beau understood that part of this related to their adventures in the New World. Kate had always been a great friend to his mother and he had always, ungraciously, said that this was because she recognised her own position in society. Now, finally, when he couldn't tell her, he realised how wrong he had been and what a pompous snob he was. Lord and Lady Falmouth had acknowledged Ginifur as one of their friends and she had been well received in most of the large houses of the upper classes. No, he had wronged both his father and his mother and he wished that he could tell them and make amends. As unlikely as it was, even if his mother should make a remarkable recovery, she would never be able to forgive him for what he had done to bring about her husbands riding accident, even if she did forgive him for the incident to her own horse. Beau sighed, no it was probably for the best, for he didn't think that he could bear to see the look of accusation and hurt in her eyes.

Jamie lifted his eyes from his mother's face, tearing himself away from the memories of her love and care throughout his life. The brothers' eyes met and held, as though a silent conversation passed between them. Then Robyn released a heart rending sob and Beau looked down at his daughter, hesitantly he lifted a hand pausing briefly before laying it on her shoulder and giving it gentle squeeze. If Robyn felt his hand she didn't lift her head or push his hand away, and he left it lie there for a moment or two.

This was a facet of Beau's character that was new. Beau cared for no one but Beau and Jamie didn't know how to deal with this new and unfamiliar brother. Dear God. . . he was angry, who wouldn't be? How could anyone's son behave as Beau had and live with the thought that he had instigated his own father's death and then gone on to repeat it? In the next incident it had been Ellen who had died in his mother's place. They had been involved in many angry exchanges over the past few days when he had threatened to prosecute Beau on three counts. The murder of his father and the attempted murder of his mother which had resulted in Ellen's death together with his involvement in the mine incident. Beau had received this threat quite calmly, giving him the feeling that it would be a relief. Jamie struggled again as he watched his brother. Was he genuinely filled with remorse or was it just an act. . . Damn him! Jamie actually found himself feeling sorry for Beau, for he had truly lost everything; he even found himself almost believing that his brother might finally and belatedly be regretful for his past behaviour and actions. Jamie inhaled deeply and Marie-Claire reached out to grasp his hand tightly.

Dickon studied his grandmother's face, every nerve within him was willing her to live. Believing that his thoughts could cross the great divide, and let her know how much they needed her; Robyn looked up and the silent message past between them as she added her thoughts to his. Robyn's eyes glazed as she saw their thoughts entwine and spiral together as they winged their way through space and time to her beloved grandmother. She picked up Ginifur's hand from the coverlet once more and kissed it gently as she finally let the tears that she had tried so hard to halt, begin to run down her cheek as she felt hope slipping away; and watched as the first tear fell with a splash upon Ginifur's hand.

Marie-Claire's attention was fixed upon Robyn and she was thinking how bereft the child would feel without her grandmother. Marie-Claire knew what it was like to be without a mother, but she had had her father. Now just as she herself had found a mother in Ginifur, she was about to loose her too. She watched as Robyn kissed her grandmother's hand and followed the voyage of the tear that fell from Robiyn's eyes. It was as though time itself was suspended; the tear fell so slowly that Marie-Claire saw it clearly from the instant that it fell from Robyn's eyes to the second that it landed on Ginifur's motionless hand.

* * *

Richard's voice was fading and Ginifur struggled to reach him but she couldn't move. Suddenly something came into her vision. . . it was a tear drop. Ginifur watched as it fell slowly through the air towards her, following its path until it fell with a splash on her hand. It was warm and full of sorrow and she knew instinctively that it was from Robyn's eyes. Eyes like Richard's and Jamie's. The grey form had faded back into the mist and Ginifur knew that Richard's words had spoken the truth. She had to go back to face whatever the problem was and with her families help she was confident they would.

Ginifur took one last look around at the pale mist and drew in a breath before she struggled to the surface.

* * *

Kate had seen a flicker of movement behind Ginifur's eyelids, now her lashes began to quiver where they lay upon her cheeks. "She lives. . . Ginifur lives." The whispered words escaped Kate's lips.; and the silence that had been briefly broken returned again as they each held their breath.

Ginifur opened her eyes. The pale mist had gone and she was in darkness, it took a moment for her eyes to adjust and focus and she wasn't aware of where she was.

Robyn broke the silence, "Oh Mama!" she exclaimed, not realising that she had omitted to use the foreword. Once again she took up the hand and kissed it eagerly. "Look Dickon, look," she repeated and she looked up at Jamie smiling, though tears still filled her eyes.

Ginifur woke to find herself in her darkened bedroom with those she loved about her and realised that she had had a close call with death, for she could still hear Richard's voice ringing in her ears.

* * *

Ginifur's recovery was slow. She wasn't bouncing back so well, she was heard to comment on more than one occasion. After her first conversation with both her sons she had come to terms with Beau's revelations extraordinarily well, though admitting that she didn't know if she would ever be able to forgive him. To give him his due neither did Beau ask for forgiveness, knowing all too well that his crimes against his father and mother were truly unforgivable. But Beau could often be seen talking to Ginifur in the lounge and sometimes even reading to her from a favourite book of poetry; at other times he would offer help with Fred. Liam's first thoughts that Beau might mean Fred harm were to be groundless and when Kate suffered a relapse Beau readily accepted the mantle of supervision. Fred actually liked him, not knowing anything of Beau's actions they got on well. They never touched on the incident at the mine; Beau changed the subject if it ever arose. He had also resumed his habit of going for long walks, and it was on one of these occasions that Daniel brought up the subject on one of his visits to see Ginifur.

Ginifur and Robyn were entertaining Rebecca, Tamsin and baby Edward in the lounge whilst Daniel and Jamie went over some details of the imminent court case when Daniel remarked. "I never really knew your brother Jamie, but I am finding it hard to understand him."

Jamie almost laughed. "You don't understand him? Dan. . . I thought I knew my brother with his jealous rages, self centred opinions and disregard for other people. As hard as it was we learned to live with that Beau. This one leaves me confused and bewildered. . . I don't know him at all and don't know what to do." Jamie admitted.

"Is it genuine, do you think?" Daniel continued as Liam entered the room.

"Ye mean, is it an act?" Liam joined in. "T'be sure, I'm not thinkin' it is at'all."

"I'm inclined to agree Dan, though I find it hard to say so. Beau has for some years now harboured a compulsive desire to be addressed as Richard and at times convulsed in a rage as the family still continued to call him Beau. I have to admit that since his return here at Christmas I have made the extra effort to use this name as often as I can to try to make him show his previous colours. . . to no avail. There hasn't been even a spark of interest, let alone anger in his eyes."

"What are you going to do? Are you going to let the authorities know of his involvement in the deaths of your father and first wife? Or are you going to forget you ever heard his admission?"

"It's not a thing you can ever forget, Dan, but I have to think of mother." Jamie explained.

"How does she feel?" Liam gave a grunt and Dan added. "A silly question, I realise, Liam. Ginny has had her world torn apart I do understand, but what I meant was, what are her thoughts on the subject of a possible prosecution being brought against her son?"

"Ginny be as muddled as we all are." Liam voiced his own thoughts on the subject.

"Truth is Daniel, Mother believes that he really is filled with remorse and that he will carry this impossible burden on his shoulders for the rest of his life. She says that sometimes it is easier to accept death than to spend the rest of your life carrying the burden of guilt and the harm that you have done to others in your lifetime. I don't know that I can entirely agree with her, but I don't know that if Beau was to be committed, judged and hanged that it would help her at all. It may be one death too many. . . I just don't know."

"Well the charges against Robert Fry have been dropped, needless to say. In any case, it would appear that he took no real active part in the incident at Wheal Jenny and even if he was implicated by his knowledge of what Henry Bishop planned to do, he is not here to stand trial." Daniel informed them before turning to Liam. "How's Kate?"

"It's failin' she is Dan'l. Dear Jesus. . . tis only the love in her that keeps her body tied t' this earth and I don' want her to suffer no more." Liam's voice cracked as he spoke and Jamie blinked back a tear and swallowed a lump in his throat. There were so few words of comfort to give and Liam saved them from searching for the right ones by excusing himself to return to Kate's side. Ginifur had made up a concoction to ease the pain and it was time for her to take another dose.

Liam met Beau as he entered the side door. "Ye're lookin' flushed lad, is it far ye've been?"

"I walked up to the headland, Liam. It's so clear you can see from the Lizard to beyond the Dodman. I called in at Rhosinnis and told Aidan that Kate has worsened, hope you don't mind. Aidan said he'd be over dreckly." He grinned; Beau never used Cornish dialect.

Liam studied him briefly. "That's good of ye lad, tis my thanks ye have."

“Don’t worry about Fred, Liam. I’ll take his food down, we’ll take a bite together and have a game of cards or two before the evening is over. Don’t fret, we only pay for pebbles.” He put his hand into his pocket and pulled out a handful of white and grey pebbles. “From Kylyn Cove,” he added with another grin. “White ones for Fred, mine are grey.”

Chapter Ten
1798

AS THE SNOWDROPS spread a sparkling white carpet beneath the skeletal shape of the grand oak tree at the bottom of the lawn, Kate gave up her fight for life on 12th January, 1798. Liam lost his soul mate, the love of his life, and Ginifur lost her closest and most beloved friend.

Kate had been a part of Tremanyon life for forty-six years. The Fierneys were also popular in the locality, even though Liam was of Irish origin and Kate from 'down west'. There wasn't a fisherman who didn't praise Liam's fishing baskets that even now he continued to fashion out of the willows from the moor. Lorna and Poppy had married local lads and Aidan had married Prue, a local girl.

Once more Tremanyon was in mourning.

Jamie and Daniel collected Saul and handed him over with Fred two days before the trial to the Sheriff, John Carr, at Bodmin where he met them at the jail. "You do realise that your evidence in the case against Henry Bishop condemns you both. You will not be able to plead not guilty to your own cases later in the day?" Sheriff John Carr made their position quite clear.

Fred spoke for both of them. "We 'ave nothin' t' look forward to Sir, only a life always 'iding, afeared t' show our faces 'n lookin' over our shoulders."

"Is there someone to act for them?" John Carr turned to Daniel.

"Yes, Fergus Malone is acting for the case against Henry Bishop and we have employed Cyril Hardy to conduct the case for the defence of Fred and Saul. I have gone over the cases with him and he will interview them tomorrow, before the court hearing.

"Cyril Hardy eh? That's cost you a pretty penny!"

"It was Jamie's wish." Daniel informed him.

"Fred wasn't really involved in the incident at the mine, only paid to deliver a message to bring me to the mine, albeit a false one. Saul is another matter, for he was involved in that incident and also witness to the murder of Walter Hawes by Henry Bishop." Jamie explained.

John Carr considered the forthcoming trials and addressed Saul. "You do realise that you could well receive a hanging sentence?"

Saul blanched. "I knows tis a possibility, Sir. Tis pure luck that I be 'ere t'day for I should be dead same as me friend, if'n Bishop

’ad ’is way. No. . . I can’t go on livin’ as I ’ave ’n if Bishop gets away with this me life i’nt worth livin’ anyways.”

“The cases come before Judge William Collicott, he’s not known for his leniency.” The dire warning was quite clear. “I will inform the jail that the barrister will be visiting you tomorrow. I understand that Captain Tremayne has arranged for food to be brought to you and a separate cell from the main one. You are very lucky.” John Carr called out to the constable to escort them down to the cells.

Fred turned to Jamie before he went through the door. “Thank ’ee Sir, for what ye’ve done for me. Whatever ’appens, I couldn’ ’ave gone on like I was.”

“Cyril Hardy has a very persuasive manner, I have not given up hope and nor should you.” Jamie grinned as he shook the man’s hand.

Daniel and Jamie spent two days and nights at Bodmin, meeting up with Fergus Malone to go over aspects of the trial against Henry Bishop and with Cyril Hardy who would be taking on the cases of Fred and Saul who would be charged together.

Liam arrived the night before the trial and early the following morning the trio made their way to the courthouse. Daniel had arranged for seats to be made available behind the prosecution council, for Dan had spent the whole of the previous day going over the evidence with him and he wanted to be near by. Fergus was a ruthless prosecuting barrister, if they had any chance of winning it was with him.

Henry Bishop’s trial was the first case to be heard at Bodmin Assize Court that day in March. As Jamie settled himself in his seat and glanced about the room, Beau entered and made his way towards them to take a seat next to Liam. It was the first time that Jamie had been forced to attend a trial at Bodmin but it was evident that the populace treated it as an event of entertainment. There were those members of the mining community, mine owners, shareholders and the like but the majority were of the lower orders, miners, peasants and peddlers. The noise was almost deafening as they called out to one another across the courtroom. For a moment their was a lull as the door opened to admit the bewigged barristers and their notaries, whilst armed guards took up their positions in front of the dock and around the room.

From behind the dock two guards appeared, one on either sight of Henry Bishop, and there was a gasp of surprise when the crowd spied the manacles about his wrists and leg irons on his ankles as he climbed the steps to the dock. He had only just settled himself in his seat when, from the side door, the jurors made their way to their seats. A motley selection of men from various trades, dressed in their Sunday best, looking uncomfortable and apprehensive, the butt of jokes from the floor and the gallery.

The Clerk of the Court rose to his feet, bringing the gavel down on his desk with a resounding crash. "The court is in session, be upstanding for The Honourable, Judge William Collicott." The door opened behind the judge's seat to reveal the splendour of William Collicott in his scarlet gown. When he had taken his seat there was much shuffling and scraping of chairs as the onlookers took theirs.

The Clerk having introduced the first case of the day, returned to his seat and Fergus took the floor to outline the case before them, but Jamie's mind was wandering and he missed the opening sentences all together.

". . . with malice and forethought set out to cold bloodedly engineer an accident at the Wheal Jenny Mine which would subsequently cause the death of one miner who had gone below to save Captain Tremayne; for the intent to murder the major shareholder of Wheal Jenny, Captain Tremayne, and the murder of Walter Hawes, ex mine Captain at the Wheal Jenny. Henry Bishop has abused his position as a wealthy mine owner to employ others to carry out his dastardly requests in the mistaken belief that he kept his own hands clean. I intend to show how a man of simple means can be caught up in another man's greed to extend his own mining interests. A man who has no scruples, who promises to give them work for carrying out these requests."

The council for the defence it appeared was relying on the fact that a man in Henry Bishop's position would not be so foolish to stoop to commit murder. . . for what reason? What benefit would Henry Bishop gain by Jamie Tremaynes death?

Jamie smiled to himself; obviously Henry Bishop's council had not been informed of the two extraordinary meetings at which he had tried to take over the Wheal Jenny mine.

Fergus Malone took to his feet yet again and shuffled a few papers on his desk. "I call the first witness for the prosecution, Fred Pengelley."

An armed guard accompanied Fred to the witness box and, at the prosecutor's request, both Fred and Saul's manacles and leg irons had been removed, for these might have had an influence on the judgement by the members of the jury. Ginifur had sent over two sets of plain workmen's clothing and Jamie had delivered them to the jail along with fresh water to wash. Three months at Tremanyon had produced a great change in Fred. He had gained his lost weight and lost his gaunt hunted look and Jamie realised now that the time that Beau had spent with him had increased Fred's confidence in himself. Across the courtroom their eyes met as Fred gave a discernible nod of his head and Jamie smiled back.

"Fred Pengelley, I would like to take your mind back to the year of ninety-four."

"Yes, Sir."

"Do you remember anything special about that year?"

"I do. Not 'ard t' remember, for I've bin outa work since ninety-four."

Fergus continued to take Fred through his part in enticing Jamie to visit Wheal Jenny, prior to the accident, before coming to his presence at the hovel on the moor the night Walter died.

Fred answered the questions well; his version of the events had not changed one iota from his first statement to Daniel.

Council for the defence attempted to discredit him on a number of occasions to no avail, and finally wound up by accusing him of making the whole episode up in retribution for being put off from the Magdalen Mine.

Saul was just as clear with his evidence and Fergus did ask him if he was aware that his testimony was a damning implication to his own part in the incident at Wheal Jenny.

"I knows that, Sir, but I don' 'ave no life now, livin' as I am."

Saul claimed that he and Ed Fisher had accompanied Henry Bishop to the hovel on the moor where Walter Hawes was hidden. According to him, Walter had put up a fight with Bishop so Saul and Ed had intervened to restrain him, where upon Henry Bishop hit him on the head with an iron bar that lay in the fireplace. That blow had killed Walter and Henry Bishop said that he would say that Saul and Ed had killed him if they didn't help him to dispose of the body. The work that they were promised was not forthcoming and then, one night when the pair were making their way home from St Austell, they were set upon and left for dead. As far as Saul was concerned there was only one reason for the attack and that was to silence them.

Once again council for the defence relied on discrediting the witness but the man's memory for detail was hard to shift. Again

Council returned to Henry Bishop's character describing him as an upright member of society and that he would bring witnesses to endorse this view.

It had been a long morning and after the evidence of the two main witnesses for the prosecution the judge called for a short recess.

Fergus turned in his seat to speak to Daniel. "I have done all I can Dan, but the defence is going to rest its case in the unreliability of two disgruntled miners who have lost their jobs. If we could have called Robert Fry as a witness I believe that he might have broken under interrogation and given evidence to save his own skin. Without this, I must tell you that I fear we may loose this case."

Jamie watched as Henry Bishop was taken below for the recess accompanied by catcalls from the crowd with a smirk on his face as he caught Jamie watching him, as though he fully expected a verdict of not guilty.

Beau excused himself and wandered outside as Jamie, Liam and Dan climbed to their feet for a moment as Fergus left the courtroom with his notary.

When the court re-assembled, Beau had not returned and Jamie feared that his brother had met up with some old friends and once again returned to his drinking habits, and that the brother of the last few months was returning to his old ways. Well it wasn't surprising, after all a leopard never changes his spots.

The floor rose to its feet once more as Judge Collicott re-entered and took his seat.

"Silence in Court." The clerk shouted out to still the noise of the crowd and when the judge was satisfied he addressed Fergus Malone.

"Have you completed the case for the prosecution?"

Fergus rose to his feet once more. "Not quite, your honour. A late witness has come forward, and I ask permission to bring him before the court."

The judge raised an eyebrow and council for the defence exchanged anxious looks with Henry Bishop who answered with a shrug of his shoulders, puzzled at who else could be called to give evidence.

As the murmur of voices grew from the crowd, Fergus raised his voice. "I call my next witness. . . Richard Claude Tremayne, known as Beau."

Jamie let out a gasp of surprise. "Beau! Dan, what is he doing? You shouldn't have let Fergus call him to stand as a witness; he will condemn himself."

The look on Daniel's face told him that he was totally unaware of this turn of events.

Beau entered the court to complete silence. There were those in the room who had drunk with Beau on many occasions; they were more than aware of his previous feelings towards his older brother and surprised that he should be called as a witness for the prosecution. Ribald comments filled the room as the clerk once more brought the gavel down with a resounding crash to bring the room to order.

In the disruption Daniel had managed to attract Fergus' attention, saying that Jamie did not want his brother to give evidence.

"Jamie's brother came to me unsolicited, insisting that I put him in the witness box." Fergus informed him "Beau is fully aware of what he is doing and the consequences which may arise. All he has told me is that he can give evidence to the fact that Henry Bishop did indeed employ others to cause the accident in which it was hoped your brother-in-law would be killed, although he cannot vouch for what happened to Walter Hawes. However, Walter's letter to his widow shows that he did indeed fear for his life and I will produce this as evidence before the end of the trial."

The clerk of the court managed to gain control of the crowd and an angry judge pronounced "Any further disruption of this court and I will clear the room."

From his position in the witness box Beau looked across the room and smiled at Jamie as he signalled for him to stand down and not put his life in danger.

When Fergus started to question Beau, Judge Collicott raised his hand in the air to ask Beau if he understood the implications of his answers. Beau said that he understood fully the things that he would divulge, and only regretted that it had taken him so long to come out and speak the truth.

The case for the defence was weak, relying on character witnesses for Henry Bishop and casting doubt on the reliability of the evidence from two witnesses who had a grudge against the defendant. With Walter's letter and Beau's timely intervention in the proceedings, it put pay to any hope that the defending council might have had. The jury had not been out for long when they filed back into the court.

Judge Collicott addressed the jury. "In the case against Henry Bishop, on the count of the murder of John Rawe by procurement have you come to a decision?"

"We have your honour." The spokesman answered

"And do you find the defendant Guilty or Not Guilty?"

There was a brief hesitation as the spokesman realised the enormity of what he was about to say. "Guilty."

There was uproar in the court from the delegation of miners from Wheal Jenny, only Jamie didn't move and it was some moments before the court could be settled to order and the judge asked the second question of the jury.

"On the second count of attempting to procure the death of Captain Jamie Tremayne do you find the defendant Guilty or Not Guilty?"

This time there was no hesitation. "Guilty, your honour."

"And on the third count, of the murder of Walter Hawes, do you find the defendant Guilty or Not Guilty?"

"Guilty."

Daniel was delighted and went to congratulate Fergus Malone but, in the uproar, Jamie slumped forwards and buried his head in his hands as he wondered what would happen to Beau now and how it would affect his mother.

The clerk of the court managed to control the crowd long enough for the judge to pass sentence. "Mr Bishop you have been found guilty of the murder of John Rawe not by your own hands but by procuring others to act for you, for attempting to have Captain Jamie Tremayne murdered, and for the murder by your own hands of Walter Hawes. You shall be taken from here to a place where you will await your own death by hanging."

Henry Bishop slumped in his chair and the crowd erupted in delight. It was some time before the crowd was ushered from the court to spill out on to the road in front of the court house, having thoroughly enjoyed the morning's entertainment.

Fred and Saul's cases came to court late that afternoon. Saul too was judged guilty by his involvement with Henry Bishop but his willingness to come forward to give evidence for the prosecution weighed in his defence and he was not given a hanging sentence but he would be transported to Botany Bay for a period of fourteen years. Everyone knew that there would be no return to Cornwall for him from the other side of the world, but Saul was quite glad to have got away with his head. Fred was judged not guilty, for the jury were convinced that he had no idea that the message to Jamie was to lure him to his death. Daniel and Jamie were delighted as were Beau and Liam and Beau slapped him on the shoulder in delight and offered to buy him a beer to celebrate.

Jamie's worries were for Beau and what his evidence might bring against him. Excusing himself Daniel told them he would meet up with them at the Coaching Inn. Jamie had made up his mind that they would not spend another night at Bodmin but make it back to Penhallow where Davey and Mary would be expecting them.

Whilst Jamie, Liam, Beau and Fred made their way through the throng, acknowledging the cheers and good wishes. Daniel and Fergus Malone were closeted with Judge William Collicott in his quarters behind the courtroom. Here they discussed Beau's evidence which sealed Henry Bishop's fate. After a great deal of persuasion by Fergus, William Collicott finally agreed that the court would take no further action in the case. Beau had not been involved in any of the actual preparations for the incident at the mine, the fact that he had known that his brother's life was in danger but did nothing to warn him was perhaps something that the brothers' had to resolve themselves. Having thanked both the judge and Fergus Malone, Daniel joined his friends to make the journey to Penhallow.

Word had reached Penhallow before they rode in. Hal had ridden to Bodmin to see if Henry Bishop would be convicted for the murder of his brother, and Grace's husband of a few hours, and had raced home with the news.

A jubilant Davey greeted them at the door announcing that Mary had hurriedly produced a celebration meal which Jamie insisted that they all share around the large table in the kitchen. When they had finished Jamie produced a bottle of brandy and they drank a toast to Fred's freedom. "So what are your plans Fred?" Jamie wanted to know. "If there is anything I can do, please ask. There will always be a job for you at Wheal Jenny."

"Well. . . Beau has asked me to 'elp 'im t' clear 'is 'ouse in Truro. After that, I'll jest wait 'n see."

Jamie glanced at Beau, wondering what his own plans were and he had noticed Fred had not referred to him as Mr Tremayne.

"I don't want the house anymore Jamie. I don't know that I want to come home to Tremanyon either. . . not long term anyway."

If Jamie was surprised he didn't show it, it was Liam who furthered the conversation. "Is it some adventure ye're seekin'?"

Beau smiled. "As always you see more than most don't you Liam? Perhaps that is it; you have had your adventure with Father in the new world. You too have seen the world Jamie, and had your adventures as well. Now you are ready to settle back in

Cornwall. Where have I travelled and what have I seen of the world? What have I done?" He gave a wry grin. "Other than cause anguish to my family. No. . . I speak the truth. Yes Liam is right; I think that it's an adventure I'm seeking. Mayhap Fred and I can have one together," but the conversation wasn't furthered and they returned to discussing the events of the day.

Before returning to Tremanyon Jamie and Daniel visited Peg Hawes. Davey had, on Jamie's instructions, found them a cottage in a hamlet not far from Wheal Jenny. Denzil and Paul were both now employed at Wheal Jenny and Maisie was delighted as her two children qualified to attend the mine school on a part time basis. The three bedroomed cottage was a little small for the two families but it had an acre of land on which they could grow food and rear chickens, and Peg also had a couple of goats which supplied them with milk and extra to make cheese. Maisie's young ones were delighted at the freedom and loved to help in the garden. Peg was delighted with her situation and when Daniel handed her Walter's few belongings she shed a tear and said that she would never be able to repay Jamie for his kindness.

Jamie had also arranged for Saul to receive better treatment during his stay in jail whilst he awaited a place on a transport ship from Plymouth, and he told him that Daniel would make enquiries to get information of him after he had sailed to Australia. It might be possible that they could arrange for him to be released to one of the free emigrants who was settling in Australia and might need a labourer to help them clear the bush.

* * *

Beau and Fred left Penhallow to ride to Truro to clear Beau's house in readiness to sell it. They returned to Tremanyon just three days later much to the surprise of Ginifur and Jamie. "You cannot possibly have cleared your house out in the time you have been away Beau." Ginifur claimed.

"To be honest with you, no, we didn't." Beau was in a good mood and laughed at Ginifur's expression. "Daniel knew someone who wanted to move to Truro. He's not married and has no furniture so was more than happy to buy the house fully furnished. There was nothing I wished to keep or take with me."

"Take with you? Where to?" Jamie was puzzled for Beau had chosen all the furniture, paintings and ornaments for the house himself, wanting only the best of everything. "Where ever you settle you will need furniture."

Beau's smile got even broader. "I think that it will all be a bit too fancy for where I plan to go."

Ginifur had not seen her son so relaxed or happy for such a long time that she found herself smiling back at him. "Where are you planning to go, Beau?"

"I wouldn't have thought of it, to tell the truth it was Daniel and Jamie who put it in my mind."

"Hold on!! What suggestions are we supposed to have made?"

"Well no. . . it wasn't so much a suggestion Jamie, but it was when you were discussing Saul's deportation to Australia that it came into my mind." Beau explained.

"Saul. . . Australia. . . " Ginifur couldn't see the connection. "What has Saul got to do with your decision?"

"Directly, nothing at all. I agree that it was when you and Dan were discussing the possibility of getting Saul released to work for a free settler clearing his land." Beau's face was quite animated as he talked. "You see they are offering free passage to Australia to anyone who is willing to settle there. Free settlers are given land, tools and implements and provisions for two years."

Ginifur was stunned by his suggestion. "Australia!! You are thinking of going to Australia?"

Jamie wasn't convinced that his brother was serious. "Beau, you will have to travel by sea. You hate water and you hate boats of any size or type."

"It won't be easy, I do realize that." Beau admitted. "And you don't need to point out my failings when looking after Kylyn and Rhosinnis. I have a lot to learn. . . I know that."

"This is a joke. You are not serious in this, surely?" Jamie studied his brother's face, he wasn't laughing now.

"I have never been more serious. Settlers also receive two years provisions and you were right when you said that if you take on convict labour they also have two years provisions and clothing for one year. Perhaps Daniel could maybe arrange for Saul to be released to me?"

Ginifur and Jamie were momentarily speechless as they tried to digest Beau's bolt from the blue when Liam walked in followed by Fred. Liam glanced about the silent room. "I'm sorry. . . we're interrupting something, I'm thinking."

"No Liam, come in. I was just telling Mother that I was thinking of going to Australia." Beau explained.

"So. . . ye've found y'ur adventure then. And what is it ye'r plannin' to do when ye get there?"

"We hope to be accepted as free settlers and granted some land which will have to be cleared first. Fred wants to join me so we should qualify for two sections which we can run beside each other. Maybe, in time, we will become respectable farmers." Beau's humour had returned. "I have already admitted my failures in that department Liam, so don't add to it."

But Liam wasn't about to point out Beau's past failings, he just nodded wisely. "Ye're finally grown up lad, and ye may have the makin' of a man who would have made your father proud. Tis a hard road ye've made your mind t' take, but if ye put y'ur heart 'n soul to it ye might prove y'urself t'be a man of substance." He grabbed Beau's hand in his, seeing for the first time tears in Beau's eyes.

Beau's smile faded as he looked into Liam's eyes. "Thank you Liam. You're a good man and I have never given you the respect you deserve. Please forgive me?"

Liam just nodded his head and added. "May God go with ye."

Turning to Ginifur Beau reached out for her hands and she gave them to him. "I can't make up for what I have done, Ma, but I hope that in time you might find room in your heart for me again. I don't know what my future holds, but I'm damned well determined to make something of myself at last. Whatever Fred and I achieve it will be for the both of us."

Ginifur managed a smile. "I expect some people might call it a foolhardy venture, but I'm not so sure. It's the sort of venture that your father would have loved to undertake. If you are serious Beau, then go with my blessing. . . and love."

Beau kissed her hands as Robyn walked into the room, wandering what was going on as she took in the expressions of their faces.

"Come in Roberta." Beau turned to his daughter.

Robyn smiled politely back at him and plucked up courage. "If you don't mind, Father, I have been Robyn to the family since I came to Tremanyon, and it is Robyn that I wish to be known as. Roberta was someone else. . . not me." She said bravely as she wondered what his response would be.

Beau actually laughed. "Well said, Robyn. And no. . . you are not a Roberta. In fact, to tell you the truth, I didn't like it overmuch either. Your grandmother named you after your Grandfather and you bear no likeness to him whatsoever. No, you are a

Tremayne through and through. I have been very foolish in more ways than one and to turn my back on my daughter was one of them. I have watched you grow from a lovely girl into a beautiful young woman that a father should be rightly proud of. I hope that one day you may find a way to forgive me."

Robyn gave him a beatific smile. "If my forgiveness helps you then you have it gladly, but believe me there is nothing to forgive. My life here has been filled with love and I have had the best mother in the world in my Grandmama. But why are you all so solemn?"

"I have decided to have an adventure, to travel to the other side of the world and maybe find my fortune."

Robyn tipped her head to one side with a quizzical expression. "I think that it must be a man thing, to go on an adventure. Dickon too thinks that he needs to see the world." She glanced at her grandmother and then out of the window at the Rhosinnis Peninsula, over Rosvarron to the one eventuality. . . the jade and blue of a Cornish sea. "But I have everything I need right here, this is my home. . . this is where I belong."

Beau studied this daughter of his who seemed to have wisdom far beyond her years. "You are one of the lucky ones, and I will think of you often. . . where ever I go." Turning to Jamie who had been taking in the various conversations quietly. "Jamie. . . is it possible for us to part as brothers and friends? My jealousy of you over the years has been a grave mistake, for I now remember all the things that you did for me when I was young. I ask you too for your forgiveness."

"As Robyn has said, if it is important for you to have my forgiveness for sibling rivalry then you may have it." Jamie found that he could go no further than that for now. . . time would tell if he could forgive him for other misdemeanours. "You may go on this adventure with my best wishes for your success."

Beau smiled happily. "I can ask for no more. . . thank you."

* * *

The cold spell of weather came suddenly to an end. Buds burst forth on the skeletal branches of the oaks and ash trees bringing much speculation as to which came into leaf first and constant repetitions of 'Ash before oak we're in for a soak. Oak before ash we're in for a splash' and spring flowers, which had been held back by the sudden drop in temperature, suddenly sprung into bloom as Beau made his plans to emigrate.

Further enquiries by Daniel proved a surprise for Beau; it appeared that as a 'gentleman' he would be welcomed with open arms and qualify for a larger tract of land which would have been surveyed before allocation. Added to this an adjoining thirty acres of land could be allocated to Fred. They would need to clear fifty percent of each parcel of land before they would qualify for the freehold, but this had been possible elsewhere so no difficulties were envisaged. A convict fleet was due to sail from Plymouth sometime in the coming summer months and there would be spaces for a number of free settlers. Beau and Fred poured over all the information that Daniel had gathered for them and attempted to make plans. When cleared it was supposed to make good sheep country and Jamie promised to send some out when Beau was ready to stock his farm.

Jamie offered to ask Jack Newton if he would give them some practical advice on stock farming and, in spite of the animosity caused by Beau sacking Jack, the bailiff at Rhosinnis was magnanimous enough to give Beau and Fred some insight into working with sheep in the time that was available, and they both did whatever chores Jack chose to give them without a murmur of discontent.

Dickon would be fourteen this year and the subject of his future could be put off no longer. Jamie had seriously hoped that his son would go on to University before coming home to Cornwall to help him with the running of the estate and the mine, but Dickon was reluctant to give up his dream. It was round the table at Rhosinnis that things came to a head.

"I don't see what the problem is." Dickon raised the question. "Father, you joined the navy as a midshipman when you were younger than I am now."

"Yes, I did. But we were not fighting a war on our own doorstep." Jamie tried to reason.

"Perhaps not, but you were involved in battles in the Americas during the Wars of Independence; and it was there, due to the death of your Captain in a battle, that you were made up to Captain yourself. You surely are not going to say that Grandfather and Grandmother were not worried about you all the time you were at sea?"

"I hate to say it, Jamie, but Dickon has a point." Marie-Claire did not want to take sides in the subject of Dickon's chosen career, for she too would hate to see him go to sea at this point in the war with France. In the silence Dickon shot her a grateful glance although his eyes swiftly returned to his father's face, but it was Marie-Claire who continued the conversation. "I know I am not Dickon's mother, Jamie, but I could love him no more than I do if I was." Marie-Claire touched upon the greatest disappointment to her, her inability to conceive a child. "It must be extremely hard to let go of your child, knowing all the dangers that face them in the wider world, and our ancestors must have sent their young sons off to war, not knowing whether they will return or not. Now it might be Dickon's time and we all fear for the worse that can befall him and not the wealth of knowledge that he could return with. I know that I didn't give great credence to Betsy's prophecies in the beginning but even I was astounded by the fact that she knew that you were in danger at the mine. Betsy was firmly convinced that Dickon would live a long and happy life at Tremanyon. It might not be wise to put too much faith in her prophesy and act irresponsibly Dickon, but if your father does let you go to sea I would suggest that you do not wilfully put your own life in danger on Betsy's promise of a long and happy life."

Jamie took a deep breath. "I am not making any promises Dickon, of course we have been aware of your desire to go to sea but I had hoped that after going to University you would return to help me run the estates here at Rhosinnis and Tremanyon and, of course, The Wheal Jenny. In time Penhallow will also need to be considered."

"It is my intention to return home, to help you and Grandmother, but like you did too, I suppose, I would like to see something of the world outside first. Robyn is content to spend the rest of her life here, in Cornwall, I want to see how other people live and work. She says that it is a 'man thing' to want to travel – perhaps she's right, I don't know."

Jamie studied his growing son; Dickon was going to be tall, possibly taller than he was. His face was taking on the stamp of a young adult. An active youngster he had never put on excess weight, his body lean and fit with no sign of 'puppy fat'. Dickon was maturing fast and Jamie had been pushing this thought to the back of his mind. He had procrastinated long enough, Dickon deserved an answer.

"I will think on it and give you my decision in a few days, first I must speak to your grandmother." Jamie would not be drawn any further on the subject but, later, with the full moon shining on the sea and through the bedroom window he continued the subject with Marie-Claire. "It is hard to let Dickon go to sea at this time of war with France, and yes I do remember my longing to go to sea too. I wanted to find out what went on beyond the Tamar, but I always believed that I would return home to the Rhosinnis Peninsula." Jamie lay on his back with his arms behind his head as he confided in his wife.

"I think that Robyn is correct when she describes it as a 'man thing' this wanting to explore the outside world, and Dickon would not be your son if he didn't too have this yearning to seek the world outside. It is impossible for me to give advice Jamie for I do not have a son, our son. Neither do I have a daughter. I pray nightly that I may be blessed and bear you a son or daughter but as the time passes I am beginning to believe that it is not to be." Her words trembled and Jamie turned on his side and drew her into his embrace. He knew how much she longed for a child of her own. Of course it would be lovely if they were blessed with a child, but for Jamie this wasn't something that was of primary importance. He loved Marie-Claire and his life could be complete without the addition of another child. But it was an important issue for a woman. She had a need to fulfil, he understood that and did not try to brush the subject aside. "If Dickon was our son, what would I think then?"

"I am sure that you would think of it objectively as you have done with Dickon. I didn't say so in front of him but, of course you were right. It could not have been easy for Mother and Father to see me go off to sea or hear that I had been sent to the Americas. I dread to think of what was going through Mother's mind all those months when she heard no news what so ever." He lay silent with his thoughts as he stared at the ceiling.

Marie-Claire was also lying on her back, light from the moon caught the crystals of the candlesticks on her dressing table and the reflections sparkled on the ceiling like stars in the night sky.

"What are you thinking?" Jamie could almost hear her mind whirring in the silence of their bedroom.

Marie-Claire didn't answer immediately, giving herself time to consider how she brought up the subject that she believed they both avoided. Jamie turned on his side, his head supported on his hand as he studied her face in the glow of the moonlight as his other hand followed a familiar path between her firm breasts towards her face. When the silence continued his caress gently pressed her face towards him. "I do realise that you long for a child of your own, my darling, but I want you to know that it is not a requirement of our marriage that you do so." Even in the dim light he could see the sparkle of tears in her eyes and the sadness written in the expression on her face. Marie-Claire's body trembled beneath his hands as she gave way to the sadness that engulfed her as she let loose a heartfelt sob. Jamie enfolded her in his strong arms, his hand reaching up to run his fingers through her luxurious curls and cradle her head into the curve of his shoulder as he tried to ease her pain with gentle words of comfort.

Marie-Claire finally allowed the tears to fall. Tears that she had managed to control for so long. It had never occurred to her that she might be barren. Barren!!. . . What a dreadfully ugly word that was, she thought to herself. It hadn't even crossed her mind during her marriage to Pierre, they had never discussed the subject of children during their time together, both living and enjoying the life of the aristocracy of France. She hadn't wanted a child then, why now? Pierre's sisters all had children, yet it had never caused her to feel the tug of maternal instincts and want a child of her own. She had even considered them an impediment and inconvenience even! How could she have believed that when she saw how much joy Ginifur's grandchildren brought to her and their parents? Her marriage to Jamie had brought her happiness that she had never dreamed of and now she longed to give him another son, or daughter. She longed to hold his child in her arms.

As the moon slowly moved across the night sky Marie-Claire's pain found release in her tears. Untangling his fingers from her hair Jamie tipped her face towards his and kissed away the remaining tears and slowly all the tension was let loose and she turned her body towards him for comfort.

Following Liam's suggestion Jamie made his way through the walled garden to the orchard where Mark told him that Ginifur had been there but had set off to walk to Quay Cottage; following the track he made his way through the wood of maturing beech trees that his mother had told him had been planted during the year of her birth. The trees would only have been saplings then, now there was a canopy of leaves above his head and squirrels scampered up the shiny grey bark to scramble amongst the over head branches. At the end of the wood a bench had been built into the side of the track that wound its way down the hill to the cottage, and it was here that he found his mother.

As he closed the gate, to keep the sheep from straying into the wood, he greeted Ginifur. "Hello Mother. Where's your shadow?"

Ginifur smiled in greeting. "I presume you mean Robyn, and she's busy turning out the linen room. She tells me that it is high time that we made an up to date inventory. She started in the wine cellar and informs me that there hasn't been an entry in Richard's catalogue of wines since he died. She has methodically organised the cellar to her satisfaction and catalogued each bottle, now she has started on the linen room, telling me that we need to replace sheets that are worn. Thankfully she has agreed that Lorna can make her own inventory of the kitchen and give her an up to the minute account of the stock there."

Jamie laughed. "A right chip off the block, wouldn't you say?" Ginifur's smile said it all. Indeed Robyn was so like her grandmother she could have been her daughter, and at this thought he added. "I hear that you have received a letter from Sara, how are they?"

Ginifur's laugh was contagious and Jamie found himself joining in as they took in the panoramic view of Falmouth Bay from the Rhosinnis Peninsula to The Lizard and the Manacles out at sea. Ginifur never tired of this view. She had been born at the cottage at the bottom of the hill and woken up beside the river for the first sixteen years of her life. It was only after Richard Tremayne purchased Tremanyon and the ruins of the burned out house that she was taken on to help his wife, Annabelle, and their two daughters Rachel and Rebecca. Then she was required to live in the house which was to become her home. Ginifur found herself looking back on those years. It would be true to say that she had faced some difficult times in the early days, but in the years since her marriage to Richard and life with their growing family they had been happy years. She missed her husband intensely, with the passing of the years she had adjusted to a life without him but there would always be an empty space in her life; never to be filled.

Jamie had been surveying the same view; his thoughts too on his life spent at Tremanyon with his family. At times he still caught himself thinking that if he had returned from sea sooner that things might have been different; perhaps his father would be here still.

Ginifur turned towards him, taking his hand in hers. "But it isn't Sara's letter which has brought you seeking me out, is it?"

Jamie found himself laughing again. "Nothing can be hidden from you, can it?"

Ginifur smiled in response. "It's Dickon isn't it?"

"Do you truly have second sight? Or did Betsy pass on her skills to you? How is it that you always know what we want before we ask?" Jamie was in wonder at her perspicacity.

"Neither of those suggestions, although I am grateful for the skills of healing that Betsy instilled in me. I think the answer simply lies in motherhood. Just simply knowing your children; learning to read their moods, sharing in their hopes and dreams, loving them in spite of their faults – for none of us is perfect." She gave a slight sigh. "So, I take it that Dickon is still set on going to sea?" Jamie nodded in answer. "It is hard to let go of those you love, Jamie. But it is only in letting go of the ties that they will find that they may still be tied by the bonds of love. Dickon is one of those, as you were. He too will return to Tremanyon for his future is here, I know it in my heart and I know it in my bones."

"You sound so very sure of this." Jamie was sceptical. "He couldn't have chosen a worse time to join the Navy, with this war with France."

"There are always wars somewhere in this world, as there are other forces at sea which are as dangerous; hurricanes, pirates, hidden rocks and hazards!" She still had a hold of his hand and glanced at it resting in hers. "We had many sleepless nights due to the situation in the American waters when you were sent there. Many didn't return it is true but that is one of the perils in a life at sea." She looked up to meet his eyes. "As hard as it is, Jamie, you have to let Dickon go and find his own place in the world. You must not think that he is turning his back on his family, for he isn't. Dickon loves his family and will return to it; just as you did. But, for now, Dickon needs to find out for himself that although the world is wide and beautiful all that he needs is here in Cornwall; on the Rhosinnis Peninsula."

"Marie-Claire agrees with you, but it was difficult for her to say so."

"Because Dickon is not her son." Ginifur nodded wisely. "But she loves him as dearly as if it was so."

"I know that. . ."

There was a pause as they both studied the far horizon before Ginifur continued the difficult subject. "It must be painful for Marie-Claire to want a child so much, yet fail to fall with child when it seems the most simple thing to do. It is a sad truth that sometimes a woman cannot fulfil this role, even though she has enough love, compassion and understanding to do so. Is it an important issue for you, Jamie?"

"Oh no! But then, I admit that I already have Dickon. My love for Marie-Claire is not driven by wanting more offspring, but how do I get her to understand that?"

"And if you didn't have Dickon?"

"That is a difficult one to answer, for I cannot imagine my life without Dickon any more than I can imagine my life without Marie-Claire. All I do know is that, should we ever be in the position of losing Dickon there could be no possibility of another child taking his place." Jamie reasoned.

"Then you have to find a way of convincing her that she is loved for herself, only Marie-Claire can find a way to accept that she cannot have a child and come to terms with it. It may be that when the pressure that she is putting on herself to conceive is taken away that she might find the situation changes." Ginifur let loose his hand. "Now. . . what are we to do about Dickon?"

"I suppose I must make the necessary arrangements for him to be interviewed for admission as a midshipman, but I tell you Mother, I will be doing it with a very heavy heart."

"It was the same for Richard, Jamie, believe me." Ginifur informed him.

"He never said so! Nor you either." Jamie was taken aback by this statement for he had believed that he had the full backing of Richard.

"No. . . He wouldn't. You had set your heart on a career at sea, always eager to hear of Edward Boscawen's latest exploits when you were only four, and you were heartbroken by his death in fifty nine. Even then you always followed any information you could find about His Majesty's ships of the line and any skirmishes they were involved in. I think we both realised even at this early age you would probably find a career in the navy. Yes there were worrying times, when we had no news, but in my heart I knew that you would return. If it is any comfort I have the same feelings for Dickon."

Jamie gave a rueful grin. "You always have the answers Mother, and the knack of placing things in order; making the undesirable, acceptable." He took in a deep breath and let it out very slowly. "Thank you, Mother. What would we all do without you?" It was only then that he noticed that the silver strands of hair amongst her dark curls were widening into silver streaks. How come he hadn't noticed this before? Jamie felt a shiver run down his spine as the unwelcome thought that the years were passing for Ginifur too and, in some circles she would already be considered an old woman.

"You will manage, Jamie, none of us is indispensable. But I have every intention of being around for a few more years yet and, should Dickon follow his wish to go to sea, I shall make it my aim to be here to welcome him home at the end of his travels; when he returns to take up his place here in Cornwall." She smiled and took a long look at the view before adding, "Now, you can see me safely home to Tremanyon." With that Jamie reached out a hand to help her to her feet, placed her arm in the crook of his elbow and they strolled home together.

It was Dickon who brought her the news that Jamie had acted on his decision, telling her excitedly that they were travelling to the admiralty for an interview. Jamie and Marie-Claire were both travelling with him and they would spend some time in London before returning home.

Meanwhile Beau and Fred had been working hard at Kylyn and Rhosinnis and Jack Newton found it hard to believe that Beau was in fact the same person who had sent him packing. During the early part of the summer they had taken their turn at 'dagging', trimming the dirty wool from around the hind quarters of the sheep where flies and maggots could cause the death of an infected animal; they had trimmed and treated their hooves for foot rot and they had taken their turn at shearing, much to the amusement of the experienced shearers. Shearing was hard work, holding the animal in a sitting position whilst you worked with a large set of shears to trim the fleece from the sheep in one complete piece, without cutting and injuring the animal. It was time consuming and a back breaking job, but after a few days they managed to do a tidy job even if not as quickly as the men employed for this task, continuing until each working day came to an end as they moved from farm to farm around the Rhosinnis Peninsula; and they fell exhausted and aching into a tin bath filled with hot water at the end of it.

Jamie, Marie-Claire, Ben and Dickon had been at Tremanyon for the day. Tomorrow they were to start the journey to take Dickon to London, and Ben would be moving back to Tremanyon until the family returned. By this time Ben felt equally at home at either Tremanyon, Rhosinnis or Penhallow and Marie-Claire was loved by him almost as much as he had loved Ellen. Robyn and Dickon had gone ahead to the drawing room and the rest of the family trailed behind as they made their way from the dining room when Beau and Fred stumbled in the side door.

Jamie burst out laughing. "You look exhausted brother! I will give you your due; I never thought that you would see the shearing through as you have done." He shook his head in wonder. "Jack said that you worked hard and he doesn't give praise lightly."

Beau and Fred grinned back, tired but happy and Jamie, who had been waiting for the old Beau to return, marvelled at the change in his brother. He treated Fred like an equal where as a few short months ago he would not have passed the time of day with him. "Have you ever sheared a sheep Jamie?" Beau wanted to know. Jamie found it hard to admit that he had done so and surprisingly declared that he had not. The pleasure on Beau's face was reward enough when he thought that at last he had done something that Jamie had not.

"But have you milked the cows yet?" Jamie asked.

"Done that too. Harry Palaughan had us bring the cows in to the parlour and milk them; we also had to hand feed the calves. Of course we won't be ready for stock for some time, but at least when they come we will know what is expected of us."

"You almost sound as if you have been enjoying yourself. Hard work is not supposed to be fun, Beau." Jamie teased his brother as Fred moved on towards the kitchen, remembering the time when Beau would not demean himself by even speaking with those who worked for him let alone actually help them.

"So. . . you are off to London to take Dickon for his interview at the Admiralty I hear. You will miss him if he goes off to sea." Beau briefly allowed himself to remember his own son, wondering what he would have made of himself and admitting, ruefully, that he probably would not have amounted to much. Now Robyn. . . his daughter was another thing. That girl was a hard worker and she would make a success of her life. "Dickon is a good lad, and you are a very lucky man, Jamie." This was praise indeed and came as a surprise to Jamie.

"Thank you, Beau. I wish that things could have been better for you." Jamie found that his feelings were honest; his words true.

"As ye sow, so shall ye reap." Beau gave a wry grin. "Biblical words, I recall. Funny thing is. . . it was Old Betsy who quoted it to me, one day when I met her in the lane. I wouldn't have taken her for a biblical person. She scared me half to death when we were children; I always thought she really was a witch. Do you reckon that old crone had second sight?"

"Mother would say there were many reasons why one would think so."

"Well I reckon she did, and she saw right through me too." Beau pushed away the memories and returned to the subject of Dickon. "If he does go off to sea, I hope he returns safely. I don't know what Mother will do with Tremanyon, I don't mind anymore. . . truly. But I reckon Dickon would make a good heir. He looks a lot like father, don't you think? But then you do too."

"So does Robyn. Perhaps you don't see it but she is a good mixture of both mother and father, and she is very much the grand-daughter of Richard Tremayne." Jamie pointed out.

"Yes, she is. Can I say something?"

"Of course."

"She is the girl that she is because of Mother and you. . . no don't interrupt please. . . she is. I was foolish to reject her because of my obsessive desire to father a son. Charlie would have been quite useless. Spoilt rotten by his mother and grandmother; he would have lost Tremanyon in no time at all. You will watch over Robyn in the years to come won't you Jamie? I believe that she is the only good thing to come from my life."

"You know that she will want for nothing Beau. Mother could love her no more, even if she had been her own daughter. In truth, having Robyn to centre her attention on helped her to come to terms with the loss of Father."

"Mmmm . . . "

"And who knows what your future has in store for you. Maybe this venture of yours will be a great success and we will see you return to Cornwall a wealthy landowner."

"No. When I go it will be goodbye, Jamie. Success or no, I will not be returning to England. I will keep in touch, to let you know how we fare, but my life here is over." There was sadness in his voice.

"That is rather drastic, don't you think?" This was the first time Jamie had heard of this suggestion.

"No. . . Realistic. I cannot expect Mother to forgive me for the things I have done and my staying here would be a living reminder to her. Believe me Jamie; it will be for the best." He clapped a hand on Jamie's shoulder. "Now how about a drink with me before dinner?"

Jamie smiled at his brother. "That's a good idea. Let us open a bottle of wine and drink a toast to your new life on the other side of the world."

I have one more thing to ask?"

"Fire away."

"Would you take me out in a boat? I think I would like to know what it feels like before I leave."

Beau laughed and Jamie couldn't help but join in.

* * *

Dickon's application was looked on favourably, Jamie Tremayne was still remembered as a fine Captain in His Majesty's Navy and this stood Dickon in good stead. His first placement came through quickly and Jamie and Marie-Claire were kept busy fitting him out and getting him measured for his uniform. As a midshipman he would be with a few other lads between the ages of 12 and 16. On ship they would learn their craft of seamanship from senior officers and their progress would depend on working hard.

Coincidentally Dickon's first assignment was to join 'The Guardian', one of the ships which would escort the convict ships to Botany Bay. Along with the convict ships another was to sail with 'freemen' who would be taking passage to start a new life in the new colony. Two of these passengers would be Beau and Fred.

Beau's first trip out in a boat was a success and he went on to make further trips in 'Guinevere' with Jacob and the crew out in to Falmouth Bay and beyond to the Manacles. He was justifiably pleased with himself; Beau's whole life had been spent fearing the sea and boats, this fear had now been conquered.

The whole family set off for Plymouth to see Dickon, Beau and Fred, set sail for the other side of the world. Two carriages were pressed into service for the journey to Plymouth where one convict ship was based and the others, from London and Portsmouth, would call in at Plymouth with the escort ships, together with the one carrying the 'freemen' and the cargo of implements and tools etc. The new crew members, the freemen from Cornwall and the convict ship would join the fleet there. Saul would be transported from Bodmin Jail in time for the departure, indeed he may already be aboard the prison ship.

In the first carriage rode Jamie and Marie-Claire, with Ginifur, Ben, Dickon and Robyn. Dickon's sack and trunk containing his spare clothes were secured on top, behind Joe. In the second carriage, driven by Alfie, rode Beau and Fred and Liam with all the things that they thought might make the trip a little more comfortable; for it would take almost a full year before they would see landfall in Australia.

As the carriages set off from Tremanyon all the staff had congregated on the lawn and beside the driveway to see Dickon off to sea and Beau off to make his fortune in Australia. More than a few of them held handkerchiefs to their eyes as they saw young Dickon all dressed up to take his place in the King's Navy. Through the village of Porthcarrow too, the villagers had lined the street to cheer and wave the popular young man off on his adventures. Ginifur tried hard to disguise her sadness but at the sight of everyone in the village turning out she could not hold the tears back any longer. Ben Nancekivel was immediately aware of her distress and took her hand in his to let her know that he was there for her support. Through the mist of tears she glanced at his caring face and gave a smile of gratitude and Ben patted her hand comfortingly while Dickon waved to the villagers as they drove slowly through the village. Blinking her tears away Ginifur turned to watch Robyn, sitting quietly beside her. Robyn's attention was all on Dickon and her eyes too were misted with tears as she turned to her grandmother and took hold of her free hand, giving it a gentle squeeze.

Jamie sat resolutely silent, his face difficult to read, but Ginifur knew exactly what thoughts were going through his mind for they would be the same ones that had raced through her own mind when she and Richard had driven off to see him set sail on his first trip to sea. Marie-Claire had her arm linked through Jamie's, her hand tightly clutching on to his sleeve; this was as upsetting for her as it was for the rest of them for she couldn't have cared for Dickon any more if he had been her own son. Benjamin too was difficult to read; Dickon was his only link with his daughter, Ellen. Yet Ginifur was convinced that amongst his sadness at the parting with his grandson, he felt enormous pride. . . as they all did. Dickon was still filled with the excitement of it all and Ginifur wondered when he would realise the enormity of all that was ahead of him; at this moment all the things that had been so familiar to him had been pushed into the past. As they left the village behind them

Dickon sat back in the seat filled with anticipation, eager to see the arrival of 'The Guardian' and impatient to be aboard; for a moment he was totally oblivious to the feelings of those accompanying him in the carriage.

Slowly Dickon became aware of Robyn, sitting across from him, and the solemn expression on her face. "You mustn't worry Robyn, I will be home long before you have missed me."

Robyn forced a smile to her face, not wanting him to remember her with tears of sadness and a miserable expression. "It will be at least two years, Dickon," she reminded him.

"The time will fly by, and think of all the stories I will have to tell when I return." Dickon turned to his father. "What was your most exciting trip, Father?"

Jamie rallied a smile. "Well . . . that would have to be the first one. The one that you are about to undertake."

"What? More than the time when you were fighting in American waters? More than the battle when you were made up to Captain?" Dickon was truly astonished that Jamie's first trip to sea was remembered as his most exciting.

"Ah . . . but think off all the new things that you are going to have to learn. All the new people you are to meet and the new friends to be made. The first time that you go aloft to the 'crows nest'. The climb up into the rigging; being more afraid of showing your fear than your fear of the climb. The sight of the deck of the ship so far below you and the horizon so far away with no sign of land in sight. Your first storm at sea, and there will be one, when everything has to be battened down and the helmsman has to be lashed to the wheel to stop him from being blown into the sea. The first time when you here the cry going up "land ahoy" and "where away?" and the answer "To port or starboard" which ever it may be. Then your first trip ashore in foreign parts, the different smells, different people, a different language and colour of their skin. All these, and many more. Each will be your first experience and they will be the ones that will remain with you long after the excitement of the battles. . . which I hope will be few."

Dickon sat back in the seat studying his grandmother. For the first time he realised that he would probably miss her the most of all . . . Grandmother . . . and Robyn, of course. Robyn was like his other half; like he supposed twins felt, each of them a part of the other. Yes he would miss Robyn. He would miss home; the

Rhosinnis Peninsula . . . and Tremanyon. Tremanyon was home. Tremanyon would always, first and foremost, be home to him and Robyn. . . to all of them.

In the carriage behind, Liam listened to Beau and Fred as they wondered what life would be like on board ship, how many like minded people would be joining them on the venture? They were all concerned for Saul, for they had heard that conditions were poor on board the convict ships. Liam told them that he had learned that a ship carrying Irish convicts would also join the convoy off the south coast of Ireland, and as he did he wondered how his countrymen would fare in this new land they were travelling to. He hoped that Beau would not be disappointed with the reality of carving a future in a new land. Liam had seen the hardship endured by settlers in a new land when he had joined Richard and Jean-Paul when they had made their voyage to Boston and traversed the wilderness to Quebec and beyond. At least they had not heard of settlers in Australia being attacked and their homesteads burned to the ground. As Liam understood it they would not have to endure the hardship of freezing winters with temperatures plummeting to well below zero. Botany Bay appeared to be favoured with a temperate climate with hot summers and mild winters. The coastal land was covered with scrub which needed to be cleared, but fertile soil lay below. Apparently some areas had already been cleared and were now farmed, growing crops and carrying stock, sheep and goats.

Liam didn't doubt that they had let themselves in for a hard life; he hoped that Beau would cope with it. If he did it could be the turning point in his life.

The carriages made a stop at Bodmin and then a further one at Tavistock, where Jamie had arranged for the horses to be changed and for refreshments to be taken. Jamie also had reserved rooms in a coaching inn at Plymouth, near the docks. The fleet of ships was due to arrive the next morning and Dickon, Beau and Fred were due to go aboard their respective ships at noon and due to sail at two in the afternoon. Ginifur wanted to wait and see them set sail so they might spend a further night in Plymouth before returning to Tremanyon the next day.

As they approached Plymouth they had their first sight of the wide estuary of the River Tamar, and moored in the centre was the prison ship. The prison ship had been waiting, mid stream, for six months until its cargo of convicts was complete and it could set sail with the convoy bound for Australia. Saul had been lucky; he had spent the last months since his conviction in a single cell at Bodmin Jail where Jamie had ensured he had received food and clothing.

Daniel had been informed that Saul had now been sent to Plymouth to join a ship for transportation to Botany Bay; but he had not been told the name of the ship. They assumed that it was the one they could now see.

As the carriage dropped into a valley they lost sight of the river and soon the outskirts of the city came into view. Not long after, the carriages pulled into the yard of the coaching inn near the docks.

Jamie assisted Ginifur to alight from the carriage and quickly ushered her inside where the inn keeper's wife showed them to the best room in the house. Ginifur had seen some awful accommodation at wayside inns and was pleasantly surprised by the fact that both the room and bed were clean and apparently free from bugs, as the proud woman assured her. A fire burned in the grate, to chase away the evening chill from the river, and a jug of hot water was quickly delivered so that Ginifur and Robyn could refresh themselves before dining.

The inn was a surprise to them all. On top of clean beds in each of their rooms, they enjoyed the comfort of a private dining room and a respectable meal. The long journey had tired them all and, in spite of the fact that Ginifur felt that she would find it impossible to sleep, they had all fallen fast asleep soon after they had put their heads on their pillows.

Breakfast was served in the private dining room where they all congregated the following morning. Needless to say there were mixed emotions.

Dickon was so excited that he was hardly able to eat. "You are wound up like a tight spring." Ginifur remarked. "You don't know when you will get your next good meal; I would advise that you take advantage of a good breakfast while you can."

"Your ship won't leave without you." Jamie added. "Believe me, your grandmother is right. You will soon be on rations that you have never had to eat before, enjoy it whilst you may," he encouraged his young son.

A shadow passed across Dickon's face. "What's the matter?" Robyn asked, immediately aware that there was something on his mind.

"I am just a little worried that I am joining the ship as a midshipman later than most boys. Usually they join at twelve or even younger," he pointed out, as if it had only just occurred to him.

"You have nothing to worry about there, and you might have the advantage of having been to sea on the fishing boats and already can use a sextant and compass to navigate. Just don't push yourself forward too much. . . listen and learn." Jamie advised.

Beau and Fred kept up an animated conversation at the same time as devouring a large plate of ham, eggs, potatoes and any number of dishes that had been put on the side table for them. Ginifur, Marie-Claire and Robyn ate little, pushing the food about on their plates as the time flew by. After Liam had eaten, Jamie asked him to find out if there was any news of the fleet whilst Dickon squirmed on his seat, eager to be off.

Liam returned with the news that the fleet was sighted and should come into harbour within the next thirty minutes. With this news it was impossible to keep Dickon seated any longer, they donned their cloaks and made their way to Plymouth Ho to watch the arrival of the fleet. Way out in front was *The Guardian* and behind that were five more ships, the names of which they could not read just yet. The convoy of ships hove to in the bay and only two ships made the journey towards the docks as Jamie hustled them all back into the carriage to go to the dock to meet them.

On the dock it became apparent that Beau and Fred were not the only Cornishmen wishing to try their luck in a new land. Men, women and children huddled together with their private possessions as they awaited their transport ship. Besides Dickon, there was another lad of similar age in midshipman's attire. He watched as Dickon's family stepped onto the dock; the only company he had was that of a young woman, presumably his mother. As Dickon spied him he gave a small smile and was pleased to find the lad beam back at him. Ginifur noticed and addressed the young woman. "Your son?" The lady nodded and made brief bob for she recognised that Ginifur was a lady of quality. "Is he to join *The Guardian* too?

"Yes Ma'am. My man was boson on *The Dart*, 'ee died at sea. There be nought that will put young Billy off though, 'ee wants t' be a sailor like 'is dad. Admiral Kemp put in a good word for un. . . reckoned as 'ow 'ee could make a lieutenant if 'ee worked 'ard enough. I tol' 'im, tis up to 'im now, 'ee must work 'ard 'n not let the Admiral down; my Bill would 'ave been some pleased I c'n tell 'ee."

Ginifur smiled. "I am sure that Billy will do his best to not let any of you down. As new midshipmen hopefully Billy and Dickon will be able to support each other, for there will be times when they suddenly feel far from home and will need a friend."

"Oh, I 'ope so." Tears filled her eyes. "I shall miss 'im dreadfully. My only child y'see."

"Dickon is Jamie's only child too, so they will have much in common." Ginifur assured the young woman.

Dickon and Billy had already exchanged greetings and were eagerly watching the arrival of their ship as it edged towards the dock with the Pilot boats guiding her in from the mid channel. Jamie was talking to the two boys, giving them last minute advice on how to behave on board. Billy looked up at him, his admiration shining on his face as he realised that Dickon's father had once been at sea too and had also been a captain of one of His Majesty's ships.

Robyn stood quietly between Marie-Claire and her grandmother, dreading the moment when Dickon would climb the gangplank and take his leave of them all.

All too soon the moment came. Down the gangplank came the First Lieutenant; glancing about him he spied the two young lads and made his way over. He saluted Jamie. "You must be Captain Tremayne, Sir. . . you are still held in high regard at the Admiralty, and now your son wants to take his place with us I hear." He turned to the boys. "Mr Tremayne and Mr Kellow, I assume. Now which of you is which?"

Jamie stood to attention and saluted first. "Mr Tremayne, Sir."

Mr Jenkins, the First Lieutenant, smiled. "So you must be Mr Kellow. I knew your dad, sailed with him on *The Dart*. He was a good boson and a good man. . . make him proud, son."

Billy Kellow stood straight and attempted a salute like Dickon. "I 'ope I will, Sir."

"Just do your best, no one can ask more of you than that." First Lieutenant Jenkins looked around him. "Now make your goodbyes, lads. Then grab your sacks and follow me, I will send two seamen to fetch your chests." He then turned back to Jamie. "I'm the First Lieutenant on board, Edward Jenkins Sir, I will be keeping a watch on the boys, never you fear." He became aware of the unshed tears in Ginifur's eyes. "Your grandson, Ma'am?" Ginifur nodded, he understood. "Don't worry your pretty little head Ma'am, I promise to keep my eye on them, I give you my word."

"Thank you kindly, Mr Jenkins." Ginifur then turned to her grandson. "Bon voyage, Dickon. May you have a fair wind and may God watch over you and bring you safely home," and Jamie remembered her saying the same words when she had first seen him off too.

Dickon was now as tall as she was and lent over to kiss her cheek whilst giving her a big hug. "I promise to take care Grandma, I will miss you so much, I know I will." For the first time a quiver touched his lips. "I will be home before you are aware I'm gone." He laughed and turned quickly away. Next he took Robyn's hands in his. "Be good, little sister. Take care of Grandma for me." He chastely kissed her cheek before shaking Liam's hand. "I know you will watch over all of them, won't you?"

"Ye can bet on it." Liam smiled at him. "Your grandmother has said it all. . . I pray that ye will come back safe."

Lastly Dickon turned to Jamie, Marie-Claire and his grandfather Ben. . . now tongue tied. . . his words failing him. He gave his grandfather a big hug, kissed Marie-Claire on her cheek and then held his hand out to his father.

Jamie grasped Dickon's now shaking hand in his firm grip. "Well, son?" Jamie found it hard to say farewell to his son; he swallowed hard.

"Thank you Father." Now the time had come for parting the enormity of the situation was finally dawning on Dickon, he found himself wanting to hug his father tight and looked up at him, still a few inches taller. Jamie recognised the small boy in his eyes and, letting go of his hand, hugged his son to him. "It's not unseemly to give your father a parting hug, Dickon. I remember well the time of my first parting on the dockside. Dear God I was so scared in those last few minutes, wondering what on earth I had let my self in for. As your grandmother has said, may God watch over you." Releasing him, once more he held out his hand and Dickon put his into it. "God speed," he said and Dickon found that he could only nod in reply. Billy had bid farewell to his mother and was waiting with Edward Jenkins. "Right lads. All aboard." The First Lieutenant gave a farewell salute to Jamie and ushered his charges up the gang plank. At the top the two boys turned and gave a farewell wave before walking out of sight and a short while later two able seamen humped the chests onto their shoulders and carried them aboard with ease.

In the meantime Beau and Fred had been instructed to join the queue of passengers for the ship that would take the freemen to Australia and they waited to find out what was happening. When Beau and Fred reached the front of the queue they were directed to another table attended by officers where Beau was greeted with open arms. They had decided to say that Fred was Beau's manservant, travelling with his master to new lands. They came back with a big grin on their faces, saying that as Beau was the only 'gentleman' on board they were to be given a separate cabin and wouldn't have to travel with the others who would spend the entire voyage in an open area, below deck, with little or no privacy. Apparently the convict ship in the estuary was full and so their ship was to carry seven male convicts and six women, all from Cornwall. They all speculated on whether Saul would be one of them.

Beau had also gleaned the information that live animals were also aboard. A flock of sheep and a ram were making the trip to see how they would fare; it was a special order for a settler who would only pay for them on safe delivery and he marvelled at the fact that they expected to keep them all alive until they got to Australia. Apparently fodder hay would be taken on in every port, and one of the settlers or convicts allocated to be shepherd for the duration. When the time came, they bade farewell to Jamie and the family, promising to write and let them know how they fared. Ginifur kissed her son goodbye and said that she hoped that he would find what he was searching for and then as Beau and Fred boarded the ship they turned away.

In silence the party left the dock and returned to the inn for refreshments. Ginifur wanted to return to wave her son and grandson farewell but there was a good hour to wait until the ships embarked. The hour flew by and they seemed to be back on the dock only minutes after they had left.

In a controlled and orderly fashion amidst shouted orders and whistled commands the two ships slipped away from the docks. Ginifur looked up at the poop deck, remembering the time when she had watched Richard and Liam set sail from Falmouth Harbour, recalling her joy and sadness as she saw Richard wave from the deck as *The White Rose* sailed away. Liam touched her arm and pointed to the aft. Two faces were looking down at them, they looked so small, so far away! But it was Dickon and Billy, Ginifur was quite sure and she took out her handkerchief and waved it. She could see the boys hesitantly look over their shoulders before giving a brief wave in reply then at the signal of a sharp whistle they both turned away and were gone.

With one hand Ginifur reached out for Liam and the other for Robin; she was finding it difficult to see, for the tears that had refused to be contained any longer spilled from eyes and ran down her cheeks. She glanced at Jamie's back, Ginifur had lost her husband, she was saying farewell to her beloved grandson and possibly she would never see her younger son again. But she still had one son; she still had Jamie.

As Ginifur watched Dickon's ship slip silently away towards the sea she gave up a heartfelt prayer that Old Betsy's prophecy would prove correct and that her grandson would indeed one day return to them. . . to Cornwall. . . to live out a happy life at Tremanyon.

* * *

TREMANYON
Book Three

IN JULY 1799 land was sighted; a dark smudge along the horizon, but they had finally reached their destination. Eleven years and six months after the First Fleet arrived to embark upon an enterprising scheme to develop a new settlement on this strange and distant shore; new immigrants would now join those first settlers' attempts to build a new life for themselves. There was nothing to greet the convicts and marines on those first ships, other than the indigenous aborigines, and Beau found himself wondering what they would find to greet them here now.

Not everyone who set out from England survived the journey; there had been losses attributed to sickness amongst the convicts but on the whole the prisoners arrived in better health than they had started out. There were crew losses too, on all ships, there always were, due to accidents on slippery decks or an insecure hold as sailors clambered in the rigging, and some occurred in violent storms . . . but not all. There had been broken limbs, minor accidents and sickness too, but all the ships that sailed from Plymouth, including the ship carrying the Irish convicts, arrived at their destination.

It was mid-winter as the fleet sailed between the two headlands but they were welcomed in sunshine and the decks were crowded as the freemen and their families jostled to catch their first glimpse of the country that was to be their new home. In front of them a huge natural harbour opened up, where the water was deep enough for ships to sail close to shore; sailing past secluded coves where turquoise waters lapped upon coral white beaches, in the late morning sun the new arrivals were treated to their first sight of exotic bird life as flocks of pink and grey galahs and green parakeets took flight from strange, ghost like trees along the shoreline. The sun, sailing high in the sky, produced a temperature that was more like a warm spring day, yet it was supposed to be winter here in the southern hemisphere. New settlers eyed this strange land with trepidation and began to realise that what had only been a dream was now reality; and some began to fear the prospect now that they had arrived. In truth very few of them had any experience of animal husbandry, or working the land and growing crops; most were escaping poverty and had been sold a dream by a government bent on building a new colony on the other side of the world. The prisoners were locked below deck until arrangements could be made for their transfer to the convict quarters ashore; if left on deck they could be tempted to jump ship and swim to the shore in an effort to escape further internment.

Captain Hardiman had not given the order for Merryn to be returned to the prisoner's quarters and she joined Beau and Fred on the quarter deck as they watched the shore draw slowly nearer. "Do you know where your farm will be?" Merryn wanted to know as she took in her surroundings; the strange grey trees, the shape of the blue mountains beyond and the township now visible ahead of them.

"No, not exactly. I have maps and details of the location, but they don't mean anything as yet. I will visit the Land Office as soon as I am able to get on shore and, hopefully, they will arrange a safe storage pen for my flock of Merinos." Beau chuckled. "I also need to make a request for convict labour to help clear the bush."

Merryn clasped a bundle of fur in her arms and a long pink tongue suddenly appeared as a glossy black nose snuggled into her neck and the young puppy licked her ear. Merryn laughed as it tickled. "I will miss you Tess," she rubbed the pup's coat affectionately as she continued. "I am sure that she will make a fine sheepdog for you, Beau." The tricoloured Collie puppy had been a gift to Beau from George Bray and his family when they parted in South Africa.

"What on earth are you talking about, Merryn?" Beau frowned as he studied the girl by his side. "You are coming with us aren't you?"

That prospect had not occurred to Merryn, she had boarded the ship as a convict and, regardless of how much she had assisted by caring for the flock of sheep aboard when the shepherd had abandoned ship, she fully expected to return to that status when she arrived at their destination. What would be expected of her then was beyond her imagination. The only information she had gleaned on her voyage had served to fill her with fear for her future. The best she could expect was that she might be expected to work as a servant for a merchant's family. The worst . . . that she might have to fight for her survival in a land where men, both convicts and freemen, far outnumbered the women. She looked up into Beau's puzzled face, how old was she? Late thirties? Yet there was still a little naivety in his expression. Merryn had grown older and wiser in the last year, she had been forced to face both fear and hardship that she hoped that Beau would never have to face. "I don't think that the authorities will be of the opinion that I be allowed to be set free, Beau. I set out from Cornwall as a prisoner, a convict . . . I expect to leave this ship as one too." She watched dispassionately as they sailed into Sydney Cove. On land the beginnings of a township spread along the shore, with the fine brick and stone residence of the first Governor of New South Wales, Governor Phillips, in a prominent position, built on rising ground with a view over the harbour.

William Trenchard had given the order for the ships to drop anchor in the cove whilst he went ashore to make arrangements for the transfer of the convicts and the unloading of the settlers and their personal belongings, together with the stores and animals to replenish the commissary stocks. William knew there was never enough to meet the demand of a growing community. It had been thought that the settlers would be self-sufficient by now, with a surplus of produce to supply to those who resided in the township; this was not happening. William had his doubts about the real success of the venture to create another new world. This country wasn't like the Americas; it was too far away for one thing. On top of this, in his opinion, there were too few who had either the incentive or the experience to create a living from this hostile land; most were escaping some disaster or failure in their life back in England. Conversely, he had been impressed with Jamie Tremayne's brother when they had paid a visit to George Bray's holding in South Africa and was still puzzled as to why he had set out on this venture; Beau's family were land owners and major stock holders in a profitable tin and copper mine, surely he had no need to be involved in the physical work to develop new land. Yet it appeared that Beau had actually experienced working with sheep; if it hadn't been for Beau and the young convict girl, the much needed flock of sheep on the Lady Penryn would never have survived the voyage. As he watched the approaching shore, from his position in the long-boat he recalled Lester Hardiman describing the young woman . . . what had he said? Unlike any convict that he had the misfortune to meet. Of course she had proclaimed her innocence, didn't they all? But, nevertheless, Lester was impressed by what he had learned of the girl on their voyage; her conduct and her behaviour threw doubts upon the charges brought against her. Lester was a good Captain, kept a disciplined ship with a crew who did not actually fear him but knew that he would not fail to pronounce punishment for an offence if it was committed. He also had a good judgement of character and was able to recognise integrity in others. Like William, Lester had never married, and in the time that he had known him he had never heard of a woman becoming close to him. In society he was popular with mothers with eligible daughters but in spite of his popularity had never become emotionally involved. So what had he seen in this girl that concerned him? William studied Beau Tremayne, sitting aft in the long-boat, he had collected the young man in order that he could make arrangements for his few sheep and goods to be unloaded, then he glanced back at the Lady Penryn, as it swung on its mooring in the bright sunlight the crew were washing down the decks and damaged sails already being attended to... and William decided that he must meet the girl, before she was cast adrift to the fate that he knew awaited her.

On the lower deck of the Lady Penryn, Merryn was spending her last hours with the sheep. Fresh water had been brought on board and both the Longwools and Merinos were drinking with relish as she gazed proudly at them. There had been no losses since leaving Cape Town, the ewes were healthy and in good condition. Merryn had asked for some new shears whilst the ship had been anchored in Table Bay and over the last few weeks she and Beau had shorn them, rolled and packed the fleeces and the sheep were a lot happier for it. The lambs were healthy and the orphans had all been fostered onto other ewes that had too much milk for their single lamb. Merryn had every right to be proud of herself, but she knew that she could not have done it without Beau . . . or little Alfie for that matter. She would miss them, both the man who had offered her a brief respite from the cramped and dirty convict quarters and the little ship's boy who had slept faithfully outside her door every night. Tears filled her eyes as she contemplated a bleak future and she made for her tiny cabin where she packed her few possessions in the small chest that Beau had found for her.

Alfie had brought her two buckets of warm water and, closing the door Merryn undressed to bathe herself from head to toe for she knew not when she would get the next opportunity and as she poured clean water over her hair tears of despair mixed with the soap and she let them flow freely.

ALSO PUBLISHED BY PALORES

All Palores titles are available from any good bookshops, Amazon or other online outlets.

TREMANYON

A Shadow Falls

After a fire destroys the house on the Manor of Tremayne, Richard Tremayne and his family return from London to Cornwall where, on the site of the ruins on the beautiful Rhosinnis Peninsula, he undertakes the building of a Georgian Manor House, Tremanyon.

Local young woman, Ginifur Retallick, is employed as a maid for his wife Annabelle and their two young daughters. Annabelle is determined to give Richard a son but, although she has given birth to two healthy children, the third child is 'still born' – casting a 'shadow' over the peninsula.

At the request of William Pitt and Lord Falmouth, Richard sails to the New World at the beginning of the French and Indian War; during the period when the English, Irish and Scots settlers were living with the constant danger of attack and their homesteads burned to the ground.

Meanwhile, in the two years Richard is absent from Cornwall, many things are changing at Tremanyon. But 'Old Betsy', the White Witch who lives on the edge of the village, promises that the shadow will be lifted.

ISBN: 978-1-906845-21-6 - Priced: £7.95

A CHRISTMAS GAME - Cheryl Hayden

In far western Cornwall, Margh Tredannack is living in newly wedded bliss. Near the banks of the Tamar, Jenna Rosewarne is promised to a loathsome cousin. In the summer of 1549, their worlds collide as the Cornish rebel against the Boy King's new English prayer book. Protest becomes war, and war becomes treason. Can anything save them?

ISBN 978-1-906845-41-4 - Priced: £12.00